# ZOMBIES

## SHAMBLING THROUGH THE AGES

**OTHER BOOKS EDITED BY STEVE BERMAN**

*So Fey: Queer Fairy Fiction*
*Magic in the Mirrorstone*
*Wilde Stories: The Year's Best Gay Speculative Fiction*
*Heiresses of Russ: The Year's Best Lesbian Speculative Fiction*
*The Touch of the Sea*
*Bad Seeds: Evil Progeny*
*Where Thy Dark Eye Glances: Queering Edgar Allan Poe*
*Bad Seeds: Evil Progeny*
*Shades of Blue and Gray: Ghosts of the Civil War*
*Handsome Devil: Tales of Sin and Seduction*

# ZOMBIES
## SHAMBLING THROUGH THE AGES

edited by
STEVE BERMAN



PRIME BOOKS

**ZOMBIES: SHAMBLING THROUGH THE AGES**


Cover art by Timothy Lantz.
Cover design by Sherin Nicole.

Prime Books
www.prime-books.com



For more information, contact Prime Books:
prime@prime-books.com

ISBN: 978-1-60701-395-2

For Kelly Link, the only person who can answer what happens next: "A leper, a gingerbread man, and a zombie stumble into a pub . . . "

# CONTENTS continued . . .

*Historians are gossips who tease the dead.*
—Voltaire

*The Past lies upon the Present like a giant's dead body.*
—Nathaniel Hawthorne

*From the October 1st, 1968 resignation speech of Dr. Stephen Berman, George Andrew Romero Professor of Folklore and Director of the Romero Center for Folklore Studies, Evans University:*

It is a sad truth that the studies of necrochronology and cryptozoology have, with this twentieth century, become as scorned in the academic community as phrenology or Lysenkoism or the once cherished field of ghost hunting. No, necrochronology, or as the mass media is wont to refer to it in baser terms, the historical study of the undead, deserves not to be relegated to roadside attractions charging a dollar or consultants for the lurid cinema plaguing drive-in movie theaters. For as long as there has been death, there has been cause for the resurgence of man, whether pure spirit, as in ghosts, or the rotting remains, the ghoul or, as some have referred to the creature, the zombie.

To deny that these ravenous entities exist is to deny the wisdom of the Ancients, to deny the work of such historians as Pliny the Elder—who was recording an undead infestation in the city of Pompeii that was wiped from memory by Vesuvius—or the writings of Eleazar ben Judah of Worms on the real reason a golem was created to deal with a revenant threat to the ghetto. "Those who cannot remember the past are condemned to repeat it." I would hate to envision a zombie outbreak because it could well lead to a veritable disaster so vast one might dare use the term apocalyptic.

That is why I have asked learned colleagues from around the globe, men and women who have spent years studying necrochronology, to present their findings tonight to you, our most gracious audience, in the hopes you will be moved to donate to the program and prevent our research from mouldering away in the university's morgue.

Alas, a number of academics who studied the prehistoric, the Iron Age, and classical eras Before Lazarus—forgive me, but, in our field, the passage of history is divided by the emergence of the most famous undead, Lazarus of Bethany. The year you call 30 C.E. to us is the year 0 A.L. As I was saying, most of the scholars studying the years Before Lazarus, or B.L., have been stranded due to the annoying mass cancellation of flights to the Eastern United States by these freak meteorological, "supposedly radioactive" disturbances. So most of the papers given tonight in my honor will focus on ghouls and zombies A.L., especially the periods of Industrialization and up to World War II.

Oh, one last thing before we begin. One of the librarians has brought to my attention that a disheveled man has been seen near the front entrance. He is most likely a student demonstrator. I would not be surprised if, upon exiting after our lectures, we find the number of these ragamuffins has exponentially multiplied. Do not be alarmed by their groaning at current political affairs or their hunger to be heard. I myself plan on exiting this building, and, most likely, my career here at Evans University, with my head held high and pushing through the mindless hordes of ignorance.

Just so we can all meet at the pub afterwards, of course. And now . . . our first speaker:

BEFORE
LAZARUS

# BLOOD MARKER

## VICTORIA JANSSEN

Lubbosh is covered head to toe in animal furs, his head mantled by a huge wolf's snarling mouth—an old kill, his proudest moment. He peers through its teeth into heavy, blowing whiteness. His flint hand axe is bound to his left palm, the stone so cold he can feel its bite through the fur wrapping. In his right hand he clasps a spear, the butt serving to find safe footing as he clambers over heaps of ice-crusted, tumbled rock. Thanks to the wind, the snowfall, he isn't leaving much of a visible trail, but his deadly pursuers can smell him.

He knows that is how they found his clan, picking them off one by one, screams swirling up into the wind, not animal or kinfolk but spirit. He caught glimpses of carnage as he raced to save his mate, his sire, old and slow. The unknown hunters appeared as his kind, clothed in gore-stained furs, but the stink of death came from their mouths. The unknown hunters ripped apart victims with hands and broken teeth. They devoured flesh uncooked and in bloody gobbets. The hunters were not story creatures but real.

With his axe, his spear, he stabbed and slashed the unknown hunters. Their rotting bodies broke but they did not fall. How can he kill the dead that still hunts? Soon he will fall as well, but he will do one thing first.

The cave lip juts; he is just tall enough to hoist himself up. The cave smells only of cold stone. There are no dead creatures here, not even bears. Once past the entrance, blown clean by wind, the floor drops. It is thickly littered with layer upon layer of bones, singed and cracked open for marrow. It is too dark to see much, but he knows there is a firepit, further back, out of the wind.

Catching his breath, he listens. Above the wind's howl, he hears other, thinner cries, advancing.

So be it. All lives come to an end. He will leave his mark first so his spirit can be proud.

Bones crackle and crunch beneath his feet. He finds the wall and follows it back. A dank breeze, bearing the faintest memory of burnt fat, brushes the skin around his eyes. He squeezes into the tunnel, back, back. His breathing speeds as the eerie wails of his pursuers come closer, begin to echo off stone. When he can progress no further, he leans his spear against the wall and struggles to untie the axe with numbed fingers. He peels free strips of hide and scores his rough palms with his axe.

The unknown hunters gurgle and growl, bones crunching beneath their shambling feet. Their foul reek obliterates all else. Lubbosh rubs his bloodied hands together and slams them against the freezing stone wall. Again, leaving wet prints he cannot see—will anyone ever see?

When the first dead hands shove into the narrow space, he batters them fruitlessly with his axe. Their clawed fingers tear through his wolf's-head, rip out fistfuls of his hair, slam Lubbosh's head against the walls to crack open his skull.

He lays one last bloodied handprint on the floor, then all is quiet.

# SELECTED SOURCES FOR THE BABYLONIAN PLAGUE OF THE DEAD (572-571 BCE)

## ALEX DALLY MacFARLANE

*Letter (clay tablet) found in the property of Kaššaya, daughter of King Nabu-kudurri-uṣur, in Uruk. Cuneiform inscription dating to the neo-Assyrian Empire:*

To the king, my lord: your servant Nabu'a. May Nabu and Marduk bless the king, my lord! On the 7th of Kislev a fox entered the Inner City, and fell into a well in the garden of Aššur. It was hauled up and killed.

*Later annotation on the letter of Nabu'a in Aramaic, using ink:*

What omen is this? What did Nabu'a prevent? It is a time of terrible plague in Babylon. With your wisdom, perhaps this tablet will help to explain one of the omens presaging the events here: the dead fox seen walking into the temple of Marduk.

*Letter (clay tablet) found in the property of Kaššaya:*

Innin-Eṭirat to Kaššaya, my sister, may Anu keep you well in this time of plague! May the plague that afflicts us in Babylon never reach the great city of Uruk!

I send this letter with four tablets that have been brought from the ruins of Nineveh in the north. Everyone in Babylon with the wisdom to understand these tablets—the omens and the measures taken as a result of them—is dead. They are dead, but they walk, they eat the flesh of living people, who then sicken and die and walk through the city, spreading the illness further. Before this terrible plague, there were four omens here in Babylon: the right-hand quadrant of the sun darkened without the moon passing across it, the king dreamed of a dead woman with teeth as sharp as knives, a dead fox was seen walking into the temple of Marduk, bones fell from the noon sky like rain.

Kaššaya, my sister, if you or your scholars can interpret the past omens described in the tablets and whether they relate to our omens, then you will know what measures to take to prevent this plague from reaching Uruk.

I have sent this letter and these tablets with a soldier I know well. I will remain within Babylon, unless the palace becomes unsafe.

• • •

*Letter (clay tablet) found in the property of Kaššaya, either an archival copy or the unsent original:*

Kaššaya to Innin-Eṭirat, my sister, may Anu keep you safe! May Nabu and Marduk keep Nabu-kudurri-uṣur, the king, our father, safe! May the great city of Babylon be unharmed by this calamity! Your letter arrived with only one tablet, carried by a woman fleeing Babylon, who tells me that she found your soldier dying on the road. I have given her food. I have ensured that she is watched for signs of this sickness.

You write: "the right-hand quadrant of the sun darkened without the moon passing across it, the King dreamed of a dead woman with teeth as sharp as knives." I too have dreamed this. I too have witnessed this brief darkening of the sun.

I have been to every temple to report the news you have sent me. Offerings are being made to every god in my name and the king's name. The signs of plague are being watched for in Uruk.

Innin-Eṭirat, my sister, may you remain safe in the palace of Babylon!

*Tablet found in the Eanna temple in Uruk:*

Eight minas and five shekels of blue-coloured wool for an ullakku garment, the property of Innin-Eṭirat, the king's daughter, brought to Eanna by Innin-Eṭirat herself on the day she arrived in Uruk, after the outbreak of the plague. Month Šabatu, 7th day, 33rd year of Nabu-kudurri-uṣur, king of Babylon.

*A story passed orally among the women of Uruk (now in southern Iraq) and surviving to this day in several variants (including a Safavid Dynasty manuscript, the only written variant), from which this original has been tentatively constructed:*

Long ago there was a terrible plague in the city of Uruk. Can you imagine! The dead in the streets of Uruk, attacking those who still lived. Feasting on those who were too slow. Even the animals could get this sickness: dead dogs and foxes ran through the city, biting the legs of the living. No offering to the gods could end this plague. No medicine could cure it.

All of Uruk's men were given bows and swords to fight the dead, but even this was not enough. Many were bitten. Many found that the dead would not die again no matter how many arrows sank into their chests—even the headless would still stumble, even the teeth would still try to bite them from the ground!

At this time lived three women, daughters of the king, called Kaššaya, Innin-Eṭirat and Ba'u-Asitu, who all owned land in Uruk.

It is said of Kaššaya that she was wise, of Innin-Eṭirat that she was determined, of Ba'u-Asitu that she was bold.

During the time of the plague, each of the daughters gathered all of the women and children working for her into her main property, each well provisioned with water and grain and dates, and built sturdy defences. There they planned to wait until the plague passed, as all terrible illnesses eventually do. They sought to keep everyone from dwelling on the horrors beyond their walls: Kaššaya organised storytelling competitions, Innin-Eṭirat led the women and children in song, Ba'u-Asitu invented a new dance every morning.

It was Ba'u-Asitu who noticed three foxes below the walls of her home.

A dead fox, its legs shattered, unable to walk but biting out at anything that passed. Two living foxes pinned it down and ate the remnants of its flesh. You wince, but such is the nature of foxes.

Ba'u-Asitu observed that when the living foxes had torn the flesh from the dead fox, it stopped trying to bite. It lay still, a skeleton, truly dead.

Being bold, she darted from the security of her walls with two other women and with great care and stealth took one of the walking dead men from outside. They covered his head with thick cloth so that he could not bite, and secured the door once they brought him inside. Then with tools they stripped the rotting flesh from him.

The bared skeleton of the man stopped moving. The teeth lay in their sockets like needles in a pouch: sharp but unused.

Ba'u-Asitu sent letters to her sisters, to the temples and to the leaders of the soldiers, telling them of this discovery. Letters were also sent to Babylon and the other cities. From then on, the living were able to fight the dead, although it was not easy and many more died.

The flesh of the dead was immediately burnt. The stench filled the city for weeks. The bones were buried far from the cities, in tracts of desert where none lingered long. The teeth were not touched with bare hands.

Eventually the plague passed, as all terrible illnesses do.

*In one oral version of this tale, Ba'u-Asitu becomes so famed for her skill at stripping the flesh from the dead that she is known as Ba'u-Asitu the Fox-Woman: an immortal figure who still hunts under an occluded moon with an army of foxes. Screams in the night are attributed to her work. The plague has never spread far again.*

*Letter (clay tablet) found in the property of Kaššaya:*

To Kaššaya, my lady, and Innin-Etirat, my lady: your servant Šamaš-ereš. May Anu and Ishtar keep you both well!

You write: "No one in Uruk or Babylon can say whether the omens we saw before the plague have appeared before. Is there anything in the ruined cities of the north that will help us understand these omens and how to respond to them?"

Nothing I have found yet will help. I do not think that this plague ever afflicted these old cities. The fox in the well of Aššur may have been alive, signifying a different omen. The omens described on the tablets found by Innin-Eṭirat's servant and lost between Babylon and Uruk may have been the same. Nothing I have found suggests that they were important.

I will continue to search the ruins.

Let us hope that this plague never afflicts Babylon again!

*Saying uttered by Uruk women when falling ill with any ailment, recorded on a tablet in Eanna temple:*

Let the foxes of Ba'u-Asitu watch over us!

# IMMORTALS

## NATE SOUTHARD

Five days after the Persians arrived at the Hot Gates, we started cutting them down. Xerxes, that mad tyrant, sent waves the size of cities at us, but our spears stuck them. Our shields held them back. Those who walked inside our spear points felt the venom of our swords. For King Leonidas, we fought. For Sparta. This is what Spartans do.

When the battle broke, we cast insults at Xerxes and his throne. Our shouts echoed through the rocky valley. We had heard such talk of his army, of his horrible legions, and still we bested the first waves he sent with only a few casualties. Our shields were too superior, a wall of bronze and wood that held back the tide of violence so that we might counter with our own.

Shortly after noon, a scout approached at a full sprint. His face flushed with panic as he shouted.

"The Immortals! Xerxes sends the Immortals!"

We had heard of the dreaded Immortals. Xerxes' finest warriors, they were said to feel no pain, to be impossible to kill. In countless battles, we had faced worse. These filthy bastards would fall like the rest. We were not afraid.

Moments later, I stood at the front of the phalanx. I saw the black wave roll toward us, a cloud of dirt and hatred in its wake. My hand felt sure, my arm strong. Their terrible mass filled the battlefield, but we choked the gates.

"Let the dogs come!" brave Demophilus said at my shoulder. He was a true friend and companion to me, and a fearless warrior. "Let us slay them one by one!"

A cheer went up, and we braced ourselves for the swarm. When a strange stench reached us while the Immortals were still at distance, I felt a small amount of wonder. These Persians smelled like death. A cunning tactic, but not one that would trample the bravery of any Greek. I heard no war cry rise up from their lines, but instead a dry rasping, like the last breath of a dying man, multiplied by thousands. I gritted my teeth and ignored the questions in my head. A soldier needs no questions, and a Spartan is greater than most soldiers.

The first line reached us, and I shouted as I drove my spear forward. The stink was unbearable as my weapon pierced black robes and entered my enemy's chest. His body shuddered, and I ripped the spear free. I expected a fountain of blood from the mortal wound I'd given him. I expected him to fall in a heap, forgotten as

I killed the next of Xerxes' precious Immortals. There was no blood, though. The man who had shuddered as my spear breached his heart did not fall or cry out in any way.

Something was wrong. I heard more of those rasps, now angry, almost hungry. Around me, I heard my fellows scream in surprise and then pain. I stabbed the man again, and this time my spear erupted from his back. He gave no sign that he felt the terrible blow, and still he did not bleed.

I looked into his hateful eyes, and I realized they were entirely white. His nose was missing, rotted away, and his lips were cracked and desiccated things stretched back to reveal a mouth of blackened teeth. My breath caught in my chest as I realized the Immortals were dead men. Somehow, Xerxes had set an army of corpses upon us.

Grabbing my spear with both hands, the rotting man dragged himself toward me. I shoved back at him, but it only brought him closer. Beside me, the phalanx began to break. I saw black-robed corpses climb over the line and drag my fellow Greeks to the ground. They bit faces and throats, and our soldiers bled more than they ever had. Demophilus thrashed beside me, one of the Immortals riding his back like an angry spider. When the dead man breached my friend's armor and bit into his throat, blood splashed across my cheek.

Dropping my spear, I ripped my sword from its scabbard and swung at the man I should have killed twice over. My blade chopped through his neck, and his body dropped as his head rolled away. At last!

I turned to Demophilus. His attacker had him pinned to the ground, still gnawing on his throat. I grabbed the horrible Immortal by what remained of his hair and jerked back his head. With my sword, I hacked at his neck. Four blows, and his skull separated from his body. I tossed the terrible thing away.

Demophilus was dead. Any fool could see it at a glance. His eyes were closed, his face washed with crimson. A wet and ragged crater replaced his once healthy throat. In the instant I had, I mourned him as best I could.

Turning away, I joined the battle anew. With each swing, I aimed for a throat, meaning to cleave head from neck. I shouted to my remaining fellows, telling them how to drop the Immortals.

A strong and violent hand grabbed my shoulder. I whirled around, ripping free of the menacing grip and cocking back my sword for a death blow. Had they flanked us?

I faced brave Demophilus. He stared at me with white eyes. Held by that cold gaze, I hesitated. My friend. My fellow. A Spartan.

Demophilus shrieked from his ruined throat, and I screamed with him.

# THE COST OF MOVING THE DEAD

E. L. KEMPER

To move your dead you must pay two *ban liang*. Not a lot.

If you didn't move them, bring them home, their restless souls roamed the countryside—your ancestor-spirits moaned and wailed for the missing, rustling through the thatch of your roof, all night long they'd call. Nobody wanted this. So the cost of moving the dead was reasonable.

The priests came to town, feet bare, bundled in brown robes, dusted by road. They passed between the mud-brick houses, trailing clouds of spiced smoke that would linger in the village for days.

When they stopped at your door you knew. Your husband, father, brother had gone north to fight the barbarians, to build the wall, and he wasn't coming home. At least not alive. So you paid. And you waited.

Months pass. One morning you wake, the crow of roosters echoing through the village. You remember you are out of oil when your front door hinge creaks, a soft stutter that makes your hair stand up. And then you forget the oil again.

Your husband, father, brother is home.

He lies across your front yard, bound to a bamboo pole, veiled in linen, small sacks of azuki beans on shoulders, hips and knees hold him down. Now the ancestor-spirits will cease their nightly clamor. Now the children will sleep in peace. You sink to your knees and reach with shaking hands to touch the bare iron nail pierced through his forehead.

He is home.

Bells rang, trickling over the blowing sands. The goats back at camp bleated and muttered, then settled into sleep once more.

Buwei followed the wall, this section as high as his hip, soon to be higher. He stopped, eyes straining in the dark for the glow of lantern and incense burner, ears straining for another clink of bells, for the shuffle-thump.

He must see Yun again. Just one last time.

Foreman Liang's orders were very clear this night. Do not venture out until sunrise.

Liang had worked the men hard, harder than usual, digging, carrying, filling the forms and tamping the walls. Pounding and hammering until the earth was hard as a rock—until wind, water and weapon couldn't tear the wall down. Then Liang filled the men full of spiced goat meat and sent them to their tents with wine to warm their bellies. Most of the men stuffed their ears with cloth, shutting out the snores of their fellows, muting the moan of the restless wind as it chased clouds of earth across the barren hillsides. And they slept.

But Buwei had to see Yun again. He had to make sure Yun's family had paid the price—could afford to. That Yun's family was bringing him home.

Bells sounded again, bright slivers of sound pricking the dark. A line of lanterns bobbed along, floating towards him. Buwei jumped to the other side of the wall and crouched in the cold, waiting for the priests to bring the *jiang shi* his way.

A scuffing slump accompanied the ringing of the bells. The tickle of incense came gusting towards Buwei, along with a rotted-meat stench that seeped into his throat until he gagged. Pack-mules followed, snorting ghosts of vapor. One shook its head and sent its bell-decked bridle jingling.

The priests walked barefoot and slow, the words of the *I Ching* spilled from their tongues. And with the priests came the *jiang shi*. They were close now, moving with a steady, lurching shuffle. Buwei hunched lower behind the wall, his hands numb, his knees turned to water.

He had to look. He had to know.

So he raised his head again, every nerve in his body protesting, twitching, urging him to run, to scream, to shut this horror away. *Jiang shi.* The dead. A nightmare told by grandmothers to pale, shivering children.

He must see Yun again.

The priests walked in a circle around the dead, penning them in with their shields of bamboo. Each shield bore the eight symbols of the *bagua*, the elements in all their forms, and was strung with mirrors swaying on black thread. With these, and the clanking bells they moved the *jiang shi*, guided them, held them at bay.

The dead were prepared well for their journey.

Buwei searched the horde of corpses, each wearing its funeral robes, hair smoothed and knotted atop its head, lashed to bamboo poles that rose like reeds from a fetid pool. Each with arms extended, fingernails grown long in the grave. A strip of yellow paper was nailed to each forehead, and the papers curled and shuddered in the wind.

The dead walked with a strange lurching hop, joints stiff and unbending. The dead had skin the color of the moon, coated in pale mold. The priests grew the mold on the corpses for three cycles. After three cycles the dead would rise, ready to go home.

Buwei searched for the familiar jaw, square and proud, the familiar arch of eyebrow, always asking and at the same time knowing, the familiar bearing, wide-shouldered and proud, arms strong and comforting against the chill of the winter nights.

It tortured him to think of Yun's spirit, tumbling with the north wind, lost and howling its loneliness across these frigid plains. Yun must return home for his body to be placed on the altar with a lantern at its feet. Home, surrounded by family in funeral white, candlelight catching their tears, incense smoke rising with their mourning chant, rising with the shadow of death.

When the buckets fell on Yun, crushing fingers into flat worms, bruising toes, Buwei had wrapped Yun's hand with a strip of his robe and traded Yun's straw slippers for his own worn leather boots and bindings. Yun worked for days, hiding his pain and the swelling. He screamed as Foreman Liang cut rotting fingers away, then the whole hand. But too late. A black line shot up Yun's arm and he slipped away, not feeling Buwei's grip on his remaining hand, not hearing Buwei's desperate prayers.

He needed to see Yun.

One priest cried out when he stumbled over a stone. As he fell he dropped his shield, his lantern and his bell. The bell tinkled as it rolled across the pebbled earth, and the priest scrambled on hands and knees after it.

Buwei couldn't breathe, his fingers dug into the wall, holding himself in place.

Two other priests rushed to assist, but not fast enough. The dead advanced on the doomed priest as he retrieved his bell. Just as his fingers grasped the cool metal, the dead fell on him. The priest's screams filled the night as the dead began to feed.

The dead were hungry. They hungered for life, for flesh, for blood.

They tore at the priest as his fellows held back the rest of the shuffling mass. With their shields and their bells and their steady recitation, the priests forced the *jiang shi* between them, leaving the fallen ones to their feast.

Soon the priest's cries ceased, and the night was filled only with the sound of the hungry dead. Joints, stiff with death, creaked and popped as the dead gnawed at their prize. When the writhing and slurping slowed, two of the priests approached the pile of corpses. Shaking their shields they reached for the bamboo poles that the *jiang shi* were lashed to and righted their charges, guiding them back to their glass-eyed brothers.

The last of the dead was pulled from the ground, with one claw dripping blood and chunks of flesh as it came, the other an aborted stump. Yun. His jaws snapped open, shut, open with yearning. His lips, now cracked and mottled by decay, smeared with the gore of his final meal—Buwei knew those lips. So often those lips had broken into smile, into laughter. Those lips were warm and soft, their touch gentle, insistent against his. On his feet he still wore the leather boots Buwei had tied with such care, those boots would bear him the countless miles of his return.

Buwei's heart slowed, each beat an ache that pressed through to his bones.

Yun. Yun was going home.

With prods and chanting and ringing of bells, the priests began to move the dead once more. Scraping along the ground the horde moved away. One priest stayed behind. He wrapped the new carcass in cloth and secured it to a mule, and together mule and priest hurried after the horde, jingling as they went.

Buwei watched until he could see them no more. The dead were going home.

One morning Yun's wife would wake to the rooster's crow, open the door to fetch some water to make rice soup for her children. She would stop. A bundle laid carefully across her front yard blocks her way, wrapped in linen, held down by small sacks of azuki beans. She sinks to her knees, tears falling from her eyes in streams. With shaking hands she reaches to touch the iron nail pierced through his forehead.

The night became quiet again and sanded wind stung Buwei's face.

Yun was going home.

# HAUNTINGS AND HUNGERS ON THE BANKS OF THE VIPASA

## RAJAN KHANNA

The summons came as Adhrit was meditating in the temple, breaking him from contemplation. He hurried to his brother's side, the raja's side, pausing only to clothe himself in his white ascetic's robes, incense still tickling at his nose.

Sankara's advisors were leaving as Adhrit entered, their faces drawn, serious. The room held the lingering odor of sweat. "What is it?" Adhrit asked when he saw his brother's pale face. Sankara's turban was askew, his habit being to rub at his forehead when he was worried.

"Alexander moves toward the Vipasa River," Sankara said. "He defeated Raja Puru, and you know Puru's strength."

Puru was something of a legend, Adhrit knew. He had more troops, more chariots, more elephants than anyone in the region. "There is still the Vipasa," Adhrit said. The river had long aided them by providing a natural boundary.

Sankara shook his head. "It won't stop him. Alexander crossed a swollen river to attack Puru. Some say he can't be defeated."

"Anyone can be defeated," Adhrit said, but he wasn't sure he believed it.

"Ramyasthana is a place of learning, of art and music and for faith. We are not warriors and now we are facing conquest."

"Is there nothing we can do?" Adhrit asked.

"I need allies who can defend us from the Macedonian." Sankara looked hard at Adhrit. "You can help me get them."

Adhrit exhaled and turned away from his brother. "Are you truly asking this?"

"I must."

Adhrit turned back to his brother, heat rising through him. "You want me to return to that life? You were the one to rescue me from it! You set my feet upon the just path and I was grateful for it!"

"I know," Sankara said. "But this is to save our home. Our family. All we know." He moved forward and placed his hands on Adhrit's shoulders. "I ask. The burden is mine."

Adhrit met his brother's gaze. "Tattva tells us life is temporary. We should meet it as we are, travelers on the right path. Like a plague, this Alexander might kill us, but our souls will move on, further on the path to moksa. Why pollute our souls—"

"The teachings say violence is allowed in situations of self-defense," Sankara said. "That's what this is—defense of our lives, our homes, our way of life." He knelt at Adhrit's feet. "Please, anujah, do this for me."

Adhrit's chest tightened. Sankara had dragged him from an evil life. And when their taata had been ready to turn his back on Adhrit, Sankara wouldn't. Sankara had saved his life, and more so, his soul. "I will do it," he said.

Yet, as he walked from the tent, that very soul felt heavy. Even sick at the thought of whom he had to return to.

In the dark, a lantern his only illumination, Adhrit wound his way through the jungle. Peacocks howled in the darkness punctuating the insects' hum. Sankara had once asked him how he found his way so easily through the jungle. "I often need escape," he'd said. He was amazed that he still knew the way.

His brother had wanted allies. Rough men. Lawbreakers and blackguards that Adhrit had known in his youth. But there was another option, of greater strength but higher price. A few killers would make little difference to an army. But the man he sought now was a different breed. It forced him to live apart.

Ekaaksh had survived the jungle by transforming himself. Just as Adhrit once had.

Their wise taata had welcomed the Jains and the followers of the Buddha into the heart of Ramyasthana and Adhrit had learned from them. It had been difficult, but the teachings gave him something to hold on to, a path to setting himself right. For years since he had prayed at the temple daily, vowing to do no harm, giving up his worldly possessions, wearing only white robes. Yet now he wore a dhoti once more, wrapped his head in a turban, shod feet that had long gone uncovered. Only his long beard marked him as monastic.

Ekaaksh's cave was filled with what appeared to be a random assortment of objects. Bowls and powders stood on surfaces of differing heights. An altar stood in the middle of the cave, containing another bowl next to a vajra and a bell. Behind it stood simple stone representations of the Vedic gods. Adhrit thought he recognized a crocodile's skull, lying next to the horns of a goat. The lamplight sent the shadows of all these things dancing on the stone walls.

"Ah." The voice came from behind him. Adhrit turned to see the familiar face: the teeth were still rotten, the one eye still blind, but Ekaaksh smiled at Adhrit. "I haven't seen you for some time."

Adhrit shrugged. "I found better things to do."

"I wish I could say the same," Ekaaksh said. "What can I do for you now? A virility charm perhaps? Or some kind of protection?"

Adhrit waved a hand in the air. Living so distant from others gave the hermit the bliss of ignorance about the wars. "I want nothing from you. The raja has need of a tantric sorcerer." The word conjured memories of other men from the past, other so-called sorcerers. Adhrit remembered one, though not his name, who drank his own urine and ate his own feces. Adhrit had been disgusted even then, but the man had said that in breaking from morality he was able to work great magics. But at what cost?

Ekaaksh stepped closer. His breath reeked. "The raja wishes my help?"

"The Macedonian sends his armies this way. Already he has defeated forces much greater than our own. We need more than men to save Ramyasthana."

Ekaaksh narrowed his eyes and rubbed his hands together. Adhrit noticed that they were stunted, small as a child's hands. "You are still shrewd to seek out sorcery."

"So you know someone who can do this?"

Ekaaksh frowned. "Me, of course. Mundane magics may earn my bread, but I know the old rituals." Ekaaksh held out a splayed hand studded with long, filthy nails. "It will be no trouble, provided the payment is—"

"You shall be paid handsomely," Adhrit said. Sankara had full coffers. Coffers that Alexander would plunder.

"Ah, good," Ekaaksh said. "Then I need you to obtain some things for me. Some I can procure myself but others . . . "

"Like what?"

"A goat, for one. And wine, the purer the better. Rice, I have. And you must meet me tomorrow night by the river. In the cemetery."

"Why there?" Adhrit asked.

Ekaaksh shook his head. He licked cracked lips. "You'll see."

Adhrit was haunted that night by dreams of Ekaaksh. The sorcerer chanted, naked and smeared with filth, while Ramyasthana's people washed away in a flood of murky water that seemed born of tears. Or blood. When he woke in the night his entire body was wet with perspiration. He walked outside to feel the faint breeze on his skin and looked out into the jungle. Somewhere out there, not too far away, was Alexander's army. How much time did they have?

The next day, Adhrit set about fetching the items that Ekaaksh had requested. Ramyasthana was a city in fear. As he visited merchants, bearing his brother's wealth, they demonstrated this, taking his payment with shaking hands. The wine merchant talked about fleeing, running into the jungle, making for the nearest city with his best stock. The fishmonger easily handed over his freshest catch. "Better you take it than the invader," he said. "It's the last I'll take from the river before he comes."

Sankara's goatherd handed over one of his best with wet eyes. "I fear they will be slaughtered," he said. "Perhaps it would be best if I did it first. Humanely."

"Courage," Adhrit said, placing a hand on the man's arm. But the word sounded empty.

As he walked the path leading out of the city, Adhrit ran into two of the priests from the temple. Their mouths were covered, but he saw their eyes travel from his face, down to his feet and the goat. "Adhrit," one of them said. "You were not at the temple today."

Adhrit flushed and looked down. "I have errands to complete for my brother." He gave them each a quick nod, then hurried away, pulling the goat a little too hard, perhaps, in his haste. He journeyed straight for the cemetery.

The cemetery stood on the other side of the Vipasa river, the running water providing a barrier between the living and the dead. Their grandfather had believed in burying the dead in the ground, returning the bodies to the cycle of life, for worms and insects and other creatures to devour. Adhrit, who had once preferred cremation, had come to appreciate that. He would visit Taata's grave often to think, to talk. Daylight made the cemetery peaceful.

But night . . . standing there, alone (except for the goat, thankfully silent), Adhrit felt uneasy. Vulnerable, as if his buried kin suspected that his transformation, his walking the right path, had been a deceit, and he was still a foolish young man of many hungers seeking excess.

His taata had been reincarnated into another form, he knew, but Adhrit still worried that some part of the man remained under the earth.

"Ah," called the voice of Ekaaksh. "You're here. And with the goat."

"My brother's goatherd claimed it was the best of his flock."

Ekaaksh shrugged and tugged on a rope that connected to a young girl.

Adhrit trembled with anger. His hand neared the hilt of his sword. "You said nothing about a girl."

Ekaaksh's eyes went to Adhrit's hand, then to the girl, then back to Adhrit. "Did you think I was going to sacrifice this young thing?" He chuckled. "I am not a monster."

Adhrit relaxed a little.

"I will be sacrificing the goat, though," Ekaaksh said.

Adhrit winced. He had been expecting it—his beliefs held that all life was sacred. And as an adherent of ahimsa he had devoted himself to doing violence to no creature. But as Sankara had said, violence was acceptable if used in self-defense. And wasn't this what he was doing?

Ekaaksh set out a bundle of cloth and unrolled it to reveal a number of metal and stone implements, including a wicked knife. Eyes down, silent, the girl knelt at his side.

"Then what is the girl for?" Adhrit asked.

"The ritual," Ekaaksh said without looking up from his tools.

"She will help you with it?"

"Oh yes. Her participation is vital."

"Look at me," Adhrit said. When Ekaaksh didn't, he said it louder. "Look at me."

Ekaaksh raised his head.

"I want a demonstration. Before you waste my time, and my brother's goat, I want you to show me what it is you're giving us. Can you do that?"

Ekaaksh pursed his lips. "Yes. That won't even require the full ritual." He stood and put one hand on the girl's head. "Stay here."

Ekaaksh moved forward into the center of the cemetery. His head tilted about as if he sought a sound, a voice. "Have you heard of the vetala?" the sorcerer asked over his shoulder.

"Children's stories," Adhrit said.

"Like many of the things in stories, they are real. Spirits of the dead who can't escape their fates. They dwell in places like this. I am going to show you one." He closed his eyes and began muttering something that Adhrit didn't recognize. He held up his hands and uttered a single, loud word. Then he exhaled loudly. "It is done."

"What?" Adhrit asked. "I see nothing."

Ekaaksh smiled. "You will."

Adhrit sighed and crossed his arms. Ekaaksh went back to his tools. The girl continued to kneel in silence. Adhrit scowled at the old man, and muttered an apology to the goat.

Then he caught sight of movement out of the corner of his eye. He turned to see the ground disturbed . . . from underneath. Two mottled limbs bloated by damp reaching, struggling to free themselves of earth.

"You may want to have your sword ready," Ekaaksh said without a glance in Adhrit's direction.

The body emerged like a wriggling worm. Dirt and grass streaked the corpse. It had been female, that much was clear from the hanging flaps of skin that had once been breasts. Upright, it paused to orient itself, then it lurched toward Adhrit on stiff limbs.

Adhrit drew his sword and held it before him. "This is the vetala?"

"The vetala is the spirit," Ekaaksh said. "But it can inhabit a corpse. Assuming someone, a talented sorcerer for instance, helps it to."

Adhrit backed away from the thing. "But why?"

"Insubstantial spirits crave solidity. Only . . . "

"Only what?" Adhrit snapped. His heart beat fiercely and sweat beaded his brown and neck.

"The process creates a terrible hunger. That thing . . . well, it won't embrace you. If it catches you, it will feast."

The vetala lurched forward with its mouth slack. Adhrit brought his sword down, but because of his haste, the blow struck the thing's shoulder at an angle. Still, he sheared through the limb sending the arm falling to the ground.

The vetala did not stop stalking him.

"It will seek prey until a truly vital organ is destroyed," Ekaaksh said. "The liver. The brain. Or heart."

The vetala swung the other arm at Adhrit and he barely managed to throw himself out of its reach. Taking a breath, he decided to test Ekaaksh's words. Taata had insisted that both sons learn how to fight, but playing the ascetic had required Adhrit forget the sword. He lashed out with the weapon, aiming for the creature's head.

He missed but struck the creature in the neck and parted the head from the shoulders. The head fell backwards onto the ground. The body continued to stumble, to walk. With a hiss, Adhrit rolled past the thing and came up over its head. The mouth still moved despite its separation from the body. Adhrit brought the sword down with all of his strength, driving it through the skull and into the brain beneath.

The corpse body fell to the ground. The head stilled.

"See?" Ekaaksh said. "I told you."

"That thing almost killed me!"

"You wanted a demonstration. I would deem that sufficient, wouldn't you?"

"And this ritual will . . . ?"

"Allow me to draw more of the vetala here, give them bodies to inhabit, give you an army. Not a sweet-smelling one, mind you." Ekaaksh laughed.

He was mad. Truly mad. Yet Adhrit imagined the sight of such creatures would unnerve even the most seasoned soldier.

He gazed back upon the limp corpse. He frowned. That had once been someone's mother or someone's daughter. Had this woman's soul moved on? Wasn't that what allowed the vetala to take them?

The five great vows Adhrit had taken tasted like bitter ashes in his mouth. "The souls of the dead are gone, Ekaaksh."

"Hmm."

"Tell me. That these are nothing but empty vessels buried in the dirt."

Ekaaksh shook his head. "You have merely replaced a physical hunger with a spiritual one. The trick about hunger, however, is that it will always return." He snorted. "At least my hungers are easier to sate. And more enjoyable.

"Now, I will need you to watch over me. Ensure that I'm not disturbed. Or attacked by a wild tiger."

Adhrit ground his teeth together but nodded.

"And you mustn't disturb me, either. Especially not when I'm coupling with the girl."

"What?" Adhrit said.

Ekaaksh shook his head. "Your vows might have doused the fire in your loins, but some of us depend upon it." He nudged the girl. "She is a prostitute. And she is being compensated."

Adhrit stalked over to the girl, placing himself between the sorcerer and her. He bent toward her. "What is your name?" he asked.

"Anjali, sir."

"You can go, Anjali," Adhrit said. "I'll not let him do this."

"No, please," she said. She stood and pulled at his shirt. "He is paying me double what I would make otherwise. While I am bleeding. And when I would normally make nothing. Please, you must. For my family."

Adhrit swallowed his bile and turned away from her. "Is she even old enough for this?"

"She is old enough to have flowered," Ekaaksh said. "Which is why she is needed."

Adhrit could feel his soul blackening at the edges.

"Shall I begin?" Ekaaksh asked.

Adhrit longed to say no. To send Ekaaksh back to his vile cave. To take the girl to the temple, clean her up. To lead a group of men to ask the Macedonian to leave beautiful Ramyasthana standing. To prostrate, to beg. But he knew that none of these things would help his brother, his people. "Begin."

He didn't watch Ekaaksh work. He stared at the sky while the goat bleated its pain, when he heard the old man's grunts as he took the girl. He imagined a great wheel, the turning cycle of reincarnation. And he pictured himself, his true self, his soul, being crushed beneath it and ground into the dirt.

Once the ritual was completed, Ekaaksh slid to the ground, his skin dripping with sweat, weariness etched into his face. "Go," he said. "Tell the raja that it is done. I will meet him on the morrow."

Adhrit did so, happy to be free of the cemetery. He stopped to rest, tossing and turning on his simple mat, but sleep eluded him. He waited for morning, then visited his brother.

Sankara listened to Adhrit's report, then nodded. "You should return to the cemetery. I need your eyes on this sorcerer. I will gather my men and join you shortly."

Adhrit returned, rousing Ekaaksh from sleep. He also made sure the girl had been paid and sent her on her way. "This business is not for you," he said.

A short while later, a pale Sankara entered the cemetery, his retinue following close behind. He was girded for battle, bearing an axe and wearing a hide vest, the inheritance of more violent ancestors. Was he anticipating heading into battle?

Ekaaksh moved forward, wiping blood and dirt from his skin. "Greetings, my raja," he said.

"Is it ready?" Sankara asked.

Ekaaksh nodded. "The ritual has been completed. The spirits have been bound."

"They will fight for us?"

"Yes," Ekaaksh said. "A bargain has been made. In return for the use of the bodies, they will follow my commands."

Sankara turned aside to Adhrit. "Is the sorcerer trustworthy?"

Adhrit snorted. "His love of wealth is. And the excesses to which that wealth can be used. He will do what is necessary for the payment you promised."

Sankara took a deep breath and looked around at the cemetery. "These are the bodies of our people. It seemed justified, but now that I look around . . . "

"They are only bodies. Their souls have moved on already." He was aware that he was trying to convince himself as well as his brother.

Sankara nodded.

"But our souls still are here, brother," Adhrit said. "And what we do here affects their journey." He clasped his brother by the arms. "There's still time to turn away from this path. We can run. Or else face Alexander knowing that we haven't sullied our souls—"

Sankara shook his head. "It is too late to turn back now," he said. "I'll not see Ramyasthana destroyed." He turned to Ekaaksh. "When can you bring them forth? And how long will they last?"

"Oh, they will not decay while the vetala are inside of them. They gain strength from the spirit. But I can not call them up until your enemies are almost upon you. As I told your brother, they have a great hunger and are driven to feed. I could hold them for some time, but their appetites will overwhelm them."

Sankara nodded. "Very well. I have scouts out monitoring the position of Alexander's forces. They will let us know when they are approaching. Then we will assemble our new army and draw them to us."

He turned back to Adhrit. "Are you ready, little brother?" he asked. "History will say that this is where we changed its course."

Adhrit said nothing. The accounting of the years meant little compared to the accounting of his soul.

Word came the next day that Alexander's forces were moving toward Ramyasthana, though they would have to cross the river first. Adhrit was given a hide vest to wear, and Ekaaksh was told to call the vetala forth.

One by one, grotesque seedlings, they sprouted. Stained and decayed corpses emerging from the earth. Adhrit began scanning the assembled creatures before forcing himself to stop. You don't want to see your father like this, he told himself. Or worse, your mother.

At last they had all emerged, hundreds of them, all stumbling about the cemetery. Sankara's troops, wide-eyed, backed away from them. Adhrit knew how they felt. One had seemed like a horror. This was an abomination. He could only hope it would fall like a hammer on Alexander's men.

"We must protect the sorcerer," Sankara told Adhrit.

Adhrit nodded.

They waited as Sankara's meager troops feinted at the enemy, their goal to draw them to the grounds outside the cemetery, where the vetala stood.

Downwind thankfully, Adhrit thought. Sweat dripped from his eyes. Burning tears. The only sound of the jungle louder than his breathing was the nearby roar of the river. At least we have the Vipasa at our backs, Adhrit thought. He jumped at every bird call, at the belch that Ekaaksh let out, at a passing monkey. Then a flock of frightened birds erupted from the trees in front of them and soldiers poured through, armed and armored.

The vetala shambled on stiff limbs and rotten old bones. The soldiers moved faster and, almost before the Macedonians knew it, they were among the corpses. The hunger within the creatures revealed itself.

Adhrit saw one of the vetala lunge forward, gripping an enemy with its thick limbs. Unnatural strength drew the armored soldier toward it, gripping it tightly. Then the vetala bit into the man's face, as a child might eat fruit. The man's cries were swallowed, literally, by the creature.

Screams filled the air as the vetala fed. Blood painted their bodies red. Adhrit spared a glance at Ekaaksh and found the sorcerer smiling at the destruction. "See?" he said. "Glorious."

Adhrit felt sick to his stomach and only the fact that he had not eaten that morning spared him from vomiting onto the ground. The display left him nauseated. The wanton violence, the death. He had given up the eating of meat so as to do less harm in the world and yet here he faced these . . . things devouring men.

We are all damned, he thought.

The vetala routed the enemy. They fell back through the jungle's trees.

Ekaaksh roared, slapping Adhrit on the back. "See what victory I have sold you?"

Adhrit shook his head. "Something's wrong. That was far too few men. Alexander's force has to be much larger than that."

"What does that mean?" Ekaaksh asked.

"I don't know," Adhrit said. "Maybe this was just to test us? Maybe they're moving in a different direction. I should follow after them." He looked at the sorcerer, who he was supposed to be protecting. "You'll just have to come with me." He grabbed the scrawny man by the arm and dragged him after the fleeing soldiers.

They plunged into the jungle, Adhrit keeping one eye on the sorcerer. Ahead of them, vetala moved like shadows through the trees. Now that they had fed, they were more limber, faster. The Macedonians, desperate to escape, looked small in number.

Adhrit made them crouch behind some trees to watch the last of the soldiers disappear into the distance. Behind them, the vetala stopped and began to return to the cemetery. "They will remain on guard?" Adhrit whispered.

Ekaaksh nodded, wiping his brow with his arm. "But their hunger has increased. I can hold them for a time, but your brother must decide how long. Perhaps this Alexander will withdraw?"

"Perhaps. But we might not know for some time."

"The quicker the better," Ekaaksh said. His eyes seemed sunken into dark pits and his hands were shaking. His control was clearly taxing him.

"Let's head back." They pushed back through the trees, in the direction of the cemetery.

"Slow down, slow down," Ekaaksh said. He yanked his arm free and stood bent over, sucking in breath. Adhrit cursed at the man, who answered in kind. Then Ekaaksh screamed and leapt, slapping at one leg.

Adhrit looked down to see the flared hood of a cobra. His sword whipped out to cut the thing in two but missed and the snake disappeared into the high grass.

Ekaaksh fell to the ground, moaning and clutching at his wound.

Adhrit remembered Sankara's words, just after they'd buried their taata: "He'll likely come back as a bull."

"No," Adhrit had said. "A cobra."

Adhrit forced the sorcerer's hand away so he could see the wound. "Can you move the leg?"

Ekaaksh whimpered. "Is it bad?"

Adhrit ground his teeth together. He'd seen bites like this twice before. Both times the men had died. And if Ekaaksh died, then what of the vetala? He gripped the sorcerer's shoulder. "Is there another way to stop the vetala?"

"Save me. Carry me to town. Or else go get help."

"I will! But I need to know what will stop the vetala."

Ekaaksh just shook his head, staring up at the sky. "No, please no."

Adhrit slapped the sorcerer's face. "Tell me how to stop them and I will get you help."

Ekaaksh's eyes focused for a moment. "A mantra. You must repeat it till the last one is stilled." His sobs interrupted the mantra. His trembling lips mangled the words. Adhrit forced him to repeat it, slapping him each time.

By the time Adhrit had committed it to memory, the sorcerer's breath came in weak rasps. Adhrit had to deny the man mercy. "Stay here," he said, in a flat, dead voice. "I'll get you help."

He ran for the banks of the river. The bridge had been taken down, the river still protected Ramyasthana. But as he reached the cemetery, he saw the vetala, as one, dropping into the banks of the Vipasa.

He pushed himself faster as hope filled his chest. The creatures would be swept away by the rough flow of the river. He stood at its edge, breathing hard, waiting to see something. Minutes passed. The vetala must now be downstream, a plague on someone else if not washed out to sea.

Then, like a lumbering, bloated crocodile, a pale, grey shape emerged from the water at the far side. Another followed. And another, until enough dripping vetala emerged to doom Ramyasthana.

"No!" Adhrit dropped his sword to the ground and began stripping off gear and clothes. Even the strongest man could barely swim the Vipasa at this time of year, but he had to try. He dove into the water and the shock of its cold took the breath from him. He pushed his arms and legs to carry him forward, even as the thrust of the river washed him further downstream. He kicked and barely came up for breath. Then he inhaled a spray of water and got swirled around by the current. His head struck hard upon a cresting rock as he was carried away.

In all things the sorcerer had been right. Alexander's scouts returned to the main force and rumors of the vetala spread. When the conqueror tried to urge his men to move on, they revolted, and he was forced to turn around, shy of the Vipasa River.

He was also right that the vetala were only bound while he lived. As he died, overcome by their hunger, they moved for nearby Ramyasthana. By the time Adhrit arrived there, no one was left alive. The vetala moved throughout the city, devouring the meat of the inhabitants, slick with blood and entrails. Some of the buildings burned, casualties of the fighting, no doubt. Bodies littered the ground like the petals of flowers.

Adhrit walked among them, tears stinging his eyes, chanting the mantra that Ekaaksh had given him. As he neared the vetala, they went rigid as he continued the chant. Then they collapsed, one by one, to the ground, lifeless corpses once more. He made three circuits of the city, until he was certain that none of the vetala remained, then he stopped, his throat raw.

Most of the dead were hard to identify, but he thought he found his brother together with his wife and children. He avoided looking at the vacated corpses. They were all just empty shells now, the souls of the people of Ramyasthana having moved on to the next step of the karmic cycle. Ramyasthana, the oasis of culture in that land, was no more. Perhaps its soul, too, waited for its next incarnation.

Adhrit once more donned the robes of the ascetic and wandered the lands. He wore a veil so as to not inhale the tiniest of insects. He went barefoot so as not to crush anything in his path. Rather than a sword, he bore a staff that jingled, warning of his presence.

He did not raise his hand to defend himself when men of the road beat him. If his lips were swollen with bruises or thirst, he still moved them to spread the word of what had happened at Ramyasthana and how straying from their path had doomed them. He taught to any who would listen the cycle of reincarnation and how enlightenment came only by walking the right path.

Still his every step away from that cemetery he had befouled pained him. He ate no meat and yet found himself salivating whenever he passed anything of flesh. Goat. Poultry. Children. The stains of his sins had not been washed away by the Vipasa or worn down by his long travels.

One night, as he sat by the road, the dark jungle at his back, before sleep came he thought he heard the hiss of a serpent. A cobra? Or was it the memory of the last breath taken by Ekaaksh. Or of Sankara. Or Ramyasthana. Or his own? His trembling hand went to his chest to assure himself he still lived.

AFTER
LAZARUS

# ANTIQUITY

# A FRENZY OF RAVENS

## CHRISTOPHER M. CEVASCO

*40 A.D. – Isle of Mona, Briton*

Alene and her father crossed swords in the shadows of the sacred grove. Great, midnight-hued birds gathered all around on gnarled oaks, watching, skittish from the clangor.

"Blade up," her father said, swinging hard toward Alene's head. "If a Roman wretch comes upon you he'll not care you're still a child. You'll have to fight like a grown warrior to stay alive." Though a druid, he was himself as much a warrior as any of the Iceni, and Alene knew he wanted her to be the same. Now more than ever. For once she did not bother to tell him thirteen summers made her no longer a child.

*Will they ever truly come?* she wondered. It was the second time these men called Romans had threatened, and just as the first time almost a hundred years before, the threat had again come to nothing. The Romans had a chief—some named him Caligula, others Imperator—and if Alene could believe the accounts, this madman called off the latest invasion while still on Gaul's shores after first ordering his warriors to gather seashells from the strand as spoils of the conquered mere. To Alene, such behavior could only mean there had been some intervention by the goddess, Boudicca, She who warded Briton, its folk, and the Iceni above all. *My prayers were answered.*

"Good," her father grunted as she shoved his blade away with her own. "That's enough for this morning. I must meet with your Uncle Hirelgdas and the others to talk of better warding ourselves in the years to come."

Whether Alene's prayers had been answered or not, the learned mystics of the Iceni and every other people had gathered from across Briton to discuss the Romans. True fear simmered among the elders; even her grim uncle, one of the fiercest warriors alive, was afraid. Alene felt it no matter how they all tried to hide it from her. She glanced up at the ravens, whose stirrings had quieted; *they* sensed it too—blood on the air—and it made their black eyes sparkle.

"I would stay a while," Alene said, "to be with the goddess."

Her father nodded and strapped his sword to his hip, then planted a kiss atop her head. There was no question of which goddess she meant; he well knew her devotion to Boudicca—the great victory goddess, known as Andraste to some, as the Morrígan to others. "Don't linger overly long. Your mother will be looking for you."

Alene nodded, then watched him melt into the woods, a tall, strong figure, his hair still dark and thick with but a hint of gray. Only when she was sure he was well away did she lay her own sword down on the mossy ground and turn to be about her business. Today she had resolved to give thanks in a way her father would not look well on.

She stripped off her cloak and tunic so she stood only in a short shift. Shivering, she knelt before the stone altar at the clearing's western edge. Alene looked around at the trees and sent her words to the gaps between the branches. "I speak to Boudicca, She Who Has Not Fallen! I am Alene, and my people are the Iceni." She paused, and her shivers worsened. "It shames me I was so frightened by the talk of Roman onslaught. I should have known you would ward us, as you've always done. I do not forget the oath I swore—to hallow myself to you if you delivered us from the wretched outlanders. So I offer myself to your gathered errand-runners. Let them drink of my lifeblood as a mark of my bond to you."

Alene took up a small blade she'd hidden earlier among the altar stones. She made a short, neat cut along each inner forearm. Then she lay back on the ground, arms akimbo, and let the blood flow.

A breeze stirred the boughs, and the ravens left their perches. Flocking about Alene, they answered her call. Dark beaks pecked at the bloody soil and the open wounds with little pinching stabs. The pain stirred her from a deepening swoon, and she heard a voice—a soughing that was part cawing, part feathered rustle. *The Lady does not take consecration lightly. Your life will be Hers. And your death. Is this your will?*

"Yes, Lady." Alene's voice was a bare whisper. "I give myself fully."

*The Lady will test you again. Temper you with hardships. More blood will be spilled, and not only your own.*

"As the Lady bids. To keep my home safe, no hardship is too great."

Awareness faded. The ravens abided, gathered about and atop her like a blanket, drinking their fill.

Then something changed.

Alene had braced herself for the pecking, and it was nothing, little worse than the cuts she'd made herself many times before. But now . . . something else entered her with each sharp pinch. Icy cold flooded her body, and some great weight—the very sky itself—pressed down on her, collapsing into her, smothering her. With it came the smell of death, of decay—a carrion smell.

She struggled but was too weak to move, let alone send off the flock. The weight lessened, and she cried out, a sound so small she was unsure if she did so in truth or only in her mind. Then the sky's press was back like a great wave, washing over her, receding, then coming again to pound her into the earth.

*I am lost.*

The birds scattered all at once, rising above the grove. The stench abated; warmth and life flowed back into her, chased away by hands lifting her, shaking her. Her uncle's hands. Hirelgdas's voice.

"Uncle?"

"Foolish girl!" Hirelgdas barked, and he struck Alene across the face. The sting of his knuckles woke her fully, and she could not stop the tears from flowing as she stared up at his angry eyes, at the dappled pattern of sunlight through leaves shifting across his shaved head as though the skin itself were moving. "Your father is a fool too, but I guessed you might be up to no good. By the gods, you are to lead your people one day! Remember that the next time you think to so carelessly cast your life away."

"I'm sorry." It came out as a sob, and Alene was ashamed as she looked down at her forearms. The bleeding had stopped, but her arms were deeply bruised around the wounds.

"Not yet you're not," he answered. "But you will be!" Then he struck her again, beating her from neck to belly with his hard fists.

Above the sound of her own cries, Alene heard a single caw from the departing birds.

*61 A.D. – Iceni Lands, Briton*

A lingering winter wind pushed in among the hawthorn and rowan. Alene looked out from the thicket on a high, moss-covered bluff over the sea of bright spring buds and tentative leaves already crowning the forest below. Out and south she looked, toward the Trinovante lands, and a little to the west, in the direction of the Roman stronghold of Kaelcolim.

No doubt that was the direction from which the emissaries would come—from that place the outlanders had founded like a scabby wound among Loegria's soft hills. They had the gall to call Kaelcolim their "provincial capital," as though Briton were no more than an insignificant afterthought to their empire over the water.

Alene shivered, and her daughter Saraid touched her elbow. "What is it, Mother?" Saraid's cheeks still held a child's round fullness, but she had Alene's high forehead over large eyes, an almost Roman nose, and pouting lips nearly the hue of spilled blood against her ivory skin. Whereas Alene's hair was a mass of amber curls, Saraid had been gifted with the straight, dark hair of Alene's own dead mother.

"Nothing, dearest," Alene answered. "It's chilly, and I should have worn a heavier cloak." She told herself it was that and not memories of the earlier Roman threat all those years ago . . . not memories of how frightened she'd been as a child. She rubbed absently at the old scars along her forearms and remembered too her vow that bygone day in the clearing and what happened when she woke aching and weak in her father's roundhouse on Mona the next morning; as she lay wrapped in blankets, a vision had come to her—Boudicca surrounded by a flurry of dark, beating wings. The goddess had looked right at her with shining eyes, fierce and awful, but also familiar somehow, which had comforted her. It was a wonder she'd kept with her always, even now that she was queen of her people. So much had changed.

"Can it be so long ago the Romans returned? After Caligula's witlessness," she mused, more to herself than to her daughter. "Seventeen summers gone, when I was newly wed to your father." Prastog was an Iceni merchant, later rewarded with a client-kingship for helping Emperor Claudius's conquering battle chiefs. Her husband had always been so quick to kneel to the outlanders, but even after all this time under the entrenched Roman governors of Briton, Queen Alene never let herself acknowledge Roman overlordship.

"I miss Father too," Saraid said.

Alene bit back tears; she had not let one fall yet and wouldn't start now. *Not on this of all days. Be strong!*

A rowan blossom rode the air until it vanished into the thicker greenery below, and Alene scowled. With her husband's death and spring's coming, the time to pay for past overweening had come. Word came to Alene daily as Roman siege after Roman siege drove high folk from their own homes across Iceni lands—men and women who had supported both her husband and the Emperor and done nothing to earn the like. But when Seneca and the others called in loans and the payments were unforthcoming, all was seized in the name of the latest emperor, Nero. Men and women were mowed down beneath Roman swords like so much wheat. Alene snorted. *The wonted Roman answer!*

"Mother, look!"

Alene looked where her daughter pointed, squinting toward the land's southernmost eyemark. A glint of sun on polished bronze was her first sight of Seneca's men just beyond the wood's edge. *The waiting is over. They've come.*

She rose from the natural stone seat, all at once unable to look away from an ancient ash tree downslope. It was bent and twisted into a tortured shape by the winds of untold storms but still clung to life on the stone and indeed put forth the first faltering black buds that meant it would live to see yet another summer in this quiet place. Nearby, a jackdaw's nest filled the newly cracked and shattered trunk of a youngish oak that jutted from the ground like some mouldering hand reaching up from the grave. The oak had been too proud to bend with the same winter winds that had taken her husband from her not two months past. The Romans were a wrathful wind, sweeping across Briton, and it was now Alene's decision how best to weather the storm. *Bend as my husband did, or stand tall like an oak as so many tried before?* All those latter folk were dead now or taken as thralls to the markets in Rome. The answer seemed clear.

"Come, Saraid." Pulling up her tunic's thick mantle and fastening it with her best brooch worn for the delegation's arrival, Alene strode from the bluff back below the surrounding trees. Saraid kept pace at her side, taking two steps for every one of her mother's. As they approached the nearby hill fort's slope, the marching Roman auxiliaries' first ranks had already rounded the curve of the southwest road. Alene made her way up from the forest bordering the hill's eastern face by hidden paths known to herself and her kin, and by the time they reached the top, the Romans were climbing the other side by way of the plainer path.

Alene's elder daughter stood behind the altar, ringed by several dozen worried Iceni high-men and women and looking comely as always, every bit the leader of their people she would one day be. If Brianne shared any of the others' misgivings, she hid it well. *Gods! She looks more like Prastog every day.* The girl had his long, sleek jawline and high cheekbones, framed by layers of her mother's amber curls. At fifteen, she was more a woman than Alene herself had been at that age, and if her swift headway in the hallowed crafts was any sign, she would one day surpass her mother in a priestess's skills.

Saraid, on the other hand, though making like headway in her studies, still had a child's eagerness, and as she stepped up to the altar, Brianne had to put a hand on her shoulder to keep the younger girl from standing on tiptoes to get a better look at the nearing soldiers. Alene stood behind her daughters and placed a hand on each. Brianne turned and flashed Prastog's crooked smile. "You've been to Boudicca's Seat. I smell the rowan in your hair. Did you summon a Telling?"

"No," Saraid answered for her, soreness heavy in her words. "She said there was no time today."

"Hush, child," Alene said, clucking her tongue. "I'll not have my daughter pouting like some spoiled Roman."

They looked back toward the road. When the delegation's rearmost at last came over the hill's crest, Brianne scoffed. "So the governor sends soldiers to treat with us. More than needed as wards for Seneca's *scribae*, that's bare enough."

Alene squeezed her daughter's shoulder with pride. "Yes, love. Suetonius makes

"Let them be!" Alene yelled, straining toward her daughters. Her hands were now tied as well, and bright, shimmering hues burst across her sight as the centurion came forward to backhand her jaw.

Alene spat a mouthful of blood at the man and lunged toward him. The centurion laughed again at her hopeless flailing, and she stilled herself.

Wiping her bloody spittle from his cheek, he leaned close to Alene. "You will learn respect soon enough." His breath stank of sour wine. Then he bid her captors bind her to the wooden staff.

"You will not do this," a small voice came, and Alene turned to see her aged uncle Hirelgdas step forward from among the gathered folk, a spear clutched in his gnarled hands. *Uncle, no.*

"Step back, old man," the centurion said, "before you hurt yourself."

Other words might have worked, but the mocking tone only goaded her uncle, reminding him of the strength that had fled him, of his once-mighty warrior status now lost to the passing of long years. "Uncle, please," Alene said, "all will be well."

Hirelgdas was not swayed. His hollow cheeks were mottled an angry red behind the droop of long, white mustaches. Alene sighed. *How I once feared his wrath . . .*

The spear came up, shakily, and the centurion answered by drawing his own short Roman sword and passing its tip almost as an afterthought through the soft flesh beneath Hirelgdas's chin. The old man's eyes went wide, then a red beard grew from his severed neck, a wash of blood leaving him in one great gout. Alene looked away as he fell, glad at least that he'd died as he had once lived, with spear in hand.

As the Romans manhandled her, no other Iceni raised a finger on her behalf, so cowed were they by their Roman overlords. *How can I blame them?* Likely they and their families had already undergone the same wretchedness in the past weeks, and there had been none to fight for them. She rued having earlier chided the uprooted folk who had gathered here, rued asking why they had not shown more backbone, why the Iceni could no longer fight even half so well as the men of Gwynedd. *What choice did they have? To resist is to be broken like the oak. Now it's my turn to be shamed.*

They stripped her.

*I am an ash. I will bend with this Roman wind.* If her open shaming was what the Romans wanted in order to forgive the debts, then they would have it. If it meant giving up her sway over Iceni lands rightfully her daughters', she would accept that. *I am an ash, and I will bend so my folk might live, so my daughters will not be made slaves, so the Iceni will not be driven into the dust.*

They tied her to the stake.

*Let the winds blow.*

The rope dug into her neck, into her ankles and arms, but she took herself away from the ache. The world around her faded as she cast her mind out from her body in the way her father had taught her to do long ago.

They scourged her.

Alene's body went rigid, and the darkness behind her eyelids filled with soothing greenery. The oaks on Mona—the druids' sacred groves—a place as yet untouched by the Romans where nothing could hurt her. As ever, she saw herself walking among the ancient boles, hands out to stroke rough bark, draw strength. And this time, something else—cold and clammy. A body.

A gray-haired druid had been bound to an oak, a rope about his waist, iron spikes through wrists and feet, crucified in the way only the Romans would do. All around her, hundreds of druids and priestesses had been similarly slain, many of the oaks themselves hacked down by cruel Roman axes. The stone altars were toppled. She smelled the smoke before she saw it, felt the heat of the fire before she saw the flames. The groves burned. It was awful—too much to bear—and Alene could not keep her thoughts bound there.

As though some great raven had snatched her into the sky, she was drawn up and away from Mona, saw it from an impossible height. In what had become an unbidden Telling, she saw all the island burning. In the smoke rising above it, Alene glimpsed the goddess, Boudicca, wreathed in flames, dying along with her people. *What sort of wretches are these Romans, not only to slay men but to murder a god? The world is lost. Lost!*

She returned to her body. The lash had fallen upon her shoulders, her back, and her buttocks more times than she could guess. Blood crept down her legs to pool on the loamy earth. As the strap fell yet again, she opened her eyes. The centurion stared at her and smiled. She pulled her lips back, giving him a rictus of grim hatred but never once letting him hear her cry out in pain.

In time the man's cast turned to one of disbelief and then boredom. When even the soldier wielding the lash faltered, the centurion grunted and motioned for her to be taken down. He retreated toward the roundhouse. Alene's bonds were cut, and her knees gave way. *The wind has passed. I was not broken.*

The Romans stepped away from her crumpled form, and her own handmaids brought her a dark wool cloak. Gathering the last of her will, Alene rose and let them settle the cloak over her shoulders, gritting her teeth as the cloth chafed her raw flesh. She looked north to the roundhouse where her daughters had been taken, and as if in answer, the centurion strode out and called for Alene.

She forced herself to walk between the soldiers who fetched her, not wanting to be dragged to her own doorstep like a sack of wheatcorn.

One of the soldiers leaned close suddenly, his lips near her ear. "I'm sorry. I would spare you this if I could, but he would have my head."

The man drew back, and Alene turned to look at him. He was young, not much older than Brianne, and from the sound of his speech, he had been one of the neighboring Catuvellauni before taking up with the Romans. His look was earnest, almost pained, and for a heartbeat Alene nearly smiled her thanks at him. Then she reminded herself that he was a troth-breaker, and she spat at his feet.

"So you will not cry out?" the centurion asked when Alene was before him. "Then we shall let your daughters do the screaming for you."

Alene's throat tightened as they drew her into her house.

She blinked in the sudden darkness. The place was a shambles—her loom toppled and broken against a wall, baskets overturned. A drinking horn that had been in her family for generations lay broken on the floor.

Then her eyes settled to the dimness.

Her daughters had been stripped. Each was bent forward and held down over one of the beds hugging the house's inner ring. Romans stood about in groups, laughing, boasting, awaiting the order.

"Stuprate them."

"Please, no!" Alene shouted, but the centurion ignored her as he and several of the waiting soldiers stepped forward, unfastening their belts. "No!"

Alene strained against the men holding her, fighting like a wild thing to free herself. One man punched her hard in the face. Her left eye began to swell shut straightaway.

Again he struck her. The crack of a tooth sounded loud in her ears.

Saraid screamed, and Alene screamed with her. "Please! They're children!" But there was a still greater wrong. Tears in her eyes, Alene stilled herself and looked toward Brianne, keeping her voice even. "Know that you defile daughters of the high ancient bloodline, the rightful leaders of a proud people. Stop now or invoke the anger of those gods who ward the Iceni!"

The centurion and his men laughed. Alene wept.

Through it all, Brianne never uttered a sound, though her younger sister screamed her throat raw as one after another, the soldiers came to her. Saraid kept struggling to get up, but one of the men always stepped forward to push her down, strike her, spit on her. It was too much, and Alene looked away. The centurion saw. "Make her watch!"

The men holding her forced Alene's head forward, fingers digging into her jaw so it popped and cracked where it met her skull. She felt a cold blade pressed against her throat by the Catuvellauni who'd spoken to her outside. Then he shifted, and his cloak fell in such a way that it was across her line of sight. "Don't move," he whispered.

*Thank you.* Her tears fell unchecked now. *Thank you.*

The kindness was short-lived. "I told you to make her watch," shouted the centurion as he strode toward them. He smashed the ivory-knobbed hilt of his sword against the young soldier's forehead, who then fell bleeding to the ground.

The centurion took his place, holding her head forward.

At every vile act she beheld, Alene now felt the lashes inflicted on her outside as though she lived them anew. She cried out.

"Boudicca! Avenge me!" But Boudicca was dead. *I saw her burning.*

The room swam and faded into murky blackness . . .

When Alene awoke, a cold stillness had fallen.

The last of the Romans were filing from the roundhouse. *My girls!*

She met Brianne's gaze first, saw the dread in her eyes. Unwontedly for her eldest, there was more sadness than anger or even hurt there. Then Brianne's gaze dropped to her sister lying so still before her. Too still.

*No.* Alene stopped breathing. *No, no, no, no, no.* She scrambled forward, saw Saraid's lifeless, staring eyes, and swept her up into her arms, sobbing as she rocked back and forth. "No, my dearest. No, no. Hush now. It will be well. No, no." She hardly knew what she said.

Brianne's arms went around them both. "We will make them pay for this, Mother."

Alene drew a heavy breath, pushing away her sobs. Brianne was trembling. She had to be strong now for her living daughter. "Yes. They will pay." *But how?* She lowered Saraid's head to her lap, supporting her limp neck with a hand as she had done when her daughter was but newly born. *Oh, my sweet babe.*

Ignoring the burning ache across her back and shoulders, Alene took up an edge of her own cloak and leaned toward Brianne, wiping away the mark of tears, the blood from her daughter's nose and split cheek. Looking up then into the darkness beneath the sloping roof, she whispered to her protectress. "Have you had enough blood yet, Lady?" She tried but failed to keep the anger from her voice. "Is this enough at last?"

She fetched Brianne's torn cloak and helped her to cover herself. She wrapped Saraid in a sheep pelt and rose, lifting her daughter's body; it felt light as a bundle of rags now that the spirit had fled her. Only then did Alene take heed of the odd quiet. No sound of wind or leaf, soldier or horse, drifted in from outside; it was as though Alene had lost all hearing save for those small sounds she and Brianne made themselves. Brianne heard it too and eyed the heavy waycloth covering the entryway.

"Stay by my side," Alene whispered and edged toward the doorway, steeling herself.

The light outside was harsh.

A large flock of ravens had settled upon the hilltop. Alene strained to open her swollen eye, not believing what she saw. The ground everywhere was black with birds. She took another step, and the muscles in her neck twitched so she almost dropped her daughter. She crouched to lay Saraid's body down carefully near the threshold. *They warned me there would be more hardship, more bloodshed. But . . . not my daughter. Not Saraid.*

Taking another faltering step, she stared out at the centurion and his men picking their way among the silent, unmoving birds toward the rest of the Roman soldiers. She turned toward her roundhouse. Ravens on its roof thatch stared back with eyes of polished jet. *Why are you here?*

A raucous caw spun her back around to face the dozen soldiers wading through the black feathers. The centurion had paused to shove several birds away with the toe of a sandal. He kicked again, more savagely, and something inside Alene jerked. Rage made her limbs quake, and the ravens themselves stirred at last. Several leapt into the air to flap about the centurion's head. He and his fellows drew swords to swat at the ravens, but soon most dropped their weapons altogether in a bid to ward eyes and faces from sharp beaks and claws.

Alene walked toward them.

"What's happening?" Brianne asked, limping at her side.

Alene shook her head, having no answer.

Twenty steps from the house, a further stirring behind them made Alene look back again. The ravens had swarmed over Saraid's body.

"No!" Alene began to run toward her, but the air around her filled with dark wings, batting at her, keeping her away. "Will *you* desecrate her now? Have the Romans not done enough?" She screamed—at the ravens, at the goddess, at the very air. At last she stopped, standing still, staring helplessly at the writhing mass overtop her daughter. One raven let out a loud screech and all at once Saraid lurched upright into a sitting posture, scattering the birds away from her.

Hope sparked in Alene's breast only to be snuffed. A lopsided grin marked Saraid's cast where one of her lips had been pulled off; her eyes were two red holes, pecked out and eaten. And yet it seemed Saraid saw, for she turned her neck until her empty gaze fell upon the centurion. She scrambled to her feet and ran toward him with the jerky lope of a drunkard.

Alene grabbed Brianne and pulled her close as Saraid—or whatever horror she had become—passed them by. An awful charnel stench swirled in her wake; Alene found herself gagging, bending over to bring up the bit of broth she'd eaten earlier in the day.

When Saraid reached the Romans, the ravens harrying the men scattered to let her pass. She jumped straightaway onto the centurion's back, biting him on the neck as though she were become a wild creature of the woods. Yowling, the centurion spun and reached back to grab Saraid, yanking her over his shoulder and slamming her to the earth. No sooner did she touch ground than she bounced back up, hissing through her exposed teeth. The centurion swung his short sword at her, a heavy downward swipe. Naked, Saraid had nothing to ward herself from the blow, which took off the left side of her face and the top of one shoulder. The blow should have felled her like a spring lamb beneath the bludgeon, but there was little enough of blood for such a wound, and only a groan from her slack throat as she threw herself back toward her attacker.

The Roman brought his sword up, and Saraid gored herself on it so its tip jutted from the small of her back. Still she kept on, pulling herself up along the blade's length with her hands until face to face with the centurion. She snaked her arms around the back of the man's neck and leaned in as if to kiss him. Her head dipped and rose over and again, great red flowers blooming on his face wherever her mouth touched him.

Alene put a hand to her own mouth and gasped. *She's . . . eating him.*

Soon the centurion's screams drowned in a gargling wetness as his own blood filled his throat. He fell back, Saraid still atop him. In spite of herself, Alene felt a satisfied smile stretch her lips.

"Mother." Brianne was sobbing beside her. "Mother!"

*No. What is happening? No. Saraid!* At last Alene tore her gaze from her impossibly risen daughter to take in the rest of the hilltop. The madness had spread. Hirelgdas had awoken too, eyes torn from his sockets by the ravens but still able to see. Soldiers struggled to take him down as her old uncle fought with an inhuman strength. In a circle around him, Romans lay dead, looking for all the world as if they had been savaged by wolves.

"Come!" Alene said to her daughter. "We must help . . . him." She had almost said *it* rather than *him*. She shoved aside such thoughts.

"Mother, no," Brianne said, tugging her arm. "We should run. Get away from here. This is all wrong."

"The Romans are wrong! They should not be here! I was wrong to appease them! Boudicca has shown me that now!" She pointed across the hilltop as she shouted, and even as Hirelgdas was at last overwhelmed and swarmed by his Roman foes, a woeful sound rose from the ranks standing beyond them. The neat lines melted into chaos, and as the bodies parted, Alene's knees buckled at what she saw.

"Prastog?" she breathed. What was left of her husband after weeks rotting in the grave had emerged from among the trees. His face was a rotten grisliness clotted with lumps of muddy earth, but she knew him from the cloak they had buried him in, from the golden bands on his gray and weeping arms, from all the finery with which she had adorned him before putting him into the stone barrow with the wheels of his war wain. With him came those men who had been laid in the earth around the barrow mound, his fellow warriors in death, bound to ward him in the hereafter and now returned with him to the world of the living.

All around the dead Iceni, the air was alive with black feathers and sharp claws; the ravens embraced the risen dead as kin, as flock. On Prastog's own shoulder, a singularly large, grub-white raven perched, and Alene knew it was the one she had insisted be put into the barrow alive with her husband to help speed him to his next life. The bird cocked its head as Prastog strode across the hilltop, pecking some little morsel from Prastog's socket, from which it had already eaten most of whatever had been left of a jellied eye.

*What is this? What's happening?* Again Alene retched, but she had nothing but bile to bring up.

What came next was not the accustomed clangor of battle; only a wet sound of rending flesh and the dull thunk of Roman blades hacking through putrid meat drifted across the hilltop. An eager roar went up from among the living Iceni witnessing the slaughter. Alene watched them join the risen dead to lay waste to the invaders. Her queasiness gave way to a queen's angry pride. She threw herself forward and took up a fallen spear. Screaming against the ache in her bleeding shoulders, she swiped at her foes.

One after another Roman came before her only to be struck down. She knew nothing else but the red death her spear brought and the black cloud of wings everywhere in between.

Only when the last *scriba* lay dead upon the ground, still clutching bloodstained wax tablets, did Alene stop to rest, to breathe.

The ravens began the grim work of eating him. A Roman feast was laid out for them.

A great cheer went up. Prastog and his risen dead did not join in the yelling—they had gathered around two soldiers, crouched over the bodies to feed like the carrion birds.

Alene looked away from the sickening scene.

The living Iceni raised arms to hail her. None among them had slain as many of their enemy as she. Their queen had become a whirling, shrieking death-bringer—a legend come to life—a goddess for whom the dead themselves fought. Standing tall and proud like a great oak, she called out their victory. "We are slaves no more!"

The Iceni chanted her name and the name of Boudicca . . . and did both not refer to her? Brianne came to Alene's side, reached out one arm toward her, but then dropped trembling to her knees at what her mother had become. Alene opened her mouth to shout again, words to take away her daughter's fear and put a wild battle-joy in its place. The sound died on her lips.

Saraid stood just beyond Brianne's shoulders, her straight, dark hair matted with blood, face torn and awful, empty sockets fixed on them both. She took a tottering step forward, then leapt onto her sister's back, teeth flashing at Brianne's bared neck.

"No!" Alene's cry came too late. A great spray of Brianne's blood filled the air before she toppled over beneath Saraid.

And the shout, one of pain and fear, disturbed the restless dead from their meal. Prastog and the others no longer crouched over the slain Romans. They turned on their kin.

"Stop! They are your own!"

The gorging ravens cawed as the bodies beneath them twitched and shuddered. The birds took flight as one empty-eyed and mauled *militus* and *scriba* after another rose. Their jaws were slack, open, no doubt hungry for warm flesh.

*We are done for.* Alene backed away as Saraid lifted her gore-stained face from Brianne's corpse and then returned to devouring her sister.

Alene turned to flee, and behind her stood the centurion, whose name she had never even learned, his face a ragged mess from Saraid's teeth and nails, his missing eyes down some raven's gullet. He stalked her, his dreadful empty gaze sapping the strength she had possessed only moments before.

At the last moment she scrambled to snatch up a nearby Roman sword—perhaps the centurion's own—and she swung at him as he lunged for her. Alene took off his right hand at the wrist, just below the metal gauntlet with which he'd earlier struck her.

His left hand came up and clawed at her, tearing an edge of her cloak. The centurion's breath was in her face then, hot and bloody, teeth snapping and flashing, tongue stiff as he hissed. Alene brought the blade up again, mashing the hilt into his mouth, shoving him away. He stumbled, righted himself, and threw himself toward her. She swung, the blow clumsy but strong, and it nearly decapitated him; his head lolled backward, dangling by a scrap of skin and sinew so it lay between his shoulder blades. *Still* he stumbled toward her.

She ran past him. A clear path opened up along a line of trees leading to the road that would take her down the hill to safety. Alene made it to the hilltop's edge and stopped.

A weird laugh overcame her. From here she could see far out across the surrounding fields, filling now with dozens—hundreds—of lurching shapes. Unearthed Iceni slaughtered by the Romans over the past weeks coming singly and in groups of two or three. The skies above them teemed with ravens, and all of them—birds and risen dead alike—streamed toward the hill.

Again Alene laughed, though her heart felt sick. *There's nowhere to go.*

She knew what had to be done. Boudicca had answered her prayers for help, for vengeance. And a most terrible vengeance had been wrought, one only a goddess swallowed by Roman fires could beget.

This was why the goddess had released her as a maiden, had let Hirelgdas pull her back from the brink.

Boudicca in her wisdom had waited for the Romans to come, to burn the groves, to slay Her druids.

A goddess of victory must be murdered for her to rise as a goddess of vengeance.

Could any less be asked of a queen? *I must die as well.* Alene looked back over her shoulder at the madness spreading over her homestead. *Better the land become a feast hall for the risen dead than a slave pen for the living.*

She sat in the roadway. Across her lap lay the Roman sword. "As my daughters serve you, Lady, so do I." She brought the blade up and drew it across the left side of her neck, opening the wellspring just beneath the skin.

Alene fell back, taking in one last glimpse of the surrounding lands, red in the setting sun's light, awash in blood. Lying on the ground, her gaze dwelt upon an overhanging tree branch thick with ravens. Their eyes glittered in her waning sight.

Her breath rasped in her throat, her limbs cramping and stiffening as though she had suddenly aged to become a feeble crone.

The ravens opened their wings and pounced.

She never felt their claws, their beaks. Rather, Alene found herself adrift in their black-feathered cloud. She looked down upon the sight of frenzied feeding on her flesh. *My vision . . . as a girl . . . not the goddess surrounded by wings . . . but myself. My dead self.*

As her corpse rose below her, Alene spread her wings to join her dark sisters. She opened her new mouth and gave voice, the sound harsh, inhuman, and hungry.

# THE WEDDING OF OSIRIS

ADAM MORROW

It was a plain, simple meal, a soldiers' supper as the emperor preferred, but the wine was strong and good, unwatered, and they ate reclining like the most luxurious of patricians on the deck of a gilded barge moored in the shallows across the river from Hermopolis, upstream of Besa. That morning they had visited the great temple of ibis-headed Thoth-Hermes in His city on the west bank and walked through the precincts Ozymandias had built a thousand years before for the eight gods of creation. Then they crossed the Father of Rivers and climbed the hill of Besa to consult the goddess's oracle. At every turn, the import of the younger man's dreams had been confirmed. Displaying no awe at the advent of the Augustus's party, the elderly priest of Besa ignored his emperor and spoke solely to the youth Antinous: "It is tonight, Lord. It can only be tonight. It must be tonight." Lowering himself to his knees, he touched his brow to the stone floor at the youth's feet. He had sent his chief acolyte down the hill with them.

After the oracle, the Augustus and his eromenos crossed the river again, leaving the acolyte of Besa to prepare for the night's ceremonies. The emperor was pensive, his beloved exalted, but they worked off their moods wrestling in the palaestra of the Greek gymnasium. The younger threw the elder and laughed seeing the emperor's surprise. Streaming with sweat, dirtied by the arena's sands, Antinous raised his fists in triumph, lifted his incomparable face to the hot Egyptian sun, and defeated Hadrian knew the boy was no longer his but he, Caesar and Augustus of Rome, was forever the boy's. He crawled across the sands and kissed the young god's feet.

In the baths, they were cleansed and pampered. The beard of the elder was oiled, combed, curled, the younger's scant stubble shaved close, both men richly perfumed. In separate chambers, they were attired and adorned, and then borne in separate boats back to the barge, forbidden to see one another.

When at dusk they were brought together again, each marvelled at the other. Hadrian found the pleated gown of an antique queen constricting and knew it fit clumsily a weathered soldier of fifty-four years—callused fingers caught and pulled at the threads of tissue-thin linen, spoiling its pleats. The collar of gold and gems weighed on his chest, making it difficult to fill his lungs, while Hathor's tall crown and the heavy wig with its infinite number of plaits and turquoise, ivory, lapis lazuli, and gold beads had already caused his head to ache. Yet Antinous saw before him Isis of the Ten Thousand Names, yielding, obliging, ferocious: his queen.

For the young Bithynian had assumed the aspect of King Osiris bearing crook and flail, Pharaoh's false golden beard fixed to his chin, his fair skin powdered green with verdigris, lips reddened with cinnabar, eyes lined black with kohl. Even had he been permitted to speak, Hadrian should have been struck dumb by the majesty and beauty of his young beloved.

They stood on the barge's deck before the acolyte of Besa, who unrolled and consulted a scroll that appeared ancient. A drop of sweat formed on his shaved scalp as he moved a stylus from one column to another, trickled down his brow, fell to the papyrus. With a frown, the acolyte brushed it away and looked up. Nodding, he began to recite the words of the hierogamy, first in Greek so groom and bride would comprehend their gravity, then the harsh syllables of the gods' ancient tongue. The priest's spells bound the two in a fashion they felt as physical, chains of iron and bronze bringing them together. It seemed to Hadrian these sacral, magical bonds were no stronger than the ties of affection and passion long between them—but a restatement, a revision, for before this instant he, Hadrian, had been the king, the husband . . . the man.

If he was no longer Augustus he could not remain the Augusta's husband. In Rome, Vibia Sabina had long ago broken her own marriage vows, so that Hadrian never regretted being apart from her, but now the priest of Besa formally dissolved the attachment. With that former marriage also vanished into nothingness all the weight of empire and history. For a moment Hadrian believed himself the careless youth he had never been, a love-struck maid. Gazing into the great eyes of Antinous-Osiris, he saw devotion, adoration, and for moments forgot the story they must enact, only knew he was chosen.

The priest spoke the final prayer, final spell, final curse. He bowed himself away.

Wife and husband—queen and king—Isis and Lord Osiris, they settled themselves on their couches to dine. For the first little while they drank the same wine from the same cup, but when the meal was consumed slaves brought new wine in separate jars and two new cups. The bride's was glass, blown and carved, through which red wine gleamed like fresh blood—the groom's hammered gold. Antinous's expression altered strangely when he sipped, for the king's wine was bitter, but then he drank deep, and set the cup aside, and rose to his feet, holding out his hands.

Somehow afraid, Hadrian swallowed his own honeyed wine. It contained a small amount of poppy's tears, he knew, their bitterness subsumed within the honey's sweet. With heavy hands, he lifted the ox-horn crown of Hathor from his own head. Moonlight and starlight gleamed on the golden sun disk between the horns, on the

enamel eyes of the cobra encircling the dis
but kept the heavy wig, and then he stood

No words were spoken. Bride reverent
When he went to remove his husband'
made in the form of a golden phallus
ribbons that held it on. Smudges of ver
of the god was not yet dead, Hadrian
of waxed, spiced linen bandage from
already more naked than any decen
with its starched apron. It was the work of a mom
god's true phallus. Hadrian was briefly disconcerted that it was

And then Osiris's hands were on his bride's body, finding the pins and brooc
that held the gown together, impatiently casting them aside. Hadrian-Isis's phallus stood up before it was unveiled, the emperor excited by his lover's unaccustomed mastery. Antinous did not remove his queen's golden collar, merely turned him brusquely and reached for the oil.

Long before Antinous's birth, as a boy in Hispania Hadrian had been for some while the eromenos of an older youth. He remembered the nearly shameful physical pleasure in being another man's woman—he had not imagined it might ever happen again, least of all that the man taking him should be his own youthful, yielding eromenos or a god—he had forgotten the initial pain. Isis cried out aloud.

When Antinous-Osiris had pleasured and bred his bride, he tenderly unfastened Isis's collar of jewelled gold and placed it around his own neck. Then, not in triumph or shame but exaltation, he moved away. Lifting green-streaked hands to the Nile of stars spread across the heavens, he uttered a wordless paean, and then, as his own dreams and the prophecies of oracles and priests uncounted required, Antinous cast himself over the barge's side into the Nile of waters.

He had expected it, dreaded it, but when the Augustus Hadrian heard the splash his lover's body made he cried out. The acolyte of Besa and the slaves and legionaries aboard the imperial barge were ready. As if he were once again tribune of the soldiers, Hadrian issued commands and, though he stood dishevelled, naked but for a woman's wig, his skin stained with smears of verdigris, and all knew his shameful subjugation, the commands were obeyed.

It was not long—and yet far too long—before the divine corpse was raised from the waters and laid upon the deck. Isis's collar still ringed Antinous's neck: it had dragged him under headfirst and the drugged wine or his own destiny had prevented him from struggling against the river's cool embrace. Weeping, bellowing, Hadrian bent over the body of his beloved, arms outstretched like the wings of a mourning nd slaves withdrew, but the priest remained, watchful,

nian ephebe was as lovely as he had ever been alive. Father Nile the painted complexion of the god, leaving the youth's skin as pale painted marble. His own eyes streaming, Hadrian tenderly brushed yelids shut, knuckled wet hair off the white brow. He kissed perfect lips already chill, that tasted and smelled of Nile water and Egyptian mud.

here is one more thing," the forgotten priest said.

Without looking up, the emperor exclaimed, "Leave me to my grief!"

The priest spoke as to a peevish child. "There is one thing more."

"You have killed my beloved, get of Typhon! Leave me, or join him in death."

"The god dies in order to live again, to grant new life to the world, but there is one thing more."

Enraged, the emperor lunged to his feet. Unafraid, the priest stood his ground. In one hand he held Hadrian's own pugio, his dagger of keen Noricum steel, in the other the golden phallus that had counterfeited Osiris's beard.

"No," said Hadrian, shaken. "I will not violate him so. *You* will not."

"Lady Isis and her sister Nephthys of the Lamentations discovered every fragment of the dismembered corpse, one in each of the kingdom's forty-two nomes—every fragment but one. The god's severed penis had been tossed into the river and eaten by fishes. The lady fashioned a new phallus for her husband, by which the dead god was able to father Lord Horus upon her. *You know this.* You know your catamite's sacrifice is useless, senseless, ridiculous, if this last act is not performed." Besa's acolyte took a breath. His next words sounded uncertain. "You need not do it yourself, the cutting."

His tears dried by bitter knowledge, the emperor turned away. The body of Antinous lay serene and lovely on the barge's deck. "No," Hadrian said again, but he was speaking to himself, and he turned farther, lifting his eyes from his dead beloved, from perfection about to be spoiled, to the serene Nile of stars flowing across the heavens. After some moments, he heard a small grunt and then a tiny splash far out on the Nile of waters.

Unable to prevent himself, Hadrian looked. The Besa priest knelt by Antinous's corpse. Pushing the base of the stiff golden phallus into the open wound, he appeared to be pleasuring the beautiful youth with his hands. It seemed the thing would not stay where it was meant to stand and the priest bent closer. Now it appeared he intended to perform an act only the most depraved whores consented to take money for.

The most depraved whores and the most devoted lovers: it was a thing Antinous had done for Hadrian and Hadrian, in dark, secret silence, for living Antinous. Horrible, grotesque—the emperor felt his own flesh begin to stiffen, to rise, as he witnessed the counterfeit of lovemaking between the priest—a eunuch, surely—and the emperor's dead beloved.

The eunuch priest shrieked when dead hands shuddered on cedar decking, jerked up to clasp his skull. The shriek was muffled when his mouth was forced onto the golden phallus—muffled abruptly enough it seemed one heard his teeth shatter.

"Antinous!" cried the emperor. The prophecies were true. The vile priest deserved such punishment for the violation he had performed. "Beloved!"

Flailing, the priest had broken free. Blood and animal noises flooded from his ruined mouth as he seemed to protest the rite had gone wrong. He still held the false phallus in his hand, like a weapon, bloodied at both ends. Clumsy, he bashed with it at the grasping hands—he lacked the sense to reach for the discarded pugio or attempt to scuttle away.

"Antinous!" the emperor called again when his beloved fastened strong fingers about the priest's throat and lurched half upright.

The body, the fatal hands, the face were Antinous's, but the expression was not. Grey lips parted, teeth bared, the corpse lunged forward and up—for a moment, it seemed the monster meant to kiss the priest like a lover, but savage teeth bit the nose from the priest's face. Before bursting blood masked it, Hadrian saw no intelligence in the adored features, no awareness, only brutal hunger. Bloody jaws champed at flesh and cartilage. Dead or swooning, the priest fell against the corpse, knocking it flat again, but the teeth kept chewing, biting at cheek and eyeball, and clawing fingers scored welts in the skin of the priest's shaven skull.

Sickened, the emperor bellowed, "A sword!" His guards were out of sight but he had commanded troops in battle: they would hear. "Bring me a sword!"

Strangely calm, Hadrian kept his distance from the one-sided battle for the moments until legionaries with bared steel arrived. Well before revivified corpse smashed its victim's skull open against the deck there was no doubt the acolyte of Besa was himself dead. Making vile slurping noises, the monster that was no longer lovely Antinous nuzzled into the shattered skull, licking and biting at the grey mush of brains.

"Give me that," Hadrian snapped when a young, unhardened legionary quavered, "Augustus?" Grabbing the soldier's sword, he said, "Stand back, all of you." As he stepped into position, he heard one of them moan and retch.

The gladius was a stabbing weapon but Hadrian felt certain stabbing would not halt a thing already dead. Holding the sword like a one-handed hatchet, he could only trust the steel was true and the young legionary kept its edges keen.

By some horrible chance, the corpse of Antinous paused in its gluttony and looked up as the blade came down, looked into its former lover's eyes. Hadrian sobbed aloud. Two necks were severed by the single blow though only one fountained fresh blood, two heads bounced across the deck, the young legionary's gladius lodged immovable in hard cedar. Hadrian released it, his hand stinging, and tried to dance back. "Another!" he howled, reaching out blindly. "Give me another sword."

For an unnaturally vital dead hand had clasped his ankle with savage, agonizing strength. The other dead arm scrabbled at the properly dead body of the priest that pinned it down and both legs flailed, drumming heels against the deck. These were not death throes: the thing had been dead already over an hour. "Damn you all, somebody give me a sword."

The hilt of a different soldier's gladius was gingerly proffered. Taking it, the emperor commanded his legionaries to stand: this was his task. He hacked the grasping arm off its decapitated body at the elbow, then at the wrist. The severed hand would not release his ankle, but the emperor bore it, limping about the deck hacking and hacking, taking no care as to which corpse he broke up, the one that moved evilly on its own or the one that was still. When the fragments were so small and broken—save the hand attempting to crush his ankle—as to be harmless, if still jolting, he came upon the head of his dead beloved.

The immortal features were fouled with blood, the eyes dimmed, but the face made vile grimaces and stained teeth chewed at its own tongue as if it were the dead priest's flesh. Publius Aelius Traianus Hadrianus Augustus used an anonymous soldier's sword to split Antinous's skull open. At last it seemed to die again. The emperor fell to his knees. "Go," he commanded with breaking voice, "all of you, go away."

Long before dawn he had managed to prise the clutching hand off his bruised ankle and crushed all of its knuckles with the blunt head of the golden phallus so it could not grasp again, and then he wept and howled like a hired mourner, shrieked like a woman, kissed his beloved's ruined hand again and again though its continued twitching horrified him.

In morning light, he crawled about the deck of the imperial barge, separating bits and gobbets of one corpse from the other. The priest's remains were merely dead meat, unmistakably so. Hadrian tossed them into a heap, uncaring. The flesh of Antinous, latest incarnation of Osiris, was unnaturally chill, dead but implicit with uncanny vitality, and the emperor made sure not to allow one fragment to touch another. When he was done, he counted. There were, as he had somehow expected, exactly forty-two.

# THE MIDDLE AGES

# THE HYENA'S BLESSING

## ALEX JEFFERS

In old tales, it's said the great king Harun ar-Rashid was wont to dress himself in merchant's or beggar's robes and wander the streets of Baghdad to learn the mind of his people. That was not the practice of Abu 'Ali, who ruled Cairo and Egypt and all of Africa and all the Levant—all the world in the eyes of those who acknowledged him al-Hakim bi Amr al-Lah, *King by God's Command*. All the world knew the caliph was in the habit at unpredictable intervals of riding alone into the desert at night, not returning to Cairo till morning. Simple people believed he consulted with angels in the wilderness—followers of the heretic ad-Darazi claimed he spoke with God Himself—some of his enemies said he went to meet with Iblis while others said it was not the evil one he consorted with but a she-devil, his lover.

I remarked to the man who wished to hire me it was a wonder Abu 'Ali had not been followed and killed before.

"Perhaps he has been," that man muttered. He was still perturbed, I believed, a person of my reputation could be so very slight and small.

"Not killed," I rejoined.

"Obviously not," was the snapped reply. The man's Baghdadi accent was strong but I did not know whether he was an agent of al-Qadir or of some other enemy of al-Hakim. There were so many: the Sunni caliph in Iraq—the Qarmatiyya dervishes of Bahrain—the kafir king in Constantinople—in Egypt itself, Abu 'Ali's jealous elder sister, or quarrelling factions within his army, Turk and Berber ever jousting for advantage. Ad-Darazi's disciples, too, for all they proclaimed al-Hakim the earthly manifestation of God, were said not to forgive him for having their heretic sheikh executed.

"Is it certain he goes alone? Al-Hakim—"

"Do not grant him that title!"

"He is not known as a swordsman," I continued mildly, "or any kind of fighter."

"Perhaps he is guarded by jinn! Are you afraid?"

"A wise man is cautious." I looked the Baghdadi in the eye. "You will have been told my history or you would not seek me out."

He lowered his gaze. "All our agents swear he goes alone. He is too proud not to go alone, just himself and his donkey." Raising his eyes again, he attempted to appear stern. Seated, he was a foot taller than I, slow, well fed—succulent. "You may hire assistants—*you* need not face him alone."

I smiled. "Perhaps."

"Half now," the man said, unnerved, "half when you succeed."

"The entire sum now," I said agreeably. "A generous additional gift if you see me again." I did not intend to look for him. There was a man in Beirut needed an introduction to sharp steel.

"You will simply take it and ride away from Cairo."

"Perhaps." I smiled wider.

After some moments, the Baghdadi grunted and passed over the purse. Weighing it in my hand, I determined it was near enough the agreed amount I needn't count the individual coins, and pushed it into my sleeve. "I will do this for you," I said. "Be assured. The next night al-Hakim ventures alone into the desert."

A grimace twisted the man's face as if he had smelled a foul odor. "See that you perform the task," he said through his teeth, rose, and went away. It was he who stank, of human fear.

"Go with God," I said to his back.

When he had passed the door, I requested another cup of tea. It was a Berber shop so the tea was brewed with mint, something I'd taken a liking to. I had not previously been hired to murder so exalted a man as a caliph, false or not. An interesting prospect. I pondered whether it was a feat I might add to my clandestine legend or if it was best left unspoken. Then I recalled the money in my sleeve. Added to what I had already hidden away, I believed, it would be more than sufficient for my return to the Lebanon, where my legend was not a thing I wanted known, and to hire an assassin there. I had failed killing him once. Attempting yourself to kill the man you loathe is never wise.

Having finished my tea, I left the city and walked into the desert. Not as al-Hakim would set out one night soon, for it was morning daylight and I did not ride. Horses, donkeys, camels, mules—they do not like me: I do not like them except, now and then, to eat.

My way led past al-Qarafa, the city's vast necropolis at the base of the Muqattam Hills, a centuries-old city in itself. I made sure not to approach very near. It was a place I found oppressive—ostentatious, offensive. At the Hour, all persons will be raised again to flesh for judgment whether the mortal body was or was not buried, with or without pomp. Until then, the person should be remembered, mourned, celebrated, but the body is not the man: the corpse is simply meat, human carrion.

I am not a scholar. My belief may be misapprehension or heresy. I do not apologize for it. Almighty God will judge me at the Hour.

All belief aside, I skirted wide past the necropolis—its hazards were not a matter of belief. At times one thought more conscious beings dwelled there than dead. Besides custodians and guards, there were entire colleges of sufi saints and acolytes, grave robbers, bandits, displaced fellahin inhabiting tombs far grander and more solid than the shacks they had left behind. The feline tribes mostly avoided the place, but foxes, jackals, wild dogs, and feral dogs denned in sepulchres and roamed the cemetery's avenues. Hyenas, though of course I am not fearful of hyenas. Kites, carrion crows, vultures—I despise vultures. Of direst concern, any site where the dead are laid attracts that ravenous variety of jinn called ghul. Cowardly, they prefer to wait till night to clothe themselves in the flesh of the recent dead and hunt down helpless sleeping prey, but I have met those shambling nightmares in daylight more than once. Not yet at al-Qarafa, if only because I avoided it.

Noon arrived overhead before I reached the place I was going. I heard the calls of muezzins from the city's minarets behind me and, although I am not a good Muslim, I found a stretch of clean sand, performed tayammum, then as-salah az-zuhr. After my prayers, it was not long before I came upon the den I had scouted and claimed when I first arrived in the vicinity of Cairo. No creature had visited it in my absence beyond the usual bugs and small vermin. The dimness and cool within were pleasant. It would be pleasant to sleep—I have always found it more restful to sleep in daylight than through the night—but for now it was necessary to continue counterfeiting an ordinary man. I dug up my locked chest. It was gratifyingly heavy, heavier still when I added al-Hakim's unnamed enemy's gold.

For some while I sat before the open chest, remembering the man in Beirut I intended having killed. He was not a clever man, but wealthy and influential: a merchant who also owned properties within the town and farmland without—who served, unappointed, as neighborhood qadi although his knowledge of the subtleties of law was no better than my own. A greedy, corrupt man for all his shows of piety. He cheated his clients and relatives, demanded ruinous rents of his tenants, issued no legal judgment without a bribe, thrashed his servants, and whipped his slaves. Beirut's Christians and Jews, native and foreign, it was said, lived peaceably only on his sufferance and paid dearly for the privilege. A kind of living ghul, I thought, preying on the helpless and unwary.

All that to the side. An assassin for hire, I am no model of good action myself. It was not my place to judge him for sins against God or other men—leave that to Munkar and Nakir when he lay in his grave, to God Himself at the end of time. The man had taken something precious to me, spoiled it, killed it. He would die.

I buried the chest again. Leaving the den, I set out back to the city, steering wide again of the necropolis. At the edge of a field rustling with young wheat, I scented the burrow of a family of jumping mice. It had been some days since I tasted fresh kill, so I plunged my hand into the earth and grabbed one of the animals before it or its fellows could wake. The blood was hot and good, the flesh savory, and the tiny bones crunched nicely between my teeth.

Within Cairo's walls, I made my way to the hammam, for the jumping mouse's blood had heated my own. The youthful attendant recoiled from my stink until I paid him. Then, knowing me well enough, he bathed me thoroughly, served me mint tea after, and served the needs of my body and blood. He called himself Jabr and, although he was merely handsome and sometimes clumsy, he was a welcome comfort and a consolation when Farid came too much to mind.

Farid! Farid was a rare white rose in a waste of stinging nettles—a springing fountain in the desert—a slender cypress standing tall and straight amid twisted, dwarfish pines—the fragrance of attars, the song of nightingales, the brilliant spark of sapphires and rubies, the refrain of an incomparable ghazal, the forbidden flavor of wine. Ah, Farid . . . . Farid was dead. Stolen, violated, murdered.

I waited three nights outside the gates of the caliph's palace—lurking in a dark alley across the way, huddled against winter chill in a black wool jellabiya, my face and the white taqiya on my head hidden in the drapes of a loose black shemagh. I feel the cold more severely, I believe, than men born in human skin, for when snow fell in the mountains of the Lebanon in my youth I never went about in the form of a man but always on four feet, clothed in fur.

I am of the tribe of al-Dabeyoun: that is, I was born in a den in the hills, furred, blind, deaf, toothless. I wrestled weakly with my sister and brother for our dam's teats, nuzzled and sucked at the carrion bones our sire brought. I was speechless, thoughtless, an animal. Some time after my eyes and ears opened and teeth began to sprout in my jaws, our sire failed to return from his nightly forage. Taken by hunters, I would guess later when I learned to think and reason. They do not generally find our flesh good to eat, humans, but they have always liked killing us. Killing us, and telling unkind, untrue stories about us.

We seldom kill livestock: unlike wolves and dogs, we prefer to hunt and forage alone and none of us is large enough to take down a full-grown sheep easily, let alone a cow. We might scavenge a carcass killed by wolves, dogs, lions, but that's a different story. We (I wearing human skin the exception) are too wary to attack men until driven to it. We laugh not out of savagery or amusement as men believe but fear, unease. We are not the unholy companions of witches and necromancers—I have never met such a person. We are not a species of jinn. No ghul can adopt the form of a hyena or assume a dead hyena's flesh—they are hateful, unclean entities which we despise. Very few hyenas can learn to take the form of a living man or woman. Besides myself, in all my travels I have encountered only three.

My brother and sister and I had wide eyes, open ears, strong jaws with able teeth. We wrestled and nipped and played about the sandy floor of our den—we were learning to prefer meat to milk but our dam had not yet taken us out under the sky and the moon to teach us scavenging, foraging, killing.

She did not come home.

We were animals, cubs, unaware of time. Perhaps it was only a day later, perhaps five, that—squabbling and hungry—I employed my powerful jaws and able teeth to gash open my sister's belly and drag out her entrails. Her blood was so hot, so sweet. It was some while before I would permit my brother a turn at her carcass.

Possibly he was cleverer than I. When I woke from glutted slumber he was gone, our sister's ravaged corpse dragged away with him. Disconsolate, I crunched up and swallowed down the single shinbone he had left me, and then I made to follow him.

The world outside the den was terrifyingly big, hurtfully bright: it was day. Whining, giggling with unease, I retreated to the comforting dark.

Hunger drove me out at dusk. I followed the trail my brother had made dragging what was left of our sister. I began to smell fresher blood and to hear noises, horrible noises, chuckles and coughs and chirps. Peering between a rock and a leafy bush, I saw a wake of black vultures squabbling over the corpse of my small brother and our sister's few disjointed bones.

I do not remember a great deal of what followed. Where I stumbled, what I ate, where I slept, how I avoided becoming prey, for how many nights and days. I smelled meat. Not fresh, but fresh enough. I had come, I recognize now, upon a graveyard, a human graveyard. A paltry place outside a paltry village. Stumbling among the narrow hummocked or sunken graves, I followed the ripe scent. As I came nearer, I became aware of a different, lighter odor—living meat.

I saw the living meat first, an oddly formed animal. I was not so famished its largeness didn't make me wary, but neither did it fill me with revulsion and horror as the vultures had. It bore a kind of plumage that confused its shape but I recognized that it stood easily on its hind legs while its forepaws covered its mouth and muffled its low-pitched cries. Keeping to downwind shadows, I prowled about, my attention divided between the peculiar creature and the turned earth that covered the dead meat. I was so very hungry.

The earth shifted. Possibly because I was an unreasoning animal, possibly because I was an inexperienced cub, although I knew the buried meat was dead I was less startled by the physical action of a forepaw very like the living creature's thrusting out of the quaking soil to scrabble at the air than by its size. It seemed twice as large as the standing animal's. Then the meat bucked its shoulder and hip and began to wriggle its entire carcass from the ground.

I had gone down to a crouch. I felt the mane rise along my spine. Meanwhile, the living animal's cries had grown higher pitched, louder, and I could sense its terror. *Its*—his. *It* was Farid, a boy of nine summers whose beloved father had died of a sudden fever the afternoon before. Hours after the funeral, Farid had returned to his baba's grave, hours after his baba's soul had answered the angels' three questions and been dispatched to await the day of resurrection. Farid's uncle, that vile man with sons of his own at his house in Beirut, had beaten him.

All this I learned later, after I learned to be a human boy myself, to speak and listen and understand.

The ghul that had taken possession of Farid's father's corpse levered itself from the soil, tearing away its linen shroud. It had been laid to rest on its side, turned toward the holy city and, by some luck, facing me. Its senses were confused and its slight intelligence overwhelmed by hunger—it knew there were two living creatures nearby, two prey, and that the boy was more suitable but I was closer.

But I also was consumed by hunger. Somehow, too, I hated the monster, even more than I had hated the vultures. As it lurched to its knees and reached for me with clawed hands, I leapt from my crouch. My jaws latched on its swollen belly, teeth ripped through skin and muscle. The corpse had been dead too long for blood to burst or flood but bad air blew between my teeth, and then offal tumbled from the gash. The ghul's odious taint had already suffused the meat—it tasted bitter on my tongue, burning.

A living man, any animal, would have gone down. Neither the ghul nor the meat it animated was alive. Its fists bashed at me, pushing me off, and its small dull teeth clashed. It was strong, unnaturally strong, strong as death itself.

On the far side of the violated grave, Farid stood trembling but as rooted as a tree. His whimpers and gasps came thick as moths about a flame. I do not know if a ghul has the capacity to hear but it was well aware of Farid's presence. I do know a ghul will choose human over animal prey every time—perhaps flesh animated by true intelligence is more nourishing. Once the ghul had tossed me aside, it clambered to its feet and turned toward the boy. When loops of trailing entrails threatened to tangle its legs, it paused a moment only to rip them from the wound in its gut.

I was bruised but not hurt. I felt powerful unanimal emotions which, when I look back, I see were the true sign I was unlike other hyenas: anger. A brilliant fury that the monster mistook me for so little threat. A dreadful *wanting* to kill the thing that was entirely separate from my hunger, and a thrilling fear that I could not kill it for it was so much bigger and stronger than I and already dead. A hot, despairing compassion for the terrified boy who was its true prey. A potent, uncanny cunning.

In an instant more I had leapt again and locked my teeth in the tendons at the back of the corpse's knee and severed them. It did not understand it was lamed until it attempted another step and collapsed. The boy uttered a series of full-throated shrieks as I snapped at the fallen corpse's thrashing limbs, ripping muscles and tendons, cracking bones. As long as it was able, it beat at me with its hands, but I was too clever, too fast. My jaws clamped around its throat—if it were a living creature requiring breath it should have strangled before I crushed its spine.

Retching, I retreated. The vile thing twitched and shuddered on the disturbed earth, body too damaged for unnatural will to command, will too potent to subside or withdraw. Its dead eyes brightened with hatred as it gazed on me, and I stumbled farther back, and then the eyes dulled as the ghul acknowledged the wreck of its corporeal weapon and withdrew.

Stumbling again, I collided with petrified Farid, who moaned and crumpled. I knew no way to comfort him in my natural form—I knew that whatever savage beast he took me for would frighten him nearly as much as the ghul. I did not understand why I needed to comfort him, but it was a compelling need so I rubbed my great head against his flank and made mewling sounds in my throat and patted at him with my paw until it became a delicate, hairless, uncallused human hand. Farid did not witness the transmutation of my flesh for he had fainted. When I was entirely changed, I dug up loose earth with my clever new paws and buried the broken corpse of his father again—the notion of feeding upon it revolted me although I was still famished. Then I curled up in the graveyard dirt beside the other boy and slept.

The clopping of hooves on stone paving roused me from memory. Blinking away sorrowful visions of Farid's face as I had seen it first with human vision, I shifted position slightly and pulled the shemagh lower to hide the shine from my eyes. The guards across the way closed the palace gates behind the caliph slumped in his donkey's saddle. I saw little to distinguish al-Hakim from a humble fellah riding home from the city market to his small farm or the grandee's tomb he had appropriated at al-Qarafa. Perhaps the jellabiya's wool was of tighter weave but its dull black was as drab, perhaps the caliph's mount was better fed, better groomed. I saw no evidence this sayyid's flesh encompassed, as his followers believed, the living light of God, still less—as ad-Darazi had proclaimed—God's essential nature: he appeared merely a man, this caliph of all Islam: a man weary of the world before his time. I was the cure for his weariness, I told myself, though I would make sure he never knew it.

I let him ride a little way ahead before I began to follow, keeping to shadow and darting as stealthily as if I had returned to my natural form. He passed through the wealthy quarters surrounding the palace with their high walls around subtle gardens and luxurious residences. When he came to the city gate, the guards required a word before they recognized him and let him pass. He did not appear to resent their suspicions. Slipping through after, I heard the younger guard marvel the caliph should be so courteous.

Once al-Hakim had ridden beyond the slumbering slums outside the gate, I must fall farther behind in order not to be seen. I felt no worry about losing him, however. The moon was full and high in the cold dome of sky sequinned with an infinite number of brittle stars. The worry came when I realized he had chosen the well travelled road to al-Qarafa. Killing him within sight of the city of the dead would be unwise.

In the event, he turned his donkey off the road soon after the domes and towers of the necropolis became visible under moonlight, riding into the Muqattam foothills without benefit of a path. The terrain was uncertain but the donkey sure footed—as was I, following unseen. We climbed some distance, eventually reaching a kind of vale among higher ridges. When I looked back, I saw the great walled bulk of the city reduced to an architect's model, gates marked by candle flames. Beyond ran the wide expanse of the river like black glass that reflected moon and stars. Below, nearer, torches and cooking fires burned among the avenues of al-Qarafa. I could not actually smell the smoke but it seemed to me I could, and underlying it the faint perfume of corruption although, in desiccated Egypt, rot is not so pervasive as in damper climates.

I turned again to look for the caliph. He had dismounted and hobbled his donkey. I saw the patient animal but had to glance about to find the man. Kneeling some feet away, al-Hakim was still as a wind-weathered boulder, nearly indistinguishable from the landscape, the contours and folds of his garments carved by moonlight into solid rock. He faced away from me, oriented, I imagined, on the qibla axis toward the holy city.

Like any predator, an assassin cannot afford scruples. It would be best for me simply to dispatch al-Hakim, here where the corpse would not be found without search, and then go on about my other business. But like any other predator I am prey to curiosity and, as a man prone to reflection myself, I wondered about his purpose in retreating to the wilderness. It had never been a requirement of my meditations that I go into seclusion . . . but I was not a descendant of the blessed Messenger of God who received God's words from the angel Jibril during his own retreats to isolated Hira.

Careful to remain upwind of the donkey, I made my silent way around the vale until I could see al-Hakim's face where he knelt so still, and then I settled to my haunches. I believe I have never seen a visage so rapt, so joyously calm, as the caliph's that night. It seemed I could make out every detail as if I sat in the sand just before him, as the student sits before his teacher. His eyes were open but unseeing, upraised toward the heavens. I seemed to see every thread of silver in the beard of a man past his youth—the slight smile on parted lips—the fans of wrinkles at the corners of his eyes and the deep lines on his brow. I seemed to see an unearthly radiance within his eyes.

This was a nonsense, a distraction. I lowered my gaze. Those who claimed Abu 'Ali as the true and only caliph and imam, heir of 'Ali and Hasan and Husayn, believed he was the earthly vessel of God's immortal light and revelation, but I was not of their number. I had experience of things other men would call miraculous, uncanny—my own existence—but I had never encountered evidence of God's hand interfering in the day-to-day business of men or beasts.

I glanced again at the caliph. Now the very skin of his face and the hands loose in his lap appeared to glow with the same radiance, as if a pure white flame burned within his flesh. Before I could be snared by wonder I turned away. Whatever Abu 'Ali was, what his followers believed and enemies feared or something else again, I had entered into a bargain with the Baghdadi in that Cairo teashop: he had fulfilled his part and now was the time for me to do mine. To kill this person without passion or prejudice, as I had slain many others before and would again.

I reached to loosen my keen steel dagger in its sheath . . . hesitated. The *man* I was hesitated, awed.

I was not only a man. A hyena, innocent of reason, knows neither awe nor sentiment. Loosening the garments that clothed human flesh, I set aside my equivocal, scrupulous humanity, and the hyena shuddered off heavy wool and linen fabrics weighted with a man's pungent sweat and the stenches of the city.

Four footed, naked in my winter pelt, I took two steps away from the man's garments and sat again, lifted my muzzle to sniff at the air, looked about. Hyena eyes saw more keenly in the night. The other man, my prey, knelt unmoving in his place. His donkey waited patiently. On the mild, persistent dry breeze up from the lowlands, I scented carrion, a smell that caused saliva to flood my mouth and dragged a whimper up my throat.

Not dead meat only. I scented the dire, deathless odor of ghul that is not truly a smell, and the mane between my shoulders and down my spine rose. As I brought myself to my feet, I heard the thumps and scrapes of dead men's feet on sand and rock, and the caliph's donkey, my fellow animal, also heard or scented something amiss, lifted its head, uneasy. Uncomfortably sympathetic, I seemed to feel the beast's shudder in my own muscles, the resistance when it tried to take a step against the hobble between its ankles, and then the donkey brayed.

The piteous cry would wake the dead had they not already been awakened. I discovered I had retreated some steps from the pile of clothing I would wish to don if I allowed myself to become a man again. Backed up against an immovable boulder, I had gone to a crouch. The giggling cry of my kind that so disturbs the ears of men rattled my throat.

In the vale below, the panicked donkey broke its mercifully loose hobble. With another bray, it cantered past its unmoving master, away from the approaching ghuls.

I saw them now, the shambling dead. More than two—my hyena mind incapable of counting: a number, five or seven or ten, both dead women and dead men clambering clumsily up from the plain. Some still wore tatters of the stained white linen wrapped about them before they were laid to rest in al-Qarafa but most staggered naked in their desiccated skin that clung to shrunken muscle and sharp bone. A lambent glow flickered in the deep sockets of their eyes, a light harsh and dry as smoldering coals, unlike the liquid reflections on a living person's eyes or the supernal, unwavering luster I had witnessed in the eyes of contemplative al-Hakim.

Startled, I looked for him, the caliph. Serenely unaware, he had not stirred from his posture of meditation or rapture, facing away from advancing slaughter. With hyena's eyes, I saw the radiance within him, liquid as mercury or molten steel but calm, untroubled. A remnant of the scrupulous man in the beast of prey's skull wished to warn him but the beast was near panic with horror and loathing and the assassin reflected I had been paid to see him dead: it was not required my own teeth or claws or steel release the life from his flesh.

The scrape of bone bound by withered gristle to bone against stone and sand had carried all the wake of ghuls into the vale. Like a pack of starved pariah dogs, they shuffled or staggered after their leader, a corpse somewhat fresher, still fleshy, whose gait was nearly a stride, whose hands were raised in skeletal claws, whose leathery lips were drawn back in a rictus snarl from dry ivory teeth, whose sunken eyes burned with unholy fire. Cringing, whimpering my giggle of horror, I shrank back against rock that prevented flight, that offered no protection.

At last the caliph seemed to become aware of approaching doom. First he bowed toward the holy city, touching his brow and his palms to the earth, and then he rose to his feet, graceful as a crane. For a moment, he gazed into the defile where his panicked mount had fled. The skin of upraised hands and face gleamed silver in moonlight as he began to turn, his eyes glowed brighter still, like flame behind glass, as if he were a lantern of flesh scarcely tempered enough to contain the radiance within.

His motion was slow, unhurried. When he faced me, he seemed to pause for an instant, and I felt he had known my presence all along, as man and now as animal, my intent—known, acknowledged . . . forgiven. His radiance suffused me to bursting, and my substance melted from brute hyena to the chilled, naked flesh of a man capable of wonder, and al-Hakim bi Amr al-Lah continued to turn.

The caliph did not awe the ghuls. I could not look away. It seemed, indeed, that the pure light he barely contained irritated or attracted them, for their shuffle quickened, their clawed hands waved aimlessly, their dry joints creaked and groaned, and al-Hakim waited. I could not look away.

Unlike animals, even unlike men, they were clumsy killing him though he did not struggle, inept, unclean. His radiance brightened and brightened as they ripped at his garments and tore his flesh. His brilliant blood fountained over them, refreshing their dried-out meat and sinew, smelling rich and fragrant, increasing their frenzy. One wrenched his left arm from the shoulder and staggered away, gnawing at unclean fingers while two others fought to dispossess it of its prize. The uncomplaining body of the caliph collapsed beneath the weight of the ravening ghuls but his being continued to shine, to shine, pulsing like the beat of a laboring heart.

I could not look away until the caliph's illumination flared up like the dawn, blinding me, and was catastrophically snuffed out. As I collapsed into darkness, I continued to hear the dreadful clacking and grinding of the ghuls' weak jaws and dull teeth, the blows of their boney hands against sodden flesh.

In my faint, I found myself once again in the house in Beirut where that man had brought his orphaned nephew and Farid's peculiar, savage companion. He liked to have me there, bound, raging, while he abused my friend. Farid sobbed under his uncle's brutal weight, moaned when the man's prick stabbed into him, howled when he was slapped and buffetted, gurgled when he was choked. The man laughed when the boy died—then shrieked when the snarling hyena slipped free of bonds meant to hold a human child and stalked across the floor toward him, stiff legged, bristling.

I was too small, too young, too weak. He was too big, that man. I caught his hand in vengeful jaws, crushed its bones and mangled its flesh, but he beat me off with the other, breaking several of my ribs. I had no choice but to flee that charnel room, that house, that city, into the countryside and then the mountains. I learned later that Farid's uncle's hand had had to be cut off but he survived.

Dawn woke me, a naked, shivering man curled up on myself on rocky ground in the Muqattam Hills outside Cairo, above the necropolis of al-Qarafa. Coming to myself, I found my discarded clothing and weapons a few steps away. Dressed but still chilled through, I began to remember the events of the night.

The ghuls were gone, vanished like dreams to their graves or tombs. The sand and soil of the vale below me showed their passage and passion, as if disturbed by the hooves of a multitude of goats. Of al-Hakim bi Amr al-Lah, caliph of Islam, remained only the rags of his garments, black wool and white linen stained rusty by blood—not even bones.

I turned east toward the sun and the holy city to which the Hajj had not yet brought me, and I knelt. I performed tayammum, then as-salah al-fajr. During my prayers, the caliph's donkey returned ambling from whatever sanctuary it had discovered in the night. It approached the heap of rags as if it smelled its master, then shied back from the scent of blood.

The caliph's donkey was no concern of mine. The caliph's death was not my concern, his blood did not stain my hand or steel or teeth—the fatal light he contained all the years of his reign had passed to his young son in the palace in Cairo, under the regency of his wicked aunt.

I went away from that place. Going wide around al-Qarafa when I reached the plain, I found my den and slept dreamless through the heat of the day. At dusk, I dug up my hoard of gold, distributed the coins among purses and pouches about my person. And then, avoiding the gates of Cairo and the other habitations of men, I set out afoot on the road to Beirut.

# THE GOOD SHEPHERDESS

S. J. CHAMBERS

**May __, 1431**

My very dear and kind friend, the seignior and Baron de Rais, Marshal of France, the Maiden sends you her last final message via this courier, Jeudon. The Voices have told her with whom you fought in glorious battle at Orleans, Jargeau, and Paris that you have abandoned her to her fate, and that you believe the lies that the Maiden did not serve the King of the World, but a Dark Prince.

But what her inquisitors do not understand is that there are no Kings or Princes of this world; only the Great Old Ones who know nothing of Love, and only of Domination. And for France to remain free and pure from the British swine they control, Jehanne the Maiden had to give Him her soul.

*The Voices tell me how to speak, how to move, whom to sacrifice. They have silenced my reflections, devoured my pieties, and possessed my tongue, forking and gilding it in blasphemies of our Lord and Mother. When my thought is effortless, it is* their *thought. For my thought is . . . buried . . . buried under my service to them. They disguise all I say within semantics, and in an effort to protect me, make my meaning obscure. Unless it is about war—on that they have always been clear.*

*I used to be a pious girl; but what I have learned from battle, Gilles, is that our God is a delusion, and what we serve is more terrible than that wrath the Church teaches us to fear. There is no forgiveness in resurrection—only hunger, only servitude.*

The Maiden knows why the Marshal flees Rouen—he saw things about the Maiden too terrific to explain to himself, much less before the Magistrate. The Baron's account is cast in a doubting veil leading to darkness. But the Voices have always shown the Maiden the way; and now they want to show you—who witnessed her fall thrice, and her rising thrice—they want to explain.

What I want to tell you is that I am not guilty of evil, nor am I guilty of miracles. I heard the call, it is true, when I was thirteen, when the stars seiged my family's pasture. It was dusk, and I was wandering back home after herding our flock to the next meadow, and I saw in the lavender sky several stars appear, twinkle, and then fall, their fiery tails whipping overhead and bombarding the field. One landed behind me, and I was taken under.

During Orleans, there was an arrow in her neck that brought forth little blood. While others around her grappled and died from their penetrating shafts, the Maiden merely snapped it from her throat, while still charging the Anglo savages, leading her flock to victory against les Tourelles. At the battle's end, de Rais saw nothing but a slight pink lump under the Maiden's healed neck.

I awoke face down in a water trough. My clothes were charred; my arms and legs were raw and red. My right leg dangled over the trough's edge—the bone snapped in twain—but I felt no pain and found I could walk with the lame leg dragging in the dirt. I wandered homeward, passing scorched pastures filled with black-baked sheep, until upon a hill I was accosted by a robèd-priest. He held a spade, and when I tried to pass him, he raised it to halt me.

"Do you love France, Maiden?" he croaked. I struggled to ignore him, to pass by him as quickly as my lame leg would allow, but something within me seemed to burst forth:

The Maiden would die for France.

"What of your soul, Maiden?"

*I succeeded in silencing myself, but this angered him and he grabbed my arm, clapping his palm right over a burn, but all I felt was the dull and slimy texture of his webbèd hand.*

*"Would you give France your soul, if you knew it would save Her?" I wrestled from his grip, but he held up the spade, and in the moonlight I saw my face—or what had been left of it after the starry blast. My long hair, uncut for twelve years, had been singed to the skull. How had I survived?*

*"Here, Maiden, take this, for it is from the King of the World, who demands you do his bidding and go forth and fight. With this, you will live a thousand lives, and die a thousand deaths—you will be resurrected and live through Him, and in every battle you will be victor and all of France will be in your debt. Go to Glory, Maiden, go to Him. You can sit and weave wool and bear children who will be captured and tainted by English blood, or you can go forth and bear arms and save all of France's children from tyranny."*

Then there was the battle of Jargeau where after ducking a cannonball, the Marshal heard the cold crunch of stone against armor. The ball had stuck the Maiden's armored skull. She stood before him, her armor covered in British blood and her helmet dented where the cannonball had landed. She was merely stunned.

The monk pulled back his cowl, revealing a round and noseless face whose amphibious features would have been disconcerting had I not been distracted by his pale, bald pate gleaming in the moonlight.

The Baron de Rais shouted after her in between gutting a British page and beheading a fallen cavalryman. He saw her take off her helmet, lick the flesh off her sword, and return the Baron's gaze, smiling and winking at him with the common bloodlust of friend-soldiers.

And that baldness was more than a naked skull—it appeared succulent, somehow appetizing—like a plucked chicken, a debristled boar, a sheared lamb, braised frog's legs. I knew he was lying to me about something, about his King of the World, about the War, and in my mind swam a drowning vision of a battle under seas, of gilled soldiers charging with our heralds, blue and gold, yet in the middle the fleur-de-lys seemed garnished with animated arabesques that reached up to me through the water trough I had awakened in.

*I wanted to run from this man, return to the warm hearth of my family's farm, but the same instinct that forced my voice,*

Hunger.

*forced my hand into taking the spade.*

The Maiden became hungry with the soldier's appetite—for blood and flesh sacrificed to the Mother Country, to the Dreaded Father. It was an appetite that appealed to the Baron de Rais, that allowed him to assist the Maiden and look the other way.

*He was calling to me, Gilles, and spoke to me of life and death on this Earth, and spoke to me of our Mother Country, and how my answer would render me His puppet, and lead France and Him to victory.*

Finally, running at top speed in a charge on Paris, the Maiden was penetrated again by an English bolt to the knee. Rather than topple like a hunted fawn, her pace was unhalted, the bolt unnoticed, and she outran the pages, splitting the skulls of several

British swine in twain with her sword hilt, not once letting the Herald brush against the soil or become speckled with their blood.

Victorious at battle's end, the Maiden congratulated her soldiers and sent them to the farmer's fields to gather the night's dinner. She stayed behind, and knew not the Marshal tarried to inquire about the still protruding bolt in her knee. Before he could speak to her, he saw her sever and hold before her one of the split-skulls, which she shelled and slurped—like an oyster— he muscle from within. Then, hiding himself, the Baron de Rais watched her graze among the corpses, her cuts and lesions erased from her skin, and the precarious bolt pushed out from the bone and muscle, extruded from healing tissue, until it simply fell to the ground.

The priest knelt, placing his salient pate before me. He began chanting words from another time, another era, and while they fell on my ears foreign and brusque as English, within me the words translated: "Eat," he said, "For He waits—." Then he looked up at me teary-eyed:

"I am the good Shepherd," he said. "The good Shepherd giveth his life for the sheep."

The Hunger then became overwhelming and I fell upon him and with strength never before experienced, I broke his skull. I pondered the grey oozing muscle—so this was what was inside mankind—and devoured it.

*Afterwards, I looked at my reflection in the bloodied spade and saw my face restored. My leg was healed, my wounds sealed, the only remaining traces of my devastation were my ruined clothes and singed hair.*

A Philosopher in Chinon once told the Maiden at court that scholars have always wondered where the soul was. He scoffed when the Maiden told him it rested in the mind.

*I fled to the woods, and in an open field under the blinding light of the moon the Voices began. They began as one—the priest's voice spoke to me in a language not of this Earth, not of Christ's kingdom, and well outside the Mother's loving grasp; yet I understood, and they guided me through visions and instructed me on how to speak, how to move, whom to sacrifice, whom to save—all to ensure the Maiden would lead the Mother Country to Victory.*

*All one can do is serve—is sacrifice—a soul for country—.*

They are to burn the Maiden at the stake.

*I am relieved to go to the fire. To be relieved of these Voices, of these souls, of Him.*

But be not afraid, Baron de Rais, the Dreaded One is calling, and he is calling for you.

I am the good Shepherdess.

The Maiden begs of you to build an army of souls for the Great One—and save all of France's children from Burgundy, Britain, and the Old Ones they serve.

*The good Shepherdess giveth her life for the sheep.*

*Jehanne*

# THE FLEDGLINGS OF TIME


## CARRIE LABEN


You have to be careful, especially of the little ones. They're clumsy but they're faster than they look. Half-grown ones like to throw rocks at things. Also watch out for the ones who drink too much. The crazy ones. The angry ones. Sometimes they go crazy-angry together, from bad teeth I guess. Teeth are a burden feathered races are well rid of. Nothing but trouble.

The crazy-angry ones start by killing each other, not in the normal thinning-the-flock way, or pecking the sick to death like the rooks do, but groups of them travel about killing each other. It seems like good times because there is plenty to eat, but it can turn bad in a hurry because crazy-angry doesn't stop, and sometimes they get to where they kill anything they catch, not just each other. Then there are fires. The ones that survive sit in the ashes with dogs they've caught, or cats or sheep or their own young, gnawing on their heads. Easing the pain in their teeth with grinding on a skull, like we polish our beaks.

The upside to the crazy-angry ones is that if you find one dead—really dead, it's important to make sure, the best sign is if the head's smashed in—they're the tastiest. They're soft and come apart like they've been rotting for weeks, but they haven't been picked over by the dogs and rats already. The eyes, the genitals, all the good bits of the guts, still right there and waiting for you. Gobs of fat and marrow, and the brains, the brains are sweet and rich, not like any other brains you'll ever taste.

Of course, you don't see them go crazy-angry very often any more, sometimes in the dark north when the winters have been mild and every so often near Porton Down. The crazy-angry ones went the way of the wolves and wildcats. But there was a time when crazy-angry humans appeared in great herds, and even came into the city itself.

We lived in the tower then, not yet banished to the countryside in favor of the Clipped-wings who gobble up their mutton and strut for them now and imitate their bleating calls for attention. I had a story from our grandmother, who had it from twenty-three generations ago. It was a strange time, only a season long, and yet on the strength of it our family has dreamed of going back to the tower ever since.

Underneath the tower, you see, there was a head. The head of a human, full of teeth, buried with all the meat still on in their wasteful way. This human was attacked by a crazy-angry enemy, and so weakened that his followers pecked him to death with their swords. They cached his head beneath the ground, and built the tower around and above, and burned the rest of his body. This annoyed us. We wanted to taste his sweet brains.

Years went by, generations, and though we knew the brains were probably rotted and gone, we never forgot the site of the cache. There were plenty of other humans to scavenge—they left their dead lying about more often in those days, not bothering to lock them in boxes or poison the bodies as they do now. Sometimes they even hung a soft rotting corpse in a cage for us, like they hang out seeds for the smaller birds. I don't know why they stopped. The world was better in those days. But sometimes, gorged on dead humans or on pigs or horses or the other rotting things they brought in their wake, one or two of us would scrape the earth and stones with our beaks, just to see if the earth was shallow enough to turn up its treat.

At the time of this story there were two human nestlings in the tower, being watched over by their uncle, much as I watch over you while our parents are foraging. We took some interest in these boys, though the young of families with shiny plumage were usually given prompt burials, not left about to be eaten. We were more immediately interested in the many beheadings that went on in those days. But it was important to keep an eye on the doings of the humans with the rich plumage, because you could follow them to the sites where plenty of humans and horses lay dead. They were better than wolves in this way. These nestlings were also worth keeping an eye on because they were boisterous and prone to give chase and, as I told you, the small ones are faster than they look.

There was also a drunk one—well several drunk ones, there always are, but a drunk one in this well-plumaged family, who we also kept one eye on. You always have to keep a lot of eyes, and that is why flock and family are so important. We were half keeping an eye on him as a threat, and half because it seemed likely that he might fall into a ditch and not be retrieved for some time. The other brothers did not look out for him as brothers should.

Our very own many-greats-grandmother, she was the one tasked with keeping an eye on the oldest living human brother, the one who had brought the nestlings to the tower. She'd been watching him since he first came to the tower, when his older brother was still alive. Sometimes she would follow him for great distances—this was when she was a nest-helper, before she mated, and finding the scenes of battles meant not only the chance to gorge but also an opportunity to meet plenty of young males, some of whom might even have territories of their own. This wanderlust has always run strong in our family, and it's served us well because every time we've been evicted—from the tower, from the city, from the rich plowed fields and the sunny southern lands—we've been able to survive. In time, to return. I suspect this is why we are so fond of humans, though they chase us and throw rocks as you've discovered. They, too, bounce back.

And our greats-grandmother was very fond of the human she watched. The way she told the story she liked his face—it was a bit more intelligent, more bird-like, than the faces of the other humans, and the way he moved likewise, with just a trace of a strut and not so unnaturally erect as the others. At times, when she fell to daydreaming about a nest of her own and young, she'd have to resist the temptation to stuff choice bits of meat down his throat. He'd started riding into battles when he was little more than a fledgling himself by human standards, and she'd followed him many times thinking that she might end up feasting on his eyes, but as it didn't happen, she grew more and more attached. That was the only defense she could ever offer for what she did.

The nestlings, yes. I'm getting to that. At that time our greats-grandmother's older half brother, himself still a nest-helper as well, was watching the nestlings. He'd been attached to the drunk brother, before, and seen him drowned in a barrel; sharing his sister's fanciful nature, he was prone to mope about this, and his new humans were too young to follow into battle—in fact, they never left the tower. Moreover it was a stormy year, and everyone was roost-weary and bored. The nest-helpers decided to go and dig for the legendary cache that they'd heard so much about.

The earth was rain-wet, soft and rich with insects. They had few other duties; thanks to executions in that year their youngest brothers and sisters were well-nourished without their parents needing to range too far from the tower. They made more progress than anyone had before towards uncovering the cache. And then the human nestlings, bored themselves, I suppose, for humans do bore easily, came wandering out into the yard.

They rushed the flock and scattered them, laughing, throwing clods of mud. Then they noticed the hole. The bigger one found a stick and poked about; before long the little one joined in. With thumbs and sticks they could dig much faster than any raven.

They turned up the skull and made their hooting noises of wonder. The younger one had it at first, but the older took it from him after a brief struggle and began to clean it, holding it up to the drizzle, poking his fingers into the muddy eye sockets. The jaw unhinged and fell away. The little one swooped on it but his older brother tugged it back. A classic squabble over prey, and all our ancestors could do was sit and watch while the head they'd dreamed so much of was tucked under a stubby human arm and rushed back inside the tower with the younger brother giving chase.

Their only comfort was that it was clear, from the state of the thing, that none of the delicious brains were left. Still they felt rather embarrassed of themselves, getting out-scavenged like that, and decided not to tell any of the older birds what had happened.

A few days later, the human nestlings were ill. They lay moaning in their beds while adults flocked around them offering food that they refused. Greats-grandmother's older brother began complaining that he should get to watch her human, and she should be stuck with the ones who never went anywhere and then died for a change. But when she tried to perch on their windowsill to see where the skull they'd stolen had gone, he chased her off.

It was early in the morning of the next day when a man came running to her human in a frenzy, plumage in disarray. She was intrigued, hoping this would lead them to another battle or perhaps a fire or outbreak of disease. But as she tilted her head to catch their inflections—sometimes, she said, it almost seemed as though they had a language and that she could understand a bit of it—an outcry went up from her brothers and sisters outside, a call of sheer delight, of feasting to come.

The human nestlings, her older brother croaked out with a combination of sadness and pride, had gone crazy-angry, right there in the heart of the city, in the heart of the tower. Already they'd seized one of the nest-helpers that tended them and started gnawing out the pain of their teeth. The rest had fled the room and blocked up the door.

The family settled in to wait. There was great jostling on the windowsill as they all vied to keep watch, and our greats-grandmother even ventured into the room. She bragged that she was the first to steal a scrap, a torn-away flap of flesh from the cheek, right under the beaks of the two crazy-angry humans. And as if she'd regained some honor, she caught sight as she flew away of the empty-eyed skull beneath a bed.

The sun had crossed its peak when the two tired of their kill, but there was still plenty of meat left, more indeed scattered about the room than eaten—one of the odd habits of humans that you'll learn very well. They fell to scratching at the door, emitting deep moaning cries, so intent on getting out that the others felt brave enough to follow greats-grandmother's example and start to scavenge their first of what they hoped would be many rich meals.

Of course, this meant that there was no challenge left, and greats-grandmother soon had her fill. She also remembered the interrupted alarm that had called her away from her human, and even if a battle or a plague wasn't going to impress the family much now, she still felt she should find out what she could.

She found him with his flock around, deep in the anxious chatter that she associated with feasting, the tones and calls that they always made in the times leading up to battles, fresh executions, even the drowning of her older brother's human. Soon they rose, and she followed them from window to window until they came to the other side of the door where the moaning was.

Her human twisted his face as she'd seen him do in battle, and gestured at a few members of his flock. They unlocked the doors. She could hear her feeding family retreat in a rustle of wings.

The nestlings rushed out and were caught in arms as thick as nets. Most of the humans, except the largest and strongest, retreated with their faces in their hands, but her human stayed. She watched him as his nephews were borne thrashing and biting back into their room, while sturdy members of his flock tied them to their beds, while an old white-haired human with frames around his eyes stooped to examine them. He never turned away.

She thought then, she said, of how she would feel were it her parent's nestlings that needed to be pecked to death to save the flock. But that led to thoughts of the feast that was coming, and how fat her siblings would grow on all this flesh, and she resettled her feathers and slipped away to the roost.

There followed a frustrating time. More humans went crazy-angry, but nowhere near as many as the ravens had hoped. In such a small space, the humans quickly learned not to attempt to fight or call to the crazy-angry ones; each was quickly locked in a room or bound to a bed, and then pecked to death. Most had their heads off before the sun moved halfway across the sky, but those heads were buried in short order beneath the tower walls, the same frustrating cache a dozen times over. Only the nestlings, the first to go crazy-angry, were left alive.

Greats-grandmother's thought returned to haunt her, because to her it seemed clear that her human was leading the flock, and that he was sparing those two, just as she might have been tempted to do herself in his place. It was then that she conceived her eccentric conviction that humans were too raven-like to eat, a conviction that she was the first bird on this island to hold, though it's since become trendy. Not that any of us get much opportunity to put it to the test anymore.

Greats-grandmother took this idea to her older brother, because despite their feuding she knew he was fond of his humans too, and might understand. But he scoffed at her. He called her sentimental and silly, and when she tried to explain herself again, he said she was jealous that it was his humans and not hers who had led to a feast for once. Greats-grandmother always was firm that he started the fight, though she allowed that she might have thrown the first peck.

Their parents heard them before they separated, and as they preened the mud off their feathers they were both declared to be in disgrace. They could stay out the winter but come spring they must both be off to find their own territories.

Greats-grandmother knew it was high time that she had a mate and a nest of her own, might have been pleased under other circumstances, but that didn't take away the sting of humiliation.

By now, there had been no new humans turning crazy-angry for three days. Still the nestlings lingered tied to their beds. They thrashed with as much energy as hatchlings trying to burst from the egg, although they'd had nothing to eat since their first kill. Their keepers no longer bothered to bar the door, with so many black-plumaged humans in and out to observe and cluck and try to help.

Greats-grandmother sidled up to her brother on their windowsill, ducking her head as though she wished a reconciliation. "I know," she told him, "how we can both be in the good eyes of our parents again."

He cocked his head skeptically, but he didn't flare his wings and drive her off.

"Between us, if we pick at those knots, we can set your humans free. They'll kill more of the others, and sooner or later there will be too many bodies for them to bury."

Her brother bobbed his head.

Yes, he was not as smart as our greats-grandmother—in fact he was killed by a buzzard while gorging on a horse two years later, and never did find territory or leave descendants of his own. You, however, saw it at once. That's what greats-grandmother was counting on.

So they untied the knots of the smaller human, and as he scraped on the door greats-grandmother slipped away, leaving her brother to unbind the other. She knew just where the nearest human was, and rapped at his door until he stuck his head out—just in time to see the crazy-angry nestlings stumble into the hall.

They bit only two men, both of whom were immediately pecked to death by their fellows. By the time greats-grandmother's human arrived, they were once again tied to their beds.

He looked down upon them and shook his head, seeming to sink further into his brooding posture. This time he did turn away, and as he did so two burly members of his flock unsheathed their swords and sliced the nestlings' heads from their shoulders.

They, of course, were buried at once and far deeper than the others. There was no hope of anyone, and especially not greats-grandmother's older brother, getting so much as a taste.

Greats-grandmother's human returned again and again to the nestlings' room, to stare at their beds. Greats-grandmother was seized with the desire to give him some sort of reward for behaving as she'd hoped he would. So when she was sure no-one was watching from the roost, she dropped quietly into the room and pushed the much-contested skull from beneath the bed.

Her human knelt, and called out. In moments a black-plumage human arrived and covered it with a cloth. They took it out at once, and cached it again with smoke and bells; but greats-grandmother was never able to shake the feeling that her human had not liked the gift.

She and her brother did not speak the whole winter through, and when the oak leaves had budded to the size of a squirrel's ear she set out north. She never saw her human alive again, though she, like most of the other ravens in the country, feasted at the battle where he died. She finally settled along the sea, and there we might have stayed had we not inherited her headstrong ways and her story.

Or if we had also inherited her diet. For having observed humans ourselves, few of us can believe that it is wrong to eat them. Especially not when they are crazy-angry and delicious. And all those heads still wait cached beneath the tower, with their infected teeth, to be unearthed again.

# 16$^{TH}$ AND 17$^{TH}$ CENTURIES

# HUNG FROM A HAIRY TREE

## SAMANTHA HENDERSON

The story they told many years later in Girvan Town—that a daughter of the vile brigand Sawney Beane fled her wicked life and lived a good Christian, until one day she was discovered and hanged from the Hairy Tree on Dalrymple Way for her sins—was a lie. Truth was, she knotted her own noose and took her own life on that old, moss-crusted oak beside the killing grounds. She knew herself no murderer, nor cannibal at heart, like her kin.

A year before, when she still lived in the blood-reeking coastal cave with Sawney—she would not call him Da—they snagged a gaunt pair walking the road out of Ballantrae. The man and woman staggered like pole-axed sheep, their eyes sunk deep, their mouths chattering without words. They had purple pin-marks beneath their skin, as if they were about to bloom all lavender. Their hands were torn, with old brown blood ground deep beneath nail and skin, but they didn't fight when Gar and Christie took them. The joke that day told 'round the fire was God had looked on the Beane clan with favor and sent them easy prey that offered their throats to the knife. But *she* didn't trust the sweet-musky smell of the pair; even in death they smelled like honeyed dirt. An open body should be a terrible smell, the first leap to cross before one can even think of eating another man's flesh.

But Sawney's senses had been blunted from gorging on brined meat. He ignored her warning and that day reached for her hair, as if to braid it between his chapped fingers, or to tug and bring her face closer to his filthy own. She ducked away fast, knowing no father should look at a girl, paw at a girl, the way he did. She knew that he had lain with Maggie and Elspeth, despite her brothers' growl that he had his own woman in their Ma and that their sisters needed no men but themselves.

Outside the wide flare of the mouth of the cave, she found Christie and El butchering the Ballantrae pair on the salt-gravel. They laughed at the daughter while they drained the blood into an iron pot for Ma to make pudding later. She watched as Christie dotted a red blotch on his sister El's nose, who giggled and knocked his hand away. He kissed El's cheek and patted her grimy smock; beneath it her belly swelled with Christie's child.

She looked out to the water and wondered how far she could swim, and would it wash away all the blood. For sixteen years all she had known was blood. As a child she had suckled a rag steeped in the Beane kettle, and ate a mess of stewed innards, for then she knew no better. But then she found the greasy meals made her ill, and she was the thinnest of her clan. The others mocked her lack of appetite.

She would not eat the roasted Ballantrae pair. She went hungry that night, and the next, while the rest of the clan feasted. The third night Sawney roared at her until she dipped her finger into a cup of broth—the surface had an odd sheen to it—and brought a drop to her lips to calm his anger. The taste made her gag and she hid it behind a dirty hand.

Within three days the daughter saw violet bruises bloom on the skin of her kin. Their eyes glazed as if they were drunk, and they smelled of sweet-dirt musk. Christie struck El down and gnawed her shoulder bloody before Sawney and Gar kicked him away. El screamed like a gutted sheep, like nothing human.

When she told them she would gather clean rushes for the cave-floor, they barely understood her words. She never turned back but slept in fields and trudged on roads new to her until, exhausted, she came to Girvan. The bleat of Elspeth's crying woke her every night.

The Girvan-folk looked askance at all strangers, especially one so grimy, but their minds changed when she pawned a gold chain Sawney had torn from a fine lady's neck and given the daughter when she was young, and still thought him a proper Da. She took in laundry for her living, and spoke little to anyone, but she went to church regularly, having learned some scraps of religion at her mother's knee. It was months before she took the Eucharist. She always had work from the butcher and barber, for she was accounted uncommonly good at getting out bloodstains.

Word did come at last to Girvan that Sawney Beane's clan, hollow-eyed and skin blemished with purple, boldly raided nearby farms rather than lying in wait for travelers, leaving a dozen-odd crofters gnawed to the bone in their fields before the King's Men were roused and brought the mewing lot of them to Edinburgh. The Beane Clan didn't try to flee or beg for mercy, but snapped at their captors and growled like ravenous animals. The Tollbooth jailers refused to have aught to do with them, and the King ordered them to Glasgow, for the men to be gutted and the women burned.

The gossips of Girvan would talk of little else for a fortnight. She wept for her kin. She wept for herself.

Soon after she woke with a burning thirst, a single bruise like a violet posy on her arm, and the taint of long-forgotten Ballantrae broth in her mouth. The worst was that she was hungry for more. She finished that day's washing, drying the linens before the fire and stacking them on the kitchen table. She tore her own bed-sheet lengthwise and braided it into a sturdy rope, and on her way down Dalrymple Way she stopped at the church, leaving her hoarded coins in the poor box.

After they cut her down they found a note written on her hearthstone with a charred stick: *burn me*. No record follows—perhaps they did. Or most likely, she was buried at the crossroads to keep her from rising again, as is a suicide's wont, or planted in the potter's field, for none would claim her.

# GOOD DEATHS


## PAUL M. BERGER


> *"This is the substance of the Way of the Samurai. If . . . one is able to live as though his body were already dead, he gains freedom in the Way. His whole life will be without blame, and he will succeed in his calling."*
>
> —Yamamoto Tsunetomo, *Hagakure*

The road had become a dirt track between rice fields frosted with moonlight. The gaunt mare plodded, and our little wagon jolted and swayed over the ruts.

"You see that?" Sugitani said.

Silhouetted against the stars was a lone infantryman of the army of Oda Nobunaga, conspicuous in his broad conical helmet. Heedless and gasping, he fled along a ridge as if all the hells were snatching at his heels, but there was no one behind him.

"Do you want to take him, or should I?" I asked.

"Gaki," said Sugitani. Like when we were little boys, playing tag. *You're it.* Or, *You're the ghoul.*

I grunted and stepped down off the cart. I raised my bow over my head, then drew the arrow back in the same motion that lowered it to my eye. A calm spread through me, and even before the release, I knew I had struck my target. The rush of the arrow was muted by the clatter of the bow as it spun in my grip and the string tapped the outside of my wrist. The infantryman was knocked backwards off his feet by the impact in the center of his chest.

Sugitani hadn't even stopped the horse; on a still night like this, the man's ghost was likely to harass his killers if we lingered. I was back on board in a few quick steps. Too easy. It had to be done, but there was no honor in picking off a panicked farm boy like that. Let me fight a real samurai who knows how to use his sword any day.

I hoped Sugitani would acknowledge the good shot, but he wouldn't even look at me.

"This is too much to bear!" he spat. "Are we cowards now? We should have stayed to face them and fought to the end. Or else slit our own bellies and shown them how real warriors die."

"And ignore our giri to our lord? We were ordered to fall back so that we could continue to fight," I replied.

"Our forces are scattered. How can we serve Lord Rokkaku if we can't even find him, Takeda?" Sugitani said. "If we end it now, at least he'll have the benefit of two good deaths in his name."

"We have lost our officers, but we still have our duty," I insisted. "We cannot act as free as rōnin. You know I'll follow you anywhere, but I think we should head west, towards the castle. Somewhere along the way we will find Nobunaga's forces, and then we will fight. And we will die in a way that does great credit to Lord Rokkaku."

He mulled this over, then grunted assent.

No one took his giri to our master more seriously than Sugitani. And to let Sugitani set aside that burden at the wrong time would have been to neglect my giri to him. He had been an elder brother to me as long as I could remember, closer than my blood kin. Each time he saved my life in battle or showed me the way of a righteous warrior through his own example, that obligation grew heavier.

I did not mind—there was no one I would rather have been bound to. When a man's giri and the will of his heart are in accord, his way is clear and he is happy indeed.

But when they diverge, his options are to ignore his heart, or to find an honorable way to die. Anything else will lead only to shame and disaster.

Oda Nobunaga's army had cut across Ōmi Province like a hot knife. Lord Rokkaku sent his soldiers out from Kannonji Castle to drive them back, yet we barely even slowed them down. They had deployed peasants with matchlocks and sent waves of light infantry with long spears into our formations. We were born-and-bred bushi who had trained for battle all our lives, but we could not withstand that onslaught.

Sugitani, the hero of our company, had fought his way free, and only I had managed to keep close to him. Behind us, our brothers faced the invaders, and fell. The Oda men had not even bothered to pursue us, which multiplied our disgrace. Now we were wandering alone, in a rickety cart appropriated from a peasant village.

"Let's find out what your farmer was running from," Sugitani said.

If he was deserting his unit, we'd have our fight; if it was a battle, we'd join our troops. We chose a path that led over the ridge, and then we saw what had terrified him so.

In a broad open space under the full moon, there was an entire regiment of Lord Rokkaku's men.

Every last one of them was dead.

They were spilled out across the grass, thousands of them, singly or in groups. The turf was churned to cratered mud. Pieces of armor and weapons and banners were scattered across the ground as if they had been tossed into the air. Small scavenging demons and ravens had found them days before, and every corpse was despoiled. Most were terribly mutilated, bones stripped bare and body cavities yawning and empty.

Sugitani and I walked among the fallen, trying to grasp the scope of the disaster. I had been on other battlefields after the action had passed, but they had never seemed so still, so final, or so completely given up to the dead as this. In the silver moonlight and the gathering mist, the only sound was our own breathing, and it seemed perilously loud.

"Where are the Oda?" Sugitani whispered.

I was thinking the same thing. On this field of corpses that stretched beyond sight, the only crest showing on surcoats and flags was the four diamonds of the Rokkaku clan. There was not a single Oda soldier among them.

"Maybe they took their casualties with them when they moved on?"

"Or maybe they didn't have any," he hissed.

"Are they *that* strong?"

"They could be, if their main force came through here. That means Nobunaga has probably taken Kannonji-jō already," Sugitani said.

If so, Nobunaga likely would not bother to hold the castle long. He was in a hurry to march west, on his way to deliver the pretender Ashikaga Yoshiaki to Kyōto. When they arrived, Nobunaga would force the Emperor to install Yoshiaki as shōgun. In public, he would declare his fealty, but both shōgun and Emperor would be his puppets, and then Nobunaga would rule the greater part of Nippon.

"*Now* what do you think?" Sugitani said.

"Against an army like that . . . You're right. There's nothing for it," I admitted at last. We could never redeem ourselves. Our war was futile.

Sugitani made a long exhalation and said, "Well then, let's choose a good spot."

I looked beyond the battlefield, and noticed the shape of a big old house outlined on a hilltop under the night sky. It must have been a fine residence at one time, because it had a high gate in a strong wall, over which peeked the tops of ornamental trees. It would be peaceful within the ruins of its courtyard.

I pointed. "There."

Sugitani grunted.

We took the wagon up the hillside and stood in front of the house. To our surprise, the heavy wooden gate was still standing, and it was locked. I pounded on it, and called out.

After some time, the bolt was drawn back, and the gate opened a hand's breadth. Lamplight flooded through, and we could see nothing else.

"We are Sugitani Zenjubō and Takeda Shinji, soldiers in good standing in the service of Lord Rokkaku," I announced. "We have come to humbly beg your permission to commit suicide in your garden."

The lantern was lowered a bit, and over it we could see the face of a young woman. In the flickering light, her eyes glittered.

"You have come all this way, to my home, to find your deaths?" she said. Her speech was refined; she sounded high-born, maybe from one of the old families in Kyōto. Her hair hung straight and her eyebrows were painted high up on her white forehead. She was lovely.

"Yes, ma'am," I said. "It will be quiet and clean, and very little inconvenience to you."

"Oh, I am sure it will be no inconvenience at all," she said with delicate courtesy. "We have not had visitors for so long, and it will be a pleasure to have such brave guests—even if only for a little while." The gate opened wider, and she beckoned us into the courtyard. She didn't offer her name.

The lady led us through to the garden. The many layers of her kimono sighed against each other as she walked. A household this size would have required a staff as big as a company, but the grounds were dark and quiet. She noted our surprise.

"You must excuse this state we are in," she told us. "With the war so close and all, the servants . . . "

"Of course," I said quickly. The war had taken her husband too, or she wouldn't have been the one to come to the gate.

The round moon hung over twisted red pines and a fine-leafed maple in her garden. The smooth water of a gurgling koi pond mirrored it. Lush moss filled the gaps between stepping stones. There was a broad, clear patch of raked white gravel to one side.

"I know this is barely adequate . . . " the lady started to say.

"Oh, no, ma'am," I told her. "This is absolutely perfect for our seppuku."

She dipped her head in a tiny bow.

"My lady, if it is not too much of an imposition, might we beg you for a brush and a few sheets of paper?" I said.

"Not at all." She turned back to the house.

Sugitani and I stared at the garden. You want everything to be just right for a good death, but this really was as excellent a spot as one could hope for. A single red maple leaf dropped and touched the surface of the pool, then was gone: a sad little symbol that all things pass. There was no harm in acknowledging it was a pity that it was all ending so soon, as long as the thought stayed docile and quiet.

"I'll be your second," Sugitani told me.

Which meant he would stand over me while I cut through my own abdomen, and end my suffering with a single blow when I was on the point of crying out. I would have expected no less from a brother-in-arms—but the offer meant far more in this place, where there would be no one to do the same when his turn came. It would be a long and messy trial for him.

"More giri," I said. "Right up to the end."

"Someone's got to look out for you."

"I was hoping I'd have the chance to repay it all some day."

"Don't be a fool."

The lady reappeared, walking gracefully, and bearing a brush and a carved inkstone, along with a bundle of writing paper as white as snow and a heavy white cotton tarp.

"Will these do?" she asked.

"Ah, my lady, your hospitality goes far beyond." She answered our deep formal bows with a smaller one, then stepped back to allow us to attend to our business.

Sugitani and I spread the white tarp on the white gravel. I removed my armor and laid it with my sword to one side. I would use my tantō dagger for this business, but Sugitani wore his swords in the new fashion, one long and one short without a knife, so he would have to make due with his wakizashi.

I knelt in the center of the tarp. The brush and the inkstone and the paper were before me. I contemplated the moon wavering in the pond for a few quiet breaths, and then considered my dagger; the subject of my death poem was clear to me. I suppose I had always had some version of it ready for a moment like this since I was a youth. I picked up the brush and wrote:

*Welcome to thee*
*O blade of eternity!*
*I embrace thee tonight,*
*So that we may serve together again*
*In the life to come.*

I handed the poem and writing utensils to Sugitani, holding back one sheet of the paper. He frowned at the lines I had written and said, "Ah, I see—you address it to your tantō. 'Embrace'—Very clever."

It was hardly original, but Sugitani wasn't likely to know that.

"Thank you. And it is my deep hope," I said, "that in the life to come, I may have the opportunity to serve together again with you as well."

Sugitani almost said something, then looked at me and replied with a single, stiff bow. For as long as I had known him, he had never done that.

"What are you going to write for yours?" I asked.

"I haven't decided yet." He had always been awkward when it came brush and paper.

I opened my tunic to expose my torso. I picked up the tantō and wrapped the paper around the blade for a better grip. Sugitani took his position behind me and drew his sword.

"Now, don't be impatient with the kill-stroke," I told him. "Give me the time to try to do this right."

"I will."

The lady stepped out of the shadows and stood motionless at the edge of the garden. I would have thought her sensibilities were more delicate than that. But if she wanted to watch, it was her house after all. And a witness was always welcome.

"And be sure to check your swing before it goes all the way through," I said softly. "We can't have my head bouncing around this nice lady's yard."

"I'll cut you clean," said Sugitani. "That's a promise, brother. Whenever you're ready."

I had spent my life readying myself for death; now I would prove how prepared I was. The Rokkaku family would learn of this moment one day. I had the luxury of a perfect garden under a perfect moon and the support of my best friend and a high-born lady. This would be easy—how many poor bastards died in chaos, unable to hear their own thoughts?

I focused on the blade of my dagger, on the right and welcome agony that would test me to the very end. Since Sugitani had offered to accept the unaided death, it would be small of me to go too easily. I would use the cross-cut style, which only a very few men are able to complete with grace.

With each breath my consciousness grew narrower and tighter, until the world consisted only of the certainty of the steel slicing into my flesh. I would pierce my belly with a flick of the cutting edge near the tip, not the point, and bring the blade across, cutting no deeper than the muscles of the abdominal wall. My second cut would be vertical, and if my spirit and strength did not fail me, that would be the stroke to release my innards. It would be splendid, and an inspiration to Sugitani.

At the edge of my vision I saw, but did not note, the lady step closer, and her eyes glitter with pale light. I noted only my steel and the coming challenge.

I took my dagger in both hands. The sweat from my right palm immediately dampened the paper around the steel. Just as I can know that an arrow will find its target before I even release it, I knew the cutting edge of my blade would be embraced by my entire being. All things are sorrowful because they are transient, even our bodies, even our lives, but not our actions. This act would be eternal.

With my next exhalation, I drove the knife two finger-widths deep into the left side of my abdomen. The muscles in my belly greeted the steel, and parted fluidly as I slid it past my navel. My blade was sharp. The paper around it was soaked dark red.

I saw, but did not note, that the lady's jaw unhinged and dropped open to her breast, and that her blue tongue unfurled and lolled down as far as her waist.

"No!" Sugitani cried. He leapt past me across the tarp, his sword raised to strike. "Give him his moment! Do not interfere!"

The lady tilted her head and her glance met my own eyes.

*Not now,* I thought, and with that, my focus was shattered, and the pain in my belly was unbearable. I dropped the tantō and fell forward onto my hands. I knew that I had failed utterly.

With little steps, the lady came up the path towards us. Towards me.

Sugitani stood with the point of his sword extended towards her face. She continued to approach.

"Who are you to disrupt this rite?" Sugitani demanded. "Step away, ghoul."

"I am so truly sorry." The lady kept her genteel Kyōto accent though her jaw swung loose and wide. "It was my intention to honor your bravery, and to wait until all was complete. I thought the hunger was sated for a time. But death sits heavy around him, and it calls to me. I find that I cannot summon the patience."

The garden was now a place of mists. The bright steel of Sugitani's blade was the only thing that seemed pure and real under the moonlight, and its unwavering point was nearly in her eye.

"Step away!" Sugitani said again. But she stepped forward *into* the point, and from where I crouched, for a moment the blade seemed to run right through her face and emerge from the back of her head, clean. Sugitani dropped his sword as if it had burned him, and it rang against the stepping-stones. No blow could hurt her—she was long dead, a spirit tied to this world only by her limitless need.

Panic spread from her like a chill air. I forgot my honor and scrabbled backwards until I struck the garden wall. Sugitani fell back blindly before her.

"I am so terribly sorry," said the lady. "This will all be so much easier if you would just accept your fate."

Sugitani backed up against a stand of thick bamboo stalks. He could go no further.

"Is that what you told the regiment down there?" I gasped.

The lady's head snapped to face me, and she stepped my way.

"They never even saw Nobunaga's troops, did they?" I said. "That was all you. They were good men, and they deserved the chance to prove themselves."

"I was so very hungry." The lady's sweet voice reached us as if the words were uttered by a girl in a darkened room. "And they came right to my gate . . . "

"A whole regiment—they were our brothers, and you tore them to shreds, Eater-of-Men," I answered. There were legends of creatures like her. I saw the realization light Sugitani's face, joined by a type of eagerness I did not understand.

"There is no weapon that can match your strength, lady," Sugitani said quickly. "Our clan has suffered a grievous wrong, and the army that perpetrated it is still not far ahead of us. Let us lead you to them, and we will have our revenge, and you will feast!" Even now, nothing eclipsed his awareness of his ultimate duty.

The lady raised her palm before her mouth and laughed, a sweet, trilling giggle. The cultured gesture was made a grotesque mockery by the expanse of gaping maw that her delicate hand could not begin to cover.

"Oh, I lost patience with little games of steel and fire a century before your clan claimed these hills," she answered him. "My hunger has no interest in wars. I feed when the need takes me."

The hem of her outer kimono was right before my face now. It was crimson, embroidered with a late-summer pattern of slim pampas grasses touched by a breeze. She grabbed my tunic in one fist and lifted me from the bushes, inspecting me at eye level. Beyond her black-lacquered teeth, her throat was a bottomless pit. Her tongue raised itself like a snake and probed my neck and shoulders. I was trained from childhood to risk my body as if it were already dead, but I was very afraid to die this way.

"I am *so* very, truly sorry," she told me. "I am monstrous, even in my own eyes."

"Then why not resist the impulse, my lady?" said Sugitani from behind her.

She did not take her gaze from me. "There is no resisting it," she said with regret. "The curse has only strengthened within me through the long ages. I scoffed at the enemies I made during my ascent within the Emperor's court, and I believed I had slipped beyond their reach when I died—but the Fujiwara clan had long memories and powerful priests, and they hauled my spirit back to this world with a chain forged of emptiness. I am its slave now. And you are victims of their vengeance as much as I."

She brought me close enough to kiss. Her mouth was ice-cold and bitter as poison, and so wide that when her teeth snapped shut, my head would drop into it with room to spare.

"But . . . but what if another agreed to take up your hunger for you?" Sugitani cried.

The lady froze. Her eyes glittered, and she turned to him, forgetting that I dangled in her grasp.

"Endless pardons, but would you be so kind as to say that again?" she said.

"What if another—a good man, with a true heart—offered to relieve you of your burden, and make it his own?"

Her voice was strained to breaking when she said, "Do not toy with me, bushi."

"The question is sincere."

"Then I would be free to join the dead."

"And the other?"

"Would be a jikininki, beyond life, driven by hunger for eternity."

"Such as you are now?"

She hesitated. "Not quite as I am," she said at last. "I am of the spirit world; my body was already burned when I was brought back. If the hunger entered a mortal form, it would overflow it, driving the flesh with its endless need."

He blanched. "But that flesh could still kill."

"Oh, yes. Neither sword nor spear could compare."

"In that case, my lady," said Sugitani, "I offer to accept that hunger from you."

She dropped me into the bushes and stepped very close to Sugitani.

"Take it from me," she demanded, with a different sort of hunger. "You will take it from me now."

He barely flinched. "I will take it from you willingly, but I must beg a few moments first."

"Very well," she said with effort. "You have . . . as much time as I can bear not to consume you or your companion. Do what you must do quickly. I cannot say how long that will be."

Sugitani ran over to me, collecting his dropped sword along the way. "I know how I can serve Lord Rokkaku, Takeda. But I'm going to need your help. I'm afraid you won't be able to die tonight. Can you stand?" he asked.

I tried it. "If I hold my wound closed. I'll have to bandage it." I untied my loincloth, and he helped me wrap the strip of cloth tight around my abdomen. I could walk, though blood was already starting to seep through.

"Now get your armor on. No, wait—take mine. It won't do me any good, and it's better than yours."

It was. Where mine was little more than a cuirass made of curved iron strips, his covered his arms and body with small overlapping scales of leather, lacquered rock-hard and glossy and laced together with silk. My family could never have afforded anything like that, but Sugitani's could, and he always knew how to make an impression. I donned it piece by piece as he stripped them off. It was light, tough and flexible.

He picked up my old armor, and raced to strap it on. "Oh, and you should probably take these, too." He presented me his two swords, long and short. "They draw faster than yours."

My big old tachi hung suspended from a belt, but his matched katana and wakizashi tucked into a sash, cutting edge up, in the rakish style that was just becoming popular. Dressed like him any other time, I would have felt like a daimyō's son.

Sugitani strapped my sword around his own waist. He started to pass me his iron battle-mask, then reconsidered. "I'd like to hold on to this, if you don't mind." It was shaped like the face of a grimacing demon, with staring eyes and deep creases wrinkling the forehead and nose. "I don't know what I'll look like after . . . you know. If it's bad, you shouldn't have to see that."

The lady moaned, "You will take the hunger from me now." She had stepped very close to us silently, and put a slim white hand on Sugitani's wrist.

"Apologies, my lady," he answered. "Just a few more moments."

"You will hurry." He could not remove her hand until she withdrew it herself.

"So, what exactly do you need me for?" I asked him. "You want me to help you find Nobunaga's army?"

"No, I have to find Nobunaga himself. I may not be able to get close to him on my own."

"You plan to kill Oda Nobunaga?"

"No, Takeda. I plan to eat Oda Nobunaga."

"Lord Rokkaku—"

"Lord Rokkaku will be grateful that I have eliminated his mortal enemy, and he will acknowledge my service. I want nothing more."

"But she said the hunger will overflow your body. What sort of creature would you be then?"

"I will stand with one foot in the land of the living, and one in the land of the dead. I will have my warrior's honor combined with her great hunger, as well as the endless strength that accompanies it. My duty will guide me the way a sure hand guides a sword. If a being like that fought for Lord Rokkaku, our army would be invincible. What better way to serve our master and add to his glory?"

I had no answer to that.

"With this sacrifice, I can do great good. Do not deny me this," he said.

He knew I could not. My giri was too heavy.

"I am ready, my lady," he announced. "The next time we speak, Takeda, I may not be a living man, but I will tell you what I can see of the afterlife."

He fastened his mask to his helmet, and it was the last I looked on his living face.

The lady stood before him. She was trembling with the effort the restraint cost her.

"You should know that this hunger you desire so greatly will start as a small and weak thing. It might take some little time before it fills and awakens you," she told him.

He nodded.

She turned to me. "And you should know that I cannot say if you will recognize your comrade once that occurs."

"Enough of this," Sugitani proclaimed. "I accept your curse unto my own being, so that you may be relieved of your hunger and find the rest you have sought for so long!"

She raised a hand that nearly touched him.

Sugitani sagged and collapsed. I stepped forward and caught his body in my arms.

The lady disappeared, leaving a sigh of release as loud as a shout of laughter in the air around us.

The house, the garden, the courtyard and the gate all wavered and dissolved like the illusions they were, leaving the two of us alone on a grassy hilltop in the moonlight.

I waited with Sugitani until the moon had dropped low in the sky, but I saw no movement, no sign of life. I could not tell how much longer it would be before he returned to me. I fetched the cart and loaded him into the back. The effort opened my belly, and I was careful to bind it and hide it well; there is no way to explain a seppuku wound on a living man.

Two and a half days later, the mare pulled the cart up the steep approach to Kannonji Castle. The horse had sweated and flicked her ears the whole way. There was something about Sugitani that she did not like to have so close behind her, but at least it kept her moving.

Nobunaga held the castle now. The road was busy with soldiers bearing the Oda clan's melon-flower crest.

Kannonji-jō was a hundred years old, built when it was typical to situate castles on top of remote mountains. Now they were building them like palaces and putting them in the lowlands, where they could control lines of communication. Those were all imitations of Nobunaga's own headquarters, of course. He would change the whole world to fit his tastes if we let him.

I had gone through this gate a thousand times, but this was the first time it was not a return home. The Oda guards at the gate laughed and said, "Bringing supplies *to* the castle? That was a waste of effort. Didn't anyone tell you Rokkaku and his boys left us all their best stuff when they ran off?"

Sugitani's still body was hidden under a pile of sacks and casks taken from a line of Oda porters I had killed along the way. I had fixed a rectangular melon-flower banner to the wagon; it galled me to have it standing at my shoulder.

"They shot my horse and I had to commandeer the cart," I answered. "Sorry I missed the fight here."

"It was no fight," they sneered.

My heart told me the right thing to do at that moment was to kill them, but my duty was inside the castle.

They waved me through, and I entered Kannonji-jō along with a column of marching spearmen.

The thick outer walls of the castle were gray mountain stone and pounded earth, capped at the turns with boxy wooden watchtowers. An observer walking along those ramparts would be able to see down the abrupt drop of the mountainside, and would have a long view across the valley in several directions. A square white-washed keep stood at the center of a courtyard broad enough for parade drills, and low buildings were scattered around the grounds. The Oda crest flew atop the tiled roof of the tower and on narrow banners along the walls.

I brought the wagon into the sheltered space between the wall and the closest barracks, and kicked the cargo over the side, uncovering Sugitani. He remained still and lifeless.

My heart sank. What if he never returned, and this were all for nothing? What could I do on my own, in the heart of an enemy stronghold? I could fight, of course, but it would be over quickly. At this moment Nobunaga was no doubt on a high floor of the keep, sitting on the dais of Lord Rokkaku's audience chamber, planning the next leg of his march with his retainers. The false shōgun Yoshiaki was likely with them, drawing on his negligible military experience to contribute useless advice. I wondered how I could reach them.

A messenger left the tower and sprinted across the courtyard. Almost immediately afterwards, deep drums sounded along the walls, and I heard the noise of soldiers rushing to their posts. My heart rose and I thought for a moment that perhaps Lord Rokkaku's army had been spotted, massing to re-take our castle. But the commands I heard carried a different sort of urgency, and soon I saw why.

A group of high-ranking officers stepped out of the keep's doorway and crossed the courtyard. Even at this distance I could tell they had the most elaborate and beautiful armor I had ever seen, the shimmering dark leather and steel scales laced with geometric patterns of red and gold silk. At their head was a warrior whose wide helmet was capped with a disk and tall antlers that shone with gold leaf. That helmet was meant to be recognized from far off, and it was famous. I was looking at Nobunaga.

He ignored the soldiers that sprang into formation along his path and went to a set of stone steps that led to the top of the western wall. They were going up to examine the territory below and plan their army's next move.

That narrow, confined space would be perfect for an assault, if we had a squad, or a hero.

I knelt over Sugitani. "Are you there, brother?" I shook him. "If you're ever going to come back to me, now is the time. Nobunaga's here, and we'll never get a better chance."

Blood dripped from my abdomen and spattered the rough boards of the wagon and the back of Sugitani's hand.

He twitched, and his head rolled. Behind his blackened battle mask, his eyes opened, pale and milky, shot with veins. He groaned. It was a loose, bestial sound, but I was overjoyed.

"Were you in the underworld?" I asked him. "What did you see?"

He reached for me. I lifted him upright and helped him to the edge of the wagon. His grip on me was strong, so he fell off into the dust, but I gave him space and he pulled himself to his feet.

He tested his legs with a few staggering steps. He listened and sniffed the air, and led me around the side of the barracks. The door was open. The long building was filled with young bushi, shouting and roughhousing as they loaded the Rokkaku gear that was spread across the bare wood floor into their packs.

Sugitani stood in the doorway, staring and swaying slightly. The closest men looked up and saw him, and the rest fell quiet. He took a step towards them.

"Sorry, boys, our mistake," I said, and touched Sugitani's arm. "Not them." He turned abruptly, and followed close as I headed out to the castle wall.

"There's not much time," I whispered over my shoulder. "Nobunaga's walking the wall. Are you strong now? Are you fit to do this?"

He didn't answer, but he stumbled after me. Perhaps a man who had returned from the land of the dead needed time to recall mortal speech.

"I'll guide you." I made for a set of stone-block stairs. He was agile now, suddenly quite fast, and closer than he needed to be. It took all my strength to stay ahead of him in the race to the top. He was spoiling for a fight, and I was glad to see it.

I turned right. The long straight stretch of the southern wall was ahead of us, and then the southwestern watchtower. "This way." He ran behind me, wearing my armor and my tachi and his iron mask.

Halfway across, three sentries stepped out from an alcove. They carried matchlocks, the cords smoldering.

"Hey, you," one of them muttered. "Get to your post! Don't you know the generals are coming through?"

"Orders!" I shouted, and ran past them.

Sugitani did not pass them. He chose to fight. I turned in time to see one of the sentries slide sprawling across the stone walkway with Sugitani on top of him. He ignored my tachi hanging at his side. Instead, he battered at the man with his head and face, aiming for his neck, his armpit, his nose, any spot where armor did not cover flesh. I heard his teeth snapping, but his broad helmet and the narrow mouth-slit in the mask prevented him from making contact. The sentry howled with alarm.

Sugitani reared back and pawed at his own head until the ribbons around his chin split and his helmet flew off.

His true face was a twin of the wide-eyed, contorted demon portrayed by the iron mask.

Free of the muzzle, Sugitani reached for the sentry again, and this time his teeth found his throat. With a heave of his body and a snap of his head, he tore it out. The man's startled yells turned into a spastic gurgle, and after that the only sounds came from Sugitani, who leaned in to feed on the twitching body.

The other two sentries struck him with their rifle-butts, then reversed them and speared his torso with the bayonets. He ignored it all, rending great pieces from his kill. They raised their matchlocks and shot into his body, point-blank, one after the other. He did not even look their way. In terror, they turned and ran.

Before the gunshots were done echoing off the castle walls, Sugitani sprang up and brought the two men down with great sweeps of his claws and jaws. When the top of the wall was splashed with their gore, he fed from the two new corpses, ignoring the first.

I had seen the ruin the lady had caused, so I was not surprised that this was how Sugitani fought now. But did he realize that this delay might lose us Nobunaga? How much of the bushi I knew was left in him?

"*Oi,* Sugitani!" I prodded him with my foot. "We have to hurry. This way!"

He jumped up from his meal, and I ran. I could not tell if he was following me or pursuing me.

The square mass of the watchtower loomed up before us. Inside, on the broad lower level lit only by archer's slots, an officer was shouting orders at a dozen soldiers as they frantically prepared for Nobunaga's inspection.

They all snapped to rigid attention as I ran in. I dashed past them and out the far doorway. No one followed. I turned and peered back inside the dim space.

Sugitani launched himself onto the nearest soldier the moment he entered the chamber. His attack was so brutal, so sudden, that the man's cries cut off before he struck the floor. Sugitani fed.

The other soldiers did not understand what they were seeing, but they had sense enough to draw their swords against him. Sugitani stood in the center of a whirlwind of men and steel. Some blows struck the armor he wore. Some bit into his body. None of it mattered to him. He lashed out and snatched blades, armor, limbs, until he could bring them close enough to find flesh, and then he killed with his jaws. A dozen bloody bodies lay where they had been flung, and when they were all still, he bounded back and forth, visiting each for just as long as there was still some force of life lingering within it.

A lifetime of warfare has taught me a thousand ways to wound and damage until my opponent is powerless to oppose my will. But never have I seen such savagery, such a frenzied urge to kill, as Sugitani showed me in that room.

"We have no time," I cried. "Come on!"

He looked up at me, unblinking, and wet gobbets of whatever is found inside men's chests dripped down his chin and his front. My stomach turned to ice. I searched for recognition, for signs of the brave and honorable warrior that I knew, and I found nothing. All that was left was that hunger for the spark of living things.

I knew now that if he caught me, it would not matter that we had grown up together, or that we had shed blood for each other. He would know me only as one more creature to sacrifice to his emptiness.

An aide-de-camp still in his early teens jogged up to the doorway and stepped inside with precocious hauteur. He had time to declare, "A breach of discipline has come to the attention of the generals. What's the nature of the commotion in—?" and then Sugitani knocked him halfway across the room and pinned him against a square wooden pillar. The youth tried to push him off, but Sugitani regarded his bare hands as an offering, and tore them apart with his teeth, swallowing fingers and bones whole. The boy's screams ended only after he slumped to the floor and Sugitani moved on to his head and neck.

Outside in the sunlight, the generals were on the wall, approaching the watchtower.

This thing that Sugitani had become was less than a beast. These were no bushi's actions. There was no honor in this. Even if he destroyed Nobunaga, it would mean no more to him than any of these other kills.

If he could see himself, he would know there was no duty performed, no giri satisfied, nor any bravery for Lord Rokkaku to acknowledge.

"This can't go on, brother," I said. "If the world learned of this, you could never wash the shame from your spirit."

I slid the heavy door shut. The beams of light slanting through the arrow slots became dense spears in the dimness.

"Don't go out there," I implored. "Stay with me just a little while. Maybe they'll take the west stairs down, and then I'll find some way to get you out of here."

I stepped towards him, but he was feeding, eager to consume as much as he could before the vitality left the flesh, and he ignored me.

The door slammed open.

"What the hell is going on in here?" someone shouted.

The doorway blazed with blue sky and sunlight, and the man was a dark shape against it. I saw only that his tall helmet flashed with gold as he quivered with rage, and heard in his voice a tone that took total command for granted. That could be no one but Oda Nobunaga.

Sugitani charged at him.

I could have chosen to simply do nothing, and in moments our lord's greatest enemy would be torn to shreds. But because I loved Sugitani, I could not let him reach Nobunaga.

I cast away my duty and shouted, "*Oi,* Sugitani!"

He turned to me. When I drew his katana, it came out of the scabbard as quick as thought. His right hand darted for my throat. I did not try to kill him—I had seen that was impossible. I swung, and connected, and removed his arm cleanly above the elbow.

I stepped back and raised the sword again. "Forgive me."

He lunged at me with his left. I brought the blade down on his thigh. Sugitani's sword was sharp, and it was a great sweeping blow. His leg flopped open as if it were hinged.

He fell to the floorboards, scrabbling for me, but he could not find the leverage to rise. I put a foot on the back of his neck and pinned him. He writhed and snapped, and he did not tire. I struggled to catch my breath.

"I'll say it again: What the hell is going on here?"

The Oda generals and retainers surrounded me. Each of them had his hand on a hilt. Oda Nobunaga, the most disruptive warlord the land of Nippon has seen in a hundred fifty years of civil war, stood just too far for me to reach without releasing Sugitani.

The gold on Nobunaga's helmet was the brightest thing in the room. Now I could see that he was a strong, restless man in his mid-thirties, with a bulbous nose and oddly feminine eyes.

He was a daimyō, and he was waiting for an answer.

"This man was attempting . . . something dishonorable, my lord," I answered. "I was obliged to stop him."

He looked Sugitani over carefully, and then turned his attention to me.

"If I'm not mistaken, that is not quite a man," he said.

"Perhaps not, my lord."

"Ah. It would seem I owe you my life."

I bowed.

"And you fight well," Nobunaga said. "It would please me to have you join my personal guard."

"Forgive me, sir, but I could not in good faith accept such a position," I answered.

He cocked an eyebrow. "And why is that?"

"Because I would be obliged to kill you the moment the opportunity arose, my lord."

A half dozen swords flashed as they were drawn and leveled at me.

The corner of Nobunaga's mouth twitched with amusement. "Ah. Then you would be of the Rokkaku clan, I take it."

"Yes, my lord."

"Bad luck for you and me both. Any man here would be happy to kill you, and it would be his duty to do so. Yet you have laid this giri on me, and I am loathe to disregard it. What shall I do with you?"

"Let us go, my lord," I begged. "We are done here. Let me take him away and burn the body in secret. He was a great and honorable man once, and I loved him."

"That I cannot do. The whole castle knows by now that there has been an attempt on my life. There have been murders and gunshots. They will expect a very public execution."

I hung my head. Under my heel, Sugitani continued to groan and squirm. "Then I would beg that you do it in some way that hides what he is. I would not have the depth of his shame be known, or let it taint the reputation of our master."

"I believe that would be feasible. His end would be that of a common killer."

Three days ago that would have been unthinkable. I bowed low. "You do us a great kindness, my lord."

As I have said, when a man's giri and his heart are not in accord—shame and disaster.

That day word was spread throughout the castle that one of the Rokkaku retainers had hired a band of commoners from outside their clan to assassinate Lord Nobunaga. The mercenaries had scaled the wall and slaughtered the soldiers posted there, and a sharpshooter in their party fired two matchlocks at Nobunaga as he conferred with his advisors. The accomplices had escaped, but through the heroic actions of guards nearby, the sniper was subdued, and Nobunaga was unharmed.

Lord Nobunaga decreed that since this attack on his person was based on a mere business transaction, and had its roots in neither honor nor duty, the assassin would receive the most degrading form of punishment conceivable.

A hole was dug in the center of the courtyard. The sniper was buried in it to the top of his shoulders, so that only his bare head stood out from the ground. A saw made of bamboo was left nearby, and all passers-by were encouraged to try their hand at cutting through the man's neck. A bamboo saw is a toy that can barely slice through rice-stalks. A hardy man could work it until the blade smoked yet cut less than the width of a finger. It was an exceptionally long, excruciating death.

We were indebted to Nobunaga. The deep hole served to hide Sugitani's body, so that he could be seen by the entire army, yet none would realize the extent of his wounds, or how little they hindered him. Any mortal man's mind would surely break under such torture, and the hell-born grimace that twisted his features was expected and fitting. And to those who took part in the slow execution, it seemed natural that when they approached with the saw the desperate man would defend himself the only way he could—snarling, snapping, and biting.

At the end of four days, I knelt over Sugitani and sawed until my fingers bled, guiding the dull blade between the vertebrae of his neck. When his head at last dropped loose a cheer went up, and I let him remain face down in the dust so that none would see that the eyes and jaw continued to move.

It is nearly all done now. Kannonji Castle holds no value for Nobunaga. He has abandoned it and moved on to Kyōto. I have taken away the head and body before Lord Rokkaku could return and see them. I will not fail Sugitani again. In some quiet farmhouse whose owners have been driven out by the war, I will lay him on a hero's funeral pyre. I will meditate upon the flames consuming one who let only his giri guide him, and then, without the luxury of a second standing behind me, I will complete the seppuku of a true warrior. I have killed myself before, and I know I will not need help to conquer the pain.

# DEAD RECKONING

## ELAINE PASCALE

*Roanoke, Late July, 1590*

The boy is screaming.

He is screaming and running through woods he knows as well as his own scent, but which look strange and menacing in the light of the falling sun.

*Murder.*

That was the word that was causing him to run, causing his cold skin to be scratched by low hanging branches and thorns. The scratches beget lines which beget words which beget warnings: *The woods are not for you.*

There was no reason that he had not broken free of the woods by now. He had been running for some time, screaming for even longer, and both quantities exceeded the amount necessary to traverse the woods. He had run as fast as he could. Perhaps he had gotten turned around: lost.

His feet furrowed the fallen twigs and the sound multiplied in the silent forest. His run slowed to a sporadic jog and he wondered if others were in his part of the woods, or if he was alone. He didn't know, after all he had seen, which predicament scared him more.

*The blood. His world has been tainted with blood and now everything has changed.*

The boy runs until he becomes more afraid of dropping to his knees than of anything that might be chasing him. He fears succumbing to the woods. His young mind envisions the weeds and brambles growing over his body as it lay on the forest floor. When his father had been alive, he had always spoken of new crops covering past mistakes. But the errors had been fewer when father had been there to protect them, and the boy had just witnessed the ultimate transgression.

*Murder.*

The boy feels the bushes reaching for him. He remembers the ones who had mouths like steel traps, dripping with gristle. He remembers that they devour rather than eat. He remembers that they kill without mercy. He knows that they will come after him if he does not make it through the woods. At twelve, he has lived long enough to know that there were some secrets that needed to remain hidden.

• • •

*Roanoke, February 1590*

The baby coughed.

Over and over.

His tiny fists bunched around his mouth, his thin thighs pulling up to his chest as his body was wracked by the coughs. He had passed his fourth birthday, but Elizabeth knew he had not grown in months and was undersized. He was always cold and his eyes had trouble focusing. She tried wrapping him in blankets, but he would not warm and he would not return her embraces.

When he coughed, splotches of blood speckled his fists. The blood had come from inside of him, coughed onto his hands. Elizabeth knew that that was a very bad sign.

Her happiness was dependent on him. His father was no comfort. "The angels are calling him home to the Maker," Ambrose would say. It was this blind faith that had brought them to the colony. Blind faith that kept them looking to the horizon for ships that were promised to return.

Elizabeth had seen the brown woman watching them. The woman studied the baby like a sailor studies a map, making sense of every bump and every sallow spot.

One day, after she took corn meal from the brown woman, Elizabeth tried to engage her, looking at her pleadingly. This woman, and her people, had given them so much, couldn't she give a little more? It wasn't food Elizabeth wanted; she craved answers: "My child," Elizabeth began her supplication, "he will grow strong here. Yes?"

The brown woman had shaken her head and answered, "No." That one syllable, spoken by a woman who had learned it so recently, was enough to break something stored deeply inside of Elizabeth.

While broken, Elizabeth would not give up. The baby's father, the one she was supposed to accept as her authority, wanted to leave matters to God, the God that he believed would help him to save the brown people. Ambrose had been coming to her in the night, as she slept, bent over the baby's small pile of bedding. He wanted her to conceive again, to have an heir ready as this one waned. Ambrose wanted to go forward with life and to help create the new society.

Elizabeth revoked him. She prayed. She prayed to the God she had always known, the one who had made life seem promising back in England. But the boy grew sicker and sicker. His breathing became raspy, turning him into something not human, something that once had breathed fire but now only emitted gusts of smoke. Elizabeth prayed and prayed and prayed until he died.

Once John White had returned to England for supplies, they had been left with eighty men, seventeen women and ten children. Now there were nine children.

Since baby Virginia had been born, there had been no new births. People whispered of a curse. They blamed the brown people. Elizabeth began to blame the God that had led them here.

They buried her baby without her. They tore it from her arms and buried it, while she hid inside of her house and cursed every curse she could utter. Hoarse, she remembered that the brown woman had taken pity on her; eventually she remembered the words the brown woman had taught her.

Desperate, Elizabeth ran to the beach. She could no longer rely on the God of her husband, the God of the people who brought her here—who brought her son to die. She revoked both God and husband; they had given up on her child, so she would spare no mercy for them.

The brown woman had made a promise to Elizabeth. She had looked her in the eye and promised her. The brown woman, while savage, understood pain. So Elizabeth recited the heathen words taught her, the words exchanged through whispered repetition because neither woman could read or write. "Alicarl, gaugbrojotr, istrumagi, kamphundr, kamphundr."

It was not long after saying the words that Elizabeth saw the lights summoned from the sea. Was this God coming to save her, or to take the baby?

Others had also seen the lights. The other women, who felt angry and oppressed, had seen the lights. They were whom the lights were for. As promised by the brown woman, the lights came for the powerless and gave them power. When Elizabeth said the words, only eight women saw the lights, but the lights would give them the strength of soldiers.

*Roanoke, March 1590*

The children are screaming.

They are running and screaming. They are playing a game that they always play, with sticks and rocks. They are running where they always run, minding the warning they were given to avoid the woman's house.

The woman's house is tucked into the side of a small copse. The thick trees watch her back, rendering an ambush from the rear impossible. The land falls down from her front stoop in a series of crops. She is the envy of the colony, as no one has been able to grow anything substantial. Some people whisper about her and call her "witch," especially because her garden blooms at night. Her small parcel of land is full of animal bones and there are many small scavengers creeping around the property.

A large bird has swooped upon a mouse. The woman walks past without noticing. She is called Grossi Gerta by the village children, but she has no living children of her own. Her Christian name is Agnes, but she calls herself Aegeni.

Gerta is not only the grower of crops, she is a friend of the natives. She makes secret trades with them. She has no man in her home, so she has to be savvy and wise. Perhaps the natives believe she is some sort of witch? They do like the items she has managed to acquire and give to them.

Unfortunately, she was running out of trinkets, and feared she was running out of time. Many people around her seemed to be dying. Those that were not dying spoke of fleeing. Gerta is a practical woman, so she will not run. She will not run from her formidable crops and her alliance with the natives. She also did not look away when the lights had surrounded her. She had let the lights land on her. The lights had inspected her, violated her. Now, she hides pus-filled boils: she itches, and she hungers.

Animals have disappeared. Rumors abounded of Freybug, whispers of Revenants and Phoukas. Colonists and natives alike complained of the stench of rotting deer and fish and rabbits. They looked the other way when the mauled carcasses were removed, some impaled on the decrepit posts near Gerta's property.

That did not prevent the children from forgetting their warnings and wandering onto her land. That did not serve as enough of a caution to keep the kids from chasing the rabbit into the sharp, long grass in her yard.

They didn't know that flesh kept her healthy and reduced her boils. They didn't know that if you sifted through the ashes beneath her kettle, you would find charred human bones. They didn't know what was hanging and being smoked in the back of her house or how the blood lights could create a hunger so strong that one would commit the ultimate sin against nature.

The ultimate crime.

Gerta sits in an enclosure in the thicket. She smells the children as they approach: their earnest, dirt-streaked skin and stale clothing. Their ripeness was not displeasing. In fact, it had the opposite effect: Gerta salivated and her stomach rumbled.

"Elizabeth?"

He knew she was angry with him. God had spoken to him and told him to have patience. In time, they would have many more children. They would establish the land. They just had to hold their faith in the highest regard.

"Elizabeth?"

She was not answering him. He assumed she was in their home. She had not left her bed during the day for weeks. Sometimes, at night, he suspected that she rose, but he was too tired to look after her. He had learned to sleep through the scratching. He spent most of his days constructing the church. Once that was in place, once the altar was finished, then their bad luck would end.

He felt a drop of water fall onto his wrist. Only, he was inside and he had patched the roof himself. He looked at his wrist. The drop had a yellowish quality to it. Had he not been so lost in his faith, had he not been so secure in his divine protection, he would have looked up. But he never would have allowed himself to believe that his own wife was clinging to the ceiling like a spider, a thread of drool leading from her lips.

There are now seventy-five men, seventeen women, and seven children.

*Roanoke, April 1590*

The girl is screaming.

She is screaming and standing over what she knows to be a man's hand. While she is classified as one of the women, she is still very young. She is young enough that the only male body parts she has seen are hands, beardless faces, and necks. This hand is attached to nothing. It lies on the ground, on the deadened grass, palm to the heavens as if in supplication. The hand is asking for something; for what, she does not know. Perhaps it wants to find the rest of its body. This thought confuses her. Who does the hand belong to? They had already buried several men that had been relieved of large chunks of flesh. Their bodies had been brutally ravaged, but not one had been missing an appendage.

She screams again, hoping someone would hear her, hoping that someone would know what to do next. She feels far too young to be dealing with the horrors that have befallen her people. There are whispers of there being a curse, but everyone knows the savages are after them. John White had wronged the savages and they were suffering because of it. She should have remembered the savages before she started screaming.

Someone is coming. There are sounds of someone making his or her way through the brush behind her. The girl is relieved to see it is one of the women. She would have been concerned to be alone with a man, as no one has figured out whom to pair her off with yet. She would have been in dire straits if the figure had been brown. She is relieved to see the woman, until she notices the large boils on the woman's skin, until she notices that the woman is salivating as she looks at her.

Suddenly, she finds that she can no longer scream.

There are now seventy-two men, sixteen women, and seven children.

Emme swore she would run away. She had no intention of remaining and marrying Griffen. He had been a clod back in England and a clod he would remain. Her father was pushing the union, the colony desperate for more children. Their numbers were decreasing and none of the other couples seemed to be able to add any additional souls to Roanoke. She had put off marriage long enough; her father was forcing her to move forward. Emme swore she would run away, if only she knew where she could run to.

She had been crying on the beach. She had been cursing her situation and cursing her family for forcing her to come here. She could have remained in England. She could have stayed with her cousins and ended up marrying someone wonderful. Some successful and handsome landowner, not some talentless carpenter who smelled like an animal.

She had been crying on the beach when the brown woman had found her. The brown woman had such kind and understanding eyes. The brown woman understood pain and she knew how to make it go away. The brown woman taught Emme the words: "Alicarl, gaugbrojotr, istrumagi, kamphundr, kamphundr." Later, Emme said the words and the lights came. The lights came buzzing and boldly, and they made Emme very, very hungry.

The men are laughing.

The men are laughing and joking as they build the fence that will protect the compound. They tell ribald tales as a way of distracting themselves from the task at hand: the need to put a wall between themselves and the natives. They don't realize that they are trapping themselves inside with the evil.

William and George had the first shift of sentry duty. Unknowingly, they turned their backs to the colony and watched for movement beyond. Unknowingly, they became meat at midnight.

There are now seventy men, sixteen women, and six children.

Henry came to check in for the second shift. He found no one on duty. The only person he saw was Elizabeth, wandering in the yard and scratching. He asked her if she had seen William or George. At first, she looked at him as if she had no understanding of English. Then, she shook her head and walked away. It unsettled Henry when he noticed her looking back at him and licking chapped lips.

*Roanoke, May 1590*

Grossi Gerta has grown tired of stalking children. She was a large woman with a large appetite. She had no way of seducing the men into her quarters; she was old and no longer of child-bearing age. The focus of the colony was reproduction, yet their numbers were dwindling. The few men she had managed to snare had been luck. She needed a stronger strategy.

She had seen the natives setting traps. In addition to being the grower of crops (crops which were now neglected due to her hunger), she becomes the setter of traps. Silently, she thanks the brown woman for providing her with knowledge and some lessons on knot tying. The brown woman had wanted nothing in return.

When Gerta has finished her rampage, she will be responsible for the deaths of over twenty men: men who had blamed the "savages" for their hardships.

Henry heard a scream coming from the woods.

He had been one of the most successful sentries in terms of number of nights on the job. Something was apparently scaring the other watchmen away; whenever the morning duty arrived, no night sentries could be found. Perhaps the savages were frightening the men so badly that they were turning away from their responsibilities, away from the colony. Perhaps the savages had been kidnapping the men to enslave them.

Or for reasons that were far worse.

Henry hated the night duty, but he had always been smart enough to look in all directions and never to keep his back to the compound for long.

Call it instinct or call it luck: at this rate, Henry would soon be Captain of the guards.

The scream came again, this time it was cut short. Henry could only imagine what was happening in the wooded area just beyond the fence.

"This is it," he thought, he would catch the savages in the act. They could then retaliate with a war they would surely win. They needed proof this time, to avoid another instance of harming innocents. Finding one of the tribe promoting evil would put an end to suspicion and trigger action. But did Henry really want to stumble upon a deadly struggle? His stomach sank and his genitals crawled into his body.

He lowered himself from his station and moved quietly into the thicket. He was grateful for the bit of moonlight that helped him to navigate his path. He felt as if he were staggering quickly but also moving mawkishly slow at the same time. He wanted to save whomever it was that had been screaming. Why had the screams stopped?

His question was answered when he came upon a sight too horrible to believe.

"No." That one syllable was all his brain could muster.

He saw his neighbor, Emme, bent over a child. Eating.

There are now fifty-eight men, sixteen women, and three children.

• • •

*Roanoke, June 1590*

Her parents knew, but refused to accept, what she had become.

Edward had placed Emme inside the structure he had been building as her house for after her wedding. Griffen was a carpenter, but Edward did not trust him to create a stable home for his daughter and future grandchildren. He also could not risk Griffen seeing her in her current condition. Wenefrid had bound her daughter's hands, hoping the girl would stop scratching her boils. During the day, Emme slept and Wenefrid tested seaweed and herb-based poultices. At night, Edward secured the girl, fearing she was up to evil under the influence of the moon.

Emme grew weaker and her skin grew worse. Her mother spoonfed her soup, which was immediately regurgitated. Wenefrid then came to an understanding that her husband did not entirely share, and she tried to sneak the girl hunks of raw chicken. Emme was able to keep the chicken down, but it did nothing to satisfy her hunger, nor did it have any effect on the disease that seemed to be eating her alive.

One restless night, Wenefrid stole into Emme's prison, only to find that the girl had begun to tear through her bindings. The girl looked at her with such pain, with such desolation, that Wenefrid's heart broke. She removed the casings over her daughter's hands and sprung her shackles. Then, she went willingly into her child's arms.

When Edward discovered the remains of his wife, along with his daughter no longer confined, he went much less willingly.

And Griffen, sweet and simple, allowed Emme to approach him in the night. He soon found himself united to her in a way he had never imagined.

There are now fifty men, fifteen women, and three children.

"Elizabeth?" He opened the door tentatively.

Henry knew he should not be paying her a visit alone. He had seen what had become of Emme and he suspected a similar condition was afflicting Elizabeth. He also remembered how he had loved her back home, how he had worked to put aside money so he could propose, but Ambrose had beaten him to it. He had wanted to hate the man, but Ambrose's love of God made him someone to emulate, not envy.

Ambrose's death had been so sudden. Elizabeth claimed she had found him, bludgeoned as if by a hatchet, and desecrated as only a godless savage could dare to desecrate a pious man's corpse. It had not been possible to bury Ambrose whole. Pieces of him had been torn away, the body was ragged and ripped and if Henry, upon seeing the body, had thought any less of the savages, he would have suspected that teeth had ravaged the corpse. The worst, for Henry, had been the eyes—the eyes had been removed. At that time, he could not imagine what evil the savages had had in store for those eyes. He had heard that savages sometimes consumed the heart of a warrior for strength; what had they hoped to see with Ambrose's eyes? Ambrose had been a man of letters and a disciple of God; which did they value more: a view of words from their world of blackness, or a glimpse of heaven?

The other men had not gone easily either. Each corpse told its own tale of depravity. And Henry could no longer attribute the cause to the natives.

Now that he had seen Emme, now that he suspected what he suspected, Henry faced Elizabeth's house with a mixture of fear and hope. Perhaps she was not sickly, not a monster. Perhaps he could, in some way, save her. They could leave this place together. They could start somewhere new, somewhere better. Or, they could find a way to go back home. Either way, they would be far away from this evil. More importantly, they would be together.

He was so distracted by his plan making, as he stepped into his beloved Elizabeth's home, that Henry failed to see the shadow, armed with a hatchet, moving from the darkened corner toward him.

There are now forty men, fourteen women, and three children.

*Roanoke, Late July, 1590*

"God will protect the saved from the sinners," Martyn Sutton opines during the Sunday service. Martyn had taken the pulpit after two of the original religious leaders met a tragic demise. The group knew the time had come to pray fervently. Their combined voices could catch God's benevolent ear.

The benches that had been built to accommodate them all were now mostly empty. The women itch and have great difficulties sitting still. "There exists a spiritual and divine light . . . this light shines upon the saved and allows the wicked to see the truth of their guilt."

"Amen," the men say loudly.

"This light, this divine light, will shine through the forests and lead us to a promised land . . . "

"Amen," the men echo.

"Alicarl, gaugbrojotr, istrumagi, kamphundr, kamphundr," one of the women whispers. The others giggle.

The men's heads are bowed in prayer. They do not notice the women making a movement, or they have become accustomed to the scratching and do not notice that this is different. The women have hidden weapons in their skirts and shawls. Some of the women are armed with axes, a few have muskets, all have an insatiable hunger that allows them to quickly overpower the shocked men. The women allow the remaining children to flee.

There are now no men.

*Roanoke, Early August, 1590*

It has been too long since she has had any sustenance, any flesh; Elizabeth knows she is dying. As she stumbles, gnawing on one of the few remaining bones she could find, sucking its marrow, she carves "Croatoan" into a post. She is not sure if this is the name of the brown woman's tribe or of the curse. She wants John White to know, when he finds their bodies, that the brown woman had taught her the words. John White had told them to carve a post or a tree; he had told them to add a cross if they had faced anything distressing. She decides to wait and add the cross later; after the scene at their final service, she needs distance between herself and any symbols of faith. She begins to carve the same word into a tree, but only manages "Cro" before she succumbs to her hunger.

The brown woman had done well. The curse had been overheard from stinking, hairy settlers from many generations ago. These new intruders would no longer be begging for supplies, draining the people of their resources while taking their land.

The brown woman's people had been attacked by John White, who had been seeking retribution for his original lost fifteen men. Now White had lost over one hundred.

By the time some her tribe arrive at the colony, they find twelve women: twelve very hungry women. The brown woman had heard one of the children escape into the woods. He would not survive, and, if he did, no one would believe his story. For all practical purposes, there was no one left.

The natives knew a boat was coming. The boat would see the smoke; the boat would maybe find some footprints, but nothing more.

The natives burn the women: spoiled flesh burns quickly. They sweep up the ashes, sending the remnants of the scourge back where it belongs.

# GRIT IN A DISEASED EYE

LEE THOMAS

We are abandoned. *Discovery* is under full sail, far across the bay, too distant for our meager oars. Even so, I cannot bear to order the men to cease their pursuit. It is the only hope remaining to them, though I consider their hope an illusion. The effort keeps them occupied, pumping away their dread with the exertion of muscle and bone, postponing an inevitable and tragic flood.

Icy shores and white fields surround the inlet. No prospects for a hospitable port. The water reflects the gray sky, and our pitiful shallop corrupts this water like a speck of grit in a diseased eye.

Aboard my stolen vessel, Greene and Juet carry a tale of righteous mutiny, the story of a captain obsessed and obdurate. Lies. After Murphy came down ill and then Tobin, I ordered them quarantined, but Juet insisted on delivering them to the deep. When this was done, a similar demand was made for any man showing signs of infirmity. This I refused. The compromise was hardly kinder. The shallop. Meager supplies. A hasty prayer.

The source of Murphy's and Tobin's particular malady is a mystery: perhaps a heretofore-unknown creature with a peculiar venom, or rations grown rancid during the long winter months. Perhaps it is a madness not yet documented, one that afflicts the mind when faced with such desolation of landscape. My only certainty is that my son, John, much to my misery, has become afflicted, and my refusal to leave him with the other sick men accounts for my presence on this craft.

John was loaded into the shallop unconscious and barely breathing. Then he revived, and upon waking, my boy endured an absent delirium that looked as much like drunkenness as insanity. He immediately set on Rogers, burying his teeth into the mate's wrist with so much force, his tooth broke free on the knobbed bone as he ripped away flesh and hide. He squealed in the way a pig squeals at the presentation of its slop as he gnawed the meat. I sought to constrain him, wrapping him in rope to end the flailing of his arms. But Rogers struck out enraged, sending John over the shallop's edge, and before I could offer my son rescue, Rogers incapacitated me with a vicious blow. I laid dazed in the pitching craft, mourning the loss of my boy, not knowing that he was no more lost to me in the bay than he had been in the craft.

With only enough strength to hold the rope, not enough to climb, not enough to swim, John remains in our wake, just as we remain in the wake of the *Discovery*, now a mere toy on the horizon. I see John well and clearly. His face appears just beneath the surface of the frigid bay like a spirit. His mouth remains open. His tongue lolls on the current sluicing his throat. His eyes are washed clean of color and intellect.

Until the malady afflicted him, my son had such hunger and curiosity in his eyes. A precious and forever questioning soul. The hunger remains there.

Do I grasp the rope and pull him to me, or do I join him in the frigid bay? I do not know. For now, I wait and write no more. My heart is too heavy to support the added burden of pen and page.

*Henry Hudson, 1611*

# THEATRE IS DEAD

## RAOUL WAINSCOTING

The stage was set. The crowd quieted to a murmur under the mid-afternoon sun as the narrator appeared. Entering from stage right, he glided regally to the edge of the stage. His handsome costume was new and flawless. He took a moment to study the crowd. The better-paying patrons sat comfortably in the shade on the far side of the Globe.

Squinting against the light, the narrator spoke. "Good people, hear thee now our tale of woe. The family royal Puglia, rulers of Brindisi, undone by the politics of man, while amongst them the dead do walk."

The crowd's murmur rose briefly. The rumors were true, the play did concern the postvitals. A few amongst them rose to depart, mortified by the idea of using such tragedy as entertainment. Backstage, while the narrator strolled through the introductory monologue, the cast was rushing to complete their preparations. A debut performance was always challenging, but when breaking in a new theatre, doubly so.

"Come now, into your costume!" William yanked on the cords, tugging the cape snugly about the young man's neck. "Prince Risoni enters the first scene shortly, boy!" William shoved him forward, towards his assigned post near the stage, to await his cue.

Henry Darcy, the young man in the costume of the doomed Prince Risoni, cradled his wounded hand, hidden beneath the cape. His brow was damp with pained perspiration, attributed to a mild case of stage fright. He swept the cape aside for a moment, peeking at the hand once more. It had happened in an instant, on the way to the theatre. That foul drunk, staggering along the cobbles, smelled of the sewer. Putrid and stinking, the drunk had crashed into Henry, forcing him to shove him away. As he pushed the stinking body, the old man had bitten him! Now costumed, Henry studied his hand. The arc of small, festering cuts on his palm betrayed the bite mark. But he had to go on. He needed this job, any job, and this troupe was the only one willing to take him. This was his last chance in London.

Nearby, lurking in a shadowy corner, stood the officer. Quietly, Lieutenant Richard Litchfield, of Her Majesty's Royal Navy, observed. He caught William's eyes and drew him over. William offered his hand, the pair shook, exchanging looks of tired relief. It had been a maddening few months for both of them. William thought back to their first meeting. His carriage, returning him from family business in Stratford, had struck and been overturned by an unexpected mob of postvitals on the road. His first encounter with the walking dead was terrifying. The staggering mass of rotting corpses had seized upon the coachman and his horses, giving William and the other passengers time to escape. But they were soon being pursued. A slow, relentless chase drove the passengers of the ruined coach across the field, carrying the others that could not walk. It had seemed like hours. The temptation to drop the injured and save himself had been overwhelming. Just when hope had seemed lost, help had arrived.

Richard recalled their first meeting as well. The outbreak from the small village had gone unchecked for too long. His team, atop armored horse and with their war wagon carriage, had trampled, impaled and slashed the corpses in quick order. He had personally crushed the lifelessness from the last few corpses with his metal gauntlets around their necks.

It was then that William, an enthusiastic survivor of the assault, had seized upon his plan. After hearing Richard's profane complaints of how the citizenry was too stupid to follow a few simple rules for preventing such outbreaks, he had made his offer. "Teach me these rules, as you would have them know, and I shall present them in grand form!" William had said there on the gore-soaked hillside. "Come to London with me, consult on the production of my new play. We shall take the city by storm, entertaining, educating, and making a good name for my troupe. And you, you shall gain allies in your battle."

Richard had scoffed at the idea, having no interest in sitting on the sidelines. A rising star in the Royal Navy, he had proven himself at the postvital outbreak in Portsmouth, leading his men, charging the fallen city from the docks. After that, he found himself seconded to the Royal Army, teaching them to roam the countryside, chasing down reports of the increasingly frequent outbreaks. He had no idea the power of this maddening playwright, who had the Lord Chamberlain reach out to have Richard seconded again to this new branch called "Relations with Her Majesty's Public." He had spent the last few months in frustrated misery, teaching artistic young fools to stagger and lurch in the manner of the dead. That had been easy, compared to the task of arguing with the arrogant, petulant playwright over details he was supposed to be reinforcing in their play—how to prevent the dead from rising, how to deal with those that had risen, or been bitten or befouled by them. Simple rules, needlessly complicated by their inclusion in this miserable, clichéd storyline of a fictional royal family.

William smiled. Ignorant of Richard's true feelings, he was happy to see the loyal officer standing by to the last, ready to assist during the play as needed. "We shall do well, you shall see. Your service here is most appreciated, and I shall make sure your superiors know of it, Lieutenant." William tossed off a flippant salute and returned to shuffling the cast backstage.

Onstage, the first scene had begun. Two princes of the royal Puglia family had begun their part. Their third, the quietly suffering Prince Risoni, waited for his cue. He wiped his brow again, his face growing ever paler as the throbbing in his wounded hand slowly spread up his arm.

"What hear you of Count Gemelli's plans, good brother?" asked Prince Paccheri, eldest son of the king, his majesty Fiori Puglia.

"I trust not that man, but our father's ear he doth have," replied Prince Filini, the second eldest.

"I wager it is war he doth seek, to usurp the crown, aided by our falling in battle, good brother," said Prince Paccheri.

Prince Risoni, the youngest of the three princes, lurched onto stage a few beats after his cue. He appeared somewhat dazed, raising an unexpected titter of laughter from the crowd. "How now, good brothers!" Prince Risoni finally managed to squeak through the growing pain in his arm. Backstage, Lieutenant Richard Litchfield held his ears, hiding in the shadows. He tried to block out the back-and-forth dialogue of the elder princes, as they explained for the audience the state of the conflict with the Calabria family, sworn enemies of the Puglia royal family, and how the mysterious court advisor, Count Gemelli, seemed to be making things worse.

William, seeing a lull in his backstage work, once more approached the tortured officer. "So, how do you think it is going?"

"Fine! Just stay on script and get the message across." Richard fought his urge to strangle the infuriating playwright.

William nodded. "I've been meaning to ask you, were you really there? Against the Armada? I heard some of the cast talking, they said you were." William pressed himself against the wall to let some bodies pass in the narrow space backstage, readying themselves for the upcoming onstage battle.

Richard perked up. At least this would distract him for a moment. "Yes, I was there. I was serving aboard one of the ships that met them. And, yes, the rumors are true. The dead walking amongst the crew of the Spanish galleons were a factor in their defeat. But only in part."

"And, is it true that—" William began.

Richard cut him off. "The rumors of British intrigue being the cause of the enemy vessels' infection are just that." Richard smiled at William from his shadowy hiding place. "Just rumors."

Onstage, the ambush began. The soldiers of Calabria, sworn enemies of the Puglia, swarmed onstage, all three of them. The three princes fought valiantly to fend off their attackers. Richard, backstage, shielded his eyes against the sight. No matter how he shouted at them, these actors could not manage to make a sword fight look authentic. Wild, chopping swings and lengthy pauses for heroic poses made them look like fools. But the audience lapped it up, laughing and "oohing" appropriately in time with the action. Most importantly, they gasped on cue as the brave young Prince Risoni fell, victim of a final stab from the departing, defeated enemy.

"Brother! Thou hast fallen!" shouted the elder princes, joining the brave Risoni as life failed him. The illness of the actor beneath the costume was acute. The throbbing in the wound upon his hand had spread to the rest of his body. His gasps of pain made his character's death seem all the more real. Henry Darcy joined his character in death, there upon the stage.

Even Richard had to admit, it looked pretty good.

"Now, brother, flee us to seek aid, to move our littlest brother's body," said Prince Paccheri.

"A noble carriage for his noble body," agreed Prince Filini.

The pair moved offstage, leaving the body alone. The audience murmured, some of them aware of the folly of leaving a fallen body alone, unmolested, in these dark days.

William watched as Risoni remained at rest. "Get up now, your lines!" William hissed at the prone actor. His moving soliloquy on the nature of death and the rest it might bring was going wasted! The audience rustled, curious at the pause in the action and the general state of immobility of the actor at center stage.

Richard nodded approvingly. For weeks he had battled the writer and his cast, insistent that the dead not be portrayed as speaking. As far as he could tell, the good Prince was playing dead to perfection.

"Next scene!" William signaled backstage, and the cast and crew rushed to comply. The narrator rushed onstage to explain to the crowd the terrible mistake the elder princes had made, leaving a recently-fallen body untended. While the chances were slim, the horrible new condition that afflicted those rare few might lead the body to rise again. A mindless killer, wandering, feeding, spreading the curse to others through their wounds.

The prince's body was dragged offstage as the intrigue between Count Gemelli and Queen Bavette was established. He had dirt on her, and it would prevent her from disrupting his plans for disposing of King Fiori.

The body of Prince Risoni continued to play its part. That which had killed him, so painfully, was now reanimating him. Slowly, the body of the costumed Henry Darcy twitched upon the wooden floor and began to rise.

"Funeral scene!" William signaled backstage and the cast and crew set to work. The costumer rushed to Prince Risoni, ready to throw a damp gray cloth over the actor's head, the better to appear a lifeless corpse. Upon seeing the actor, he decided the Prince didn't need it. Someone else must have already prepared the actor, he already looked the part. Risoni's body let out a low moan, reaching for the man, the hunger for flesh already consuming what passed for its mind.

"Come on!" Prince Paccheri and King Fiori grabbed Risoni's barely-animated corpse and dragged it onstage, flopping it onto the flimsy bench next to the trapdoor in the stage. The scene was set, the body was atop the Puglia family's royal crypt, and the rest of the royals had assembled for the ceremony.

"Curse be to mine enemies, having our son from us ta'en!" King Fiori bemoaned his loss, shaking his fist skyward. The actors playing Queen Bavette and Princess Barbina wailed in falsetto at their loss. Count Gemelli skulked in the corner, lurking, to remind the audience of his evil, traitorous nature.

"We beseech thee, look with favor upon . . . ," the priest began, as the body of Prince Risoni began to rise from its prone position. "Not yet!" hissed the priest, pushing the corpse back down onto the table.

Backstage, William grimaced at the miscue by the young actor.

The funeral continued, with soliloquies on the nature of life and death bursting forth from the King and Queen. Frequent interruptions by the body at the center disturbed them, the actor apparently wildly confused as to when it was his turn. The trapdoor was slid open and the body was hoisted off the table by the cast for its deposit into the crypt.

The dead Risoni flailed, this time on cue, and gripped a convenient arm, that of the actor wearing the wig and dress of Queen Bavette. The cast gasped and erupted with a horrified "Zounds!" to emphasize their surprise over the rise of the dead. The audience was less impressed, having seen it coming due to the frequent miscues by the dead actor.

Prince Paccheri immediately drew his stage sword and moved to dispose of the animated corpse. Just as quickly, the King, reinforcing the family's tragic misunderstanding, ordered him to hold. "Thine own brother thou wouldst stab in death? What manner of love is this?" questioned King Fiori.

"One speaketh so often of that which is rotten in Denmark, what say you of the rot before thee?" retorted the Prince, gesturing widely at the struggling corpse.

Risoni's body lurched again in their arms, tugging itself towards the Queen. It clamped its jaw around the arm it held, digging its teeth in. The Queen, played by one of the eldest boys in the cast, howled and cursed as the actor tried to tug away, his artificial royal bosom shaking with the effort. "Not so hard, you fool!" he hissed at the corpse as he saw blood erupt from his broken skin.

Risoni's body was now poised over the trapdoor, and the rest of the cast, upset with the actor's fumbling of the scene, simply dropped it through the hole. The fierce grip of its hand and jaw dragged Queen Bavette along with it, through the trapdoor. The unexpected headfirst dive of the Queen and the howls of painful surprise echoing beneath the stage shocked the audience with its realism.

Backstage, William howled in pain of his own. "She's not supposed to go in there! Just Risoni! He gets buried, then comes back up! What are they doing out there? We need the Queen for act two! And three!" He stomped his feet and flailed his arms for an immediate scene change.

Richard, meanwhile, had grown suspicious. Drawing a hidden dagger from under his uniform, he grabbed a stagehand and dragged him along as he sought access. "If I'm not out before the next scene ends, set fire to the theatre!" Richard hissed at the shaken stagehand.

"I don't think Mister Shak—" the frightened stagehand began.

"I don't care what he thinks, we have a bigger problem than some botched lines!" The officer dove below through another trapdoor, barely touching the ladder during the short drop. He disappeared into the dark space beneath, seeking his prey.

The next scene began quietly. The priest and the nefarious Count Gemelli were discussing the latest developments, explaining to the audience the reasons for the rise of the dead prince. They carefully recited the checklist of the ways one might ensure that the recently-deceased would not rise again, as well as delivering a tedious lecture on the nature of the bites they leave. The more astute audience members wondered why they seemed to be avoiding any mention of the departed Queen. The occasional muffled thumping and moaning noises coming from beneath the stage only added to their confusion. William was incensed by the noises and sought out someone to explain the activity. The stagehands claimed ignorance of anyone doing work below.

Richard reappeared with a streak of blood across the breast of his uniform and some sticky mess upon his fearsome dagger, but it was the angry look upon his face that scattered the cast and crew as he stalked through the backstage spaces, hunting.

"What have you been doing down there?" William demanded, furious over the awful noises he had heard.

"The Queen is dead," Richard stated flatly.

"Yes, I know, those damned fools. What were they thinking? We'll need Princess Barbina to step up for some additional lines." William snapped his fingers, then jabbed them at King Fiori, who nodded and went to find the boy wearing her dress.

"We require Prince Risoni for the next scene, did you manage to retrieve him?"

"No. But I shall. You need to stop the show. There is a . . . " Richard spoke through tightly-gritted teeth.

"Stop the show? On opening day? I think not!" William laughed, pointing to usher the next group onto stage. "You just sit back here, keep out of the way. And find Prince Risoni for me!" William scampered off to correct the order of the Calabrian soldiers, lining up for their next entrance.

"I intend to." Richard stalked off to explore another corner of the backstage maze, hopeful that the mindless corpse had not discovered an exit.

Minutes later, the officer had cornered his prey. The walking dead weren't terribly clever, but they had their moments. Having found its way out from the depths beneath the stage, the lifeless Prince Risoni was now hopelessly tangled in the costumer's line of over-sized dresses. Richard aimed his dagger, intending to stab the lengthy blade through one hazy white eye and into its brain, ending the poor actor's new existence. His thrust was interrupted by William and one of his crew swooping in and whisking the lifeless creature away. He was required on stage.

"William!" Thundered Richard, catching up and spinning the playwright around to face him. "That is a postvital, it must be ended!"

"Oh, please, you do carry on. He's just acting the part, staying in character!" William dismissed the officer with a deferential wave.

But Prince Risoni was not interested in his entrance. It had taken the opportunity to attack the stagehand escorting it. The youngest Prince's teeth ripped at the neck of the poor man, as it dragged him down to the floor. William leaped in to cover the victim's mouth, muffling the scream, lest it erupt from backstage and ruin the performance.

"Move!" Richard demanded, shoving William aside with a swift boot. "I must do this!" He stared into the stagehand's eyes, hoping he understood and would forgive him. The stagehand fought to escape, kicking and clawing at the Prince tearing at his throat. The lifeless corpse's grip was broken and the stagehand rolled away, clutching at the wound on his neck. Richard could see it was not immediately fatal, a shallower cut than he had expected.

"Don't! I'm fine!" The stagehand protested through pain-clenched teeth. On his knees, he backed away from Richard.

"You know I have to, you're going to be one of them soon. You know this is the right thing, for everyone." The officer moved closer, preparing to stab at the stagehand, to end his suffering and prevent the foulness from spreading.

Behind him, William saw his opportunity. He scooped up the momentarily sated Prince Risoni's body and aimed it towards the stage. The Prince's lifeless face appeared strangely pleased with itself, its grey tongue probed at a trickle of blood running down its jaw.

"William! No!" Richard objected, caught in a rare moment of indecision between the two that must be put down. The stagehand took the opportunity to flee. Awkwardly, he rose and staggered painfully away from Richard, seeking refuge. In the other direction, William and the Prince reached the stage, only a few beats after the corpse's cue. With a forceful shove in the back, the lifeless Prince Risoni was propelled, staggering awkwardly, onto stage. William wrung his hands nervously. Something was terribly wrong here.

Onstage, the trio of lusty harlots had been awaiting the entrance of the Prince. They were played by the same trio of boys that served as the soldiers of the Calabria family, well-practiced for their rapid costume change. The lifeless one's escape from the crypt was to be observed in the village below the Castle Puglia, thus fueling rumors to the other royals that their dead Prince still walked. And the play needed some saucy language to keep the audience interested during the second act.

"How stiffly thou movest," observed the first of the town harlots, in his best falsetto.

"Tis good, for the stiffer thou art, the greater thy use shall be," suggested the second, earning a rowdy chuckle from the crowd.

"Stiff he does move, but perchance to remain so as I should require?" agreed the third, causing the trio to laugh and point at the Prince. The dead one took no offense, but staggered forward, its arms raised in anticipation. It began to moan, its breathless voice rising as it called out, eager to feed.

The trio of harlots used wild gestures to feign offense at the smell of the walking dead.

"Thy breath stinketh of the dirt, good sir!" the first fanned her hand before her nose.

"A horse, a horse," the second harlot began, "thou stinkest as doth a horse!" The trio broke down laughing at this.

Backstage, Richard finished chasing the bitten stagehand and gave him a thorough skull-stabbing. Disposing of the body through a trapdoor, he turned again to the primary problem, the wandering Prince Risoni. Rushing towards the stage, he was stopped by the other two princes.

"You can't go out there! You'll ruin the scene!" Prince Paccheri objected, as they struggled to keep the officer from his duty.

"I must! It will kill them!"

"He's just acting, you should be proud, he's doing that walk you taught us better than anyone." Prince Filini noted with admiration.

On stage, the harlots began to taunt the poor Prince, running to and fro, their dresses lifted immodestly for better mobility.

"Staggerest thou as if from a tankard house fled!" the first one cried.

"Thy odor precedes you, and doth linger well after!" the second one offered.

"Hence, rotten thing—" The third one's line was cut off by Prince Risoni grabbing the harlot as she passed. "Hey, wait, that isn't in the—" the harlot said as the dead one struggled to bite at the tempting neck flesh. The pair stumbled, tripping and staggering backwards, locked in a struggle. The other two actors chased after, leading the entire ensemble on stage to crash out of sight and back into the wings together. Horrible screams were heard from the now-hidden party.

The audience, confused, began to grumble louder. Some howling and hissing of disapproval erupted. William struggled to keep the play moving. He shooed the next scene onto stage early, with whispered instructions to stretch their part out, as the Calabrian soldiers might not be immediately available for their entrance.

William was right about that. The three young men set to play those soldiers, and more recently the town harlots, were being efficiently dispatched by Richard. When William found him, the officer's blood-soaked uniform sleeve rose and fell again, putting to rest the last of the three new postvitals, before they could rise and kill.

"You must end this, sir!" Richard demanded as he rose to meet William with a glare. "It is over! We must clear out the theatre, save the patrons."

William, shaking with panic, lashed out at him. "No! We have to go on. Our generous benefactor, the Lord Chamberlain, the other investors, they need this to work. I need this to work, I am gambling my reputation, my fortune on this."

"You won't have enough actors to go on, they are already infecting each other!" Richard gestured at the new corpses at his feet. "Listen to the crowd!"

Indeed, the crowd was turning. The raucous noise of hissing and hooting was growing as the dwindling cast made the best of the scene. Backstage, the shadowy forms of Prince Risoni and its newly-deceased companions staggered haltingly in the shadows, eager to feed on their former colleagues.

William sagged. It was true. His mind reeled as his carefully-crafted denial collapsed on him. The terror of his first encounter, that day with the carriage, came back to him. The horrible noises they made. The sight of them tearing apart the coachman. He shivered at the memory. They were here.

Onstage, the remaining members of the royal family delayed, improvising lines as they awaited the surprise arrival of the traitorous Count Gemelli and his allies, the now-missing soldiers of Calabria. They turned as one when they caught sight of an entrance. King Fiori began to stride onto stage to demand answers from his formerly-loyal court advisor. Only a few of the audience members, seated at just the right angle, witnessed the King's just-as-sudden exit, clawing at the wood of the stage as unseen forces dragged him away by his ankles. His screams were short-lived.

The actors stood silent, waiting for direction. The audience responded, renewing their howling and shouting, many moving to depart. A few token rotten vegetables were launched towards the stage, as if testing their range before a full volley.

Richard shook the playwright by the shoulders with gore-soaked hands. "End this!"

"I have an idea," William rasped, his throat dried by fear. He gulped loudly as the sounds of violence grew around them.

A bold voice shouted over the chaos in the theatre. A resplendently gaudy royal costume strode onto stage. It was Richard, officer of the Royal Navy, dressed as the King. The new King Fiori, with loud and efficient shouting, belted out the lines that William had pressed upon him. His words were orders, jarring the other actors and silencing, for the moment, the audience.

"My family, my kingdom, it is undone!" shouted Richard. "Undone by our lack of wit. Ignorant we were of this vile scourge, this walking of the damned dead!"

Stumbling, William entered, clad in the trademark green suit of Count Gemelli. The stains of blood from the recently-slain actor hardly showed at all through the dark color. "I beseech you sire, forgive me now ere this wretched scum taketh me!"

It was a significant leap forward in the script, but the remaining cast, two Princes and the Princess, stood their ground, waiting to see what would happen next.

"Another day shall I deal with thy traitorous nature, Count. For now, we must fight to live!" The new King Fiori began to whisper quick commands at the cast. The Princes drew their stage swords. They turned as one, backs to the audience, and waited. The silence in the theatre was such that everyone could hear them. The postvitals. Former cast and stagehands, moaning and thumping about backstage. They were coming.

"This royal throne we defend to the last!" King Fiori waved his own sword, one not fashioned for the stage, but for real combat. He handed his dagger to Princess Barbina, a slender actor, who held it nervously with both hands.

A shadow broke the entrance to stage right. "But soft! What corpse through yonder window breaks?" William, as Count Gemelli, stammered.

"The first thing we do, let's kill all the postvitals!" Richard, the new King Fiori, waved his sword and attacked the shambling forms emerging from backstage. The audience shouted with enthusiasm, hoping for a blood-soaked finale to save the day. They were quieted with shock at how real the blood looked, spurting from the newly-decapitated body of the first one to emerge from backstage. Richard's sword was a blur as the crowd screamed for more of the amazing tricks of costume and makeup that made such a graphic death possible on stage.

The battle was upon them. The actors stabbed and clubbed their weapons against the lumbering wall of corpses taking the stage, while Richard's sword carved great gashes in their necks and gouged deeply into their eye sockets. As the horrible, gruesome battle played out on the stage, the audience that had remained was enthralled. Prince Paccheri was the first to fall, taken down by teeth clamped upon his jugular. Prince Filini joined him soon after, the pair set upon by the grotesque creatures. Richard moved quickly to disown the lot of them of the contents of their skulls.

William himself managed to club and push back one of his stagehand's corpses, nearly tossing himself from the stage in the effort. The corpse he clubbed spun about, halting itself as it faced the unguarded back of Princess Barbina. The actor in the dress was distracted, attempting to dislodge his dagger from the neck of a fallen corpse, and was set upon without warning.

The carnage ran its course. It came down to William and Richard, as Count Gemelli and King Fiori, backed up against the edge of the stage. The last of the postvitals moved forward. It was the former Henry Darcy. The tattered, blood-soaked remains of Prince Risoni's costume hung about him like wet feathers. The body shuffled towards the pair of survivors, slowly. Richard reached into his costume and pulled out his last surprise, a small pistol, which he moved to charge with powder and ball. The hungry moaning of the corpse grew louder, deeper, as the corpse neared, arms outstretched.

"We're supposed to die now," William admonished in a quiet whisper to his officer. "The script says everyone dies, the lesson of not heeding the rules about these creatures."

Richard paused and stared at the playwright incredulously.

"This is a tragedy, it has to end this way," William explained.

Richard nodded and smiled. "Fine. Follow my lead."

As the arms of the corpse reached for the pair, they fell down, shouting with feigned pain. The surprised corpse halted, seemingly wondering where its prey had gone. And then it noticed the audience. It moaned loudly, hungrily.

Richard lifted his body up, on one arm, as if to gasp out a final, breathless proclamation. Instead, the silence of the theatre was broken by the sudden explosion of Richard's pistol. The crowd screamed in shock and awe as the corpse's skull volcanically erupted blood and brain and bone. The wrecked body of Prince Risoni fell to the stage for the last time.

The bodies, the living, the dead, and the dead-again, lay still on the stage as the audience went mad. The screams and cheers put to shame their earlier protests.

Lying prone on the stage, the playwright and the officer spoke to each other with short shouts over the noise.

"I think I'm starting to like the theatre, William." Richard said, a gruesome smile spreading on his gore-spattered face.

"Yes. But I don't know how we're going to manage to top this one. Or even put it on again. We deviated from the script rather sharply." William sighed heavily and then laughed.

"And you seem to be short a few actors." The pair laughed uncomfortably before rising to take their bows. The audience, too stunned to wonder why the other actors remained motionless, showered them with thunderous applause.

The next day, the word was out. It was said that the play was an unconventional, uncompromising, revolutionary look at the future of theatre. The signs went up around the Globe, announcing a temporary hiatus for some necessary upgrades. This move only stoked the rumors. The next week, the advertisements went out. New actors were required for an expanded version of the hit new play. Other ads sought out new stagehands, with preference given to those with experience in animal handling. The theatre was besieged. Quietly, elsewhere in London, a new program for dealing with outbreaks was established. The disposal of postvitals went on as it had previously, but stories were told of some Royal Army squads conducting careful round-ups of the walking dead. Hushed voices explained it to be part of an experimental, more humane, less traumatic program for disposing of the problem.

The next month, the theatre reopened with a new cast and expanded costuming and makeup magic. It was said that the actors playing the postvitals in the cast were masterful in their impersonation, and the way they died on stage was simply the most realistic depiction of graphic, bloody violence the stage had ever seen.

# 18TH CENTURY

# DEATHLESS

## ED KURTZ

On the road to Nebolchi, Evgeny folded his hands in his lap and lowered his chin to his breast. The carriage bounced over the uneven road, the driver whipping the horses into a frenzy. Above Evgeny's head a cage of iron rattled so relentlessly he barely noticed the clamor anymore. His orders demanded he make the village by Saturday, and he was not one to disappoint. A beardless boyar of the Tsar's new Russia, he did only what he was told and he did it to the letter. Nebolchi would be reached in time, and if the specimen did in fact exist as the letters to Areskin attested, Evgeny would not fail in bringing the curiosity back with him to St. Petersburg.

Robert Areskin, the Tsar's surgeon-in-residence, had come into possession of the letters at the end of a chain of custody leading back to a prominent household in the German Suburbs of Moscow, where talk erupted like fire of a revenant terrifying the simple-minded farmers of the outlying *pogost* village. Accompanied by a small cadre of soldiers, Areskin arrived unannounced at the house to demand the letters be handed over forthwith, which they were without incident. In conference with the keeper of the Tsar's Rarities and Scientific Collections, Areskin formally concluded that the revenant—named only the "specimen" in writing—be assessed immediately and confiscated for the collection should it be verified. Thus was Evgeny Tretyakov elected to the task.

A bachelor with little but his loyalty to the state, Evgeny accepted his commission with zeal, if not a spot of skepticism. His narrow house in St. Petersburg tended to grow cold and lonely in the long winter months, and though he shuddered still in the frigid confines of the carriage, even the strange and timid man assigned to him was welcome company.

His companion and secretary for the journey, Yefim Azhishchenkov, scribbled ceaselessly on leaf after leaf of paper as they trundled eastward, recording his every thought and observation for their liege's eventual satisfaction. Though the notes he made would no doubt prove useful to posterity, particularly once Yefim had the opportunity to witness the specimen at Nebolchi, Evgeny could not help but find the fellow a poor secretary at best for recording his own notions rather than those of his immediate superior. Evgeny too had observations, although these largely concerned how futile he expected the quest would turn out to be. Revenant, indeed.

Yefim was a small man with tiny black eyes who legally retained his beard, as the tax medallion he wore around his neck testified. If Peter could not force every man in Russia to modernize and Westernize, he would at least bolster the state coffers with the stubborn's own coin. The diminutive secretary did not often speak, though now he raised his head, stroked his wiry black beard, and made the sign of the cross—three fingers, right to left.

"Do you know of Koschei the Deathless?" he asked, his voice thin and docile.

"I knew a Koschei once," answered Evgeny. "Koschei Dobrynin. He was Streltsy, participated in the revolt against the Tsar." He chuckled and shook his head. "By fire and knout I assure you he is quite dead."

"Not this Koschei," said Yefim. "He could not die. He hides his soul—sometimes in an animal, or an egg—so that he cannot be killed. It is an old story."

"I do not know it," groused Evgeny, "but it seems unwise to tell tales of men who by chicanery do not die. Only through our Lord Jesus are we truly deathless."

"Always he tricks young men into fighting him," the secretary continued, unabated. "He steals their wives and daughters, and they come with swords and knives, but always Koschei kills them."

Evgeny snorted. "Peasant nonsense."

"Only a story."

"Skirting quite close to blasphemy, Yefim. Careful, there."

The secretary bowed his head, dropped his eyes to the papers on his lap.

"That does not sound much like our Rostislav, anyway," Evgeny continued, tapping a finger on the sheaf of letters on the seat beside him.

"I have not read them," said Yefim with evident disappointment.

"State secrets."

The secretary fell silent thereafter, and before long resumed scratching out his thoughts on a fresh page. Evgeny Tretyakov touched his bald pate and glanced out at the passing farmland, lying largely fallow for the winter. In the middle distance he espied a young man and woman traipsing nude across a thin layer of snow, white steam billowing off their pale bodies, from the bathhouse they undoubtedly just exited. Country people, he mused, were decidedly different. Whatever Peter did in the cities, in St. Petersburg and Moscow, to transform Muscovy into something like the maritime nations the Tsar so loved and envied, the folk of the land never changed.

Neither, Evgeny considered, did their superstitious beliefs. The Orthodox Church and its Patriarch could exercise all the power given to them by God Almighty in the urban centers, but out here in the nation's hinterlands things were categorically different. Out here people still believed in spirits and witches, Baba Yaga in her cabin on chicken feet and the dead come back to life. No one in St. Petersburg expected Evgeny to come back with anything apart from a shaking head and bitter laugh, a wasted journey behind him. Yet every possibility had to be investigated. The insatiable curiosity of Muscovy's Tsar demanded it.

Whilst Yefim filled his pages, Evgeny took up the letters bound in leather from the seat beside him and untied the string that held them. Only four in total, the letters grew more urgent in chronology, begging somebody to come to Nebolchi, to bring a Father, to rid the village of the devil among them. They were not all written by the same hand. The first and third were signed by the *pogost* priest, darkly hinting at Peter's Western inclinations and the evil with which they were plaguing Russia. The second was written by a village administrator who feared for the safety and souls of his family. The fourth and last letter came into Moscow's German Suburb from the hand of a visiting scholar who claimed to be inscribing the very words of the revenant's own mother. Certain that God had forgotten or forsaken her, she demanded someone in Moscow alert Patriarch Feofan of her distress lest the devil's influence in Nebolchi spread to the whole of the empire.

"Rubbish," hissed Evgeny, his mind flashing back to Koschei and his eyes rolling over the shaky, uncertain handwriting.

"We shall find out soon enough," answered Yefim without looking up from his work. He had managed to get ink in his beard and his dark eyes squinted in the failing light.

"Yes," Evgeny agreed. "I suppose we shall."

Like everything built by human hands in the country, the house to which they traveled was constructed entirely of wood and clay, a simple single-story box with a stone chimney belching gray smoke at the back. Thin, piebald goats shivered in the dancing light of the carriage lanterns, hedged in a crude pen on the east side of the house, and to the west were a trio of hastily built wooden crosses jutting from the frozen earth. The carriage slowed to a halt and Evgeny reached across to touch his sleeping secretary's knee.

"We have arrived."

"It must be the middle of the night," complained Yefim, pulling his coat tightly over his chest. His words were expelled in a white fume.

"Indeed it is. Come."

Clutching one another against the cold, the two men climbed out of the carriage and stood in the shadows, facing the house. Evgeny shot a glance at the driver, who sucked at a long-stemmed pipe and nodded as one fighting off exhaustion.

"Should we have found an inn?" Yefim wondered aloud.

"I very much doubt there is one. No matter—these people called for us. We came."

With that Evgeny advanced to the door, leaving his secretary by the carriage door, and rapped three times in rapid succession upon the hard, weathered wood. A soft murmur arose from within the house, and a moment later a faint glow illumined the cracks around the door.

Evgeny opened his mouth to speak, but found that he had forgotten the name of the family who dwelt there. Instead, he knocked once more and called out, "We have come from St. Petersburg pursuant to your request."

For several long minutes there came no reply and the light emanating through the cracks did not waver. Evgeny shivered, hugged himself, and grunted.

"It is really quite cold out here and I suspect you have a fire indoors," he bellowed impatiently. "I shouldn't like to think you would keep the Tsar's own men freezing out here in the dark."

"You are from the Tsar?" came a timid voice.

"We are the Tsar's men," Evgeny answered honestly and evasively. Peter would know nothing of this expedition if it was not successful. The Emperor and Autocrat of All the Russias would only become aware if the specimen was true and returned to Peter's Kunstkamera in St. Petersburg to be studied, catalogued, and kept.

"You come for Rostislav?" squeaked the tremulous voice.

"Yes. Now for God's sakes let us inside. It's damnably cold out here."

The woman fell silent and the door did not open. Evgeny sighed heavily and pulled the string to release the door from its latch. It swung in, revealing a dark, musty room with a small fire flickering in the stone hearth. A shirtless man with a thick tangle of white hair stoked the embers while the woman—small and fat, her red face framed by a heavy woolen shawl wrapped around her hair—stood before Evgeny and glowered.

"Take him," she grunted. "Take Rostislav, but take him now. Tonight."

"I shall have to see him first, *sudárynya*. See him and examine him."

"Shut the fucking door," barked the man at the hearth. He did not turn around, but continued poking at the fire as he swore at their visitor.

Evgeny grimaced but did as he was told. He pushed the door closed and reaffixed the string. The woman crossed her arms over her full bosom and worked her jaw, her small eyes fixed on the man from the Tsar.

"It is true, you know," she said. "Everything you have heard. It is all true."

"That is what I am here to determine."

"And when you see? That our Rostislav is . . . what he is?"

"In that case he shall be taken back with us, for study in the Tsar's Kunstkamera."

"I do not like anything about this," the woman groused. "But if you are to see him before you make up your mind, you had better come along."

"Go see him," bellowed the man at the hearth. "Go see that damned devil."

The woman curled her upper lip and for a moment Evgeny thought her eyes were sparkling with tears. Instead, she squinted in the darkness and waddled toward the shadows painting the far corner of the cabin. There she fumbled for a moment in the darkness before a candle flared to life, revealing a second door at the backside of the room. She heaved a sigh and shook her head, and then proceeded through the door.

A foul stench rushed into Evgeny's nostrils like an evil wind the moment he stepped into the other room. It was like nothing he had ever smelled before: nauseatingly sweet like rotten fruit with a thick, musky undertone. The odor was immediately accompanied with a low, raspy moan. He went stock still and narrowed his eyes in the dull glow of the candle light.

"Quiet now, my son," the woman whispered. "Quiet."

Rostislav responded with a wet puling sound. Evgeny grasped the door jamb and waited for his eyes to grow accustomed to the lower light. As the room came into better focus, he realized that the floor was littered with feathers, fur, and small bones. The tableau looked to him as though a wolf had gotten into a menagerie. He swallowed and dragged a stinking breath in through his mouth.

The woman knelt down beside a prostrate form on the floor, bringing the candle down low. The form belonged to a man dressed in tattered brown rags, his feet bare. His wrists and ankles were bound tightly together with leather straps, his neck secured likewise and affixed by a large iron nail to the wall. Evgeny looked from the man's startling state of confinement to his slack, pale face and gasped. Rostislav's skin was gray and weathered beyond his possible years; his mouth hung open and mewled pathetically. He had few teeth and his eyes were wide and haunted. Only a few sprouts of thin, white hair sprang from his spotted scalp. He juddered like a drunk in need of vodka. Evgeny thought him the saddest human being he had ever seen.

The woman gently touched the top of her son's head and cooed into his ear.

Evgeny said, "This, then, is Rostislav?"

"Yes," she said sadly. "This is my son."

"Why is he imprisoned in this way?"

"Did you read my letter? The man said he wrote everything I told to him."

"I want to hear it from you, madam."

Her face tightened and her mouth drew into a small frown.

"My Rostislav is not himself anymore. He does not know what he does, but he . . . hurts things."

Taking another step into the room, Evgeny laced his fingers over his belly and said, "Tell me."

"He died," she said.

"He does not look much dead to me."

"He did then. After. We found him in the wood, cold as the ground and white as smoke. There was no mark on him. We brought him home, my husband and me, and the father came to pray with us before we buried him. It is hard work to dig a grave in the winter, so we were waiting for men from the village."

"So you were mistaken," Evgeny said. "About the boy's death, I mean."

"Oh, no. It was no mistake. Rostislav was dead. The father made sure of it—no blood moved in him."

The son jerked his head to the side and grunted angrily. His mother's eyes softened as she glanced at him.

"Still his blood does not move. He is not alive, sir, but he is not dead either."

"A revenant."

"If that is what you call it. He was laid out in the front room, and we slept close by. It was me who awoke to see him. He was standing up, a shadow in the dying embers of the fire. I spoke his name and he groaned, as he does now. Rostislav does not make words anymore. He is not himself."

"What happened next?"

"When I said his name, my husband awoke. He thought our son to be an intruder, so he leapt from the floor and attacked him. Rostislav went mad, shrieking and shaking all over. There was a terrible fight, and in the end my poor husband lost two fingers."

"I noticed that," said Evgeny. "How did that happen, exactly?"

"Why, my son bit them off," she said as though it was evident.

"He *bit* them off?"

The woman nodded once. "And swallowed them."

"God in heaven."

"Always he is hungry now. He screams terribly when there is no meat for him to eat. Sir, he did not know what he had done. Now I give him chickens, rabbits. The poor boy, he will not eat if the meat is cooked. That upsets him the most."

"He eats them raw?"

She snorted.

"He eats them *alive*."

Evgeny stepped back again, crossed himself. The woman hefted herself back to her feet and smoothed out her plain, worn skirts. In the front room, voices arose. Evgeny leaned through the door to find Yefim with his palms turned out to Rostislav's father, shaking his head and pleading for the man to be calm.

"Take him, damn you!" the man barked at the secretary. "Take him away. We cannot kill what is already dead or I'd have done it by now. So take him from us and be gone from here."

A choking sob emanated from the back room. It was followed shortly thereafter by a deep, savage growl. Yefim turned his gaze from the man to Evgeny, his eyebrows raised and hands tugging at his beard.

"Did you see it?"

"I saw it," Evgeny replied.

"What shall we do?"

Evgeny looked to the man's right hand, curled into a gnarled fist bereft of its pinky and ring fingers. All that remained of the missing digits was a crusty mass of scabs. The man opened his fist and allowed Evgeny to see his ruined hand more clearly. A fire burned in the wounded man's eyes.

"Bring down the cage from the carriage, Yefim," Evgeny said. "Have the driver assist you. We are taking Rostislav to St. Petersburg after all."

On the bank of Fontanka River, where it flowed into the colossal Neva, there stood a surprisingly modest palace of just two stories and fourteen rooms. Surrounded by a sumptuous garden, the palace's façade was yellow and featured reliefs of subjects mythological in origin between the first and second story windows. A harbor of no great size was built up to the front entrance, permitting the palace's owner to sail directly to the door, and the encompassing gardens were filled with flora from all over Europe, a tranquil grotto, and several spouting fountains. The Dutch-style structure, with its enormous windows and high roof, was the Summer Palace of Tsar Peter, who was nowhere to be found among its oaken panels and tapestries and ornate stoves. For it was winter still, and the only men to wander the palace's hallways and rooms were those appointed by Areskin to inventory the Tsar's collection of artifacts on the second floor. And among these men were Evgeny Tretyakov and Yefim Azhishchenkov, the latter poking at coals in the painted stove whilst the former pled the case for Rostislav's addition to the kunstkamera.

"I think perhaps you misapprehend the meaning of the term," Areskin trilled in English, causing Evgeny to bring Yefim into the argument to translate. "A freak is by definition a human being born significantly different from the normal, functioning person. A dwarf, for example—"

The Scotsman gestured with his silver-handled cane toward the small form of a taxidermied man, no taller than three feet, supported by an iron rod at the back. The stuffed corpse wore the costume of a clown; its glass eyes shone blue and stared permanently across the cluttered room.

"Or this one," Areskin continued, clopping his elaborately buckled shoes over to a row of large jars filled to the brim with yellow fluid. Crammed into one of them was a human fetus with two distinct heads. "Two heads, Tretyakov. The very essence of freakdom."

Yefim chattered quietly in Russian, conveying the Surgeon-in-Residence's musical yet incomprehensible words, as Evgeny's face reddened and his Adam's apple bobbed up and down. The Scotsman was impossible; a tremendous curiosity lay within reach, ready to be met with the Tsar's wonder and approval, yet all Areskin wanted were bones and trinkets and toys.

"This fellow Rostislav, on the other hand . . . " Areskin screwed his mouth up to one side and took a deep breath, permitting a moment of silence so that the incessant moaning from the adjoining room could be clearly heard. " . . . while obviously a madman, is by no means a freak nor is he suited to this collection. That man belongs in an asylum. Or perhaps the gibbet, seeing how he gravely assaulted his own father, as you say.

"Our directive according to the code of law is to deliver unto this assemblage freaks or other curiosities found, Mr. Tretyakov. I hardly think any one of us finds a garden variety lunatic all that curious, do you?"

"That madman," Evgeny said through clenched teeth, "is dead."

"So you have claimed," Areskin scoffed. "A revenant, was it not? I suppose one of your *upir* is what you take this poor soul to be?"

"No, not precisely, but a dead man who walks. He is cold to the touch, he does not breathe regularly. His blood does not move. See for yourself, Doctor Areskin, and you will know that Rostislav is no poor soul or any other type of being with a soul. I know not how he walks, why he cries out like one in pain. I know not the source of his rage, nor why he attacks when he does. But I do know that there is nothing human in that boy, and that he ingested his father's digits, and that is most assuredly quite curious, indeed."

"Rostislav the Deathless," Yefim muttered.

Areskin planted a hand on the hip of his waistcoat, his laced sleeves flouncing as he exhaled with force.

"Firstly, this is utter nonsense. A living dead man—really, Tretyakov. Secondly, and I dare say more importantly, when the Tsar and his family return here in the summer, do you honestly expect them to live with that devilish moaning night and day? One can hear it throughout the whole of the house, and likely out in the gardens."

"But Doctor, it was you who sent us to investigate . . . "

"And investigate you did, Mr. Tretyakov. All such claims must be examined should the resources to do so be available."

"You also instructed me to bring the specimen back to St. Petersburg should I deem the claim true."

"Here you demonstrate your severe lack in judgment, sir. The claim is clearly not true—I cannot say what I might have expected, a dancing skeleton perhaps, but all you have done is bring a raving imbecile into the home of the Emperor himself. A dangerous one as well, from the looks of it. Very poor judgment indeed."

The Scot shook his head, nearly dislodging the brown wig from its placement upon his pate, and skulked off to the windows where a pair of bright-faced young men chattered over a wooden crate packed with small skulls. Areskin pointed at one with the end of his cane and knelt down to examine it. He had clearly closed the book on the issue of Rostislav.

Yefim grabbed his beard and shot a glance to the adjacent room, whence the sorrowful mewling continued unabated.

"What shall we do with him, then?" the secretary asked.

"It will be the knout for me if he stays here another minute," Evgeny groused.

"These foreigners," Yefim said, pulling his thick eyebrows into a tight knit. "Ordering us all about. That would never happen when Feodor was tsar . . . "

Evgeny slapped his secretary hard across the face with an open hand, stunning him into silence.

"You ought to be more cautious in your choice of words about our government," Evgeny said evenly. Yefim's eyes welled up, but he nodded and looked away. "Go retrieve those boys that brought him up so we can take him back down."

"And then where?"

*Where?*

Evgeny squashed his brow into a tight knit and considered his duty. Someday, he reckoned, His Majesty might hear word of the spectacular discovery Robert Areskin had turned away from inclusion in the kunstkamera. And against that day, Evgeny found it wise that Rostislav be cared for. His lot, after all, was service to the throne, not to a foreigner who could not even converse in Russian.

"I do not know, Yefim. To my own house, I suppose, until I determine his fate. And I suspect he will be wanting something to eat, don't you?"

Yefim's mouth stretched down into a grimace as he turned to the stairs to fetch the boys.

Evgeny Tretyakov's house was considerably less regal than the Tsar's modest summer palace: wooden with no reliefs, two stories but only five rooms. He employed no servants and he had no wife to clean or cook for him. The holes in his only frock coat were patched by himself; he was his own haberdasher and cobbler. And by the time Yefim's boys left at the purple approach of dusk, there was nobody remaining to look after Rostislav but Evgeny.

He lighted every lamp and candle in the main room as well as a pipe, a western vice only recently permitted by law, and pondered what to do about the moaning corpse upstairs.

He had spoken to the Tsar's Surgeon-in-Residence about Rostislav's soullessness, but he considered now that he was in no position to judge whether or not the boy remained in possession of his soul. When a person died, Evgeny knew, his soul was transported back to God, to the Kingdom of Heaven, but what became of a young man who subsequently returned to life? His thoughts turned naturally to Lazarus, whereupon he sprang up to seize the Bible from the mantle, but the Word had nothing to say on the subject. Perhaps, he thought, the Lord restored the soul of Lazarus alongside his life. The notion seemed theologically sound, yet far less so in the case of the caged boy from Nebolchi.

Rostislav was no Lazarus, and whatever power had restored life to his bones seemed to Evgeny less than the Most Holy. Whether or not dangerously so he had yet to determine.

Returning the Bible to the mantle, he let the fire warm his stocking feet for a moment before the muffled moans exploded into desperate howling. Evgeny jumped, then cursed, and bolted for the stairs with a candle in hand. He stumbled on the landing, composed himself. Drew a deep, cold breath into his lungs. With a tremulous hand he pushed open the second door in the narrow hallway and held the candle up to cast its weak, guttering light on the iron cell in the center of the room.

Rostislav remained fettered, the cage locked. In the candlelight his gray, drawn face looked more ghoulish than ever—the small flame flickered and caused shadows to dance over the contours of his jutting cheekbones. The movement was like squirming maggots. Evgeny sneered.

The revenant bellowed. His shriveled lips receded from large, rotting teeth between which a pale tongue writhed. The jaw opened impossibly wide, as though Rostislav hoped it would make his howls louder. His yellow eyes shimmered mournfully beneath a trembling brow. He gripped the bars of the cage with pale, leathery hands that were bound at the wrists and screamed. And screamed. And screamed.

"Enough, Rostislav!" Evgeny roared. "Enough."

Though his maw remained open, Rostislav's screams died down to a pitiful squawk before he fell silent. His fingers loosened around the bars, and Evgeny saw how only a few of them had any vestiges of the nails left on them. Rostislav crooked his head to the side and moaned softly, his foggy eyes trained on Evgeny.

"You unfortunate wretch," said Evgeny, pursing his lips and meeting Rostislav's gaze. "What on earth could have done this to you?"

By way of response, the wretch poked a gnarled forefinger into his mouth, groaned pitifully, and bit down with all the force he could muster. His eyes bulged as the digit snapped free of the hand, and with a tightly knotted brow Rostislav swallowed his own finger.

"Christ have mercy," Evgeny cried, covering his own mouth with his hand and taking a few steps back, away from the cage. "Lord Jesus Christ, why have you forsaken this boy?"

The revenant boy heaved and shook, but he did not cry. Evgeny decided the boy could not cry, even if he wanted to. So in his stead, Evgeny shed tears for the both of them. And when he was nearly done, wiping his nose on the sleeve of his blouse, he whispered, "Do not do that again, you poor man. I shall bring you what you require."

The man on the ground rose up enough to take the small copper bowl handed down to him by the Orthodox priest. He accepted the gift with both hands, smiled a largely toothless smile, and brought the bowl up to his soot-black nose to sniff at its contents. From the safe embrace of the shadows catty-corner to the church, Evgeny observed as the man's grin then faded away.

"Cool water and chicken fat, is it?" growled the man.

The priest, his alabaster face masked almost entirely by a thick nest of dark hair, straightened up and nodded.

"I can offer but little, my friend. But please accept this small bounty and consider the gifts of Christ."

"Such gifts," spoke the man, leaning back now against the wooden outer wall of the meager church. "Such miracles."

The priest smiled and his cheeks reddened in the moments before the man hurled the bowl at the father's head, nicking him by the edge against the forehead and digging out a broad wound that spilled a curtain of blood over the holy man's left eye.

"Tell your Christ to fuck off, charlatan!" barked the wretch. "I do not want his shit poor gifts."

The back of Evgeny's neck burned at the outrage. Scampering off, the priest held both hands to the seeping gash and muttered curses through his beard as he vanished into the church. The man on the ground chortled and kicked at the air, his mirth tainted by rage.

"Chicken water!" he bellowed at the night. Men and some few women detoured in wide arcs to avoid his immediate sphere of hate and madness. "Christ piss!"

There were, Evgeny knew, a multitude of such wasted souls staggering the streets and alleys of Muscovy's cities, in St. Petersburg and Moscow. Madmen and women, the sick and the forgotten. Worse still for them if they were foreigners or Jews, but this man appeared to be neither. Merely an angry rascal, too hateful to take an offer of sustenance from a man of God on high. Filthy and unkempt, the man nonetheless looked well enough to work, to push a plough or carry a musket. It was the wretch at home who could not care for himself, whose infirmity relegated him to another's charge. This man, conversely, cried foul at the loving assistance of Christ's own proxy. A wastrel. Unrepentant.

Ideal.

Upon approaching the man, Evgeny extended his palms in a gesture of peace. The man brought his shaggy black eyebrows into a squashed point and growled. To Evgeny he very nearly sounded like a revenant himself.

"Rather than chicken water, how might you like roasted chicken?" he asked the wretch. "And vodka? It is a good stock, believe me."

"Why should I believe anyone?"

"What have you got to lose?"

"And why should a man like you wish to feed one like me?"

"Compassion, my brother. I have more than I need and you have nothing."

"Then share it with that fucking priest and bugger him after," barked the man. "I will not be indebted to you."

"I am truly sorry to hear that," said Evgeny with sorrow in his voice. "Should you see me again, my offer remains. Be well, friend."

Turning on his heel, Evgeny commenced a fast walk back from whence he came, toward his home in the southern quarter. He was in no way startled by the quick steps that sounded behind him, slapping at the paving stones in his wake.

"You," huffed the man. "You—wait."

Evgeny halted, turned about, and lifted his mouth in the smallest smile.

"My brother," he said softly, and he embraced the man, who did not resist.

The chicken was tender and moist, almost perfectly browned on the skin. Evgeny himself was no cook—he had plied the man with cups of vodka before stepping out again to procure the bird from the woman at a nearby hostelry. The man, who said his name was Lev, devoured the lion's share of the chicken, leaving little for his host, and took to cracking the bones open in order to suck at the marrow. His only conversation outside of pleasurable grunts were compliments about the repast.

"Good, good."

Evgeny filled his cup again. Lev poured it down as though it was water.

"This life," said Evgeny at great length, "cannot be an easy way."

"It is not, brother," said Lev, adopting the term of endearment now that he was drunk.

"Tell me, have you prayed for better?"

"I never pray. No use in it, friend. Once I did, but things only got worse. Now I ignore God and God ignores me. We have an understanding."

"I see."

*For Thou art not a God that hath pleasure in wickedness; neither shall evil dwell with Thee.* The Psalmist's words played through Evgeny's head like music. *Neither shall evil dwell with thee.*

*And a man who ignores God . . .*

The carcass was picked clean and the vodka running low when Evgeny poured the last of it between their two cups. The men touched cups and swallowed their liquor, and as Lev wiped his lips dry, his host leaned back on his chair.

"I should like you to meet someone," he said. "A man. Someone I believe will make an extraordinary difference with regard to your circumstances."

"My circumstances will not change, brother. Some are princes, and some are like me. The street needs men to keep it warm, I reckon."

"Must you be that man, Lev?"

"I don't know. I think so. I think I must."

"Will you at least see this man? Hear what he has to say? Perhaps you will find he offers to you something you have not considered. A way out, I mean."

Lev laughed bitterly and ran his tongue along the inside of his cup.

"The only way out for me, friend," he said, "is death."

"Perhaps."

"I know it. Now, I know it."

"And until then?"

"I suffer."

"Then if you must suffer, it could not possibly harm you to meet him. Just for a few minutes. See what he has to give you, and if you find you do not want it, you can return to your place on the street."

Lev narrowed his eyes to slits and regarded Evgeny for a moment. He then raised his cup and said, "Have you more?"

Evgeny grinned and rose from the table.

"I have. Just a moment."

He stepped into the pantry and returned with a fresh flagon, from which he filled his guest's cup to the brim yet again. Lev drank deeply of the vodka, swallowing it all in two gulps, and gasped with satisfaction.

"All right," he rasped. "I will meet your man."

Evgeny withdrew an iron key from the pocket of his waistcoat as he opened the door. He then bent at the waist to retrieve the lamp from the hallway floor.

"The matches are in the room, I'm afraid."

"What's the key for?"

"What this man has to offer is safely secured. I shouldn't want to give it to just anyone."

"No," agreed Lev. "I'd think you wouldn't."

In a moment, there was the scratch of metal on metal, and then the squeal of moving hinges. Lev shifted his stance. A match struck, close to his face, filling his nostrils with the odor of sulfur. The lamp in Evgeny's hand came alight, and the light cast a dull saffron glow across the small, musty room. As the sulfur smell dissipated, another, ranker one took its place in Lev's nose. He frowned, covered his face with his hand. And before he could inquire into the source of the fetid stench his eyes fell upon the open cage on the floor.

All that he managed to say was, "What's—?"

Then Rostislav was upon him, and Lev's words were transformed into shrieks.

The revenant sprang from the cell the moment the door swung open; soundlessly, his feet padded over the floorboards, past Evgeny at whom he softly grunted. He eschewed the light—it hurt his eyes—preferring instead to crouch in the shadows. It was from the shadows he noticed the newcomer, the dirty stranger, at whom Evgeny made a gesture of . . . offering?

A nod. Evgeny stepped back two paces, three. The shadows crept back over the stranger as the lamp retreated from him.

"What's—?"

The revenant lunged. One hand tightened around the man's throat, the other tore at the filthy rags wrapped around his neck and shoulders. Teeth gnashed. The man struggled. The revenant was stronger. Flesh came apart like well-done meat. Blood pulsed in spurts that filled the revenant's mouth, warmed his throat. The shrieks did not last long.

And Evgeny muttered from the doorway, "Good, son. Good, good."

Having twice walked the circumference of the royal gardens, Evgeny and Yefim made their way to the riverbank and followed the water beside what few small frigates sailed past.

"A prison would be best for the boy," the secretary opined, one hand behind his back and the other worrying his beard. "If indeed he has killed a man, you are obliged to report the murder."

"I feel equally obliged to care for Rostislav's needs," said Evgeny. "It was I who brought him here, after all. I who separated him from his family and whatever care and limited structure they offered him."

"He is not natural. You know he isn't."

Evgeny nodded gravely. "He smells awful now. I suspect he is . . . rotting."

"Leprosy?"

"Something else," Evgeny said.

Yefim stopped walking. "Something worse?"

"Something happened to that boy in the wood where he was found in this condition. His mother did not appear to know what it was, and I believe her. But something happened, which by God's gracious gifts should have ended his suffering."

"Perhaps it not a gift from God that causes him to persist so."

"I am no priest nor am I theologian. Talk of devilry is not first among my priorities at this point, Yefim, but . . . "

"But Rostislav is no mere madman, is he?"

"Our Rostislav is a walking corpse. I am certain of this, though I know not how it is possible."

"Must you know? Are all of the world's worst secrets ours to discover?"

"If I mean to help the boy, then yes."

"I say you chain him with stones and throw him in the Fontanka."

"Should I become a murd—?" Evgeny swallowed the word, remembering Lev.

"Can you murder what is already dead?"

Evgeny shook his head and squeezed his eyes shut. The wretch he had fed to Rostislav deserved what befell him—of this Evgeny was absolutely certain—yet still, Evgeny could hardly go on luring sinners and blasphemers into the revenant's hungry grasp. People would take notice. Authorities. Worse, he fretted over what effect such a pattern might have on his own everlasting soul.

Or upon Rostislav's, if indeed he had one.

*Hidden someplace, in an animal, or an egg.*

"Dear God, what a quandary."

The men walked some more in silence until they reached a bend in the river, whereupon Yefim gently guided his superior back round to return to the gardens. At some length, the secretary asked, "Do you suppose he still has a soul?"

Evgeny froze stiff and bore a wide-eyed gaze at the still waters. In lieu of answering him, he swallowed noisily and whispered, "I must go back to Nebolchi."

"And there?"

"Pray I learn what to do, Yefim."

Rather than the ramshackle house to which he first was driven, Evgeny instructed the carriage driver to find the *pogost*'s church. Daylight remained on the horizon when the modest church came into view, and the wheels had barely time to stop revolving before Evgeny hopped to the ground and hurried to the doors, leaving Yefim in the carriage—beneath Rostislav. As one of the doors opened into the dark church, a haggard priest with a patchy gray beard stepped out into the snow and held up a crumpled letter—Evgeny's, which had preceded him from St. Petersburg.

"Tretyakov," grumbled the priest.

"The wood, father—will you take me there?"

The priest drew a deep breath into his chest and moved his cloudy gray eyes up to the carriage, to the iron cage secured to its top. Thick carpets covered the cell almost completely, but there remained a sliver through which empty, yellow eyes stared back at the priest.

"You will not save him," the priest growled. "Already he is in Satan's grasp."

At the name of the adversary, he made the sign of the cross and gritted his teeth. White steam trailed out his mouth as he whispered a short prayer.

"Cannot every man be saved?"

"Every man, yes. But that—" He gestured with evident repulsion at Rostislav. "—is no man."

"He was. Once."

"And the Devil was once an angel, Tretyakov. There are crimes against God Almighty that cannot be undone. Come—I will take you."

The priest stuffed the letter into his cloak and set off on foot, ignoring the carriage and waiting for no one. Affronted, Evgeny hurried after him and seized the priest by the elbow.

"Where are you going?"

"To show you what you want to see, naturally. Those damned woods."

Evgeny scrambled to get Rostislav down from his cell in time to catch up with their guide. The boy moaned and squirmed every inch of the way, but Evgeny succeeded in goading him to the ground beside him. A leather collar was secured around the revenant's neck, attached to a long strap. Evgeny grasped the strap tight and fell into a trot, chasing after the priest. Yefim loped a safe distance behind, his leery eyes fixed on the revenant.

"Father," Evgeny cried. "Wait."

The old priest dismissed him with a wave of his hand and trudged on. Before long, they neared a dense copse to which the priest raced. By the time Evgeny and Rostislav reached the edge of the trees, the priest was standing stoically with a grim look for his charges.

"I do not see why you must bring that *dydko* along," he groused.

"Do you know where he was found or do you not?"

"I know."

"Take us, priest."

"As you wish, *boyar*."

The father ducked under a tangle of branches and slipped into the shade of the boughs. In a second, he was gone. Evgeny followed, scratching his face on the rough branches, dragging Rostislav behind. When he emerged on the other side, he found himself in a cramped clearing and espied the priest vanishing again into the trees. Evgeny heaved a sigh and glanced back at his ward. The boy's left cheek was shredded by the branches, the gray skin sloughing off like wax. There was no blood. Rostislav did not appear to notice.

Evgeny tugged the strap and rushed after the priest.

Two dozen men in fur hats and kaftans embellished with regimental colors awaited them in the next clearing. A quarter of them were armed with pikes only; another quarter gripped sharp-edged bardiches in their pink, frozen hands. The remaining half held matchlock muskets at the ready. The regiment appeared to Evgeny prepared for war.

The priest stood a few yards from the tree line, stock still and glaring angrily at the soldiers. Among the armed men, one stepped forward, his face grim and hands unoccupied by any weapon.

"Leave this place, father," the officer barked. "Evil lives here."

"What good is a priest, if not against evil?"

"Hunters die here," replied the officer. "But they do not remain dead. But you know this, do you not?"

"I know this," agreed the priest.

"Then you believe your prayers will cleanse this place?"

Before the father could answer, one of the regiment cried out, "Look! A *dydko*!"

A great commotion broke out among the soldiers as they clattered their arms and moved awkwardly, noisily forward, toward Evgeny and Yefim and their rotting charge. The secretary yelped and moved behind a scrawny tree. Evgeny felt his skin prickle as he widened his eyes and shook his head.

"I am here in service to the Tsar," he bellowed, his voice tremulous.

"Is that then the Tsar's devil?" shouted back a sneering soldier. "What proof have you?"

"What is your purpose here?" Evgeny challenged the regiment, ignoring the soldier's inquiry. "Who is in command? What do you intend to do?"

"They've come to see for themselves," Yefim muttered from the relative safety of his hiding place. "To see the evil this place brings."

Evgeny scowled at his secretary before the clatter of rifles returned his attention to the regiment.

"No, please. No—I've come here to save this boy."

The priest twisted at the waist to shoot a blistering glare at him.

"Be silent," he hissed.

"Can the damned be saved?" asked the officer in charge.

Rostislav growled low in his throat and bent at the knees. Evgeny grimaced, reached out to calm the boy, but the boy's face twisted into a snarling rage and he snapped his teeth at Evgeny, who jerked back in shock.

Yefim whined and dropped into a crouch. The priest snorted in contempt.

Then: a musket bucked with smoke and thunder, startling Evgeny who fell into a squat as Rostislav's head was halved by the soldier's iron ball. Crown, brow and right eye were gone in an instant, leaving only the revenant's gaping jaw, one rolling yellow eye, and a split nose gushing black ooze that once was the boy's blood.

Evgeny bellowed with sorrow and rage as Rostislav slumped, his ruined head spilling brains blackened with decay. The officer screamed incomprehensibly, upbraiding the young kaftaned soldier for his pique. And the priest merely walked calmly back to the thick foliage, chuckling bitterly as he murmured an angry prayer to his God.

"You fool," Evgeny sobbed at the soldier as he knelt to drape his frock coat over what remained of Rostislav. Even the young soldier himself appeared startled by the smoking musket in his red, cold-raw hands. "You damned fool."

As though by way of reply, the wood came alive with a chorus of mournful moans. Evgeny cracked open his swollen, wet eyes to barely make out the silhouetted shapes emerging on all sides from the trees. More shots cracked out and a tightly formed group of six men with pikes and axes separated from the regiment with blades out.

Some terrified solider cried, "What is this place?"

At this, Yefim Azhishchenkov crossed himself and erupted into peals of raspy laughter until a musket ball found his heart and dropped him into the cold, wet snow.

In the frozen midday air, Evgeny crawled on hands and knees through the slush toward a felled tree blanketed in lichen and snow. On the other side of the rotting wood, a group of four or five figures milled about, sated from their feast. There, the snow was stained black and red by the steaming lumps of flesh and entrails that remained of the regiment, of those who had not made it out of the wood. Upon heaving his cold form up on the downed trunk, Evgeny's bleary eyes espied three more among the gathering dead, their gray faces buried in the torsos and thighs of the Tsar's soldiers who had not survived the brief, one-sided battle.

His mind strained at the impossible task of interpreting what he barely saw. Dead men and women, their skin tight and colorless and flecked with gore, feeding on the hot corpses of a half dozen slain men barely out of boyhood—luckless Yefim among them. His tongue pulsed inside his cold mouth. Focus dissipated like steam.

*What is this place?*

He crept away in the direction from which he had come, more trouble than he was worth to the slavering things whose pantry was well enough stocked for the time being. Heads rose from the outraged corpses of the soldiery, jaws dripping with gore, but the dead were slowed by their satisfaction, their wicked repast. One by one, they all returned to the work at hand.

Along the path back to the *pogost*, Evgeny found what was left of the priest. He lay in a tangle of icy brambles, his face chewed away to the bone. A lunatic grin spread across the bloody skull, and a rush of blood to his head forced Evgeny to fold over, whereupon he vomited into the nettles. Behind him, in the clearing, the moans resumed. A cluster of wet, black magpies took flight from the treetops. They too fled the forest of the damned.

When he staggered out of the wood, Evgeny caught sight of the carriage in the middle distance, still before the humble church. The nags blew white steam from their nostrils that matched the woodsmoke rising from a dozen tumbledown houses spotting the hills. Curling his hands into fists at his sides, he fell into an obdurate march for the carriage, his sights set hard on St. Petersburg. The driver would complain, but Evgeny would refuse to wait another minute. Time was short.

Areskin had to see.

"Freaks or other curiosities found," he growled low beneath his frozen breath as the driver snapped awake and took notice of him.

"Terrible cold out here," the driver said. "Haven't they an inn round here?"

He rubbed his hands together but went rigid when the howls from deep in the wood echoed out over the still, gray afternoon.

"I shall show that officious son of the devil *freaks* and *curiosities*," Evgeny seethed at the startled driver as he climbed into the carriage and slammed the door shut. He then punched the roof and bellowed, "Come on, then—back home."

"But your man, Gospodin Azhishchenkov . . . "

"Is dead," barked Evgeny, as bereaved as he was enraged. "As will you be should you delay me further, you mooncalf. *Go.*"

The prodigal son was coming home, Hell in his wake. Faces flickered like candle flames in his mind: Rostislav, Yefim, Lev.

So much death.

So much deathlessness.

*Koschei was dead—long live Koschei.*

All stories seemed somehow true, now.

And as the carriage bounced back to the Tsar's western city, Evgeny resolved to take His Majesty's surgeon-in-residence to Nebolchi . . .

. . . or else bring Nebolchi's damned, as many as he could, to him. For the good of Muscovy, for the need to sate Peter's great curiosity, for the love of Christ Jesus Almighty—the Neva would run red before Evgeny was rebuffed again, and Rus would fall to an inexorable plague of living corpses not even the Turks could best before the end.

Then, of the whole of the earth Robert Areskin would ask: *What is this place?*

Like the deathless, Evgeny Tretyakov whimpered and moaned for the preponderance of the journey back to St. Petersburg.

# TANTIVY

## MOLLY TANZER

**tantivy (tan-TIV-ee)**
*adv.*
At full gallop. *To ride tantivy.*
*exclamation*
(Used as a hunting cry when the chase is at full speed.)

"But surely you don't mean this will be *your first time*?"

Sir George Partridge's tone was warm and soft as amber velvet, sweet and rich as whipped syllabub. Only with the utmost difficulty did James keep himself from smiling. If the old fop was already playing at double entendres they might as well pop the champagne and publish the banns.

James checked himself. The thing was not done yet. He still had work to do.

"Indeed, my lord, this will be my first . . . first *Wicht*-hunt," replied James, feigning shyness. After a well-timed trembling gasp he took a seat on a convenient rose-upholstered chaise, hoping his pose offered the illusion of innocence, perhaps even swooning. This put Sir George in the position of towering over him, which was James' purpose. Sir George was famously confident in the seductive power of his arch manners and robust physique. He looked too pleased, too flushed under his powder. James hoped the man would keep drinking claret at the same rate—that would help his chances, too.

"But how can that be?" said Sir George.

"Beg pardon? It is *so* noisy . . . "

Sir George lowered himself to sit beside James, a little closer than was needed to be heard even in the loud, crowded parlor. *Excellent.*

"I asked how could it be that you've never been on a hunt before?"

James stuck to the truth. It was easier that way. "Mother forbade it. My eldest brother—he died after being thrown from a horse whilst fox-hunting. I don't remember it, I was still in swaddling clothes. But after that, you see, Mother refused to let any of the rest of us ride for fear of another tragedy."

"And your father stood for such nonsense?" The older gentleman took another sip of wine and licked a crimson drop from his lips before cocking a painted eyebrow at James. "Accidents happen all the time. If your brother—God rest his soul—had died of choking on a chicken bone, would your mother have forbidden poultry to be served at table?"

"I could not say, m'lord," said James. "My mother is very fond of fowl, but she was never one to join the hunt."

"More Juno than Artemis, then. Well, as is proper, being a wife and mother, I suppose. But what of her son, I wonder?"

"What of me?"

Sir George grinned. "Are you more a Lelantos or a Philomelos? I myself consider Dionysos my patron god, but I have been known to cast my eyes heavenward to do honor to Orion, as I shall do tomorrow."

What on earth was the old fart on about? "I'm not sure I—"

"A shame. Your Classical education has been neglected. Well, I am an expert on all matters Greek and can help you with that." Sir George put his hand on James' knee and squeezed it so hard James winced. But he did not attempt to free himself. He had come as suppliant to Grampnell Hall for this, after all. "I can't let my sister become affianced to someone *uneducated*, now can I?"

James' heart began to pound and he felt the stirrings of panic in his breast; obtaining Miss Aliza Partridge's substantial dowry was the only hope for his family's finances. Here he'd been convinced he was doing well in his suit, but if he went and soured this interview the family's debts would . . . he couldn't think about that, not now. He had to concentrate on the task at hand, perhaps by further playing up his eagerness to become husband to Miss Aliza Partridge and wife to her brother. James could only parlay his sole inheritance, his handsome countenance, after all.

"My apologies, Sir George, my education has not been of the highest—"

"Oh. come now. James, I'm just teasing you. My expectations of you are quite low." Sir George sighed as if suddenly bored. He snapped for a servant to refill his glass. "She loves you, and that matters more to me than anything."

"Really, sir?" James thought he might choke on his false cloying sweetness.

"Within reason." Sir George stood and went over to the window overlooking the eastern side of the vast estate. James followed him. "It's devilish fun, *Wicht*-hunting. Better by far than chasing reynards. I insist you ride with us. On a hunt a man shows his true cloth."

James did not feign his shudder of revulsion. He wasn't afraid of doing what he must to win over Sir George when it came to the boudoir, but he knew enough of *Wicht*-hunting, the blood-sport *à la mode,* to know it sounded utterly dreadful. Riding down a quarry that looked human—had *been* human, once—seemed ghastly.

"My sister has always been attracted to sensitive souls, " remarked Sir George. "If you are to pluck Miss Partridge—for my sister will, I assure you, make quite a mess of all the pretty wedding-linens I'll be forced to pay for—you will have to inure yourself to a bit of screaming." He smiled when James raised an artful handkerchief to obscure an equally artful expression of alarm. "You seem more frightened than excited about the wedding-bed, my boy. Doesn't the prospect of riding Aliza ragged please you? Why, just look at her."

James glanced across the busy parlor to the lovely girl in a mantua that was, oddly, the same blue-green of her brother's eyes. She was whispering something to James' second-youngest sister, Elinor, as they stood together, giggling and colluding as if they were the only two at the party. Well, good show, Elinor. Aliza's affection for the chit could only help James.

"She is extremely lovely," admitted James, but he bit his lip as he turned back to Sir George. "It's just . . . I should hate to hurt her, even a little—even once."

His host leaned closer. Those gaudy, painted lips almost brushed James' cheek. "See here, my boy, tomorrow, on the hunt, you must ride with me, it will be safer that way for you, I think. You can follow my lead, and I'll show you how it's done. And once you've heard the horns blowing, the hounds baying, whipped a horse into a lather in pursuit of your quarry—well perhaps after that you'll find the prospect of *hard riding* more . . . appealing."

"Appealing" had less than nothing to do with the matter, mused James, as Sir George staggered off to greet another of his many guests. Even if Aliza had been born with a hound's face and her brother a tail, needs must when the Devil drives.

Galloping full-tilt after the hounds was rather fun, James decided, as his bay gelding leapt over a low thicket, hot on the heels of Sir George's black stallion. The morning air was bracing, the smell of grass and heather churned up by hoof and paw and foot pleasing, his thighs ached pleasantly from the horse exercise over the green rolling hills.

Best of all, the hounds had yet to scent a single *Wicht*.

Sir George was out of sorts about the situation. A flop of a hunt would haunt him, socially speaking. He had bragged so often of stocking his grounds with those who had fallen prey to that awful plague sweeping across the noblesse's Jamaica plantations that if no *Wicht* could be flushed out he was at risk of becoming a laughingstock. Not that James particularly cared about the man's reputation, only his purse strings.

The dogs snuffled and barked and whined and frolicked to no end. Everyone in the hunting-party looked very disappointed indeed, but James hoped things would continue on in this manner. Eventually the nobles would get bored, and then they could go back and eat dinner without his having to watch the dogs tear what had so recently been a human limb from limb.

"I say," shouted a gentleman in a blue coat, as they reined up at the edge of a thick wood, "this is rather rum, eh, Sir George? They're not tricky devils like foxes, you know, to hide and put the hounds off their scent. Could someone have poached all your game?"

"Bronson would have noticed," shouted Sir George back at the man, but all the same James thought he looked worried.

Then Sir George's prize bitch scent-hound, who had been sniffing back and forth along the wood's edge, put her nose in the air and bayed excitedly. All the dogs raced to her side, plunging as a single great panting yelping body into the forest. The gentleman and few ladies of the hunting party (Aliza and Elinor had surprised James by tagging along) cheered, the master of the hunt blew his horn, and all spurred their horses into the brush.

James alone hung back, keeping his bay at a walk as they entered the shadowy forest, one hand holding onto his hat so no stray bough would knock it from his head. His father had been forced to settle some debts by selling most his stables when James was just a boy, and as a result he was not the surest of riders even over good terrain—to say nothing of dense woodland.

That, and he hoped Sir George, who had promised so ardently to look after him, would notice his absence and come back. Alone. James was willing to bet that a bored, rich molly like Sir George would be charmed by lovemaking *al fresco*, and his place would be secured.

Once under the trees the day felt darker, almost solemn, as the noisy hunting party moved out of earshot and the woods pressed in around him. He neither heard nor saw animals about and told himself that even songbirds would be frightened off by baying hounds. The only sounds were the champing and tramping of his horse and his own light breathing. It was almost eerie, the silence, and the mist, churned up by the bay's slow hoof-falls, looked ghostly and strange.

James came into a small clearing and reined in his horse. He wished he could have brought a sword, but it was not tradition. The dogs would do the work for the hunting-party, rending the *Wicht* to pieces while their masters remained on horseback. It had struck him suddenly that there was a potential problem with this particular gambit: If a *Wicht* were to break from one of the deeper thickets, startling his horse into stumbling or throwing him, no one would be there to help. Indeed, no one would know, not for hours. It was an unsettling thought—and it preoccupied him so wholly that when a dark shape crashed into the clearing he screamed and nearly lost his seat.

"Why, it's only me, James," said Sir George, when James had recovered himself. He wore an unsettling smile that did not entirely put the image of those poor plague-victims who had died and then risen again, hungry for flesh, out of James' mind. "I lost sight of you and came back to make sure you were all right."

James sighed in genuine relief. "Please don't think less of me, Sir George, but galloping through a wood was nothing I felt myself capable of."

"No?"

"I'm . . . not the most experienced rider." Sir George wasn't the *only* master of the entendre at Grampnell Hall.

Sir George laughed, and then, to James' joy, swung himself out of the saddle. "Come down off of that horse for a moment, my lad," he said, offering James his hand as he struggled off the tall bay. "Rest your legs. The party's gone ahead and we shall have some quiet time together—we should have some, do you not think, if we are to be brothers?"

"If you say so, Sir George."

"I do say so."

The day was cool, but it was James' shiver of victory that prompted Sir George to gallantly offer him his coat—and several nips from his flask of Armagnac. The fine brandy warmed James quicker than the large hunting frock, and it smelled better too, but it also made him far more relaxed than he thought safe. He refused further tipples. Things could still go wrong, he had to play his part as best as he could—so when Sir George proposed they sit a spell under a linden tree and enjoy the peaceful morning, James agreed readily.

"I don't think we shall make a huntsman out of you, my boy, but that's all right," said Sir George.

"Is it?"

"Yes, yes, of course. All we shall require of you is that you get sons on my sister."

The man was a liar, but James pretended ignorance. "I . . . will do my best to fulfill all my duties to your family . . . if I am to become a part of it, of course."

"All your duties?" Sir George settled in beside James, hesitated, then to James' surprise instead of making a move, he tilted James's face upward by the chin to look right up at him. "My boy, you . . . seem like a nice young man. I wonder—rather, I find myself wondering . . . "

*Here it is at last,* thought James. "Sir George?"

But Sir George was hesitating further; the man seemed genuinely nervous! How queer. From everything James' mother told him before putting him and his sister into a rented coach to attend this ghastly summer hunting-party, James should have found it challenging to keep the man off him with a cudgel and three trained mastiffs.

"I am well aware that your family's situation puts you into a difficult position," Sir George said in a hushed tone, as if fearful of being overheard. "You must marry well, as your sisters, while beautiful, have nothing to offer a man of means—less than you, and that is saying quite a lot."

James opened his mouth to protest the implication, but Sir George did it for him.

"I'm not saying you don't love my dearest Aliza; your attentions toward her are clear enough. But . . . I've noticed your attentions toward me, and if they are done out of interest—I know my reputation—I should hate to take advantage of you, dear boy. I may have *appetites*, but they are . . . if not pure, then at least they are honest. I am not interested in what is unwillingly given. If you have made up to me to secure your situation with Aliza, tell me now and I shall leave you be and bless your marriage just the same. You're her choice, for whatever reason, and I am no ogre. But . . . but if you be true, and want me . . . "

Sir George's honesty so unsettled James he found himself at a loss for words. He turned away, partially to hide his features less they show guile, partly to think clearly without that man staring him down.

James desired Aliza purely for her dowry, nothing more. Indeed, given his choice he would be more inclined to welcome Sir George's advances (well, if the man had been three stone lighter and a decade younger) but that adage about beggars and choosing was all too true. No, he could not afford to trust in Sir George, no matter how sincere the man seemed, and so instead of confessing all, he turned back with a shy smile on his face,

"I find myself at a crossroads, and do not know which path to walk," he said so softly Sir George had to lean in close to hear him. "Both of you are so wonderful, so beautiful, so—*oh dear God!*"

Sir George hastily buttoned up his breeches but it wasn't the sight of the man's admittedly enormous cockstand that had so alarmed James. No, it was the pair of filmy, hungry, dead eyes winking at him from the linden-boughs; the skeletal, naked body, the clutching, bony hands and feet that dug into the wood of the tree as it perched there. Lank hair framed its awful face, and its open mouth was full of blackened teeth. James had had no warning of its approach. How the deuce had something so rotten moved through the branches so quietly?

"Sir George," whispered James. He'd been so focused on his future prospects that he'd completely forgotten his current peril: This wood was, after all, deliberately stocked with horrible monsters! "A . . . it's a *Wicht*, look there, it—"

"Good heavens!" cried Sir George. He leaped to his feet, stumbling in his haste to gain the musket lying against a tree to their left. He flailed, but though hardy, his not-insubstantial weight was against him and he fell into the side of his black stallion. The spirited animal reared and screamed; Sir George backed away from its slashing hooves but stopped when the *Wicht* screamed too, a disgusting throaty sound.

Then half a dozen more pairs of eyes in drawn, cadaverous faces were staring at them from every direction.

The gun was no use now, if it ever really had been, so in desperation James took off running for the edge of the forest. He had no idea how fast the creatures were, so he ran pell-mell through the brush, heedless of the thorns that tore his jacket and branches that cut and whipped his face. When Sir George caught up with him, looking far worse for the tribulations of the dense forest and the running, James felt a brief flash of guilt—he had left Sir George to his fate but if there was any time that the philosophy of "every man for himself" might be ethical it was when a herd of flesh-eating monsters had silently surrounded you.

He skidded to a halt when he heard a sound like baying—perhaps the hunting party had returned for them—but then realized the ululating yelps were nothing like a hound-pack. The *Wicht* were *calling* to one another, they were behind him and to his right, so he zig-zagged away from them as quick as he could, waving at Sir George to follow.

"They're hunting us," gasped the older man.

"I know," panted James, not slowing his pace one bit. "Can't say if it's by sight or smell, but if we could make for a stream . . . "

"This way," said Sir George, and with surprising lightness of foot headed into a denser patch of forest.

Eventually the sound of water reached James' ears along with the hunting cries of the *Wicht*-pack. He dared to hope—they might just get away, maybe—but when they charged into the clearing he stopped short, all thoughts of his peril driven from his mind.

Of all the sights he had expected to see during this trip that had been, at one time, a pleasure-party, he had not dreamed of finding his sister Elinor naked with her face obscenely buried between the bare creamy thighs of the girl who, at one time—a lifetime ago, perhaps—he had hoped to make his fiancée. They writhed and moaned with pleasure atop a makeshift bed of their shed skirts; it was shocking, the juxtaposition of danger and heedless pleasure, and for some reason it made him laugh.

"James!" cried Elinor, sitting up in alarm at the unexpected intrusion. Her face was smeared with something that glistened in the watery filtered sunlight. "What are you doing here? What—oh no! James!"

"Run for it, ladies," cried Sir George, dashing forward and grabbing both girls by their slender wrists. Though naked as the day they were born they followed him, splashing into and up along the burbling stream. James made to follow when his shock wore off, but he tripped over his own feet and landed face down in the forest loam, dazed.

As claws closed around James' neck and limbs and he felt multiple sets of soft but persistent teeth champing at various parts of his body, James laughed again. So that was why Aliza had been so eager to affiance herself to a penniless boy like him. Elinor *had* introduced them, after all, the minx. And here he'd thought he could tell hunter from hunted!

And then the forest darkened around him, and his laugh became a scream.

# CINEREOUS

## LIVIA LLEWELLYN

**Paris**
**October, 1799**

The nails on the heels of Olympe Léon's boots are the only sounds in the silence of night's chilly end. Click click click through indigo air, like the metallic beat of a metronome's righteous heart. As always, when she sees her destination at the end of rue Saint-Martin, rising black and monolithic against the encroaching country and the graying sky, her heart and feet skip beats. She thinks of each single drop of blood, spurting and squirting from the bright flat mouths of the necks, and her small callused hands and wide bowls to catch them all. Olympe, like all the assistants, is very proud of her training, and very afraid of losing her place, very afraid of sinking back into the city's bowels, never to return. She never misses a drop.

The building has no name. It never has. Inside the courtyard, men in effluvia-stained coats scurry back and forth to one of the three large guillotines sitting on the worn packed earth. Scientists and doctors and handlers, carrying out their part of the Forbidden Experiment. Olympe and the young assistants are forbidden to venture beyond the warren of labs and rooms on the ground floor. The rules of their mysterious, tight-knit society haven't stopped her, but after two years, she has still only seen glimpses of the eight labyrinthine stories that loom in a perfect square around the courtyard, occasional flashes of people moving up and down the wide staircases, and the constant winking of the stairwell candle flames high above her like trapped stars in the artificial night. Most floors are reserved for research. The top two floors, merged long ago into a single high-walled prison, are where the Forbidden Experiment has taken place for over twenty years now, and only handlers are allowed inside. Thick-limbed men swathed in heavy layers of leather and chain mail, with animal-faced masks and gloves of unyielding steel, unlock the doors to the top floor once every week, and venture into a metal-bar-ceilinged warren of broken rooms and passages, untamed flora and small creeping fauna, a facsimile and perversion of the natural world, open to the elements yet contained and confined. And after a time, each handler emerges with a young boy or girl who howls and shits and pisses and bites like a wolf, a child who has had no interaction with the civilized world since birth. Enfants sauvages. Some are sent to labs on the middle floors for dissection and vivisection and resurrection, some are taken to the

Mirabelle's first visitor of the day. A handler has one of the diseased sauvages locked in an iron jacket attached to a long pole at the back, which he uses to push the body forward—a device the handlers created for when the creatures are ill, when they don't want contact with the body. It lunges and stumbles on twig-thin legs, reaches out with broken-fingered arms, as all the creatures do, but giant strands of spittle hang from the cracked black lips, and its pallor is that of a corpse, as if every particle of health has been siphoned away. And its movements are slow, Olympe notes; sluggish and confused as if fighting off fever or waking from the too-long grip of a terrible dream. One low continual moan issues from deep within its ribcage, not the high healthy roar she's used to hearing. Around the handler and creature, physicians and scientists scurry, already throwing out theories and furiously writing down notes. One of those physicians is Marie François Xavier Bichet, favorite student to the now-deceased founder of their society, Pierre-Joseph Desault—whose own head, it is whispered, now sits blinking and gaping in some forgotten corner of the building. Bichet never appears in the courtyard unless occasion merits, unless some important discovery is about to be made.

Olympe steps to the end of the table and grabs a bowl, hugging it to her chest like a shield as the phalanx of chaos approaches. The blade rises to the top of Mirabelle, and the executioner locks the déclic and release handle into place. Lorilleaux is several meters away, on the opposite side of the table. Olympe likes his gentle disposition, but she's never seen anyone who can make a living lifting heads from dead bodies yet tremble like a girl at the sight of anything worse than a bruise. He'll never be a doctor. The handler has unlatched the pole from the metal chest plate, and another handler is removing it from the sauvage, who claws and paws at the man's mask, trying to scrape through the layers of protection to get at the man inside. Seconds later, the man forgotten, it swivels its head like a mad dog, snapping and biting at the soft bits of ash floating around them like dead fireflies. For what reason it does these things, Olympe cannot fathom. The men scribble faster, and Olympe reaches into her pocket, touches her little notebook as a reminder that she'll do the same thing later, when she has the chance. There is no time, now, though: the first handler is maneuvering the creature's head into Mirabelle's curved base while the executioner lowers the lunette over the top of its neck. The second handler stands at the back of the bascule, holding the creature's constantly flailing legs together with one massive hand as he keeps it still against the plank with another hand flat against its back. For the first time she can recall, Olympe is revolted at the sight of so much physical corruption and decay. Black and blue discolorations entirely cover the almost skeletal body, and there are perhaps a hundred shallow and deep cuts on the creature, yet no bleeding or discharge. Her lips curl slightly—it can't be possible, but it looks like some of the vertebrae are poking out through the skin.

And now the first handler steps back, and the executioner motions them forward. Lorilleaux and Olympe take their places, she with her copper bowl to the side, and Lorilleaux with his spidery hands reaching out to clasp the creature's jerking head. He makes a wet grunt of disgust as his fingers sink into the filthy tangle of hair and soft skin. For once Olympe can't blame him. Everyone waits. Lorilleaux buries his nose into his shoulder and violently shudders. She knows he's swallowing his own bile. Beneath his grip, the head keeps moving. Finally he lifts his own, and gives a single definitive nod. The sequence of events is practiced and swift. Once Lorilleaux nods, the executioner shouts out as he pulls the lever, Mirabelle's blade shoots down swift and straight, right through the creature's head. Lorilleaux pulls the head away and holds it up for immediate inspection, while Olympe takes one step in and holds her copper bowl under the neck, catching as much of the blood as possible. As she holds the bowl, scientists will switch out the bowls for her, take quick samples from the flow, and attempt to measure the rate, thickness and amount of drainage. It's all clockwork, performed by them at least a thousand times. Nothing should go wrong.

Lorilleaux gives his nod. The executioner shouts out, and the head in Lorilleaux's grasp turns sharp and strong. He lets out a scream. The blade comes down and severs the head, and Lorilleaux drops it, whipping his hands away and shouting in pain. The head comes down on Olympe's feet, and instinctively, she drops her bowl and reaches down to grab it, her fingers outstretched as she's seen Lorilleaux do a thousand times. As her hand moves down, the head moves, and suddenly there is pain, unlike anything she has felt before. An animal-like roar erupts from her throat, and she raises her hand, the head still attached, its teeth moving back and forth across her finger like a miniature saw. She can feel the blood in her veins grow cold, the world turn black at the edges, and everything grows dull and murky. Doctors surround her, using the calipers and any other instrument they can find to pry the horrible object from her body. And then it is all suddenly over, and the head is gone. Olympe holds her hand up to her face, steaming rivulets of red running down her trembling flesh and disappearing in the sleeves of her clothes. One finger is crooked, torn and almost bit in half at the knuckle. When she speaks, it's as if the timorous, childish words are coming from any place other than her mouth.

*—I've been bit.*

Activity at the other guillotines has ceased. Olympe finds Nana at her side, guiding her across the eerily silenced courtyard to the holding rooms. Lorilleaux runs ahead, his blood-spattered boots echoing back and forth between the stone walls. The air feels too warm, and the ash, the ever-constant smell of burning flesh, the thick scratch against the back of her tongue—Olympe halts, bends over, and vomits. Bits of black spatter against their boots. A frisson of terror washes through her. Those black clots are her blood, darkened from sitting in her stomach for hours as it curdled into something else. Nana waits until she's finished, then guides her forward again, through the holding rooms and into a corner of a makeshift medical lab, where a physician is already bandaging up an ashen-faced Lorilleaux. He'll never be anything more than an assistant. He can't handle change or pain. Olympe sits down, props her elbow upright against the table, and studies her finger. Already the edges of the wound are drying out, cracking slightly. Moistening a rag with her spittle, she wipes away the blood, and leans in, squinting. A low moan escapes her lips, barely a feather's breath. Tiny veins of blue and black thread away from the edges of the bite marks, a network that spreads as she watches, slow but sure. Around the lines, soft gray blossoms up from within. Olympe grabs a roll of linen and quickly begins wrapping her hand. The doctor doesn't protest. They all know how hard she works, how quick and smart she is. Several tears drop onto the cream fabric as she pins the ends tight, then rolls down her stained overcoat sleeve. She'll be fine, she tells herself as she rises from her seat, ignoring Nana's steadying hand. She's going to go far.

After a few sips of water, Olympe makes her way back outside and back across the courtyard to Mirabelle. Already the blood has been washed away with buckets of scalding water that sends steam curling into the air, and the remaining assistants and doctors are placing equipment into straw-filled barrows to be wheeled back inside. The tracks of another wheelbarrow lead to the back of the building, where the remains will be sent first to the morgue, and then, in pieces, to other labs on other floors. Bichet and a group of the older scientists gather at the far end of the table, staring at an amber liquid-filled glass container set at its edge. Hair floats in the liquid like seaweed. Normally Olympe wouldn't dare approach these important men, who know her only as a pair of disembodied hands holding a blood-filled copper bowl. She sidles along the table, her uninjured hand touching the edge casually, as if it's not necessary to keep her balance. When she gets to the edge of the group, Bichet straightens, and waves her closer. The men move aside: they're making way for *her*. Little trickles of sweat run down the sides of her face. She feels like her body is pushing all the fluids out, squeezing out every last drop of moisture, to make room for the gray blooms and the black veins.

Bichet reaches out and grabs the top of the container, twisting it around with his nimble surgeon's hand. Olympe crouches down until her chin rests on the tabletop, as though she were five again. The waves of blackened hair make way for a face, bruised and contorted. The eyes are clouded over, but open, and they blink, and they see Olympe. *Tête vivante*, someone whispers. Smears of blood stick to the lips, preserved by the fluid. Some of it is hers. A part of her will always be in that jar, trapped between the lips of something that is not dead or alive. The mouth opens in a soundless cry, and a piece of tooth floats out, disappearing in the waving hair. Olympe turns and runs from the table, stumbling across the courtyard back to the safety of the holding rooms. Behind her, loud laughter floats and tumbles and mixes with the snowy crematory ash.

Time and the day and the ashes in the air sift past Olympe in an increasing haze of detachment and low-grade pain. She hovers near the door of the holding room, watching the handlers walk to and fro with their living cargo. None of the sauvages that they take to the guillotines are ill, as far as she can tell. Men walk back and forth between the assistants, jars and dishes and bowls filling and emptying. Heads, feet, bones, blood. A farmers' market of grotesqueries and abominations. And in the distance the fires eat away at the remains, vomiting out the bits onto their heads. She stares into the distance. Her face is somewhere else. She can't feel her lips. Everyone in the courtyard coughs, hocks, spits. Something happened today that she should be weeping about, but she can't remember. She holds up her bandaged hand. The nails are black as onyx. They look oddly fetching.

It's the ash. They got it, all of them, everything in the building, from the burning dead.

Ouroboros. Disease is.

Nana is helping her into her scarf and coat. Is the day over? For some reason she refuses to take off her laboratory overcoat. Outside, the courtyard is pitch black, silent until tomorrow morning when the blades come back to life. Someone walks her through the thick double gates. His face is familiar, pretty and delicious. Outside, the world is eerily calm. She hears the roar of the furnaces now, all the machinery hidden within and without the building that keeps it alive to gobble them all up in the name of Science. The rest of rue Saint-Martin lies before her like a dried-up river, pointing a dim, insurmountable way back into Paris proper. Lights twinkle overhead in the black of night. Olympe sighs. She knows what those are. She breathes them in as she drags her feet down the raggedy sides of the road.

A lamppost or a tree trunk is at her back. The night is cold. She should feel it, but she doesn't. She should care, but.

She is going to go far.

It was the ash.

It was the ash.

Olympe wills her numb fingers to begin a laborious creep through the layers of fabric, toward her notebook and pencil, though she cannot feel their progress or lack thereof. No matter, she must somehow write down her observations and present them to the others in the morning, before the disease spreads further. This knowledge will be the society's salvation, it's debridement, and her way out. Respect, at last. Olympe will be taken seriously, taken under wing. She will become a scholar, a doctor, a brilliant beacon of light, and an example to all women of France. She stares down. Her hand is a hand that is not her hand and it is all the way on the other side of Paris or perhaps even the world and she does not know what it is at all or what it holds. At the quiet end of the street, the building stands tall and funereal against scrabbly trees and darkling sky. The river of Time rushes steadily into and through her, filling her up until all she sees and feels and hears is a great slow blanket of nothingness: and stops. Disconnected images fill her mind, images of each silky shining drop of blood out there in the world, spurting and squirting from the bright flat mouths of necks, and her small callused hands and the wide bowl of her mouth to catch them all. Warm red, squirming and streaming behind the outlines of the shapes so rapidly approaching. Bright red, to push the gray of the world away.

# 19TH CENTURY

# THE WAILING HILLS

## L LARK

### Part I.

*Northwestern Oregon*
*1811*

Margaret is thirteen when her sister dies for the fourth time. Her mother doesn't bother to call for the settlement's lone doctor, who has already pronounced Ruth deceased on two occasions. She burns Ruth's death sheets in the backyard, while Margaret laments her boring and unhappy life in the darkness of the cellar, tugging at beaver pelts that hang against the wall in layers.

It is infection this time around. One of the neighbor's dogs had latched onto Ruth's arm, and two days later, the wound had puckered and violet lines forged a trail map towards her heart.

The dog had been shot. Ruth's brain had been scorched by fever. Margaret thinks the dog was the lucky one.

Now, Margaret knows, the Chinook men who come to trade with their mother will wait silently for Ruth to reemerge from the cabin, freshly resurrected. With her pale gold hair and flushed cheeks, she looks otherworldly. Ruth will touch their hands and whisper the prayer of Saint Hubert, patron of hunters and the ill. She will tuck sprigs of lavender into their thick braids.

Margaret watches out the window as they disappear back into the forest. The air is full of thick, yellow mist. It seems like any step could be the last before the edge of the world.

That evening, Ruth sniggers about the Indian's superstitions while she and Margaret sew patches onto their father's winter coat. It is October, but unusually cool. In the firelight, Ruth's eyes are a dull black that remind Margaret of a newborn seal. She is eating pink apple slices from a tray, one after the other.

Ruth is three years older than her. Before her first death, she spent Sunday afternoons in the doctor's small practice, reading the encyclopedias he'd brought with him from cities, far in the east. She would return to the cabin with words like *gravitation*, *electricity*, and *atmosphere*—words that Margaret cherished for their beauty and inherent danger. Ruth had learned to set rabbit traps from the

Chinook boys, knew how to introduce herself in French, and often feigned bouts of homesickness for a Europe she had never visited.

She had recently begun a correspondence with a third cousin in England, who'd sent her a pamphlet of atheistic literature. Ruth had declared over breakfast that God did not exist and announced her self-initiation into the Cult of Reason.

Their mother had crossed herself and said nothing.

Margaret's hair is black and lank. Her skin is dark like an Indian's, and she has a long crooked nose to match. She has recently gone through a growth spurt, and though she now towers over Ruth, she is unused to the awkward new length in her limbs. When sitting, she keeps her arms and legs folded tightly, minimizing the amount of space she occupies.

Margaret has only ever read the Bible, is prone to daydreaming, and though she recognizes every herb that grows within a five-mile radius of their cabin, she only knows them by their Indian nicknames—Crow's Foot, Deer Tail, Death's Bell.

Still, Margaret loves her sister with an intensity that frightens her.

She wants to ask Ruth how she can dismiss the gods of the Chinook when she is so very like one herself, but is too dangerous to speak to her in that way. She is prone to sudden changes in mood, tantrums, and Margaret does not want to spend all night sewing alone in the darkness.

Their cabin is two miles from the small cluster of wooden buildings that make up an unnamed trading post along the river, where their father once bought whiskey and beaver skins. The home is balanced on the side of a tall hill that looms over the Oregon coast. In the garden, the sagebrush and horsetail grass sway like water. Margaret's window is next to the chicken coop, and the room is filled with their gentle cooing at twilight.

From the edge of the forest, the grandiose outlines of the Cascade Mountains stretch into the north and south. Margaret hates only their immensity, but she sometimes catches Ruth staring at their silhouettes in the night, fingernails curled into her palm.

They have all learned to be afraid of the wilderness. In Oregon, the days are short and dark, and at night, beasts with giant teeth and claws vie for overlapping territories. The forests are deep and unexplored, and the Chinook have warned Margaret about the spirits that live in the rifts and hollows of the Wailing Hills, at the base of the mountains.

"Can you believe it?" Ruth says, without looking up. To her left is an open book, and her gaze shifts between it and the tattered elbow patch she is repairing. The corners of the pages are damp with apple juice.

"Believe what?" Margaret says, startled to be addressed by Ruth directly.

"The Indians. They say there is a giant bear in the woods. They say it's eating all the animals. Nothing left to hunt."

Three months previous, their mother had saved the lives of two Chinook youngsters with cholera, and they have co-existed amicably ever since, trading small European luxuries from the ships for meats and honey. As a result of this, the other families at the trading post have ostracized Margaret's mother.

Margaret does not understand this. The Chinook have taught her which plants and mushrooms can feed them and which can clean their wounds. A boy with cheekbones like oyster shells had given Ruth a carved bone pendant in the shape of a raven.

"A bear," Ruth repeats flatly, staring into the fire.

Margaret has seen a bear once, high on the side of a cliff, and three summers ago, only half of the Prestons' boy had been found in the woods. Margaret had not seen the body, but she has imagined it many times, scattered across the field like he had been shattered by the wind.

"Maybe there is one," she says.

"Oh, stop it with that nonsense," Ruth says, and they return to their comfortable agreement of silence.

That night, Margaret cracks her windows and listens for the huffing and pounding of a bear pushing its way through the trees, but hears nothing.

Margaret has only been present for Ruth's third and fourth deaths. During the second, cholera, a priest had ushered Margaret out of the room once Ruth's pulse had begun to falter.

Ruth was alone for the first. Margaret has envisioned the sequence of events many times, but has never had the courage to ask Ruth what really happened the morning two Chinook fisherman found her dead at the bottom of Dogwood Gorge.

She'd left the cabin the afternoon before to pick huckleberries at the end of an old trapper trail, and their mother had waited all night by the window for her to return, saying the prayers of Saint Anthony, patron of lost things. In the morning, their cabin smelled like herbs the Indians burned to keep away mosquitoes, and Margaret woke to find her mother in the front yard, staring beyond the tree line.

Two Chinook men carried Ruth's body on a plank between them, a cloak draped over her face. One of them, Chanko, was the father of one of the children their mother had nursed back to health. He had a kind face, and deep blue veins in his forearms.

Margaret had seen Chanko dipping in and out of the shadows on their property at night, and often he brought their mother gifts of fur and lovely beaded necklaces that sat at the base of her throat. He'd once had a wife who died of an illness he would not speak of; when Margaret has asked her name, he had refused to answer, but touched the long scars that bleached his skin from throat to chest.

There was a deep bite on Ruth's left shoulder, violet and bruised in the places where her blouse was torn. Margaret could not look directly at it. The sight of blood and Ruth's stiff wrists and ankles made her lightheaded. She kept her eyes trained on the laundry blowing back and forth above the garden, and Ruth's favorite black gown filling with air.

In Margaret's peripheral vision, her mother sank to her knees as the men lowered the plank to the ground. The fir trees heaved and whined in the Pacific winds. When her mother began to wail, it reminded Margaret too much of Ruth slaughtering wild hares in the winter.

Then it was over, and the next time Margaret looked back, Ruth was sitting up with the cloak pushed back on her shoulders. There was a bruise the color of seawater on her left cheekbone, and she was breathing hard into her cupped hands.

Ruth was covered in bits of the forest—sheets of birch bark, violently yellow pollen, a dragonfly's wing on her left knee—as if it had blanketed her completely while she slept. No one said anything. No one helped Ruth up from the ground.

Eventually, she stood by herself, shaking the leaves from her hair. She seemed dazed, but otherwise unharmed.

"I-I lost my footing and fell," she said, even though no one had yet spoken about her miraculous resurrection or cruel practical joke.

For a long moment, Margaret hated her sister with such intensity her vision went white. But Ruth was aloof, and stubborn, and ignored Margaret whenever convenient, but Ruth was not cruel.

One of the men who'd carried her reached out to touch her wrist, as if to confirm he wasn't dreaming. Ruth only looked confused when their mother began to sob into her hair. She touched Ruth's eyelashes, her jawline, tangled her fingers into Ruth's ponytail. The men stepped back, uncomfortable to be witnessing such a private moment.

Margaret did not entirely understand their expressions. It was the same look she'd once seen in her father's eyes, when a pack of wolves wandered too close to their cabin in the winter, and he'd sat all night by the window with his musket, eyes locked on the tree line.

Eventually, their mother accepted that Ruth had slipped and knocked herself out on the tumble down the gorge. She spoke with the Indians in hushed voices for a long time, and then sent the men away with half a pound of tea, a dozen sewing needles, and several satchels of gunpowder.

Both Ruth and her mother seemed oblivious to Margaret's presence, even though she followed them into the house, hovering silently like a ghost.

When Margaret asked about the bite, neither one of them answered her. Her mother shushed her and fussed with Ruth's bruised eye. Ruth stared into the fireplace, blowing on the surface of her tea. The white raven pendant at her throat was still caked in dried blood.

"Be more careful next time," their mother said, pressing a wet rag against Ruth's cheekbone. "I couldn't stand to lose you too."

And then Ruth didn't die again. And again.

It isn't until after Ruth's fourth death that Margaret realizes the store of canned fruits, grain, and dried meat they have been stockpiling for the winter is only half what it used to be. Without their father's hunting, they've had to rely on trading for meat, but visits from the Chinook have become less frequent. Ruth brags that they are wary of her, that they think she is some kind of demigod, but Margaret cannot help but remember what they said.

*"They say there is giant bear in the woods. They say it's eating all the animals."*

Two nights ago, Margaret heard something huffing and gurgling outside of her window. She'd lay curled on her side, clutching the iron knife she'd snuck out of the kitchen, and the sound had come perilously close to her window before passing.

Margaret did not sleep that night. She'd bitten the tips off all her fingernails before morning, and over breakfast, her hands ached as she gripped her spoon.

She has to confront her mother about the missing food that afternoon. Margaret finds her on all fours in the garden, yanking weeds up by the root, soil trapped in the pitted skin of her knees and elbows. In the sunlight, her hair mother's hair looks almost white.

Margaret has ruddy, dark hair like her father. It dries out and cracks in the heat of summer, and then again in the cold of winter.

"There's something you need to see," Margaret says.

Her mother looks up, squinting.

When Margaret leads her to the storage shed out back, her mother says nothing at all. She covers her mouth with her hand, and presses her back against the wall as if she has been struck with a sudden exhaustion. Margaret can see sweat pooling in her collarbones.

"What are we going to do?" Margaret asks, feeling her heart struggle against her breastbone. She tries not to think of winter, rolling in from the east, and the low grey skies beneath which nothing grows.

"Don't tell Ruth about this," her mother says.

Margaret doesn't understand why.

The next morning, Margaret wakes to find a dead elk at the edge of their property. She has stumbled upon dead animals in the forest before—raccoons and opossums with moss growing in their ears and armpits—but never before has she seen a corpse so unrecognizable. If it were not for the great set of antlers jutting out of the ground like tree branches, the mass of meat and tendon could belong to anything.

There are small teeth marks on the bits of exposed bone, like scavengers have gnawed at the carcass. She buries what remains with wet leaves and branches, but takes a tooth to keep in her pocket, for protection.

Margaret tries to distract herself with work. She scrubs the mold gathering around the windows. She tends to the chickens, and picks berries in the forest, and spends her evenings knitting large pairs of gloves and socks for her father's return.

"He'll be home soon," their mother assures them, weaving a rosary between her fingers. He'd left in June to hunt beaver in the north, expecting to be back by early August. It is nearly November now, but their mother insists he will be home before Ruth's birthday, on the first day of winter.

Margaret stopped believing this some time ago, but she would never voice this to Ruth or her mother. She knows how important it is for them to keep her ignorant. So she mends her father's clothes, and stores food enough for four, and smiles politely when others in the settlement inquire about her family.

She also notices that Ruth can't stop eating.

Strawberries by the dozen, entire loaves of bread, strip after strip of dried salmon. Margaret catches her eating leaves of wild sorrel, until all that's left is a white pulp of roots and fiber, poking out of the soil.

Ruth disappears into the woods for half the day and returns with dead rabbits, which she carries in bunches by the foot. She roasts them in olive oil, pacing by the oven with her arms crossed, silent. After dinner, she eats great chunks of bread pudding, chewing with her mouth open. Margaret hears her sneaking out of her room to visit the kitchen in the middle of the night.

November becomes December. Their father does not return. The rain arrives and stays, turning the sky the color of tin. Ruth eats and eats, and the Chinook cease to visit, except for when Margaret catches sight of them in her peripheral vision, moving in silhouette through the trees with their bows drawn. As the days become short and dark, Margaret cannot help but feel that there are eyes in the forest, narrowed and focused on her.

Ruth dies once that month, breaking her neck on a tumble from a wild apple tree. Margaret is not there when it happens, but arrives a moment before Ruth returns to life. In a moment of furious courage, Margaret reaches out to touch Ruth's hand and finds it cold and oily, like beeswax.

The crows arrive before Ruth awakens, circling in the updraft. Margaret hates the crows. In the winter, they look like ink stains against the white sky, and they draw bears and coyotes out from the wilderness. Margaret carries her father's musket strapped to her back, but she has never shot at anything aside from empty mason jars he let her use as targets.

She waves the birds off, until Ruth reawakens in spasms, hollow-eyed and pale.

Margaret cannot entirely process what happens next.

The motions are quick and dreamlike. Ruth reaches out and snatches one of the crows that has wandered close. A moment later, Margaret can see blood on Ruth's face through the curtain of feathers, and there is a sound like fabric being ripped apart. The birds all take to the air at once, and Margaret stumbles back, falling elbow-first onto the rocks behind her.

The butt of the gun collides painfully with her shoulder and her vision blurs. It hurts, but she is too afraid to look away from the flurry of wings and limbs in front of her. Margaret lurches to her feet, raising her arms to swat at the birds, but the crows are gone by the time she nears Ruth, who is still slumped forward on the ground.

"Ruth?" Margaret whispers, although she can barely hear the word over the panicked screams of the birds in the air above them.

Ruth doesn't answer. There is dirt beneath her fingers, and her torso is swaying rhythmically, like she's been sampling the whiskey their mother distills through the summer.

"Ruth?"

Ruth finally looks up. The skin around her eyes is pale blue and damp, and there is down stuck to the drying blood around her mouth. She does not look afraid, or even remotely startled by what has just happened. She is encircled by what remains of three dead birds, and a fourth whose left wing twitches, until Ruth snatches it up and takes a bite from its midsection.

Margaret cannot tell if the strange, guttural noise that follows comes from Ruth or the crow. She turns and vomits in to the ferns, feeling her stomach acids burn a path up to her throat.

In her peripheral vision, she sees Ruth amble to her feet.

"I'm sorry, I'm sorry" Ruth calls, "I didn't mean to do that. I'm hungry."

Margaret takes a step back, and then another. From this distance, Ruth's cheeks are rosebud pink, but her eyes look opaque and white. Margaret tries not the think about the stories the Indians tell about ghosts with unquenchable appetites, who must eat and eat and eat.

Margaret is too afraid to answer her. She runs.

Ruth does not chase her. Margaret makes it halfway home before she has to stop and bend over to breathe through her mouth. The rain has started up again, falling heavily on her neck and shoulders. She tries to listen through the storm, for the pop of a breaking twig or the huff of a predator sniffing in interest, but the pine trees are roaring in the wind.

When she can flex her hands again, Margaret grips the musket and places her index finger gingerly over the trigger. She does not actually know what she will do if Ruth appears, but the gun feels good in her hands—like strength and potential energy.

Their cabin can't be more than a mile away, but the earth seems to dip beneath her heels. Margaret nearly sinks her boot into a raccoon carcass slowly being swallowed by the mud. Its fur is dark, but the chunks of flesh missing from its throat and stomach are obvious. As is the bone crow pendent, tangled in the animal's ribcage.

Margaret says a word that she's glad her mother is not around to hear, and stumbles forward.

Somewhere from the east, she thinks she hears someone calling her name, but she is too afraid to stop running. By the time the lights of the cabin appear, Margaret feels like she did last winter, when she'd slipped beneath the ice of a frozen lake and her heart had seized with cold.

Her mother is standing with a flintlock trade gun at their door. The veins in her forearms are thick and swollen, as she pulls Margaret through the doorway and into the cabin with a deep grunt.

"Ruth," she gasps, crumpling into her mother's arms. The cabin is dry but cold, and their guns are silver-blue in the diffuse light. There is a sound in Margaret's ears, like the world spinning and spinning on its axis. Her mother drops a hand unto her shoulder, heavy and solid.

"I heard you screaming," her mother says.

"It was Ruth," Margaret finally gasps, "She ate the birds—"

Her mother shushes her.

"She'll be fine. She's just sick. She's just hungry," she says, which is not what Margaret expected to hear.

• • •

**Part II.**

Ruth does return that night, but they don't know it until the chickens begin to scream. Before it happens, both Margaret and her mother are sitting by the fireplace, guns cocked against the wall. The fire hisses and rattles like a snake. It does not seem to help the cold that soaks in through the porous wood of their cabin.

Her mother's eyes don't stray from the front window.

"Shouldn't we go look for her?" Margaret asks. It is late, but she knows she cannot sleep. There is adrenaline rushing through her, and her veins feel scraped out and raw. Margaret thinks the fear she feels has nothing to do with Ruth, wandering outside in the darkness. She is afraid of the winter, and the empty storehouse, and the dead animals in the forest.

"No," her mother says, and Margaret does not think she has ever heard her voice so resolute. "She'll be fine on her own. She's just hungry."

"Did she eat all the—"

"Hush. I don't want her to hear us through the walls."

It is only a moment later that the chickens begin to wail and beat their wings against the walls of their coop. Her mother reaches out and clutches her wrist so hard, Margaret is sure it will be bruised in the morning.

She twists her arm out of her mother's grip, and snatches her musket up. Margaret runs before her mother has the chance to scream after her, rushing unprepared into the cold. It hits her with the force of a blow, and Margaret nearly drops the gun, fingers twitching uncontrollably.

She sees Ruth's silhouette bent into the chicken coop, and calls out, "Stop!"

Ruth does not. She reaches in and pulls a hen out by the neck, snapping it with an audible pop. Margaret is glad the bird is dead when Ruth takes a bite from its torso, feathers in a whirlwind around her.

"Ruth," she repeats, "I'm going to shoot you."

It is a lie. Margaret does not think she could kill her sister, no matter how impermanent it might be. Still, she raises her musket into the air and sends off a shot, whose echo bounces back and forth between the hills.

Ruth drops, but it is not a bullet that hits her, it is an arrow. Margaret does not see it immediately. Ruth's body jerks twice before stilling, in a way that reminds Margaret of waking from dreams where she falls and falls. The arrow is lodged in between Ruth's ribs, and the stiff red leaves dangling from its end tells Margaret that it is a Chinook weapon.

She squints out into the forest, and sees Chanko at the edge of the tree line, flanked by two large men in bearskin cloaks. They approach Ruth's body with their bows drawn, walking in long silent strides.

"How long until she wakes?" one of them grunts, aiming his arrow at the soft pulp behind Ruth's left ear. She looks pale blue in the light that slips through the fir trees, too still to be asleep.

"Four minutes, five at most," Margaret says, sensing her mother approach from behind and freeze mid-motion, the barrel of her gun lost in the billowing fabric of her skirts.

"Let's get her inside," Chanko tells them, with such authority in his voice that it is impossible to disobey.

They lock Ruth in her mother's bedroom closet, jamming a chair against the door. Her mother does not cry; her eyes seem sad and angry all at once, but she does not cry, even when Chanko unceremoniously drops Ruth's body on a pile of ancient blankets.

"What's wrong with her?" Margaret asks, once the door has been secured. Even the spiders have crawled out from the gaps in the walls, looking jolly and interested, a myriad of eyes twinkling in the candlelight.

Chanko is silent for a long time. Margaret hears her mother give a half-sob, a soft whine like a dog's, but she catches herself before he answers.

"She has the hunger sickness. There is nothing we can do for her now."

Before Margaret can answer, Ruth's fists are beating on the other side of the door.

"Margaret," she calls, "Maggie. Please. Let me out."

"There is nothing more we can do for you," Chanko repeats, shouldering his bow and giving a vague gesture to the two men behind him. His voice is difficult to hear over Ruth's pounding, and the sound of her violent exhalations. "There will never be enough for her to eat. It would not be wise to let her out again. Ever."

They leave without another word, but Chanko places his hand heavily on Margaret's shoulder. For a moment, their gazes meet, and Margaret feels fuzzy and disoriented. He tips forward to kiss her forehead, and his shadow looks crooked and enormous against the walls of the cabin.

"I don't understand. What do we do?" Margaret says.

Chanko only shakes his head.

Ruth never stops pounding.

That evening, neither Margaret nor her mother sleep. It is impossible, with the sound of Ruth's voice wailing incoherently, like she is in pain or deep religious ecstasy. Margaret imagines Ruth's hands turning purple and bruised, but her voice does not falter once through the night. She begs for food and water, but Margaret is too afraid to open the door, remembering the blood around Ruth's mouth, and the birds entombed in their own feathers. It is the blood, more than anything, that Margaret cannot get out of her mind—blood on Ruth's gown, blood on the moss growing in the crooks of the trees, a trail of blood that winds through their house like a dry creek in the summer.

Her mother seems catatonic, staring out the window as the sun rises behind clouds in the east. Margaret waits by the closet door through the evening with her musket mounted against her shoulder, unsure of whether or not she will be able to shoot Ruth, if that moment should ever come.

It does in three days time.

By then, Margaret feels woozy from lack of sleep, but her mother seems to doze off at any moment—at the breakfast table, in the rosemary bushes in the garden, in the outhouse. Margaret gathers food in the daytime, canning fruits and drying the salmon that she catches in nets by the riverside, knowing it might never be enough for three to survive the coming months of cold. She daydreams often, of her father materializing at the forest's edge, a band of mountain men behind him. She daydreams of the elk meat, and strawberries, and roasted potatoes they will carry with them, and the enormous feast they will enjoy for his homecoming.

Occasionally, Margaret mashes oats into a thick paste she can slide beneath the closet door on a tray, but Ruth can only ever be appeased for a few moments. Afterwards, she screams and pounds and pounds, and Margaret does not sleep.

The New Year comes and goes with nothing to mark it but Ruth's voice shouting obscenities late into the night. Margaret spends as much time out of the cabin as possible, lips and eyelids numbing from the cold as she stares at the edge of the forest, wishing for the Chinook to appear.

In retrospect, it is stupid to leave her mother alone in the house for so long, but Margaret is delirious from the lack of sleep. Shadows curl and shift at the edge of her vision. Any rustle in the grass becomes a rattlesnake, coiled and ready to spring.

She hears the screaming from the garden. For a moment, she cannot be sure if the sound is coming from the crows gathering on their rooftop, or from inside. Margaret has taken to keeping her musket at all times, and she draws it as she sprints towards the front door, her heart squirming furiously beneath her breastplate like a trapped mouse.

She kicks the door in with the heel of her boot, shell shocked by the sudden warmth. The painting of her grandmother above the fireplace seems to watch with her pupils dilated and mouth ajar.

Margaret has to resist the urge to reach into her pocket and palm the elk tooth as she pushes the door to her mother's room open with her hip, a thousand prayers tingling in her mouth. She knows that she will kill Ruth before she has time to process the scene before her.

Her mother lies contorted on the floor, in a growing pool of her own pink blood. Ruth is curled over her like a coyote, her hair matted into thick clumps that hang over her eyes. The fingers of one hand are sunken into her mother's torso, and the other is holding a chunk of violet matter, which Ruth takes clumsy bites from.

There is an ignored tray of bread and honey, overturned on the bedroom floor. Behind Ruth, the closet door has swung open, and Margaret can see their winter coats hanging tattered by the threads of their shoulders.

Margaret shoots. Her finger seems to take action before her brain can send the command out from its center. Ruth's shoulder evaporates into red mist, and she slumps to the ground, a thin line of blood spilling from the corner of her mouth.

Margaret suppresses a sob, and lowers her musket. She can feel the vertebrae in her spine clanging painfully against one another. She approaches the two bodies slowly, half-surprised each time her foot settles successfully on the wooden floor. Both Ruth and her mother are still curved against each other like two parts of a shell. Neither one of them moves.

Margaret reaches down and presses two fingers against the base of her mother's throat. She feels nothing, as she expected to, but it is impossible to handle the rush of grief that follows, especially with Ruth's eyes, open and staring and waiting.

Ruth body is heavy and bloated with food. Margaret cannot breathe by the time she manages to drag her sister back into the closet, and wedges the door shut with furniture from the room.

Her mother's body is different. Margaret does not know what to do about that. She hovers over it for a moment, before leaving the room and closing the door behind her, feeling sick from the smell of copper and flour and sugar.

She presses her back against the door and slides down, hair tangling in the latch. Margaret hears Ruth begin pounding in the closet before she has the chance to steady her breathing.

"Please," Ruth cries, "Please, please, please. I'm so hungry."

Margaret does not cry, but she does not open the door.

She knows she will never open the door again.

Chanko arrives in the morning with the two men who helped him capture Ruth in the first place. By the time they appear on the front porch, pushing through the cold fog, Ruth has been pounding at the closet door for at least seven hours. Margaret feels delirious and weightless, like she could float away with any step. When she opens the door, and sees the three men back-lit at her door, her knees nearly give out.

"Thank you," she whispers, even though she's certain that she will hate what is about to happen. All three of the men are armed and wearing the same elk skins the Chinook take to war. Chanko's hands are cold when they envelope hers.

"Where is your mother?" Chanko asks, in his long vowels. "Has Ruth bitten you?"

Margaret shakes her head, and imagines she sees the same swell of grief in his eyes that she felt in hers. Margaret's body responds in a manner she does not understand, forehead colliding with Chanko's chest involuntarily.

"What do we do? What happened to Ruth?" she says.

Chanko draws back, backlit and enormous, like a fir tree.

"It is an old sickness from the forest. Your sister cannot die," he says, "And she will never stop eating. We know where to take her."

The other men enter the cabin without Margaret's permission. Against the simple backdrop of their living space, they look like architectural marvels, all straight lines and strength. Margaret is dwarfed by their blue shadows, spreading across the floor and walls.

"I shot her," she says to Chanko, unbidden.

"She cannot die. We have to lock her away."

"But she'll starve." Margaret says.

"She cannot die," Chanko repeats, in a way that signals Margaret to say no more.

Margaret does not cry when the men shoot through the closet door, shattering the wood to reveal Ruth slumped over dead on the other side. She does not cry when Chanko binds her mouth and arms with strips of hide and drops her body into large linen sack, stained with burgundy splotches.

Margaret is unable to shift her eyes away from Ruth's blue fingernails, peeking out from the top of the sack.

"This has happened before," Chanko says, the split ends of his hair brushing against the scars on his collarbone. "Come with us."

Margaret follows, because she has no other choice, watching Ruth's limp body bob in the sack ahead of her. They move quickly through the forest. Branches scratch against Margaret's neck, and more than once, she feels tendrils of poison oak brush against her wrist, sending fire up the hair on her forearms.

The rain has cleared and the trees are black against sky. The air is so thick Margaret thinks flowers could grow in it, even in these darkest nights of winter. There is fresh snow on the hills around them, meaning soon there will be snow in their valley, meaning soon Margaret will have nothing to eat. Already her stomach feels as though it is made of glass, but Margaret ignores it.

She cannot afford to wonder if this is how Ruth felt, before she lost control completely.

They walk for seven miles, perhaps eight. Ruth returns to life and dies twice in the interim; each time, the Chinook toss her bag to the ground and swing their clubs against it until her screaming ends. Margaret wants to cry, but more for Ruth's hunger than her terrible propensity for dying—they are her ninth, and tenth deaths, respectively, and frankly, Margaret is no longer shocked each time her limbs flail during a resurrection.

The smell of gunpowder keeps the animals away from the trail, but occasionally Margaret sees the twin rings of an owl's eyes, starring through a hollow in the trees. When she feels as though she can walk no longer, Chanko breaks her off thick pieces of elk jerky which take so long to chew they lose all flavor before Margaret can swallow them. She washes them down with half-frozen water from the creek, so cold it hurts her teeth.

She asks where they are going only once, but Chanko presses his palm to her mouth.

"There are more dangerous things in these forests than bears," he says.

They walk until reaching the rocky, uphill paths leading to the foothills of the mountains. This is the farthest Margaret has traveled from her home since infancy. The air here is thinner than on the coast, and Margaret has to breath twice as often to sustain herself. She knows these lands only by the nickname the Chinook have given it, the Wailing Hills. Both she and Ruth had been forbidden to wander this far.

The Indians do not stop until they reach the mouth of a shallow cave that faces east. The man who is carrying Ruth drops her carelessly to the ground. In the pink light, Margaret can see they stand in a landscape of cliffs and stone towers. There are four more caves within seeing distance, but these have been barricaded shut with rocks and petrified branches. Margaret thinks she hears the muted scream of an animal, but it might just be the crows, rising with the dawn.

Chanko mutters something in the language of the Chinook as they seal Ruth's body in with boulders and the cracked bark of an enormous tree. Margaret does not help. She is improperly dressed for the low morning temperatures, and it is difficult to move her wrists and fingers. It helps distract her from the thought of returning to the cabin, and what she will find there.

"You can never return here," Chanko says, taking Margaret's wrist in his hand. The calluses on his index finger hurt her skin. If she tries hard, she can pretend that the high-pitched wail rising up around them is nothing more than the wind moving through the pine trees. "Come with me."

Her mother's body is missing by the time Margaret returns to the cabin, exhausted and weak, late that afternoon. Chanko stares at the irregular brown stain where her body lay earlier for a long time, but he says nothing.

"I must bury my mother," Margaret says, when Chanko orders her to collect her clothing and what food and pelts remain from their cabin.

"Someone has already done it for you," he tells her, and falls silent when she insists on being taken to the gravesite. In frustration she raises her musket towards Chanko's chest. She has been a killer once already, after all.

Chanko moves her gun aside with his hand, and tells Margaret, "If you want to survive the winter, gather your things. Now."

Margaret wants the butt of her musket to collide with his face. She wants to run away, run into the forest, and unearth Ruth from the frozen ground. She wants to curse at Chanko, to tell him to go to hell, to tell him that she will never come and live with savage Indians, no matter how much she sees her own dark eyes mirrored in his.

Instead, she gathers her coats from the floor of her room and piles the beaver pelts in the basement into a rusting wheelbarrow. The muscles hugging her spine ache from walking, and grief. Chanko nods in approval when she appears at the front porch, careful not to let emotion show on her face. She had refused to surrender her musket, and its barrel presses against her shoulders, warmed by the heat radiating off her.

Chanko walks into the forest. Margaret follows.

## Part III.

Margaret lives with the Chinook for forty years before she visits her sister again. It is winter once more. The skies are the same silver of the past, but now Margaret is a widow, and the mother of a boy who does not speak English. In the summer, she still swims naked in the creek that runs through their territory, but there is a constant pain in her left knee and a hunger that never entirely leaves her. It is quiet and only resurges in odd moments, when she thinks of her mother, kneeling in prayer before the windowsill, or Ruth, reading by firelight.

By the time Chanko dies—shot by white traders, who flood their lands after gold has been found in their rivers—Margaret is able to speak to him in his own language. She is there when he passes, their fingers interlocked by the bedside.

Margaret prays to St. Joseph, father of Christ, while the Chinook doctor behind her prays to the vast spirits of the mountains that surround them.

"Whatever you do, never let them go," he says, with his last halting breath.

Until now, Margaret has obeyed him.

The trek to the Wailing Hills nearly destroys her left leg. She is limping by the time she reaches Ruth's resting place. Margaret slumps against a boulder, cold air forming frost in her lungs.

For a long time, the landscape is silent. The hills block her from the distant whirr of the Pacific to the west, and the day is too still for the trees to speak in their creaking, secret language.

Margaret feels her spine curl involuntarily, and draws her cloak around her. She looks like an Indian to the whites now. Her hair dangles down in braids to her waist, equal parts black and gray. As a result of cataracts, she is nearly blind in her right eye, but her hearing is sharper than ever—sometimes in the night, Margaret imagines herself to be an owl, listening to field mice padding through the leaves.

Margaret closes her eyes, and thinks she hears a faint screaming, like mist rising from the rocks. She tries to ignore the dead raccoon, cradled between two boulders. There are plenty of scavengers in the caves.

"I'm sorry," Margaret says, to no one.

Only the hills answer her.

*Northwestern Oregon*
*Present Day*

They find the caves on the third day of their hike, and by then, both Steven and his wife are exhausted, mildly arthritic, and smelling vaguely of wet dog. It has been raining for three days. Their backpacks are sagging and heavy, and the shallow caves are the perfect place to dig out their protein bars and eat, watching the droplets gather in the puddles at the cave's entrance.

Later, when the skies clear, they explore the bare, lunar landscape of the hills. Steven finds two femur bones and what is clearly a human molar, tucked away in the rocks.

"I want to go," Anne says, when she sees them, clutching at his sleeve. She is from Chicago, squeamish and uneasy in the wilderness. Last night, they'd heard something passing through the ferns around their tent, and she'd slept the rest of the evening with his army knife clenched in her right hand.

"You know, Indians used to live in this forest," Steven says, pocketing the tooth. He has a young nephew, back in Illinois, who wants a souvenir from Oregon. "One day, American settlers found their colony empty, except for a few fresh corpses.

Smallpox is the official story, but the trappers who found them said it looked like they'd been eaten."

Steven grins at his wife's silhouette in the rain. He loves to make Anne jumpy; sometimes, he makes her lead on the trail just to watch her twist and squirm whenever she walks into a spider web. Steven hunches over, so that shadows fill the hollow spaces beneath his eyebrows. He does his best Boris Karloff impression.

"They say there is a giant bear in these woods. They say it craves human flesh."

Anne hits him on the arm, and laughs. The raindrops on her eyelashes look heavy, and blink on and off like traffic lights.

"Come on," she says, "Let's get out of here."

The rain stops that evening, and the skies fill with the strange, bright light of the western stars. Steven builds a decent fire, and they eat baked beans out of aluminum water cans. They make love to warm their joint sleeping bag, and Steven falls asleep immediately after, snoring in even cycles like a washing machine.

Anne stays awake late into the night, unable to sleep with the constant sighs and exhalations of the animals in the woods around them. She tries her best not to listen to the movement of soft, padded feet around their campsite, or what might be fingers shifting through their food packs.

And when the long, low frequency growl of something hungry approaches their tent, she closes her eyes and pretends to be home, far from the fearsome things living in the forest.

# AS THE CROW FLIES

RITA OAKES

> *"The revenant knows nothing of strategy or tactics. He wakes from death without fear. He marches to no drummer but his own insatiable hunger."*
>
> **Etienne Jean René Feraud**

**Russia, November 28–29, 1812**

*There are forces a man should not have to fight. Not this side of the gates of Hell.* Captain Etienne Feraud, of Emperor Napoleon's 5th Hussars, called his ragged troops to a halt within a small evergreen wood. *Cavalry unhorsed are worse than useless. God has a terrible sense of humor, certainly.*

Lice-ridden, starving, frost-bitten, his men turned faces to him that even now held an unshakable faith—faith in him and faith in their Emperor. *So few and still so trusting.*

They had done all he'd asked. Endured march and fusillade, bayonet and world-shaking artillery, and when in triumph they entered the wondrous capital of the tsars, instead of relaxation and plunder, their reward proved an inferno and the snapping jaws of the hungry dead.

The emperor had passed that very afternoon, leaving the remnants of the finest army on the continent to its wretched fate. With any luck, the dead city of Moscow and its unholy inhabitants had burned entirely to ash in the weeks since the retreat began.

Etienne reached inside his greatcoat and pulled forth a brass spyglass, a gift from his lover before departing for the Russian campaign. *Martin. The tales I might tell you.* But he wouldn't. Even if fortune permitted him to live to see France again he would keep talk of revenants from tainting Martin's sunny nature. Etienne blinked back a wash of sentiment, put the glass to his eye, and peered through the fringe of trees.

The land sloped down to a snaking river. Two makeshift bridges had been thrown across it by General Eblé's pontonniers. The broader of the two, for artillery, had collapsed, and Etienne could make out small figures in the icy water working to repair it. Crowds of soldiers and civilians, mostly on foot but some miraculously retaining their mounts, swelled and surged at the remaining bridge, eager to cross before Cossacks or revenants fell upon them.

"Orders?" Gerard asked, the habitual challenge in his tone.

His elder brother was unquestionably brave, but frequently quarrelsome. Oftentimes cruel, Gerard Feraud had been reduced in rank more than once for insubordination, and Etienne cursed the fate that had forced Gerard into the tatters of his own regiment.

Etienne took the spyglass from his eye, studied Gerard's frost-rimed beard, the wind-burned patches of skin beneath his eyes, the never-quite-absent air of a rabid wolf in his manner.

"Set the watch," Etienne said.

His preference would have been to cross the bridge and camp on the other side of the ice-filled torrent, but it would take all night from the look of things. And footing would be treacherous. He'd lost too many men to relish pitching the rest of them into the water. Better to cross in the morning.

*Provided Cossacks and the revenants do not attack in the night.*

Bent with a bag over one shoulder that bulged with plunder, Gerard nodded curtly and set off to post sentries. As Etienne watched his brother crunch across the ice-crusted snow, he noticed the bag seemed to writhe.

Etienne rubbed gritty eyes with his thumb and forefinger. *What I would not give for a soft bed, a blazing fire, and a full bottle of cognac. And for Martin in sweet dalliance beside me.*

But Martin was thousands of leagues away on a small horse farm in Picardy. Etienne was glad of it—glad that Martin's gentle nature need never witness the brutal waste of thousands of good horses, nor the horror of those who refused to stay dead.

Fires dotted the grounds where men kindled flames with pine boughs for their meager camp. Discipline was holding and the men had not yet resorted to plundering each other—unlike some of the other regiments. The road from Moscow was littered with riches looted from a city now abandoned—gold and jewels gave no warmth, filled no bellies—only served to weigh a man down, step after exhausting step.

They were a far cry from the five hundred thousand enthusiastic men who had crossed the Nieman in the summer.

Etienne moved among the men, asking after this one's frostbitten toes—that one's rasping cough—a pause to remind another of their valorous charge just three months before at the redoubt at Borodino—remarking on the courage of still another in the less glorious but more dangerous recent affair of the revenants in Moscow—a clap upon the shoulder, a word, a memory—reading moods as his thermometer read the falling temperatures—steadying those most likely to break.

And steadying himself in turn. For the sake of his men Etienne kept madness from gnawing its way through the stubborn bone of his skull—kept the nightmares tamped down as thoroughly as tobacco in his broken pipe. On the march he managed better—one foot planted mindlessly before the other. The nights—the nights were different. Too much time to think in darkness.

Etienne circled back to the edge of the wood. Gerard crouched over a merry blaze, roasting a black bird spitted upon his saber. The stench of burnt feathers and roasting meat filled Etienne with nausea.

"What is that?"

"Crow. Froze in mid-flight and fell to earth like a stone at my feet. Lucky." Gerard tore off a chunk of the half raw, half-charred flesh.

Gerard had never been a generous man, especially toward the brother he held in near-contempt, but he offered his bounty with grease-slick fingers. Bound by shared misery, had warmth kindled in his heart after all these years?

"Eat," Gerard said.

Etienne shook his head. Though his last meal—an unsatisfying handful of frozen cabbage stalks, had been hours—perhaps even days ago—the smell and sight—even the thought—of eating meat revolted him. The bitter smell of seared feathers conjured the burning city—the ripping of bone and muscle reminded him of the first victims he'd seen fall to the revenants.

"Eat." Gerard shook the rent fowl at him. The faded sleeve of his uniform was discolored where the chevrons of a sergeant's rank had been removed. Gerard had not volunteered the tale of his most recent disgrace and Etienne had not asked.

"It fell at your feet, not mine," Etienne said. "I'm not hungry."

Gerard's eyes went flat, as if dead. A dangerous look Etienne remembered from childhood. Gerard never liked being spurned. And whatever truce there might have been between them swirled away into spark and ash.

Huddled inside his coat, Etienne turned from the fire, made another circuit of the camp. *I should have accepted the execrable bird. I am supposed to be the polite one.*

When they were boys, Gerard had always been the favored son—in spite of his tempers. High spirited, their maman said, though she would beat either of them with a stout wooden spoon for the slightest transgression. She was too busy running a bustling inn to brook youthful nonsense. Though Etienne tried to be a dutiful son, especially since their soldier father's visits home were all too rare, he could not help but note that the shine of pride in her eyes when her boys were clever or obedient never shone as brightly for her youngest.

Gerard loved little so well as tormenting his younger brother—a pinch, a punch, a horse turd dropped down the collar of his clean shirt. Etienne bore it with puzzled stoicism or the unequal scuffles common between brothers and rivals.

*Now is not the time for nostalgia.*

Etienne returned to Gerard's side. Gerard barely acknowledged him, tossed the stripped clean bones of the crow onto the fire. Etienne settled himself for sleep—close enough to the flames he would not freeze to death in the night—yet not so close the warmth would rouse the lice in his uniform to their maddening quick-march.

He closed his eyes, not truly expecting sleep—he'd managed only light dozes since marching from Moscow—but a little reprieve from the weariness of body and soul he carried as surely as Gerard carried his bag.

*A summer day in boyhood. The brothers were mucking out the inn stable, the air sweet with the smell of horse and hay, straw and dung. Dust motes danced sleepily in a shaft of sunlight at the open door. A fine day, except for Gerard's constant teasing. Etienne had had enough and Fanchon, the stray dog Etienne had patiently tamed with kind words and pilfered table scraps, had had enough, too.*

*She growled, which Gerard found funny, and snarled, which he did not. He launched a kick at her. She dodged, barked a warning Gerard did not heed. Fanchon darted back and nipped him on the calf, which surprised Gerard so much he fell into a pile of fresh horse manure.*

*Etienne laughed.*

*Gerard sprang to his feet, face purple.*

*Etienne braced himself for the inevitable drubbing, but Gerard seized Fanchon instead, throwing her against the stone stable wall with so much force Etienne heard bones snap.*

*Fanchon gave one high-pitched yelp and tried to flee, but her hind legs refused to work.*

*Gerard advanced. He kicked her, time and again, while Etienne pummeled and pulled and shouted for him to stop, but Gerard was older, stronger, and filled with rage.*

*The ostler, a grizzled campaigner who had served with their father, barked an order which pierced Gerard's madness. "Off with you, boy," he said. "You're scaring the horses."*

*Etienne gathered Fanchon in his arms. She licked his hand. The ostler shook his head. "That boy's got the devil in him." He knelt beside Etienne, deftly ran his hands along Fanchon's sides.*

*"Help her," Etienne said.*

*"Nothing I can do for her boy, but end her suffering."*

Etienne opened his eyes. No true sleep had claimed him—only unpleasant memory. Why must he think of Fanchon now? His head ached with weariness and hunger. Shooting pains darted up his legs. His feet spasmed. Etienne rose to walk the cramps out.

His steps crunched in the snow. Muskets stood in regular stacks. A watcher at each campfire huddled in misery, feeding pine boughs to the flames while his comrades slept. The more fortunate wrapped themselves in plundered furs or rugs. Men snored, coughed, broke wind. A sentry stamped his feet and blew upon his hands for warmth, breath clouding white in the icy air.

Etienne's chest tightened. He loved these men and yet he could not save them, any more than he had been able to save Fanchon so long ago.

It lacked an hour of dawn when Etienne returned to his bedroll. Gerard hunched beside his fire, staring into the flames, the ever-present bag at his side. His eyes looked sunken, his cheeks flushed.

"You have not slept," Etienne said.

Gerard shrugged.

The bundle moved as if something squirmed within. For a confusing moment Etienne wondered if Gerard had bagged Fanchon and a litter of unwanted puppies to toss into the river. Etienne blinked.

*Has hunger addled my wits?*

"What is in your bag?" Etienne asked.

"Treasure."

"Show me."

Gerard put a protective hand upon the bag, a sullen expression on his face. "You should have eaten."

"Show me what is in the bag."

Etienne was certain he would disobey—that the ancient dynamic of older brother versus younger might prove stronger than military rank. But Gerard shrugged, untied the bag. "Look for yourself."

Etienne bent to peer inside. Difficult to see in the darkness, so he seized a brand from the fire, held it carefully over the bag. Even with the light it took him a moment to understand what he saw.

Not a writhing mass of puppies. Not a crop of strange, partially furred melons. It was the wrong season for melons. Not cabbages.

Etienne straightened abruptly when the eyes of one opened to reveal a milky stare.

Heads. Severed heads. Heads of revenants, gray-skinned, relentless jaws gnawing at strips of cloth gagging them—presumably to prevent their teeth rending the faces of their tumbled, dead fellows. In spite of himself, Etienne retreated a step, just managing not to trip and end up ingloriously on his backside.

"A curious treasure," Etienne murmured, gratified that his voice remained calm in spite of his startlement. No, not startlement. Fear.

A soldier faced many kinds of fear: the dry-mouthed fear of a cavalry charge, which had the benefit of shared excitement and potential glory; the itching fear of self-doubt and dormant cowardice; the bowel-twisting fear of a surgeon's knife; but this—this was a primitive and solitary fear—that of dark places and slithering things and churning guts gone to water.

He dropped the burning branch back onto the fire. "And what are your plans for this . . . treasure?"

"I shall give them to maman. We'll put them in a vitrine and charge a fee to see them. People will come from leagues around and the inn will prosper." Gerard tied the bag securely.

"You think our mother will enjoy such a gift?"

"She is a practical woman."

*As a soldier's widow must be.*

Before the order to burn the wretched things to ash could pass Etienne's lips, a trooper ran up to them in a state of agitation. "My captain! The pickets report Russians in the trees!"

"Cossacks?"

"Revenants!"

Dawn brightened the wooded gloom. Etienne's men had broken camp and formed up, waiting for orders. They looked as little rested as he felt. Nervous. Tired, hungry men facing an enemy that could not die had a right to be nervous. Through his spyglass, Etienne studied the line of revenants staggering through the trees.

Men. Women. Russians. No few of their own men, who had perished before he'd learned to destroy the brains to prevent their rising. Some were partially burned. All were hideous. All were hungry.

*So much for the hope they had all perished in Moscow.*

Cossacks on sturdy horses darted in and out of the trees at a tantalizing distance in front of the revenants, teasing them with the promise of warm, living meat.

*Luring them to us. Bastards.*

Etienne called a trio of skirmishers to him. "Bring down those horses," he said. "Then fall back toward the river."

"Yes, my captain," they said in unison, saluting smartly in spite of tattered uniforms and skeletal aspects. But for their air of purpose and clear eyes, Etienne would be hard pressed to distinguish them from the revenants themselves.

*Perhaps we are already dead and this is our sojourn in Hell.*

He hated to sacrifice horses, even Russian ones, but they were a bigger target than their riders, and Etienne possessed no sharpshooters. The revenants would fall ravenously on horse and rider. It would buy his men time. The Cossacks would learn to regret their battle tactics.

Etienne ordered the rest of his men out of the wood, down the slope toward the river. He swept his glass over the bridges. The wider bridge had been repaired overnight, but both were littered with bodies of men, horses, abandoned caissons, stranded artillery, and overturned baggage carts. Fires dotted the near bank where stragglers camped.

*Why the hell didn't they cross?*

Perhaps they were discouraged by the congestion he'd seen yesterday when it took hours to move even a few meters. Perhaps, like him, they had decided to wait for daylight: thousands of soldiers—wounded perhaps, or sick—malingering or separated from their regiments—or perhaps remnants of regiments that had almost ceased to exist following battles at Smolensk or Borodino or Moscow. Uniformed Poles, Württembergers, Westphalians, Italians, Dutch, and French formed a polyglot tangle within the Grande Armée. Civilians, too: émigrés, actresses, wives, whores, cantinières, merchants—Etienne had seen them trundling in the wake of the main column, shocked and dispirited and facing an uncertain future. None of them had been able to match the emperor's headlong flight.

And the rumors: The English had taken Paris. Napoleon, dithering uncharacteristically for days in the Kremlin, was ill. He had been bitten, his blood tainted. The emperor was a revenant.

Etienne believed none of it. If the emperor had been a revenant, he would have no reason to flee. And Napoleon feared nothing. More likely he needed to deal with matters of state.

Leaving the rest of them to perform rear guard action. *We die arms in hand.* That was the regimental motto. Never mind that he could muster too few officers and too few NCOs for effective coordination of his squadron. Never mind that they lacked horses, food, and any hope of re-supply.

Although the sun had risen, a scan of the stragglers' camp showed no efforts to rouse themselves and begin the crossing.

At the sound of musket shots, Etienne returned his attention to the wood.

*We can't allow the revenants to cross. The bridges will have to be destroyed.*

Etienne glanced at Gerard. Shadowed eyes lent his visage a skeletal appearance. His face had lost color, except for the stain of fever high on his cheeks.

*He's ill and won't admit it.*

"Go down to the river," Etienne said. "Find out who, if anyone, is in command there. Tell them the stragglers must cross now. Tell them the revenants are in the woods. We will hold here as long as we can."

Gerard flushed. "You seek to deny me my place in battle?"

"I seek a soldier capable of carrying out his orders!"

Gerard hesitated long enough for insolence, and then loped down the hill toward the river, his bag of heads bouncing on one shoulder. Etienne realized that once again he had neglected to order his brother to dispose of the grim trophies.

The skirmishers broke from the trees and raced toward Etienne. "My captain," one said. D'Hubert, his name was, a soldier so young his cheeks bore not even the first fuzz of beard. "The revenants—there are so many. They paused to feed upon the horses, but stripped them to bone in seconds. They will soon be upon us."

Etienne nodded, managed to keep the dismay from his expression. The last thing the men needed was to see him waiver. "Well done," he said.

He trained his glass upon the trees.

*Martin. I would have written you, but I broke up my travel desk for kindling days ago. My words would not have made it past the Emperor's censors, in any case. Nor is it likely I could have kept the ink from freezing.*

A ragged line of revenants lurched from the wood.

"Steady," Etienne told his troops. He formed them in a line three deep. "Courage. Hold the line and hold your fire."

In the course of the retreat, most of his hussars had replaced their shorter carbines with the heavier infantry musket, lifting them from dead or dying unfortunates fallen out on the march. With bayonet fixed, the musket was a formidable weapon, though hardly an accurate one.

Volleys of musket fire, so deadly against massed troops, were not so effective against revenants, impervious to pain or the most catastrophic wounds. Hunger spurred the ravening dead ever onward. That had been Etienne's first lesson in Moscow: to forget what he already knew of war. Though a musket ball to the head would drop a revenant, few soldiers could manage so lucky a shot.

Etienne longed for the feel of a horse between his legs, snorting and bunched and eager to charge. His hussars no doubt felt the same. Fighting on foot lacked the power and dash of all their campaigns before Moscow.

But their horses were dead—of exhaustion and hunger, of shot and ball. A solder must adapt to survive.

"My brave ones," he told the assembled men, "my comrades. We have faced enemies before—and we have been victorious. Many of us may die today—our efforts may not be recorded in any bulletin or journal—our glory may be lost to history. I am proud of you—proud to fight beside you. We make our stand here—the revenants must not cross the river to imperil our beloved empire." Etienne drew his saber, raised it high. "For honor! For France! For our emperor!"

The enthusiastic chorus of "Vive l'empereur!" from his weary men made Etienne's eyes sting and blur. He blinked back tears.

The revenants fell upon them.

The battle raged in near silence. Revenants used no weapons beyond hands and teeth, had no need of breath or battle cry, and did not scream in spite of grievous wounds. They smelled of spoiled meat. For the first time, Etienne was glad of the cold—without it the stench of the revenants would have been much, much worse.

The hussars struck with bayonets, aiming for eye sockets, or the soft bones of nasal passages, or up through the roof of the mouth—anything to destroy a revenant brainpan. The length of an outthrust musket kept the soldier relatively safe from the revenant he'd engaged, though others could swarm and overwhelm him.

The men behind protected against such disaster, using a club, a saber, or sometimes even the butt of his musket to shatter revenant skulls. Etienne witnessed one hussar raise and bring down a medieval mace to deadly effect. He must have looted it from some noble's collection in Moscow.

A musket would fire occasionally, very sharp in the chill air, when bayonet became stuck in bone and tissue. At point blank range, accuracy was no longer a challenge. Once a hussar had fired his weapon, he stepped back to reload and the second and third man in line moved forward.

All along the line, the hussars fought in relay fashion, in continual snakish, writhing movement, while the revenants struggled to climb over the growing pile of their downed fellows.

The hussars grunted, gasped, sometimes cursed. Their breath plumed in frosty air. They were tiring.

And the revenants kept coming.

Etienne risked a glance toward the river. A handful of stragglers had begun crossing the bridge, but the bulk remained in camp as if lost in some sort of torpor.

*What the devil has Gerard been doing all this time? Those people need to cross now!*

He had no time to fret over his brother. The line was wavering. To his right, d'Hubert stumbled and went down before one of the revenants. His comrades were battling others.

Etienne ran to the hussar, kicked the revenant aside, and clove the creature's skull with his saber. He wrenched the blade free, hauled the fallen soldier upright. "Are you bitten?"

Breathless, the young hussar shook his head.

"Carry on."

Another glance toward the river. No sign of Gerard and no movement in the camp.

*Damn them! I'll not sacrifice my men for imbeciles who make no effort to save themselves.*

"Fall back!" he ordered. "Fall back to the bridge!"

They retreated in good order. The number of revenants had thinned. The remaining shambling corpses appeared baffled by the wall of felled dead they must clamber over. A few found their way around the barricade and shambled in slow but relentless pursuit.

*The dead never tire.*

Etienne followed in his troopers' wake, using his blade against the skulls of scattered revenants who drew too close. The saber sliced neatly at first, but repeated use turned it more into a bludgeon than an edged weapon.

More revenants spilled from the woods.

"Cross the bridge! Double quick!" He grabbed the arm of the nearest soldier. "We must set fire to the bridges as soon as we cross. Pitch, oil, gunpowder—anything that will burn—pass the word."

"Yes, my captain."

Etienne maneuvered the men from line to column to cross the nearest and most narrow of the twin bridges. Etienne's attention roved among the closing revenants, the progress of his men, and the still silent camp of stragglers. The revenants were beginning to shift their attention from the hussars to the stragglers' camp.

*They had their chance.* Still, guilt twisted in Etienne like a bayonet.

On closer examination, the bridge proved a precarious thing, only about five meters wide and perhaps a hundred meters long, built of supports which resembled sawhorses, and covered with planks the pontonniers had had no time to secure. Mounds of corpses were heaped upon it: horses trapped when their legs stepped into gaps caused by shifting boards, soldiers felled by musket ball and cannonade, civilians crushed or trodden upon in some prior mêlée. Corpses lay four or six deep, horses, men, women, mashed past all recognition, making it nearly impossible to tell where one body ended and another began, flattened by the tread of so many relentless feet.

The frozen corpses made for grim mortar and uncertain footing, Etienne discovered. The dead beneath his feet were firm, unyielding as wood or stone, but ice-coated and slippery. He fell once, worried more about revenants than patches of frozen blood.

*Careful. Surviving the revenants will do you no good if you slip into the river.*

Etienne sweated with effort, the dampness turning to ice on his face. Adrenaline had carried him through the battle, but the strength it lent was tenuous and fleeting. After the initial shock, a plunge into the waters of the Berezina might prove as pleasant as a tumble into a featherbed.

*I'm so tired.*

*Martin would never forgive me.*

*I can't abandon the regiment.*

Etienne stumbled, nearly fell, but a hand steadied him.

"Lean on me, my captain," d'Hubert said.

The two scrambled the rest of the way across the bridge. Etienne's legs trembled with fatigue. His numbed feet barely registered the step onto frozen marshland.

An anxious glance back revealed no revenant looming behind. The bridge lay empty. Etienne sheathed his saber, pulled the spyglass from his coat. A flock of crows had settled on the pile of slain revenants. Black wings shone darkly in the morning sunlight as they fed. The tide of revenants spilling from the woods had slowed, and turned toward the encamped stragglers, who appeared unaware or uncaring.

Etienne could see no sign of Gerard on the opposite bank. *Where the hell is he?*

"My captain," d'Hubert whispered.

Etienne returned the spyglass to his pocket. "What is it?"

D'Hubert had come to attention.

A general stood before them. General Eblé. Etienne recovered quickly from his surprise, drew himself up, and saluted.

Eblé said, "You are no more than just in time, Captain . . . ?"

"Captain Etienne Feraud, my general, at your service."

Eblé was a handsome man of middle years, clean-shaven, with a slight dimple in his chin. His expressive eyes were bloodshot from lack of sleep.

"Captain Feraud," he said. "You have done well."

"Thank you, my general."

General Eblé offered Etienne a flask. A pleasant warmth spread as Etienne took a swallow of excellent brandy. "Thank you, my general."

Etienne passed the flask to d'Hubert, who hesitated briefly at such impropriety, then took a deep gulp before returning it to the general.

"Fall in with the others," Etienne ordered d'Hubert, who snapped a smart salute and scurried away with seeming relief.

Eblé gazed across the river with a mournful expression. "We must fire the bridges, of course."

"Yes, my general."

"Too many of my boys died building them," Eblé said. "But the army survives and we managed to save some of the artillery."

Etienne scanned his troops to see if Gerard had somehow crossed ahead of them. He had not. *Damn you, Gerard! What will I tell our mother?*

"My general, I request permission to return to the other bank. I gave my brother the task of rousing the stragglers and—"

Eblé gave him a sympathetic clasp upon the shoulder. "Denied. It is too late for that. And the stragglers . . . I tried myself to rouse them earlier. They are stupefied with exhaustion, insensible to their danger as stone. They have given up. We have not that luxury. We must do our duty."

"But my brother—"

"Perhaps he will find another ford down river. I will mention both of you favorably in my report. His name and rank?"

"Gerard Feraud. Private Feraud."

Eblé nodded. "Take your men to Vilna for resupply at the depot there. Good luck to you, Captain. My boys and I will take care of the bridges."

"Understood, my general."

Etienne's men trudged along in column westward toward Vilna. Music should direct the pace—a drummer's tattoo, or a series of marching songs. But they'd lost their drummer long ago and the men were too weary, too hungry, and too dispirited to sing. Etienne followed.

Behind, a great cry rose up from the Berezina, a wail like thousands of tormented souls at their first taste of Hell. Etienne jerked to a halt. He fumbled for his spyglass with icy fingers.

The stragglers were now under full attack. Reinforcements of revenants poured by the hundreds from the woods, joining those thinned by recent battle. Eblé, true to his word, had fired both bridges. Flames surged across the river. Oily smoke smeared the sky.

Galvanized at last, stragglers fought desperately hand to hand. Some raced to the bridges and flung themselves into the conflagration. Still others jumped into the river in a mad attempt to swim across, but the current swept them away.

*This is what Hell looks like. This is what Hell sounds like. Good God.*

Etienne scanned the far bank for Gerard or his bag of severed heads. He could well imagine him attacking the revenants with the same berserker fury he had turned on Fanchon. Weakened by fever, Gerard would quickly grow weary—his opponents never would.

He saw no sign of Gerard. Soon smoke obscured everything.

*I could never forgive you for Fanchon—or for being mother's favorite—but that is no proper death for a hussar. You offered to share with me and I repaid you with—*

"My captain," d'Hubert said.

Startled, Etienne lost his grip on the spyglass. It slipped from his hand. He swore.

"My captain," d'Hubert said again, stooping to retrieve the glass from the frozen earth. "You do not look well." He surrendered the brass tube to Etienne. The lens had cracked.

"None of us look well," Etienne said, returning the broken spyglass to his pocket.

A crow plummeted to earth at their feet. "One for the stew pot," d'Hubert said, brightening as he picked the thing up by its feet.

"No!" Etienne put all the force of years in command into that one word.

Shocked, d'Hubert dropped the bird and stood to strict attention.

"It is a carrion-eater," Etienne said, more gently. "And most likely has eaten of the revenants we have slain. Do you really want to risk putting it in your belly?"

The memory of Gerard offering him a bit of ill-cooked crow flesh made Etienne's empty stomach spasm and yet at the same time, filled him with guilt. Like the space left by an extracted tooth, he probed Gerard's absence, worried at the novelty of it, missed the solid, though painful, physicality of him. *How can I mourn a brother I never loved?*

D'Hubert, too young to dissemble, struggled earnestly with the dilemma of the dead crow. A starving man learns not to be overly particular where food is concerned. Discipline could only stretch so far, Etienne knew.

"Pah!" d'Hubert said at last, and kicked the dead bird aside.

"Good man," Etienne said. He filled his voice with false heartiness. "We shall find more wholesome food in Vilna. It's fifty leagues, as the crow flies." He clapped d'Hubert upon the shoulder and the pair hastened to rejoin the column.

*As the crow flies.*

Blood drained abruptly from Etienne's face. Faithful d'Hubert gripped his arm to prevent Etienne's collapse onto the snow.

*Men who eat bread made with tainted rye sicken and die. Ofttimes they first go mad.*

Might tainted fowl not have the same effect? Could that explain Gerard's failure to rejoin the squadron?

Etienne tried to push the thought away. Gerard had always been half mad. And many of the men were sick: fevers, dysentery, typhus, simple exhaustion. Perhaps Gerard had fallen into the river. Perhaps he had simply deserted. Certainly taking orders from a younger brother chafed him.

Yet the possibility remained that the corruption of the revenants could reside in the guts of a carrion eater. How many soldiers could resist the bounty of a dead bird falling like some dark manna from the sky? Suppose they left the revenants behind in Russia, only to produce new revenants in their very midst?

*How far might a crow actually fly?*

# SENECA FALLS: FIRST RECORDED OUTBREAK OF STRAIN Z

## RECOVERED BY DAYNA INGRAM

*The following, believed to be a chapter excised from her 1898 biography* Eighty Years And More, *was found among Elizabeth Cady Stanton's estate in a file marked: "Incinerate upon my death." Authorities have deemed the document too vital to society's current struggle to destroy.*

Though it was perhaps the most significant chapter in my long and—if I may be so immodest, and certainly at my age I may—quite significant life, still I hesitate to include the truth of those two short days as a chapter in these memoirs. As much as I do not care to admit it, I am frightened. But of what do I have to be frightened? I am an old woman now and the only person I might betray has long ago passed on. She swore me to secrecy that night—more for the one sin than for the other—and I, though the record shall prove it quite contrary to my nature, I have bitten my tongue on this. For her.

All my life I feel as though I have been fighting for her in the only arena I felt equipped to fight: the political arena, the constant struggle for the rights of the marginalized. I am nothing if not a powerful orator, for God blessed me with a voice and a will to speak it and I am afraid I have never been able to turn my back on the Lord's gifts. She, of course, could speak me under the proverbial table, and did on more than one occasion. It was one of the things that made her so beautiful, that stirred up those things in me. She fought for me—for my life if not for my hand. God forgive me, back then I would have traded it all for that kind of fight. A fight of the heart. But she had other, more pressing matters she had to attend to, as you will read.

Despite my fear, I have decided to write it out for you, whoever you are. Whoever would care to read the accounts of an old woman when she was but a young and impassioned fool of a girl, driven by a need for justice and equality, yes, but—but also by something too dark to name. A dark sort of longing, a dark sort of love. Never to be realized, surely, and, I thought, never to be raised up again. But, as I learned during that awful summer night in 1848, the things we thought we'd buried have a way of lurching after us.

## SENECA FALLS: FIRST RECORDED OUTBREAK OF STRAIN Z

• • •

That summer had been the stuff of nightmares, of fevered dreams, of unheard cries in the thick night air. It was the heat that broke us, and the mosquitoes, their relentless bites and buzzing. My husband had thought the country would be relaxing for me; he sent me to our new homestead to fix it up, ready it for our family, enjoy it by myself for a few weeks before the chaos of life returned. But I thrived on the chaos of my family; chasing after my little ones afforded me little time to root around inside my own head, unearthing things that were safer left lost. Alas, the children were with my mother and father, and my husband remained in Boston to tie up some things at work. So there I was, a thirty-three-year-old woman alone on a five-acre homestead in Seneca Falls, New York: a place rich in open air, that was true, and good for the lungs. But painful, painful on the brain. The cravings it brought.

After those initial weeks of ordering around the builders, the housekeepers, the landscapers—anyone who so much as stepped a toe onto my land I tasked with something—after those weeks, word came from my husband that he would be arriving later than expected. Months later, in fact. It seemed to me my fever—always biting at the back of my neck with the mosquitoes—came on stronger the instant I read that telegram. I took to my bed for days. Not even my neighbors could rouse me with their shouts and terrible rows. I was gone to the world, which held me at arms' length until my lonesomeness became a physical thing, knotted up inside my head, my chest. Gone into the arms of the darkness of sleep, which was a comfort preferable even to the sound of my husband's voice. If he were to appear just then, I think I would have throttled him for subjecting me to such loneliness.

Then, a miracle: I received a letter from Mrs. Lucretia Mott informing me of her impending visit. She would be in Seneca Falls for several days on a "political excursion," she termed it, accompanied by her husband and youngest sister, who was nearer my age. Her escorts concerned me little. All I could think was, finally. Finally, a woman with a brain between her ears. A woman who could hold a conversation about something other than crops or the weather turning or how to properly slaughter a goat. Finally, Mrs. Mott, come to save me from myself.

I did not, of course, allow myself to entertain any other thoughts of Lucretia. In fact, I prayed for the strength to let them die, those thoughts. Those memories. I prayed for the strength to greet her when she came as only another woman who shared my abolitionist interests, a woman who was my friend, my intellectual equal, and no more.

But—my strength, my strength, my strength. By the time I met her at the train station, I had no strength to speak of.

It was a sweltering day; the heat lingered in the air in oily waves, creating mirages. Everywhere, you thought you saw puddles along the road, only to come upon them and have them evaporate into dust. I dressed as coolly as my woman's modesty would allow: a skirt of loose fabric to my ankles, powder white blouse unbuttoned at the neck, the sleeves rolled up to reveal a hint of wrist. My hair was tightly pinned, in the fashion of the day, and I wore no hat so as not to trap the heat beneath. My feet sweated in my riding boots, but I wore them in case we decided to walk. Though I had hired a carriage to take me to the train station in Waterloo to meet her, I knew Mrs. Mott was a woman of simple means; she would not go in for anything so extravagant when she had two perfectly good legs to carry her.

I forced myself to think of her only as Mrs. Mott, and to remind myself that her husband would be on her arm today. Yes, on *her* arm, for whenever they linked in that way she was most assuredly in the lead. I remember walking with them from the World Anti-Slavery Convention to our rooms in London eight years ago—a first of many casual strolls—and she seemed to drag him along, his reedy fingers clutching at her elbow, exerting himself to keep up. One day she offered her arm to me. I was so frightened to take it, and abashed at my fear, that I almost laughed. But when I laid my hand on her forearm she clasped it warmly with her other hand and led me gently down the street, until at one point we were holding hands and laughing and practically skipping like school girls through the busy squares of London. I would never forget it.

Her train pulled in a few minutes after noon. The sun was at its highest and all the ladies and gentlemen with good sense were finding reasons to be inside—a shop, a bakery, the station, anything. I sent my driver on with a generous tip and stood on the platform, waving away mosquitoes until I was waving at my three visitors.

The sister, Martha Wright, approached me first, and we embraced warmly. She was, of course, sheathed in layer upon layer of dress, with a bonnet and boots, and yet somehow her youngish face avoided the gleam of the overheated. She kissed my cheek and thanked me for meeting them, and then came the husband. He wore a bright blue suit and vest, tailored to his unusual short height, which I judged to be only a head taller than myself. I didn't even have to tilt my head back to look into his eyes. His smile was generous and spread wide across his shaven face, and he tipped his wide-brimmed hat to me, his hair molded into a perfect silver bowl thanks to some slick oil. I insisted on shaking his hand, which he was ready for and took graciously. Then he stepped aside, and all that remained was Lucretia.

With her, I did have to tilt back my head to see her eyes. The sun caught them and lighted them a brilliant green. Her face, though hardened by the years since I'd last looked upon it, remained soft at the corners of those eyes and around her mouth. Her thin lips pressed together in a closed smile, and I wished they'd open—open, open, open to reveal what was forbidden to me. A curl of brown hair escaped from beneath her bonnet to hang charmingly across her forehead. Her skin was pink and slick with heat. I drew closer to her but she held her gloved hand out to shake mine. I was meant to take this as a sign of respect, so I did.

"Mrs. Stanton, you are so kind to receive us," she said. Her formality did not surprise me, considering the company she kept, but it stung nonetheless. This is meant to be a confession of the truth and so I must hold nothing back. It hurt me deeply, a mortal wound, that she could not even say my name.

"Lucretia," I said her name with as much passion as our audience would allow. She did not even blink. "It's so lovely to see you again." I turned to her family, "To see all of you."

A moment of shared pleasantries, and then Lucretia got down to business: "I'd like to visit the Wesleyan Methodist church in Seneca Falls. I've written the pastor there and he's expecting me this evening."

"Of course. May I ask why?"

"My sister is plotting to change the world," Martha put in with a sisterly leer.

"I dislike that word, 'plotting.'" Lucretia screwed up her face, as if she had just smelled something foul. "I simply wish to put into action all the myriad things you and I, Mrs. Stanton, have so frequently discussed. It is time, it's beyond time, to elevate the voices of women in these United States. I mean to do that, and I know you mean to help me."

Mr. Mott reached out a hand to pat Lucretia's shoulder, saying softly, admiringly, "My darling."

"You know me well, Lucretia," I said. "I'll fetch us a carriage."

"Nonsense," she said, "The day is fine. We'll walk." And she began to lead us in long strides out of the station.

"It's three miles," I argued, though I knew it was futile.

"Lucretia loathes idleness, Mrs. Stanton," Martha said, taking her sister's hand in hers as much to slow her down as to convey companionship. "Makes her feel old."

"I am old," Lucretia said, smiling. She was fifty-five, and looked it, but her spirit was younger than all of us. "And when my body gives out, you can cart me around by any means you like. Until that day, I will walk, and wear my blisters with pride."

All of us laughed, and, laughing, Mr. Mott kissed Mrs. Mott on the forehead and started off in the opposite direction down the heat-heavy street.

"Mr. Mott—" I began to call after him, but Lucretia interrupted: "Mr. Mott will be staying with friends here in Waterloo."

Despite the heat and my lingering fever, I shivered. "But—"

"Just us ladies," Martha said gaily. "Now, wouldn't you like to hear all about my sister's plot to empower all us fine American women?"

Lucretia playfully pinched her sister's arm for her repeated use of the word "plot." As we hiked our way back to Seneca Falls beneath the wrathful eye of the sun, Lucretia spoke at length about an idea to draw up a declaration of women's rights and to hold a democratic convention to debate and vote on the issues. It was her hope that a convention, spread over two days at the Methodist church, would garner attention not only from local newspapers but from papers states away. It would be exactly like the sewing circles where we discussed these issues among ourselves, but the larger scale would spread the message farther and wider. Martha worried that press coverage might not be desirable, as most journalists were certain to paint such a convention as the fanciful flights of "unnatural women," but I disagreed: "Even if the convention is mocked and ridiculed, our ideas will be out there. There will be no danger of the Women Question dying for want of notice." Lucretia smiled at me, then looked at her feet.

We reached Seneca Falls as the sun was setting, the darkening sky streaked a rich crimson. We stepped into a little café whose owner kept it open late in summers, and nourished ourselves with water and sandwiches. It was here Martha decided to wait for us as Lucretia and I went on to speak with the Methodist pastor.

The building was a solid brown brick square with two front-facing windows flanking wide double doors. These were shut against us, locked or barred from the inside as Lucretia tried tugging then pushing with only slight give. I peered into the windows only to be met by a curtained darkness.

"You said the pastor was expecting you."

"That is what I said." Lucretia pulled roughly at the fingertips of her right glove until the thing slipped off. She pounded on the door with her naked fist.

From inside, I heard a low moaning like that of a keening calf. I pressed my ear to the window pane and plugged my other ear with an index finger. The moaning echoed through the hollow belly of the church, vibrating the pane against my cheek. Then suddenly there was a great crash, as a table or perhaps a pew turned over, and the sound of glass shattering, and a man's voice shouting. The moaning grew sharper in pitch then abruptly cut off. Lucretia grabbed my shoulders and pulled me roughly from the window.

"We'll return another night," she said. A knuckle of her de-gloved hand brushed the underside of my chin. My shivers returned. Before she could release me, I clasped my hand around hers, skin to skin, cold and warm at the same time. "Lucretia—"

But there was a loud scraping sound of wood on wood, and something heavy tossed to the ground, and the double doors opened.

An older gentleman—older than Lucretia—stood in the darkened doorway, his white mussed hair standing out against the shadows. As the sun slowly died behind us, it washed his face in a thick orange light, which was creased and worn like an old pair of trousers. His shirt was nearly as wrinkled as his skin, unbuttoned to an absurd degree down his chest, his hair there sticking out in white puffs. One suspender drooped down his left shoulder, and he reached a shaking hand to pull it back into place.

"What do you want?"

"Pastor Simon," Lucretia nodded at him but stepped no closer. "My name is Lucretia Mott. You invited me here through our correspondence. I hope I have not mistaken the date."

The pastor squinted his eyes in puzzlement, then widened them in recognition. "Of course! Oh, my dear lady, forgive me. If I don't write things down, often and in quite conspicuous notice of my face, I forget so easily these days. I'd forget to put on my underpants if it weren't for my wife."

When neither of us laughed at his lewd jest, he shook his head and apologized. He motioned for us to step inside, but as we moved forward, the deep, rattling moan started up again. I saw Pastor Simon's shoulders tense, and he turned to shout into the darkness: "Quiet her! For the Lord's sake, woman, keep her quiet!"

He backed out of the doorway, swinging the doors shut. He turned to us but held the doors closed behind his back. "I must apologize again. I-it isn't a good time. My granddaughter, she's come down with a bad fever, and her mother, my daughter-in-law . . . well, she's her first child and she needs a lot of help to care for her. A lot of help."

"Malaria,"[1] I said. "It's been bad all summer."

He nodded, wiping with his shoulder a bead of sweat that sprouted along his stubbled chin. "If you don't mind, we'll speak out here. The fever . . . it's mighty contagious."

"Of course." Lucretia told the pastor about her intentions for the women's convention, asked when the church might be available to host it, even offered to pay the man a little coin for the use of the place. He graciously refused any remuneration, but hinted strongly that a little goodwill in return for the use of the space would not go unappreciated—a warm dish to eat, a hand-knit sweater for his granddaughter, some light landscaping around the churchyard if the husbands were up to it. Lucretia handled the negotiations and within minutes it was set: in two weeks' time we would hold our first very public women's rights convention here.

On the walk back to the café to fetch Martha, I turned to Lucretia. "Well, that

[1] Strain Z often presents with similar symptoms to malaria, as do Strains V and X. See Appendix IV.

was strange." She made no reply. "Did you not find Pastor Simon's behavior at all strange?"

"I find all behavior strange," Lucretia said, eyes straight ahead on our destination. "Especially male behavior. Sickness is weakness and weakness irritates men because it so intimidates them. Pastor Simon is unused to weakness presenting itself so close to him. He fears it will rub off on him."

"Well, if it's truly that contagious—"

"Illness is a weakness of the body. He—all men—fears a weakness of something greater."

"The mind?" I ventured.

She looked at me. "The heart."

And then we had reached Martha.

Over the following two weeks, I heard nothing from Lucretia. She returned none of my letters. I only knew the convention was still set because it was announced in *The North Star*. It was my own fault she ignored me. I could not blame her. I had pushed things too far.

That very night after we had secured the Methodist Church, Lucretia was in a sullen mood. With the disappearance of the sun, the heat had fizzled down to a mild, not unpleasant warmth. Arriving at my home, all three of us removed our boots and set about soaking our tired feet. Martha attempted to jest with her sister but Lucretia was silent, fully focused on the task of washing her feet. After a light meal, Martha retired to the guest room—my eldest's room, actually, but he would not have use of it for several weeks—and Lucretia and I were left alone.

By candlelight, Lucretia's skin softened and a healthy color returned to her cheeks. I studied her for a while but she took no notice. Lost inside her brilliant mind. How I'd do anything to be allowed to know her thoughts, her innermost secrets and wishes.

I was a young girl, then. I had experienced much yet so little of the world, and I thought I knew everything. I thought I knew what was right and what was wrong, and that I, through sheer willpower, could make right the wrong things.

Eight years ago, Lucretia thought the same.

Having been barred, due to our sex, from the convention proceedings in London, we had had hours to wile away until some man—a husband or a friend or an empathetic stranger—would report to us the day's events. It was during one of these lingering afternoons that the rain kept Lucretia and me indoors, holed up in my room playing cards to avoid the bustle of the overcrowded common area. We had been on the edge of something the entire week; we felt it like something hot passing between us when we looked at each other, when we passed each other without touching, so careful not to touch. But this day, I went to pick up a card, and she put her hand out to pick up one as well. Our fingers met and that sealed it. We both stood, and she planted both hands on the sides of my face, her fingers snagging in my curls. She pulled me to her and kissed me in a manner entirely unbecoming of a married woman, a manner which I quickly copied and which went on for several yearning seconds. Afterwards, she apologized and left the room. From then on I could not get her alone to speak of it. I would allude to it in my letters and she would pretend I had never mentioned it. She erased it. I tried as well. But.

But here we were. Alone.

"May I help you? I have this balm . . . ." When Lucretia did not look up from working her fingers between her toes, I spread a bit of the ointment on my hand and laid it on the arch of her right foot. She jerked slightly but did not pull away. I rubbed her feet in silence.

"That feels nice." Her eyes were closed, the candlelight casting shadows over the bottom half of her face. She had removed her bonnet and her hair hung loosely to her shoulders.

"I've waited," I started, my mouth gone dry around the words. "I've waited so long . . . to touch you again."

"Cady," she said, and my heart quickened. Cady was her private name for me. She had accidentally referred to me as Miss Cady when we first met, before my husband appeared. After that, when we were alone—before the kiss—she would call me Miss Cady, or simply Cady, with a wink and a smile that instantly made her ten years younger.

She said it now not with a smile but with a sigh, and yet it gave my fool heart hope.

"Lucretia, please." I rose from her feet, bending closer to her face. "Please do not deny me. I have been so lonely here. Please."

"Do not beg me."

"Why?" Our faces were a breath away from each other, we barely had to whisper to be heard. I cupped her cheek to my palm and she did not try to stop me. "Why should I not beg you? Because I am a woman and above begging? Because I—"

"Because I would submit." She sounded so tired. "Because I would submit to you."

Just then my neighbor's youngest daughter, a skinny, jittery girl of twelve years, skittered through the back door into my darkening kitchen.

"Mrs. Stanen! Mrs. Stanen!" None of the country children could quite pronounce my name correctly. "Please come, please! Daddy's hurting Momma again!"

"Has he been drinking?" I asked the child.

"A barrel full," she said, one foot out the door. I wished I could be certain she was exaggerating.

"What is it?" Lucretia was already lacing up her boots. I dried my hands on a towel and set to lacing mine as well, explaining as I did: "The Cookes. Large family down the road, father takes to beating the wife when he's fallen gullet first into his cups. I've broken up their rows more times than I can count." I grabbed the rolling pin from the counter on the way out the door.

We raced through the breezy night on the heels of the Cooke daughter, Lucretia keeping pace like a woman half her age. The breeze brought the smell of burning to our noses, and soon enough we could see a deep orange glow against the backdrop of night. The fire was burning uncontrolled in the Cooke's front yard; while it was not entirely unusual for folks to burn their garbage out here—or to cook their freshest kill of deer or slaughtered goat on a spit above a roaring bonfire—this fire was a haphazard thing. Dangerous embers blew this way and that in the wind. Patches of the unkempt lawn were already ablaze. A rocking chair lay a few feet from the primary fire, flames licking up its wooden spine. I sent the Cooke girl to the well. When she was gone, the father emerged from the house, hoisting a nest of blankets above his head which he then chucked at the flames. They smothered half the fire, clearly not the desired effect, so Cooke picked up the rocking chair and threw it on top. The blankets quickly caught fire.

"Mister Cooke, you'll bring your entire house down!" I screamed at him.

He looked in my direction, but his eyes filled with smoke. "It's all tainted," he roared back. "Tainted with sick!"

His wife came out, bloodied in the face, and they began to scream at each other. While his back was turned to me I brought the rolling pin around beneath his chin and pulled him back with both hands and all my strength. Caught off guard, he folded easily, falling to his knees with a grunt and swiping at my arms.

"Calm down, Mister Cooke!" This was not the first time I had pulled Cooke off his wife. There was always a row over one thing or another that needed to be quelled, not just in this household, and for some reason the neighbor children had taken to alerting me whenever this task needed doing. Mayhap I had the biggest rolling pin in town.

He continued to wail about sickness, and his wife sat in the grass and cried. Several of the smaller children appeared in the open doorway of the house, sleepy eyed, their bedclothes soiled. When the Cooke girl ran back into the yard from the well, Lucretia retrieved the bucket from her and dumped the water over Mister Cooke's head, then handed it back to the girl for another round.

The cold shocked Cooke into silence. I tightened the rolling pin against his neck and spoke harshly into his ear. "Now calm down. No squabble is worth burning your house over. Unchecked, your fire may burn the next farm down, and the next. I know that's not what you want, so calm down now, Mister Cooke. Just calm down."

"Why is he so upset?" Lucretia asked Mrs. Cooke.

It took her a moment to pull herself together enough to respond. "The children. The children have been sick. They cry and they want. It's too much wanting for him. He went to hit the littlest one and got bit. That's what brung on the madness."

"Gotta burn it out," Mister Cooke said. "Burn it out."[2]

The girl returned with another pail of water and dumped it over the primary fire. Smoke plumed into the air with a hiss.

We stayed with the Cookes until all the smaller fires were out and the wife had settled the children back into bed. I explained to Mister Cooke that it was the season for fever, and it would burn itself out, as he insisted it do, with a little patience and perhaps some medicine. I promised to return with food and medicine in the morning. All the fight had gone out of him, slumped there in my arms, and so I sent him back inside.

During the short walk back home, Lucretia asked me about the fever, how bad it was here. "Flares up in the hottest months of summer," I told her. "It can lay you up for weeks, months. Even I have a touch of it now."

She held her knuckles to my forehead. "You don't feel warm."

I took her hand and held it in mine. "I can."

She bent her head forward and allowed me one quick, chaste kiss on the place her knuckles had been. "You are a good woman, Elizabeth. I'm certain your husband thinks so too."

And she said not another word to me that night, and in the morning she and Martha were gone.

I sat in a chair at the front of the church, looking at the crowd of forty or so women and a handful of men. We had started later than intended, having arrived at the church hours before only to discover the doors barred against us once again. Eventually, the Smiths' youngest, a spritely lad of no more than six, volunteered to be hoisted through a side window and then unlock the doors for us. We hastily scanned the church proper for Pastor Simon, but every second we delayed the

[2] Before this document surfaced, it was commonly believed that initial discoverers of Strain Z assumed its means of contagion were tactile. Much time was wasted on erroneous preventative measures, such as the burning cleanse illustrated here. For more on this topic, read Dr. Blackthorne's *On Methods of Contagion During the First Zombie Insurgence.*

proceedings was one more second for those assembled to entertain doubts as to the validity of our cause. So we got to it.

I listened to James Mott open our convention for the rights of women. It was only proper etiquette at the time to have a gentleman be the first to address the audience, and Mr. Mott was a decent enough speaker; his voice was soft and coaxing, taking you by the hand to lead you through his words. I waited with bated breath for Lucretia to speak, for she was a powerful orator. When she spoke, she held nothing back; there was something wild inside her, a caged animal that almost escaped on every word, and her listeners clung to the faintest syllable, eager for the animal's release. She kept you waiting and waiting and wanting and wanting.

We had printed up a program for the day, and while Mr. Mott gave a quick summary of the accomplishments of democracy in our free country, I checked the schedule. We had decided, through correspondence filtered by Martha, that James would open the convention, and then Lucretia would speak about the specifics of our goals, and then we would present the Declaration of Sentiments, which she and I seemed to have been working on all our lives, and finally open the floor for debate. I thrived on a good debate. As passionate a speaker as Lucretia was, I was a fierce debater. Counterarguments fell to the ground beneath the sharp slice of my words.

But this first day, we would never get to the debate, though certain accounts claim otherwise. Which is all to the good; I am the first to break our vow. Here is the truth of that day, if you think you can stomach it:

Lucretia was winding down her speech, on the verge of introducing the Sentiments. The sun came in heavy through the windows at the sides of the church, bathing the attendees in a light and warmth that should have weighed them down, but they were buoyed by Lucretia's words. We were all at attention. And so when she abruptly cut off mid-sentence, we held our breath. Then she looked to her left, and I, from my vantage point, looked across the stage. From the back room stepped a little girl, no more than eight or nine, her white dress stained dark by something we could all smell the moment she appeared. It covered her face too, especially around her mouth, but in the forever silence of that moment I would be surprised to learn that any of us thought, "That child is covered in blood."

One of the female attendees in the front row stood up. She made to take a step toward the child, but Lucretia held a stiff arm out to her: stay put. The child's eyes rose to meet Lucretia's, and though I was seated fifteen feet away I could tell there was no light in them. The silence stretched, and the child smiled—*smiled* beneath all that filth, her teeth rotted with the same stuff, she *smiled*—and then emitted a horrible sound, something close to shrieking but more guttural, and she launched herself at Lucretia.

There was no hesitation in Lucretia; she moved her body as surely as she spoke her words. She planted her left leg and brought her right leg around to connect her boot with the child's head. Over the collective gasp of the attendees, over my shout, you could hear the snapping of the skull. The child slumped to the ground as if her shrieking were the only thing keeping her upright, and when Lucretia's kick cut that off the rest of the body followed suit.

I leapt up, instinct pushing me to check on the girl, but Lucretia grabbed me as I attempted to run past. "No," she warned. "She may not be dead."

"Dead?" I could not believe what I was hearing. "Dead? You struck a child, Lucretia! You want her dead?"

By this time others were getting to their feet, shouting and demanding answers. Above this din there came the sound of something else: someone screaming.

Still grasping my shoulders, Lucretia called to her husband, "James, bar the doors!"

He raced to the front of the church, dodging upset attendees with a nimbleness even I haven't known since my youth. He pulled the heavy oak bar through the handles of the double doors. It was slow enough work that someone could have stopped him, but just then the screaming rose and, alongside it, a terrible, rattling moan.[3]

Suddenly, the crowd on the left side of the church swelled outwards. In the center of their scattered ring was one of the little Cooke children, my neighbor. He had latched himself onto the shoulder of Mr. Cooke, who shook him violently with no result. Mrs. Cooke screamed, holding onto her other three children, who cried or looked at the floor. Spittle flew from Mr. Cooke's mouth as he pounded on his son's head, but the jaw was set and the child continued to moan into his father's shoulder in something akin to ecstasy.

The rest was pandemonium. I cannot say exactly how Lucretia and James did it; they moved with such grace, such purpose, as though they had rehearsed. James hooked his arms underneath Cooke's armpits and yanked him back as Lucretia—who had left my side so quickly I had not even realized she had gone—gripped the boy's neck and gave it a sharp, violent twist. His jaw popped loose from his father's arms with a sound like the opening of a pressurized jar. Lucretia dragged the boy by his neck to the right of the stage, where she opened a small broom closet there and tossed him unceremoniously inside. James brought the father, who struggled weakly against him, and threw him in as well. Then they closed the door and cast around for something with which to bar it.

[3] The pre-attack moan described here has only been recorded in cases of Strain Z infection. For more on strain differentiation, see Appendix IX.

Shock had gripped the attendees like paralysis. Plenty of mouths flapped but no legs moved. Women who'd brought their children held them tighter and wept, and women who'd brought their men allowed themselves to be held. A young lad towards the back had gotten up and made for the door, but suddenly Martha Wright was there, holding him off with no more than the unsympathetic look in her eye.

Finally, James found a brass candlestick to shove through the door handle of the broom closet. When he got it in place, pounding started up inside and Cooke called out to be released. His wife, hearing him, started toward the closet, wailing.

"You can't do this to him!" She cried, dragging her children with her. "What are you doing to him?"

"Please," James began in his soft tones.

"You must sit down," Lucretia demanded. "All of you, sit down. Everything will be explained. Sit down."

Even in the midst of chaos her voice had power, and some sat. James had to cajole the wife a little more to get her to sit with her children, the eldest daughter helping James, whispering soothing things into her mother's ear.

Like all the rest I was shocked. But not paralyzed. I had it in my head that I would flee. Whatever was happening here I did not want to see it. I did not want to see Lucretia, whom I'd never even witnessed smack down a fly, callously strike children and rip them so violently away from their parents. I could not, in those wild moments, think of what the children had done to warrant their fate. I could not think of the blood, or the sounds they made, or the pale, stony look of their small, blank eyes.

I stumbled backwards into something and tripped. It was the little girl in the white dress; I'd tripped over her prone body, landing bottom first on her small thighs. The stink coming off her was awful; it reminded me of the smell of a freshly slaughtered pig. Hand to my nostrils, I bent to examine her, to help her, and she jerked up. My heart caught in my throat as her ruined face shot toward me; I do not think I had time even to yell. But someone else's hand was quicker, catching the girl under her chin and flinging her back so forcefully that her already damaged skull cracked hard against the floor. Then those hands were on me, pressed against the sides of my shaking cheeks, and I was looking into a woman's eyes, and it was Lucretia.

"Cady," she said. "Cady. Did she bite you? Tell me—oh, Lord, please tell me!—did she bite you?"

I think I made a sound, something like a whimper or a bleat, and then all I remember is a welcoming darkness as my body invited me to black out and I, with proper feminine grace, accepted.

• • •

Waking up was something of a dream. The soft light of the setting sun peeked through the half-shuttered windows of the pastor's office. The fogginess of my recent unconsciousness had not quite left me, and the haze of my vision combined with the light made Lucretia's features as she worked diligently to undress me appear absolutely angelic. She gently untucked my blouse from the waistband of my ankle-length skirt. Her other hand swirled a bit of rag in a small porcelain water dish near my elbow. She began to unfasten my buttons. I allowed her to undo all but the final two over my chest before I grew nervous.

I cleared my throat. "Lucretia—"

She drew her hands away from my breasts. "Try not to move too quickly."

I was sprawled atop the pastor's modest wooden desk. Lucretia supported me by my shoulders as I sat up. As blood rushed back into my brain and my wits returned, so too did the images of the horror I'd just witnessed in the church. My hands began to shake with the memory, and Lucretia held them between her own, her palms damp with water from the washbasin.

"Tell me it was all a hallucination." I could not bring myself to look into her eyes, into the eyes of someone who could hurt a child. "Tell me I am going mad, please. You could never do what I have seen you do."

"Madness would be a simpler explanation," she said. "But a false one."

She wiped her thumb across my cheek, and as my pulse quickened I turned my face from hers.

"Elizabeth, I must examine you for bites."

"Bites? What sort of bites?" I could only think of mosquitoes. "Do you think— Was it malaria? That fevered girl—?"

"It's no fever,"[4] Lucretia said. Her fingers went to my final two fastened buttons. "It is an infection. That unfortunate child had it, and the Cooke child as well. And now the father is infected. The disease is spread through a transmission of bodily fluids. One bite—the saliva of the infected introduced into the veins of the victim—is all it takes."

She spoke low but sternly, inviting no debate, while her fingers brushed the skin along my breastbone, inviting goose pimples. My blouse slipped down my shoulders and I arched my back, a reflex that once I realized I had done it I was too embarrassed to undo. Lucretia placed a gentle hand between my shoulder blades and slowly ran the fingers of her other hand underneath my

---

[4] This assessment is not entirely correct. Mrs. Mott's discussion of the disease on the following pages is also flawed. For a more comprehensive understanding, see Dr. Heinrich's *The Anatomy of Strain Z.*

undergarments. It was here that I gave serious consideration to the idea that this "bite examination" might be pretense, but I was certainly not going to deny Lucretia her pleasure.

"What," I forced my tongue, gone dry, to move. "What does it do? The infection."

"First, it kills you. It attacks your organs, beginning with your heart." Lucretia's hand rested against the flesh covering my own heart. Her eyes found mine, that unnatural green vibrating with purpose. "Once it has shut down your body, it reanimates your corpse."

I gasped, raising my chest against her palm, and she turned to the washbasin as she continued. "That girl you encountered out there—I'm positive she is the pastor's granddaughter." She brought the moistened rag to wipe away a crimson spot on my collarbone—a droplet of the granddaughter's stained spittle, most like. "When we first met Pastor Simon and heard his granddaughter's wail, I feared she might have been succumbing to the illness. But this is the Devil's disease,[5] and if anyone would be spared, I thought, certainly it would be the granddaughter of a man of God." She dropped the bloody rag into the washbasin and pulled my blouse back over my shoulders. "I was foolish to hope such things. The Devil's disease spares no one."

She began to refasten my buttons. I asked, "Where are Pastor Simon and his family?

"I've locked them in the basement." She ran her hands down the length of my skirt, checking for rips or tears the size of a little girl's teeth. "I fear they are all sombies now."

I bent forward and caught her wrist at my knee. "Sombies?"

She pulled away from me and continued her skirt check. When she reached my ankles, she moved her hands beneath my hem and felt the flesh there. "Somnambulists. Walkers through the repose of death. The shortening to 'sombie' was a crude jest of one ancestor or another, but it persevered."[6]

Slowly, she walked her fingers over the flesh of my calves, circling every inch at least twice as she moved up toward my knees. I closed my eyes and shivered through the heat.

"How do you . . . " My breath caught in my chest as her fingers found the sensitive skin at the back of my knees. "How do you know all this?"

"My family belongs to a secret order of sombie quellers."

I could not stop my breath from coming in rapid, shallow bursts as her hands

---

[5] This is the first recorded supposition that Strain Z's origins may be supernatural. For a full list of origin theories, see Appendix II.

[6] This is the only known document which refers to the infected as "sombies." For a deeper etymological exploration, see Dr. Vidal's *Etymology of the Undead*.

crested my knees and skimmed over my thighs. My breath catches even now, writing this some forty years later, and I am tempted to embellish the truth. Alas, her hands stopped abruptly. I opened my eyes to watch her pull the hem back to my ankles and settle it prudently.

"The Mott family are quellers as well. Our history with the Devil's disease dates back centuries."[7] She patted my leg as though I were a treasured pet and she my doting grandmother. "No bites," she said.

She moved away from me and all my heat went with her. I pushed myself up from the pastor's desk to stand beside it. "If the disease dates back centuries, that means there is no cure."

"No." She took the tainted wash water to the window to release it, but encountered some difficulty opening the pane and so left the dish on the sill. She sighed heavily and turned back to me. "There are no preventative measures either. Once a person is bitten, they are already dead. When they reanimate as a sombie, it is important for you to understand that what you are seeing—the thing that looks like a person and walks like a person and hungers like a person—that thing is only a corpse. Do you understand, Elizabeth? You cannot kill a sombie. You only de-animate it. Understand?"

"Yes." I swallowed hard, thinking of the pastor's granddaughter, the viscera lacing her chin. "I think so."

Lucretia stepped toward me and gripped my upper arm. My breathing quickened again and I brought my hand to her bare neck. She did not stop me, but stared me down with her emerald eyes, asking, "Can you do it?"

"Oh, yes," I said, leaning into her. My lips barely grazed hers before she stiffened her arm and held me at bay.

"No, Cady. De-animate a sombie. Can you do that?"

Sighing, I leaned further into her, resting my forehead against her chin because, in my distraught state, she was finally allowing me to touch her. "Lucretia. I do believe I have gone mad."

One finger beneath my chin, she titled my head up to look at her. "And I with you," she said. Her breath was hot against me, her mouth so close I could fight against it no longer. I brought my mouth to hers and kissed her. When she did not resist me, I opened our mouths and gave her my tongue and kissed her as deeply as my shame would allow.

After a time—an oasis of bliss amongst the terrors behind and awaiting us—Lucretia broke our kiss and stepped away from me. She retrieved a thick disciplinary

---

[7] Unfortunately, neither the Motts nor the Coffins kept written records of their "sombie queller" heritage.

paddle that hung on one wall of the Pastor's office and handed it to me. "Will you help me, Cady?"

Her taste was fresh inside me, and tasting her, I wanted more. Taking the paddle, I could think of only one thing standing between us. "Wouldn't you prefer your husband?"

"He has an entire congregation to keep calm." She took up one of the tall brass candleholders that sat near the door and tested its weight by slapping it several times against her palm. "I think we drew the longer straw on this one."

It was rare to hear such a jest from her, at least lately. I hefted the paddle. "What do I do?"

"Stay behind me. Sombies are slow but do not let them get too close; if they can smell you, their hunger quickens and so do their reflexes."

"You keep saying that, about their hunger. For what do they hunger?"

Lucretia reached out and with one hand fastened a button near my neck that she had missed. "Your flesh."

She tore her eyes from me and cleared her throat, heading toward a door at the back of the Pastor's office. "You can break as many bones as you like," she said over her shoulder. "But the sombies will not stop moving until you take out their brains." She threw open the door to the darkened basement staircase. "Aim for their skulls."

The stench reached us first—the granddaughter's slaughterhouse odor tenfold. I put my arm around my face and breathed into my elbow as I followed Lucretia's descent down the staircase. There was a scuffling some yards away from us in the darkness and a symphony of low moans started up the instant our feet hit the basement's dirt floor. I clutched at Lucretia's back, on the verge of shouting that we should go back up for a candle, but Lucretia was ahead of me. Deftly, she turned and struck a match against the rough edge of my disciplinary paddle. The match head was a pinprick of light until she threw it out into the darkness and it caught in the soiled rags of the thing that used to be Pastor Simon.

He was on his knees in the dirt—I saw quickly that his kneeling was not in prayer but rather due in large part to his vivid lack of either calf. The match's flame licked along the lapel of his torn shirt. As I watched it dance up his torso toward his gaping, black hole of a mouth, another pinprick of light flew against him, and another, until he was engulfed. Strangely, his moaning remained steady, a yearning rather than a wail of pain.

"Here they come," Lucretia said.

And come they did.

By the wavering light of the burning pastor, I followed the slow progression of three shadows further back into the basement until they revealed themselves as the shambling forms of the pastor's unfortunate family: An older woman, the pastor's wife, whose face was half gone, replaced by pulsating fly larvae; and her adult children, the man moving with sure strides on his supposedly dead legs, the only indications of his corpsehood being the loss of an arm that had been messily amputated at the shoulder and a fist-sized hole bored straight through his neck; his wife, the pastor's daughter-in-law, was more pieces than wholes; it looked as though rats—or perhaps her own forsaken daughter—had gnawed at every exposed bit of flesh.

The son moved ahead of the others, taking no care to avoid stepping over his aflame father, who writhed miserably in the dirt. The son's trouser leg caught fire but this, too, did not slow him down. When he was within striking distance of Lucretia, she brought the brass candlestick down a fraction of a second too late. It glanced off his left ear and smacked down onto his shoulder; I heard the bone splinter and saw the blood spurt, but the sombie son did not even recoil. He held his arms out for Lucretia and bared his dripping teeth at her. She wound up for another shot, but I saw the pastor's wife closing in on her flank.

"On your right!" I shouted to her, and moved in to block the son's path. I swung low to take him out at the knees, but misaimed and found his hip. This tripped him up slightly but he did not fall; his moan renewed itself.

Somewhere behind me, I heard the thwack of Lucretia's candleholder against soft flesh and decaying bone. I swiped again for the son's knees and to my astonishment he sidestepped me. Then his hands were gripping my shoulders and his moan was directly against my ear, the smell of death striking me like a physical thing.

In a panic, I threw my elbow up and connected with his jaw, which clacked and splintered. I swatted at his head with the paddle, connecting a few times until his grip on me loosened enough so I could stumble back. My ankle began to burn, and I looked to see a hand of flame curling around my flesh.

Pastor Simon had managed to crawl his way into my fray. Furiously, I stamped on his arm, as if trying to put him out. The arm broke off at the elbow and I was able to rip free. I backed up a pace but he continued to pull himself forward on his remaining arm.

I wanted to shout for Lucretia but she was somewhere in the shadows, grappling with the wife and daughter; I could hear her candleholder thwacking, a reassuring sound in the near-darkness. I will confess—for near the end of one's life is the time for confessions—that I not only thought about fleeing from that basement but took several steps toward that end. The son caught me, however, and clamped his injured jaw upon my shoulder, but could not summon the pressure enough to break my skin. A few well-placed whacks with the paddle, punctuated by my own hoarse screams, and the son finally fell. I did not stop whacking his head until there was no head left to whack.

The flames had nearly died away upon the Pastor's back. He was nearly a skeleton, his moaning died out too, as he struggled, even then, to pull his bones across the floor. I brought the paddle down edgewise and severed his skull from his neck. The final flame whiffed out and I was sheathed in darkness. I listened for Lucretia's thwacking but was met with silence: no grunting, no scuffling, no moaning.[8]

Backing toward the staircase, I called for her. Nothing. I held the paddle out before me, prepared to start swinging wildly, and backed up until my heels met the bottom stair. I turned to ascend, too cowardly to wait or to search, but something pulled against my elbow and I sliced the paddle through the air. It slapped hard against Lucretia's palm as she caught it. A little light from the office upstairs revealed only one side of Lucretia's face, slick with a sombie's excretions, one emerald eye gone dark. She frightened me then, more than any walking corpse.

"It's finished," she said.

We ran up the stairs and locked the door behind us. Lucretia held me tightly as I struggled to control my breathing. Repeatedly I closed my eyes against the things I had just seen, the things I had just done. I dropped the paddle on the floor.

"You do this," I said, forcing myself to look at her dirtied face. "You do this so easily."

She wiped some of the horror off onto her sleeve. "Why do you assume because I do it well that it is easy?"

I felt the gunk smeared across my own face. "Lucretia, I . . . I don't think I can do this again. Mister Cooke is my neighbor. He's not altogether a bad man, only uneducated and poorly—"

"James can handle the Cookes." She leveled her eyes at me and instantly they softened. "You were braver today than I have ever seen you. I would not ask any more of you today."

"And tomorrow?" I wiped my thumb across her bottom lip, which trembled beneath my touch. "What will you ask of me tomorrow?"

She leaned closer, but stopped herself. "Cady. Your husband."

I pushed away from her, exasperated. "You hide behind him like a shield. What of *your* husband?"

"James and I have an arrangement," she said. "We married out of familial obligation. We are, neither one of us, bound to the other."

---

[8] A live-action dramatization of this struggle has been created as an invaluable resource for learning basic combat techniques when defending oneself against a Strain Z zombie (Caution: certain techniques displayed here will not work against Strain V's or W's). A link to the download code can be found in Appendix X.

I smiled and reached for her. "All settled then."

She held me back. "Cady—"

"Do you think I want to hurt my husband? I do love him, do not mistake me. Only . . . only he is not here. And I . . . I . . . I am so *hungry*."

We were pressed together again, and her mouth was almost mine, but just then the office door creaked open and Martha strode into the room. Lucretia spun away from me as if I were aflame.

"Sorry to interrupt," Martha said unapologetically. She looked at Lucretia. "Pastor Simon?" Lucretia gave a curt nod. "Good. We need your help out here. The Cooke wife is insisting we release her husband and son, and everyone is restless to leave. James can't convince them alone. We need both of you."

Lucretia nodded again and followed Martha out of the office. Wearily, I stooped to retrieve the well-used disciplinary paddle and left the office as well.

In the spirit of confession, I must tell you I have paused in my retelling to pour myself a glass of brandy. A tall glass. All that I have recounted to you here is nothing in comparison to what I must now put to paper for the first time. Not to belittle the lost lives of the Simons, or the horrible sin Lucretia and I perpetuated in that basement, but what we allowed to become of the Cookes . . . . Lucretia would say—and did say then—that it was an unfortunate but necessary sacrifice. She spoke a lot about sacrifices that night. I did not possess the constitution to argue against her then—in anything—but I worry now. Will I be denied the Kingdom for my sins that night? In the fight against the Devil's disease, are all sins forgiven? Or is it just your poor luck—your pitiable fate—to fall into such a mess and be forced to choose between Eternal Life and "sacrifices"?

I'll take you back there now.

Night had fallen and the great room of the church proper was lit by candles and oil lamps. Someone had covered Granddaughter Simon's body with their coat. James Mott had explained the sombie situation to the assemblage. Things were mostly quiet as groups formed to talk amongst themselves, weigh the options, convince each other this was not some sort of collectively experienced nightmare. But towards the front of the church, near the broom closet, the Cooke wife was causing a stir, shouting and crying that she needed her husband, that he was hurt and her son was sick, and what right had we to detain him. Lucretia and James put their heads together in secrecy while Martha went back to guarding the exit doors with her steely glare and I held Mrs. Cooke's arm, patting and cooing at her as if she were a distressed bird.

Finally, Lucretia turned to face the assemblage and stamped her foot for silence. The crowd shifted to face her, and then the hall grew silent, save for the intermittent sobs of Mrs. Cooke and the rhythmic thumping of her husband's body against the broom closet door.

"Ladies and Gentlemen," Lucretia began, unaware of or ignoring the absurdity of such a formal address in this situation. "Friends. I fully understand and appreciate how difficult it must be for you to digest all that you have been told about what you have just witnessed. It is devastating, and in that devastation it is all too tempting to doubt the explanation you have been given. To fight against the stark truth of what decency now commands you to do. Decency, you think, has fled this place, hand in hand with your sanity. But I stand here begging you to believe in this fight. To believe in the sombie threat. And above all, to believe that what I do now, I do for your safety. I do out of the strongest sense of decency, out of the strongest love I have for you and for this country."

Lucretia approached Mrs. Cooke and held out her hand. "Mrs. Cooke," she said. "If you refuse to believe that your husband is lost to the living world, then I shall take you to him."

Mrs. Cooke gasped back tears and, nodding furiously, took Lucretia's hand and followed her to the broom closet door. Stirs of protests and questions rose like a swelling tide amongst the crowd, and James attempted to quell them with his soft, even tones and soothing eyes.

I raced after Lucretia and stayed her arm. "What are you doing?"

"The people must see the threat," she said. "They must not be able to misconstrue it or excuse it away as madness or a dream. It is unfortunate, Cady, it is. But it is a necessary sacrifice. If you wish to be absolved of this, then look away, and be assured there was nothing you could do to stop me."

"My husband! My son!" Wailed Mrs. Cooke. "Let me see them! Let me in!"

And so Lucretia let her in, or rather, she let Mister Cooke and his young son out. I watched Mrs. Cooke's face light up for the reunion, and fall and cringe and turn ugly with regret and pain when Cooke descended upon her. A cacophony of screams rose up from the crowd behind me, and I tore my eyes from the cannibalistic reunion, and ran, hands pressed tightly over my ears, to huddle between the far wall and a boxy piano. I stayed that way for a long time. When finally I let my hands fall away from my ears, Lucretia was speechifying again, with assists from Mr. Mott. They were convincing the congregation that it was vital they witness Mrs. Cooke's dismemberment and consequential transformation so they could no longer deny the severity and immediacy of the sombie threat. They were asking permission to "put down" the Cooke family. They were not asking it directly, or taking votes, but the question was implicit. And all of us who turned our faces away and fled to far corners, all of us who wept for the remaining Cooke children who wept for their dying or dead parents and brother, all of us who kept our arms at our sides and our tongues in our mouths—all of us indulged in the sin of complicity that night.

There was a resurgence of the sombie moan that was becoming all too familiar, and then a series of blunt strikes, and one by one the moans cut off. Murmurs and sobs undulated through the crowd. Finally, Lucretia came and knelt before me.

"I'm sorry, Cady." She tried to lift my chin to look at her but I refused. "I'm sorry you had to see who I truly am."

I heard her telling the assemblage that James would take the bodies into the churchyard to burn. She argued the importance of discretion, briefly recalling, by way of example, some incident in Philadelphia with a Mr. Valdemar which a dreary poet, a Mr. Woe or Poe or some such, kindly painted as a work of fiction. I heard her then tell the congregation about the warning signs of a sombie infection, but how she believed it was now contained, and if they should find that it was not, she prayed they would have the heart and the decency to quell it themselves.[9]

And then I heard her say: "As tragic as tonight has been, the tragedy would be ever worsened if we were to leave here forgetting the impetus for our union in the first place. We joined together tonight not out of desire but out of the deepest of human need: the need for what is right."

I was drawn out of hiding by the subtle change in Lucretia's voice, from commanding to near-pleading. I stood across from her, the distance clogged by the attentive bodies of our humble congregation. Although throughout her impromptu speech she never once made eye contact with me, I knew the truth of her words were meant only for my ears. Ostensibly, she spoke about the rights of women and the importance of keeping the sombie threat a secret lest it incite unchecked panic; but something stirred within me and I knew, undoubtedly, she was truly speaking of her passion for me—her *need* for me.

Lucretia continued: "Can you weigh our fight for civil liberties against the fight for liberation from the sombie threat? One must, if it is to exist at all, exist in the open, unfettered by our fears and reservations of usurping tradition or emasculating our male counterparts. The other, if we as a species are to exist at all, must be dealt with through discreet means, through a terrible grace relying on strength and sacrifice. We can accomplish both of these things here tonight.

"You who have witnessed what I have done for you this night—you will say, it came at the cost of moral degradation. But I will say to you there is already a kind of moral stagnation in this country. There is . . . there is . . . "

[9] The next instance of Strain Z in the United States was not recorded until 1874 in Vermont.

She seemed to cast about for some great metaphor that eluded her. Cautiously, I raised my voice and offered: "There is war, slavery, drunkenness, licentiousness, and gluttony." Lucretia looked at me with appreciation, and my voice swelled. "All of these . . . these abominations and deformities have been brought fully into the light, yet with idiotic laughter we hug those monsters to our breasts and rush on to destruction. Our churches are multiplying on all sides. Our missionary societies, Sunday schools, and prayer meetings and innumerable charitable and reform organizations are all in operation. But still the tide of vice is swelling, and threatens the destruction of everything, and the battlements of righteousness are weak against the raging elements of sin and death."

"The world waits the coming of some new element," Lucretia took up the charge. As she and I spoke in turns, we moved towards each other through the pews, looking into the eyes of each member of the assemblage as we strode forth. "Some purifying power, some spirit of mercy and love."

"The voice of woman has been silenced in the state, the church, and the home," I said, "but man cannot fulfill his destiny alone. He cannot redeem his race unaided."

"There are deep and tender chords of sympathy and love in the hearts of the downfallen and oppressed that woman can touch more skillfully than man." Lucretia said. "There are evils more dire that walk among God's kingdom than man knows how to handle. You have seen me handle this evil tonight. You have seen what a woman is willing to do—what a woman must do—to secure safety and justice for everyone."

"I have seen what a woman must do," I said, and this time I spoke directly to Lucretia, and she listened. "I have seen her fight with her full heart for what she knows to be right, and in so fighting, I have seen her suffering. Only when she allowed her heart to surrender—to surrender to decency, to surrender to hope—did her suffering ebb. Lucretia Mott—tonight you have shown us all the power and the passion of a woman when she is fighting for her love—of civil rights."

We now stood an arm's length apart from each other, and though Lucretia kept her arms at her sides, she reached across that space with her smile. She said, "We do not expect our path will be strewn with the flowers of popular applause—"

She paused here to allow the audience a hard-earned laugh. I nodded at her hidden meaning and took up her smile. Facing the congregation, I concluded our speech, saying, "But over the thorns of bigotry and prejudice will be our way. And on our banners will beat the dark storm clouds of opposition from those who have entrenched themselves behind the stormy bulwarks of custom and authority, and who have fortified their position by every means, holy and unholy. But we will steadfastly abide the result. Unmoved we will bear it aloft. Undauntedly we will unfurl it to the gale. For we know that the storm cannot rend from it a shred, that the electric flash will but more clearly show to us the glorious words inscribed upon it: Equality of Rights."

There was some applause, and then much discussion of how we would discreetly handle all that had transpired this night. Our friend Mister Douglass of *The North Star* agreed to report nothing out of the ordinary in tomorrow's early edition. Everyone vowed their silence on the matter, and the Cooke children were remanded to a kindly older couple who promised to seek out their next of kin. Most everyone agreed they would return on the morrow for the proper convention, feigning as if they had already experienced a full day of proceedings, and bringing with them many family and acquaintances who were unable—much to their good fortune—to attend this evening.

Much later that night, after the plans had been planned and the plots had been plotted, I met with Lucretia Mott in a secluded location under the cover of darkness. She swore many things to me, and I to her. But I shall stop here, for I have already given up too many of the lady's secrets.

# PEGLEG AND PADDY SAVE THE WORLD

## JONATHAN MABERRY

I know what you've heard, but Pat O'Leary's cow didn't have nothing to do with it. Not like they said in the papers. The way them reporters put it, you'd have thought the damn cow was playing with matches. I mean, sure, it started in the cowshed, but that cow was long dead by that point, and really it was Pat himself who lit it. I helped him do it. And that meteor shower some folks talked about—you see, that happened beforehand. It didn't start the fire, either, but it sure as hell *caused* it.

You have to understand what the West Side of Chicago was like back then. Pat had a nice little place on DeKoven Street—just enough land to grow some spuds and raise a few chickens. The cow was a skinny old milker, and she was of that age where her milk was too sour and her beef would probably be too tough. Pat O'Leary wanted to sell her to some drovers who were looking to lay down some jerky for a drive down to Abilene, but the missus would have none of it.

"Elsie's like one of the family!" Catherine protested. "Aunt Sophie gave her to me when she was just a heifer."

I knew Pat had to bite his tongue not to ask if Catherine meant when the cow was a heifer or when Sophie was. By that point in their marriage Pat's tongue was crisscrossed with healed-over bite marks.

Catherine finished up by saying, "Selling that cow'd be like selling Aunt Sophie herself off by the pound."

Over whiskey that night, Pat confided in me that if he could find a buyer for Sophie, he'd love to sell the old bitch. "She eats twice as much as the damn cow and don't smell half as good."

I agreed and we drank on it. Shame the way she went. The cow, I mean. I wouldn't wish that on a three-legged dog. As for Sophie . . . well, I guess in a way I feel sorry for her, too. And for the rest of them that went to meet their maker that night, the ones who perished in the fire . . . and the ones who died before.

The fire started Sunday night, but the problem started way sooner, just past midnight on a hot Tuesday morning. That was a strange autumn. Drier than it should have been, and with a steady wind that you'd have thought blew straight in off a desert. I never saw anything like it except the Santa Anas, but this was Illinois, not California. Father Callahan had a grand ol' time with it, saying that it was the hot breath of Hell blowing hard on all us sinners. Yeah, yeah, whatever, but we wasn't sinning any worse that year than we had the year before and the year before that. Conner O'Malley was still sneaking into the Daleys' back door every Saturday night, the Kennedy twins were still stealing hogs, and Pat and I were still making cheap whiskey and selling it in premium bottles to the pubs who sold it to travelers heading west. No reason Hell should have breathed any harder that year than any other.

What was different that year was not what we sinners were doing but what those saints were up to, 'cause we had shooting stars every night for a week. The good father had something to say about that, too. It was the flaming sword of St. Michael and his lot, reminding us of why we were tossed out of Eden. That man could make a hellfire and brimstone sermon out of a field full of fuzzy bunnies, I swear to God.

On the first night there was just a handful of little ones, like Chinese fireworks way out over Lake Michigan. But the second night there was a big ball of light—Biela's Comet, the reporter from the *Tribune* called it—and it just burst apart up there and balls of fire came araining down everywhere.

Paddy and I were up at the still and we were trying to sort out how to make Mean-Dog Mulligan pay the six months' worth of whiskey fees he owed us. Mean-Dog was a man who earned his nickname and he was bigger than both of us put together, so when we came asking for our cash and he told us to piss off, we did. We only said anything out loud about it when we were a good six blocks from his place.

"We've got to sort him out," I told Paddy, "or everyone'll take a cue from him and then where will we be?"

Pat was feeling low. Mean-Dog had smacked him around a bit, just for show, and my poor lad was in the doldrums. His wife was pretty but she was a nag; her aunt Sophie was more terrifying than the red Indians who still haunted some of these woods, and Mean-Dog Mulligan was turning us into laughingstocks. Pat wanted to brood, and brooding over a still of fresh whiskey at least took some of the sting out. It was after our fourth cup that we saw the comet.

Now, I've seen comets before. I seen them out at sea before I lost my leg, and I seen 'em out over the plains when I was running with the Scobie gang. I know what they look like, but this one was just a bit different. It was green, for one thing. Comets don't burn green, not any I've seen or heard about. This one was a sickly green, too, the color of bad liver, and it scorched a path through the air. Most of it burned up in the sky, and that's a good thing, but one piece of it came down hard by the edge of the lake, right smack down next to Aunt Sophie's cottage.

Pat and I were sitting out in our lean-to in a stand of pines, drinking toasts in honor of Mean-Dog developing a wasting sickness, when the green thing came burning down out of the sky and smacked into the ground not fifty feet from

Sophie's place. There was a sound like fifty cannons firing all at once, and the shock rolled up the hill to where we sat. Knocked both of us off our stools and tipped over the still.

"Pegleg!" Pat Paddy yelled as he landed on his ass. "The brew!"

I lunged for the barrel and caught it before it tilted too far, but a gallon of it splashed me in the face and half-drowned me. That's just a comment, not a complaint. I steadied the pot as I stood up. My clothes were soaked with whiskey, but I was too shocked to even suck my shirttails. I stood staring down the slope. Sophie's cottage still stood, but it was surrounded by towering flames. Green flames—and that wasn't the whiskey talking. There were real green flames licking at the night, catching the grass, burning the trees that edged her property line.

"That's Sophie's place," I said.

He wiped his face and squinted through the smoke. "Yeah, sure is."

"She's about to catch fire."

He belched. "If I'm lucky."

I grinned at him. It was easy to see his point. Except for Catherine there was nobody alive who could stand Aunt Sophie. She was fat and foul, and you couldn't please her if you handed her a deed to a gold mine. Not even Father Callahan liked her, and he was sort of required to by license.

We stood there and watched as the green fire crept along the garden path toward her door. "Suppose we should go down there and kind of rescue her, like," I suggested.

He bent and picked up a tin cup, dipped it in the barrel, drank a slug, and handed it to me. "I suppose."

"Catherine will be mighty upset if we let her burn."

"I expect."

We could hear her screaming then as she finally realized that Father Callahan's hellfire had come aknocking. Considering her evil ways, she probably thought that's just what it was, and had it been, not even she could have found fault with the reasoning.

"Come on," Pat finally said, tugging on my sleeve, "I guess we'd better haul her fat ass outta there or I'll never hear the end of it from the wife."

"Be the Christian thing to do," I agreed; though, truth to tell, we didn't so much as hustle down the slope to her place as sort of saunter.

That's what saved our lives in the end, 'cause we were still only halfway down when the second piece of the comet hit. This time it hit her cottage fair and square.

It was like the fist of God—if His fist was ever green, mind—punching down from Heaven and smashing right through her roof. The whole house just flew apart, the roof blew off, the windows turned to glittery dust, and the log walls splintered into matchwood. The force of it was so strong that it just plain sucked the air out of the fire, like blowing out a candle.

Patrick started running about then, and since he has two legs and I got this peg, I followed along as best I could. Took us maybe ten minutes to get all the way down there.

By that time, Sophie Kilpatrick was deader'n a doornail.

We stopped outside the jagged edge of what had been her north wall and stared at her just lying there amid the wreckage. Her bed was smashed flat, the legs broken; the dresser and rocker were in pieces, all the crockery in fragments. In the midst of it, still wearing her white nightgown and bonnet, was Sophie, her arms and legs spread like a starfish, her mouth open like a bass, her goggling eyes staring straight up at Heaven in the most accusing sort of way.

We exchanged a look and crept inside.

"She looks dead," he said.

"Of course she's dead, Pat; a comet done just fell on her."

The fire was out but there was still a bit of green glow coming off her and we crept closer still.

"What in tarnation is that?"

"Dunno," I said. There were bits and pieces of green rock scattered around her, and they glowed like they had a light inside. Kind of pulsed in a way, like a slow heartbeat. Sophie was dusted with glowing green powder. It was on her gown and her hands and her face. A little piece of the rock pulsed inside her mouth, like she'd gasped it in as it all happened.

"What's that green stuff?"

"Must be that comet they been talking about in the papers. Biela's Comet, they been calling it."

"Why'd it fall on Sophie?"

"Well, Paddy, I don't think it *meant* to."

He grunted as he stared down at her. The green pulsing of the rock made it seem like she was breathing, and a couple of times he bent close to make sure.

"Damn," he said after he checked the third time, "I didn't think she'd ever die. Didn't think she could!"

"God kills everything," I said, quoting one of Father Callahan's cheerier observations. "Shame it didn't fall on Mean-Dog Mulligan."

"Yeah, but I thought Sophie was too damn ornery to die. Besides, I always figured the Devil'd do anything he could to keep her alive."

I looked at him. "Why's that?"

"He wouldn't want the competition. You know she ain't going to Heaven, and down in Hell . . . well, she'll be bossing around old Scratch and his demons before her body is even cold in the grave. Ain't nobody could be as persistently disagreeable as Aunt Sophie."

"Amen to that," I said, and sucked some whiskey out of my sleeve. Paddy noticed what I was doing and asked for a taste. I held my arm out to him. "So . . . what do you think we should do?"

Pat looked around. The fire was out, but the house was a ruin. "We can't leave her out here."

"We can call the constable," I suggested. "Except that we both smell like whiskey."

"I think we should take her up to the house, Peg."

I stared at him. "To the house? She weighs nigh on half a ton."

"She can't be more than three hundred-weight. Catherine will kill me if I leave her out here to get gnawed on by every creature in the woods. She always says I was too hard on Sophie, too mean to her. She sees me bringing Sophie's body home, sees how I cared enough to do that for her only living aunt, then she'll think better of me."

"Oh, man . . . " I complained, but Pat was adamant. Besides, when he was in his cups, Paddy complained that Catherine was not being very "wifely" lately. I think he was hoping that this would somehow charm him back onto Catherine's side of the bed. Mind you, Paddy was as drunk as a lord, so this made sense to him, and I was damn near pickled, so it more or less made sense to me, too. Father Callahan could have gotten a month's worth of hellfire sermons on the dangers of hard liquor out of the way Pat and I handled this affair. Of course, Father Callahan's dead now, so there's that.

Anyway, we wound up doing as Pat said and we near busted our guts picking up Sophie and slumping her onto a wheelbarrow. We dusted off the green stuff as best we could, but we forgot about the piece in her mouth and the action of dumping her on the 'barrow must have made that glowing green chunk slide right down her gullet. If we'd been a lot less drunk we'd have wondered about that, because on some level I was pretty sure I heard her swallow that chunk, but since she was dead and we were grunting and cursing trying to lift her, and it couldn't be real *anyway*, I didn't comment on it. All I did once she was loaded was peer at her for a second to see if that great big bosom of hers was rising and falling—which it wasn't—and then I took another suck on my sleeve.

It took nearly two hours to haul her fat ass up the hill and through the streets and down to Paddy's little place on DeKoven Street. All the time I found myself looking queer at Sophie. I hadn't liked that sound, that gulping sound, even if I wasn't sober or ballsy enough to say anything to Pat. It made me wonder, though, about that glowing green piece of comet. What the hell was that stuff, and where'd it come from? It weren't nothing normal, that's for sure.

We stood out in the street for a bit with Paddy just staring at his own front door, mopping sweat from his face, careful of the bruises from Mean-Dog. "I can't bring her in like this," he said, "it wouldn't be right."

"Let's put her in the cowshed," I suggested. "Lay her out on the straw and then we can fetch the doctor. Let him pronounce her dead all legal-like."

For some reason that sounded sensible to both of us, so that's what we did. Neither of us could bear to try and lift her again, so we tipped over the 'barrow and let her tumble out.

"Ooof!" she said.

"Excuse me," Pat said, and then we both froze.

He looked at me, and I looked at him, and we both looked at Aunt Sophie. My throat was suddenly as dry as an empty shot glass.

Paddy's face looked like he'd seen a ghost, and we were both wondering if that's what we'd just seen, in fact. We crouched over her, me still holding the arms of the 'barrow, him holding one of Sophie's wrists.

"Tell me if you feel a pulse, Paddy my lad," I whispered.

"Not a single thump," he said.

"Then did you hear her say 'ooof' or some suchlike?"

"I'd be lying if I said I didn't."

"Lying's not always a sin," I observed.

He dropped her wrist, then looked at the pale green dust on his hands—the glow had faded—and wiped his palms on his coveralls.

"Is she dead or isn't she?" I asked.

He bent, and with great reluctance pressed his ear to her chest. He listened for a long time. "There's no ghost of a heartbeat," he said.

"Be using a different word now, will ya?"

Pat nodded. "There's no heartbeat. No breath, nothing."

"Then she's dead?"

"Aye."

"But she made a sound."

Pat straightened, then snapped his fingers. "It's the death rattle," he said. "Sure and that's it. The dead exhaling a last breath."

"She's been dead these two hours and more. What's she been waiting for?"

He thought about that. "It was the stone. The green stone—it lodged in her throat and blocked the air. We must have dislodged it when we dumped her out, and that last breath came out. Just late, is all."

I was beginning to sober up and that didn't have the ring of logic it would have had an hour ago.

We stood over her for another five minutes, but Aunt Sophie just lay there, dead as can be.

"I got to go tell Catherine," Pat said eventually. "She's going to be in a state. You'd better scram. She'll know what we've been about."

"She'll know anyway. You smell as bad as I do."

"But Sophie smells worse," he said, and that was the truth of it.

So I scampered and he went in to break his wife's heart. I wasn't halfway down the street before I heard her scream.

I didn't come back until Thursday, and as I came up the street smoking my pipe, Paddy came rushing around the side of the house. I swear he was wearing the same overalls and looked like he hadn't washed or anything. The bruises had faded to the color of a rotten eggplant, but his lip was less swollen. He grabbed me by the wrist and fair wrenched my arm out dragging me back to the shed, but before he opened the door, he stopped and looked me square in the eye.

"You got to promise me to keep a secret, Pegleg."

"I always keep your secrets," I lied, and he knew I was lying.

"No, you have to really keep this one. Swear by the baby Jesus."

Paddy was borderline religious, so asking me to swear by anything holy was a big thing for him. The only other time he'd done it was right before he showed me the whiskey still.

"Okay, Paddy, I swear by the baby Jesus and His Holy Mother, too."

He stared at me for a moment before nodding; then he turned and looked up and down the alley as if all the world was leaning out to hear whatever Patrick O'Leary had to say. All I saw was a cat sitting on a stack of building bricks, distractedly licking his bollocks. In a big whisper, Paddy said, "Something's happened to Sophie."

I blinked at him a few times. "Of course something's happened to her, you daft bugger; a comet fell on her head and killed her."

He was shaking his head before I was even finished. "No . . . *since* then."

That's not a great way to ease into a conversation about the dead. "What?"

He fished a key out of his pocket, which is when I noticed the shiny new chain and padlock on the cowshed door. It must have cost Pat a week's worth of whiskey sales to buy that thing.

"Did Mean-Dog pay us now?"

Pat snorted. "He'd as soon kick me as pay us a penny of what he owes."

I nodded at the chain. "You afraid someone's going to steal her body?"

He gave me the funniest look. "I'm not afraid of anybody breaking *in.*"

Which is another of those things that don't sound good when someone says it before entering a room with a dead body in it.

He unlocked the lock; then he reached down to where his shillelagh leaned against the frame. It was made from a whopping great piece of oak root, all twisted and polished, the handle wrapped with leather.

"What's going on now, Paddy?" I asked, starting to back away, and remembering a dozen other things that needed doing. Like running and hiding and getting drunk.

"I think it was that green stuff from the comet," Paddy whispered as he slowly pushed open the door. "It did something to her. Something *unnatural.*"

"Everything about Sophie was unnatural," I reminded him.

The door swung inward with a creak and the light of day shone into the cowshed. It was ten feet wide by twenty feet deep, with a wooden rail, a manger, stalls for two cows—though Paddy only owned just the one. The scrawny milk cow Catherine doted on was lying on her side in the middle of the floor.

I mean to say what was *left* of her was lying on the floor. I tried to scream, but all that came out of my whiskey-raw throat was a crooked little screech.

The cow had been torn to pieces. Blood and gobs of meat littered the floor, and there were more splashes of blood on the wall. And right there in the middle of all that muck, sitting like the queen of all damnation, was Aunt Sophie. Her fat face and throat were covered with blood. Her cotton gown was torn and streaked with cow shit and gore. Flies buzzed around her and crawled on her face.

Aunt Sophie was gnawing on what looked like half a cow liver, and when the sunlight fell across her from the open door, she raised her head and looked right at us. Her skin was as gray-pale as the maggots that wriggled through little rips in her skin, but it was her eyes that took all the starch out of my knees. They were dry and milky, but the pupils glowed an unnatural green, just like the piece of comet that had slid down her gullet.

"Oh . . . lordy-lordy-save a sinner!" I heard someone say in an old woman's voice, and then realized that it was I speaking.

Aunt Sophie lunged at us. All of sudden she went from sitting there like a fat dead slob eating Paddy's cow to coming at us like a charging bull. I shrieked. I'm not proud; I'll admit it.

If it hadn't been for the length of chain Paddy had wound around her waist she'd have had me, too, 'cause I could no more move from where I was frozen than I could make leprechauns fly out of my bottom. Sophie's lunge was jerked to a stop with her yellow teeth not a foot from my throat.

Paddy stepped past me and raised the club. If Sophie saw it, or cared, she didn't show it.

"Get back, you fat sow!" he yelled, and took to thumping her about the face and shoulders, which did no noticeable good.

"Paddy, my dear," I croaked, "I think I've soiled myself."

Paddy stepped back, his face running sweat. "No, that's her you smell. It's too hot in this shed. She's coming up ripe." He pulled me farther back and we watched as Sophie snapped the air in our direction for a whole minute, then she lost interest and went back to gnawing on the cow.

"What's happened to her?"

"She's dead," he said.

"She can't be. I've seen dead folks before, lad, and she's a bit too spry."

He shook his head. "I checked and I checked. I even stuck her with the pitchfork. Just experimental-like, and I got them tines all the way in, but she didn't bleed."

"But . . . but . . . "

"Catherine came out here, too. Before Sophie woke back up, I mean. She took it hard and didn't want to hear about comets or nothing like that. She thinks we poisoned her with our whiskey."

"It's strong, I'll admit, but it's more likely to kill a person than make the dead wake back up again."

"I told her that and she commenced to hit me, and she hits as hard as Mean-Dog. She had a good handful of my hair and was swatting me a good un when Sophie just woke up."

"How'd Catherine take that?"

"Well, she took it poorly, the lass. At first she tried to comfort Sophie, but when the old bitch tried to bite her Catherine seemed to cool a bit toward her aunt. It wasn't until after Sophie tore the throat out of the cow that Catherine seemed to question whether Sophie was really her aunt or more of an old acquaintance of the family."

"What'd she say?"

"It's not what she said so much as it was her hitting Sophie in the back of the head with a shovel."

"That'll do 'er."

"It dropped Sophie for a while and I hustled out and bought some chain and locks. By the time I came back, Catherine was in a complete state. Sophie kept waking up, you see, and she had to clout her a fair few times to keep her tractable."

"So where's the missus now?"

"Abed. Seems she's discovered the medicinal qualities of our whiskey."

"I've been saying it for years."

He nodded and we stood there, watching Sophie eat the cow.

"So, Paddy, me old mate," I said softly, "what do you think we should do?"

"With Sophie?"

"Aye."

Paddy's bruised faced took on the one expression I would have thought impossible under the circumstances. He smiled. A great big smile that was every bit as hungry and nasty as Aunt Sophie.

It took three days of sweet talk and charm, of sweat-soaked promises and cajoling, but we finally got him to come to Paddy's cowshed. And then there he was, the Mean-Dog himself, all six-and-a-half feet of him, flanked by Killer Muldoon and Razor Riley, the three of them standing in Paddy's yard late on Sunday afternoon.

My head was ringing from a courtesy smacking Mean-Dog had given me when I'd come to his office, and Pat's lips were puffed out again, but Paddy was still smiling.

"So, lads," Mean-Dog said quietly, "tell me again why I'm here in a yard that smells of pigshit instead of at home drinking a beer."

"Cowshit," Paddy corrected him, and got a clout for it.

"We have a new business partner, Mr. Mulligan," I said. "And she told us that we can't provide no more whiskey until you and she settle accounts."

"*She*? You're working with a woman?" His voice was filled with contempt. "Who's this woman, then? Sounds like she has more mouth than she can use."

"You might be saying that," Pat agreed softly. "It's my Aunt Sophie."

I have to admit, that did give even Mean-Dog a moment's pause. There are Cherokee war parties that would go twenty miles out of their way not to cross Sophie. And that was *before* the comet.

"Sophie Kilpatrick, eh?" He looked at his two bruisers. Neither of them knew her and they weren't impressed. "Where is she?"

"In the cowshed," Pat said. "She said she wanted to meet somewhere quiet."

"Shrewd," Mean-Dog agreed, but he was still uncertain. "Lads, go in and ask Miss Sophie to come out."

The two goons shrugged and went into the shed as I inched my way toward the side alley. Pat held his ground and I don't know whether it was all the clouting 'round the head he'd been getting, or the latest batch of whiskey, or maybe he'd just reached the bottom of his own cup and couldn't take no more from anyone, but Paddy O'Leary stood there grinning at Mean-Dog as the two big men opened the shed door and went in.

Pat hadn't left a light on in there and it was a cloudy day. The goons had to feel their way in the dark. When they commenced screaming, I figured they'd found their way to Sophie. This was Sunday by now, and the cow was long gone. Sophie was feeling a mite peckish.

Mean-Dog jumped back from the doorway and dragged out his pistol with one hand and took a handful of Pat's shirt with the other. "What the hell's happening? Who's in there?"

"Just Aunt Sophie," Paddy said, and actually held his hand to God as he said it.

Mean-Dog shoved him aside and kicked open the door. That was his first mistake, because Razor Riley's head smacked him right in the face. Mean-Dog staggered back and then stood there in dumb shock as his leg-breaker's head bounced to the ground right at his feet. Riley's face wore an expression of profound shock.

"What?" Mean-Dog asked, as if anything Pat or I could say would be an adequate answer to that.

The second mistake Mean-Dog made was to get mad and go charging into the shed. We watched him enter and we both jumped as he fired two quick shots, then another, and another.

I don't know, even to this day, whether one of those shots clipped her chain or whether Sophie was even stronger than we thought she was, but a second later Mean-Dog came barreling out of the cowshed, running at full tilt, with Sophie Kilpatrick howling after him, trailing six feet of chain. She was covered in blood and the sound she made would have made a banshee take a vow of silence. They were gone down the alley in a heartbeat, and Pat and I stood there in shock for a moment, then we peered around the edge of the door into the shed.

The lower half of Razor Riley lay just about where the cow had been. Killer Muldoon was all in one piece, but there were pieces missing from him, if you follow. Sophie had her way with him and he lay dead as a mullet, his throat torn out and his blood pooled around him.

"Oh, lordy," I said. "This is bad for us, Paddy. This is jail, and skinny fellows like you and me have to wear petticoats in prison."

But there was a strange light in his eyes. Not a glowing green light—which was a comfort—but not a nice light, either. He looked down at the bodies and then over his shoulder in the direction where Sophie and Mean-Dog had vanished. He licked his bruised lips and said, "You know, Pegleg . . . there are other sonsabitches who owe us money."

"Those are bad thoughts you're having, Paddy my dear."

"I'm not saying we feed them to Sophie. But if we let it get known, so to speak. Maybe show them what's left of these lads . . . "

"Patrick O'Leary, you listen to me—we are not about being criminal masterminds here. I'm not half as smart as a fence post and you're not half as smart as me, so let's not be planning anything extravagant."

Which is when Mean-Dog Mulligan came screaming *back* into Paddy's yard. God only knows what twisted puzzle-path he took through the neighborhood, but there he was, running back toward us, his arms bleeding from a couple of bites and his big legs pumping to keep him just ahead of Sophie.

"Oh dear," Pat said in a voice that made it clear that his plan still had a few bugs to be sorted out.

"Shovel!" I said, and lunged for the one Catherine had used on her aunt. Paddy grabbed a pickaxe and we swung at the same time.

I hit Sophie fair and square in the face and the shock of it rang all the way up my arms and shivered the tool right out of my hands, but the force of the blow had its way with her and her green eyes were instantly blank. She stopped dead in her tracks and then pitched backward to measure her length on the ground.

Paddy's swing had a different effect. The big spike of the pickaxe caught Mean-Dog square in the center of the chest and, though everyone said the man had no heart, Pat and his pickaxe begged to differ. The gangster's last word was "Urk!" and he fell backward, as dead as Riley and Muldoon.

"Quick!" I said, and we fetched the broken length of chain from the shed and wound it about Sophie, pinning her arms to her body and then snugging it all with the padlock. While Pat was checking the lock I fetched the wheelbarrow, and we grunted and cursed some more as we got her onto it.

"We have to hide the bodies," I said, and Pat, too stunned to speak, just nodded. He grabbed Mean-Dog's heels and dragged him into the shed while I played a quick game of football with Razor Riley's head. Soon the three toughs were hidden in the shed. Pat closed it and we locked the door.

That left Sophie sprawled on the 'barrow, and she was already starting to show signs of waking up.

"Sweet suffering Jesus!" I yelled. "Let's get her into the hills. We can chain her to a tree by the still until we figure out what to do."

"What about them?" Pat said, jerking a thumb at the shed.

"They're not going anywhere."

We took the safest route that we could manage quickly, and if anyone did see us hauling a fat, blood-covered, struggling dead woman in chains out of town in a wheelbarrow, it never made it into an official report. We chained her to a stout oak and then hurried back. It was already dark and we were scared and exhausted and I wanted a drink so badly I could cry.

"I had a jug in the shed," Pat whispered as we crept back into his yard.

"Then consider me on the wagon, lad."

"Don't be daft. There's nothing in there that can hurt us now. And we have to decide what to do with those lads."

"God . . . this is the sort of thing that could make the mother of Jesus eat meat on Friday."

He unlocked the door and we went inside, careful not to step in blood, careful not to look at the bodies. I lit his small lantern and we closed the door so we could drink for a bit and sort things out.

After we'd both had a few pulls on the bottle, I said, "Pat, now be honest, my lad . . . you didn't think this through, now did you?"

"It worked out differently in my head." He took a drink.

"How's that?"

"Mean-Dog got scared of us and paid us, and then everyone else heard about Sophie and got scared of us, too."

"Even though she was chained up in a cowshed?"

"Well, she got out, didn't she?"

"Was that part of the plan?"

"Not as such."

"So, in the plan we just scared people with a dead fat woman in a shed."

"It sounds better when it's only a thought."

"Most things do." We toasted on that.

Mean-Dog Mulligan said, "Ooof."

"Oh dear," I said, the jug halfway to my mouth.

We both turned and there he was, Mean-Dog himself with a pickaxe in his chest and no blood left in him, struggling to sit up. Next to him, Killer Muldoon was starting to twitch. Mean-Dog looked at us, and his eyes were already glowing green.

"Was this part of the plan, then?" I whispered.

Paddy said "Eeep!" which was all he could manage.

That's how the whole lantern thing started, you see. It was never the cow, 'cause the cow was long dead by then. It was Patrick who grabbed the lantern and threw it, screaming all the while, right at Mean-Dog Mulligan.

I grabbed Pat by the shoulder and dragged him out of the shed and we slammed the door and leaned on it while Patrick fumbled the lock and chain into place.

It was another plan we hadn't thought all the way through. The shed didn't have a cow anymore, but it had plenty of straw. It fair burst into flame. We staggered back from it and then stood in his yard, feeling the hot wind blow past us, watching as the breeze blew the fire across the alley. Oddly, Paddy's house never burned down, and Catherine slept through the whole thing.

It was about nine p.m. when it started, and by midnight the fire had spread all the way across the south branch of the river. We watched the business district burn—and with it, all of the bars that bought our whiskey.

Maybe God was tired of our shenanigans, or maybe he had a little pity left for poor fools, but sometime after midnight it started to rain. They said later that if it hadn't rained, then all of Chicago would have burned. As it was, it was only half the town. The church burned down, though, and Father Callahan was roasted like a Christmas goose. Sure and the Lord had His mysterious ways.

Two other things burned up that night. Our still and Aunt Sophie. All we ever found was her skeleton and the chains wrapped around the burned stump of the oak. On the ground between her charred feet was a small lump of green rock. Neither one of us dared touch it. We just dug a hole and swatted it in with the shovel, covered it over and fled. As far as I know, it's still up there to this day.

When I think of what would have happened if we'd followed through with Pat's plan . . . or if Mean-Dog and Muldoon had gotten out and bitten someone else—who knows how fast it could have spread, or how far? It also tends to make my knees knock when I think of how many other pieces of that green comet must have fallen . . . and where those stones are. Just thinking about it's enough to make a man want to take a drink.

I would like to say that Paddy and I changed our ways after that night, that we never rebuilt the still and never took nor sold another drop of whiskey. But that would be lying, and as we both know, I never like to tell a lie.

# DEAD IN THE WATER

## RICHARD LARSON

The *Mary Celeste* was dead, but by then I was used to dead things. My lovely Elizabeth had been sketched by a street artist against the backdrop of New York Harbor, only weeks before the cough, the fever, the long night cast in shadow—the sketch which I kept now in my pocket for nights when cheap whiskey forced memories I preferred not to confront by the light of day. And Elizabeth would have insisted I stay back and recover, but I would rather burn our bed than sleep in it without her. So I took a job onboard replacing a cook taken suddenly ill, anxious to leave land behind, and something about the *Mary Celeste* made me feel at home, the way a ghost feels at home in the place where he died.

We shared a kinship early on—the way she ambled listlessly through the harbor between ships still clinging to life, ships still imagining a future in a sea where everything hasn't already been found, claimed, and plundered. For me it was all gone, and I knew that the *Mary Celeste*, too, rode the black waves, in need of neither food nor drink, sleep nor sun. Someone else with a history of unfortunate collisions. I didn't want to live, but I also knew it wasn't a choice anymore. And I saw the change, first in Captain Briggs and then the others: the way their skin changed colors overnight, growing sallow and jaundiced, then curdling like milk left in the sun. After that they kept to the darkness of the *Mary Celeste*'s cabin, the slow churning of the angry sea a call back to some ancient rhythm, some kind of shambling, a constant starving for something none of us had ever tasted.

We've tasted it now. On a ship already cursed to kill its captains, Briggs never really had a chance, but he took out two others—biting at their faces, ripping open arteries in their necks with his own mouth—before Richardson took him down, sank him in the sea after tying him to a temporary anchor. But then Richardson, too. I kicked him overboard myself, yet still he thrashed even after death, clawing his way down to the sea gods. I took the lifeboat as the others scrambled after me, falling uselessly from the deck like prisoners walking a plank. But I know *she'll* catch me. I see her back there, loping through the choppy waters, always hungry—my Elizabeth, too, hungry to the last, long after the fever claimed her, her teeth still grinding together even through all the bindings I used to keep her down. She bit me, once. And it's been slow to get to me, maybe because so much of me was already dead, but I feel it claiming me now, the *Mary Celeste* herself just biding time back there in less treacherous waters, hungry for anything that might be left behind.

For the dead are slow, but they always catch up.

# STARVATION ARMY

## JOE McKINNEY

From the window of his abominably small second-story room, Jonathan Nettle could see the alleyway where he'd found the body earlier that morning. He'd stumbled on the corpse by accident, while he was wandering the huge, unending slum of London's East End, looking for the homeless shelter on the Mile End Road where he was to take up his new post as assistant minister. He'd smelled the noisome stench moments before he came across the homeless man's body, and he'd spun on his heel and vomited all over the sidewalk when he saw the black, iridescent flies swarming around the mouth and eyes. After that, he'd stumbled out of the alleyway and grabbed the first policeman he saw. He babbled and pointed and grunted until, at last, he made himself understood enough for the policeman to follow him.

The policeman looked at the body, at the bruise-like splotches on the skin that weren't bruises, but lividity, at the emaciated, rail-skinny arms and legs, and merely nodded.

"Yer an American, ain't ye, sir?"

"Huh?" Nettle said, the back of his hand against his lips. "Uh, yes."

"What are ye doin' here in the East End?"

Nettle told him he was looking for the homeless shelter, and the policeman merely nodded. "The peg house yer lookin' for is over there," he said, and pointed over Nettle's shoulder.

Nettle could barely take his eyes off the body, but he did long enough to see the tumbledown, soot-stained building the policeman pointed out for him. He looked back at the policeman—at the bobby, he reminded himself—and said, "What . . . happened to him?"

"This bloke? Prob'ly starved to death'd be my guess, sir."

"Starved?"

"Aye," the bobby said.

Nettle had said nothing to that, only nodded as he tried to take in the wonder that a grown man could starve to death in the middle of the largest city on Earth, in the heart of the most powerful empire the world had ever known. He tried, but couldn't wrap his mind around it.

His stay was supposed to be brief, only long enough for him to get some experience with the great things William Booth and his "salvation army" were doing for the poor here in London, so he could take those practices back to his Methodist ministries in New York and Boston. But he could already tell that the "problem of the poor" that such great orators as the Reverend Merle Cary of New York had spoken of so eloquently to audiences up and down the New England seaboard all that preceding summer of 1875 was far worse than he had been led to believe.

Just then, almost as if on cue, several men began lugging bags of garbage out of the hospital across the street and dumping them on the sidewalk below Nettle's window. The bags split open on the ground and soon there was an almost liquid pile of corruption festering in the open air. Nettle watched the pile grow into a shapeless mass of rotten vegetables, scraps of meat, orange peels, and bloody surgical rags and blankets. The street was a miasma of squabbling and obscene yelling and fighting, and yet no one said a word about the garbage. Indeed, after it had been sitting there for a few minutes, children converged on it, burying their arms in it up to their shoulders, digging for any kind of food they could find and devouring it on the spot.

One boy, a stunted little runt of perhaps six years old, came up with something black that might have once been a potato, and tried to steal away with it. Several older boys surrounded him, punched him until he fell, then kicked him until he gave up the nasty potato thing he clutched near his groin.

For Nettle, it was too much. His sister Anna had snuck a dozen oranges into his luggage as a treat for him. Fully aware that indiscriminate charity is cruel, he made up his mind to be cruel. He collected the oranges in a paper sack and went down to the street.

"How old are you, son?" he asked the boy.

"Twelve, sir," the boy said.

Nettle blinked in shock. Twelve! And he had envisioned the boy a runt of six. *How this place must beat them down,* he thought.

He handed the boy the oranges, and the boy's eyes went wide, like he'd just been given all the jewels in Africa.

"Go on," Nettle said. "Enjoy."

The boy was gone faster than the sun from a November day, and Nettle, feeling a little better, went back up to his room to write a letter to his sister in New York.

The porter's name was Bill Lowell. He was a weathered, bent-back old man whose job it was to watch the door to the shelter and tell the poor wretches who came there for shelter when there was no more space available. Most nights, there was room for between twenty and fifty people, depending on the shelter's food stores and what work needed to be done—for the cost of a bed indoors and a hot meal was a day of hard, hard labor.

"We open the doors at six," Bill said to Nettle, who'd been told he'd work at each job in the shelter so he could better learn its overall operational strategy, "but the line'll start formin' 'fore noon. By four the blokes'll be lined up 'round the corner."

"Even when there's only room for a few of them?"

Bill shrugged. "We'll need to search 'em as they come inside," he said. "Sometimes, they try an' sneak tobacco inside in their brogues, and they ain't allowed that."

Nettle glanced through a window next to the door, and sure enough, a long line had already formed and was snaking its way down the sidewalk and around the corner. Word had gone out earlier that there was only room for twenty-five, and yet no one in the line seemed to want to leave his spot.

The faces he saw all looked hollow, the eyes vacuous. It wasn't until several days later that Nettle learned why everyone he saw shared the same corpselike expression. London law didn't allow the homeless to sleep outside at night. The idea was that if the homeless weren't allowed to sleep outside at night, they would find somewhere indoors to sleep. To those who only saw the problem from the stratospheric heights of wealth and power, it was a clear example of give a man a fish and he eats for a day, teach him to fish and he eats for a lifetime. The reality, though, was a homeless population that was constantly driven from one doorway to the next by the police, forced to stay awake by the toe of a boot or the bite of a baton, resulting in an expression of slack-jawed exhaustion that stared back at Nettle from every pair of eyes he met.

Bill himself had nearly shared that fate, he told Nettle. He had had a family once—a wife, three daughters, and a son—but had outlived them all. His wife and daughters he'd lost to scarlet fever, all within a month of each other, but the son survived, and had helped Bill in his work as a carpenter in days past.

One day, Bill had been carrying a load of nails that was too much for him. "Something in me back just broke," Bill said. His load of nails had spilled, and he'd ended up flat on his back, unable to get up. He was taken to a hospital, but they refused to admit him, telling him, essentially, to "walk it off."

This he had tried to do, but two hours later was on his back again. He was taken to a different hospital, and this time spent three weeks in bed. He emerged a broken man, unable to do the hard labor that was, unfortunately, the only kind of work that he and most of the men like him were qualified to do, only to learn that his son had fallen from a rooftop and died the week before his release. The boy was buried in a pauper's grave, unmarked, along with a dozen others.

He lived on the streets after that—carrying the banner, as the expression went—chased from one doorway to the next by the police, until, as luck would have it, he ended up in the Mile End Road shelter on the day they had an opening for a porter who could also do a little light carpentry. His nine-pounds-a-year salary made him a veritable Croesus among the East End's poor.

Nettle thought idly that such a man as Bill, who had narrowly escaped a cruel death by exposure and malnutrition, would be more charitable toward his fellow men, but such was not the case.

Bill, much to Nettle's unease, seemed to heartily enjoy his position of relative power over the poor, and stared down his soot-blackened nose at all who entered, demanding from each their name, age, condition of destitution, and what kind of work they were good for, before searching them all with a rough, hard hand.

In one of his searches he found a ragged pouch of tobacco inside a man's sock. Bill proceeded to beat the man with a stick he evidently left by the door for just such a purpose, and probably would have gone on beating him indefinitely, Nettle figured, had he not intervened.

When Nettle tried to berate him for his violence, Bill only scoffed. "Why 'e's nothin' but a worthless beggar, 'e is," he said, and, with all the sour disposition of a man who kicks the cat because he's afraid to kick his wife, went to the door, where a wrecked shell of a man stood on the threshold waiting for admittance, and said, "Be gone, you. Full up!"

"Please, sir," the human wreck said. "Please, I ain't 'ad food in me belly for five days."

"Full up!" Bill said.

Nettle's heart broke to see the pain in the man's eyes, and before Bill could close the door, he was at Bill's shoulder and said, "We can take this man in, I think."

"But, sir," Bill said, "there's only room for twenty-five tonight. We're full up."

"And that man," Nettle said, pointing at the bleeding bag of bones Bill had beaten for the insolence to smoke cheap tobacco, "was to be number twenty-five. Now, I believe, this man is twenty-five."

Bill said nothing, but his eyes did.

"Thank 'e, sir," said the wreck, and walked inside.

Bill's other job at the shelter, after the doors were locked and the homeless shuffled inside, was to monitor the bathing room.

Making the homeless take a bath seemed like a good idea to Nettle—that is, until he saw the process in motion. The overnighters were all lined up, and one by one let down into a dark room with a single tub of warm water and a single threadbare towel hanging from a hook on the wall. Each man used the same water and towel as the man before him, and by the time the man Nettle had forced Bill to let in got his turn, the water in that tub was a frightful stew.

But the human wreck didn't notice. He stripped off his rags and his appearance made Nettle gasp. His body had no meat on it. He was all ribs and distended belly, his back a mass of dried and fresh new blood where he'd been attacked by vermin.

He cleaned off several layers of dirt and blood and changed into a shirt and pants from the shelter's wardrobe. Then he followed the others to the dining hall for a meal of stale bread and skilly—a sort of oatmeal mixed with tepid water so unclean Nettle doubted a dog would drink it—and he would have received that meal had he not had the misfortune to pass Bill on his way inside.

"You!" Bill said, his eyes turning hard as flints with surprised anger, his tone like that of a man who's just found the boy who made his daughter pregnant and then made a run for it.

The man stopped in his tracks.

"Look who we 'ave 'ere," Bill said loudly, looking around at the crowd.

Slowly, every head in the place turned to look.

The man kept his eyes on the floor.

"I'll be damned if it ain't Barlow the Butcher. Look 'ere, we got Barlow the Butcher!"

This meant nothing to Nettle, but it clearly did to the peg-house crowd, for in short order they became a riotous mob. They fell on Barlow and began to beat on him with a savagery that would have made a tribe of cannibals blush.

Nettle waded in and pulled Barlow out of the flurry of fists. Barlow, though, didn't wait around to thank him. As soon as he was clear of the mob, he made for the door and ran off into the night.

Nettle was left with a decision to make. He was ringed by angry faces, some of them bleeding where they'd been hit by others trying to land blows on Barlow, and he had a feeling he knew what would happen if he stayed there, now that they had the taste of blood. He wisely went for the door himself, stepping out into the street in time to see Barlow, or, rather, a crowd of homeless at the end of the street, separating for Barlow, as he rounded the corner onto Stepney Green.

Nettle ran after him, and managed to follow him for a good ways before he lost him in the maze of the East End's soot-stained back alleys. He became lost in short order, every cross street and alley meeting him with endless vistas of tumbledown misery and bricks.

Walking with his head on a swivel, trying to find something familiar, he eventually stumbled onto the Brown Hay Road, where he stopped in front of an enormous abandoned warehouse. It was a blackened, eyeless hulk, not a single intact window down its entire length, and it made him feel strangely uneasy. There were, Nettle had seen already, very few empty buildings in London's East End. Real estate, *any* real estate, was at a premium, as landlords could pack as many as eight families into a home no bigger than the small, one-room apartment he had shared in New York with his mother and his sister Anna. One was more likely, he'd been told, to see a giraffe swimming down the Thames than to find an unoccupied building in the East End.

But the moldy warehouse in front of him was most certainly abandoned, and something about it made the skin crawl down his spine. And then someone was there, staggering toward him from the other side of the street. A patchwork of shadows played across the man's face, but the little Nettle could see was ghastly. The man's joints had swollen, and his body had withered away to almost nothing. His skin was black in places, almost mummified, as if it had begun to rot, and it wasn't until he got halfway across the street that Nettle could tell part of the man's leg had been torn up as if by some sort of animal.

The man raised his hands and flexed his fingers in a weak grab at Nettle, moaning as he stumbled closer. At first, Nettle thought it was just a moan, meaning nothing beyond the pain it obviously conveyed, but then he recognized the word inside the pain.

"Fooooood," the man moaned.

Nettle turned on his heel, thinking robbery, and started to walk the other way.

"Fooooood," the man groaned again.

"See here," Nettle said, "I don't have anything for you."

He was very close to running then, and had already stepped up his pace, when a hansom cab suddenly lurched around the corner at a full sprint and mowed the man down. The driver of the hansom never slowed, and a moment later, he was gone.

Nettle was frozen with shock. What was left of the man after he'd been trampled by the horses and his body sliced open and dragged by the hansom's wheels was in two gory pieces connected by a clotted smear of liquefied meat.

The man's legs were still in the street, but his torso was near the curb. Nettle staggered that way, hands over his mouth, and knelt down next to the bent over backwards mess that the hansom had made of the man.

He started to pray . . . and then the man opened his eyes.

Nettle fell backwards onto the wet cobblestones. The man's eyes were horrible, like staring into the void.

"Fooooood," he groaned, and tried to claw his way toward Nettle, his fingers digging so hard into the edges of the cobblestones that the fingernails shattered and tore loose.

Nettle got up and ran and ran and ran. He ran till he broke down, and then he cried. He was still crying when, by chance, he stumbled back onto the Mile End Road.

The next morning, still badly shaken by his encounter, Nettle packed his bags and knelt by his bed to pray. He had fully expected to leave that afternoon, but his prayers had taken him in another direction, and when he rose to his feet he had made the decision to stay, and half convinced himself that what he seen the night before couldn't have happened. He was upset, nothing more.

Nettle's faith had never led him astray, and the next few days, and a chance encounter with the man the mob had chased out of the peg house on his horrible first night there, reinforced the wisdom of the decision he had made during prayer.

Nettle took to wandering up and down the Mile End Road, watching the people as they struggled for existence, and he noticed a curious little thing. The homeless always seemed to keep one eye on the spittle-flecked sidewalks, and when they'd see a morsel, they'd snatch it up and eat it on the fly. Most, it seemed, could pluck an orange peel or an apple core from the cobblestones without ever losing a step.

Nettle had been watching people go by late one afternoon, and Barlow had been coming the other way on the same sidewalk. Barlow had stooped to pick up something nasty, and when he rose, his nose collided with Nettle's chest, for Nettle was a good six inches the taller of the two.

"Oh, hello," Nettle said, and had a devil of a time over the next few moments trying to assure the man that he had no intention of braining him to death.

They talked under the eaves of a coffee shop, and gradually the look of a rabbit trying to find an opening through a pack of hounds faded from Barlow's eyes. And then a strange thing happened. Nettle, whose over-stimulated humanitarian urges were in danger of melting down if he didn't find some specific point, some single human face to put on all this misery he had been witnessing, bought a pint of beer for Barlow, who was desperately in need of some kind person to buy him a pint of beer. It was the first pint of beer Nettle had ever bought, and it was the first full pint of beer Barlow had had in a very long time. Nettle bought a second round, and by that afternoon, as the windows of the coffee shop sizzled with rain, he had come to a conclusion. He was not going to be the salvation for *all* the world's poor—indeed, there was no way he could be, and it was vain to think so—but he could be the door to *this* man's salvation. Nettle had a project now, something he could manage.

And so they sat there in the coffee shop, the rich, well-meaning American, and the homeless, nearly starved Londoner, and the American talked about God and goodness and reward, and the Londoner drank his beer and nodded.

They met in the afternoons at the same coffee shop over the next week, and gradually Nettle began to realize that it wasn't the man's grotesque, almost troglodyte appearance that had sparked his philanthropy, but rather his cynicism. The man cared little for his own life, and not at all for anyone else's, and Nettle found it hard to believe that a creature who so hated life could actually go on living.

"Beer," Barlow said. "Beer's what makes a man feel like a man. You can take all the rest of it away, but you take away a man's beer, and there ain't no reason left for 'im to go on bein'."

Nettle squinted at his own almost untouched beer and thought about that as a philosophy of life, and it seemed tragic, empty.

"What about a family?" he asked. "A home? A wife and kids?"

Barlow snorted with laughter. "I saw enough of that growin' up," he said. "I saw what me Ma did for me old man. That was enough. Made 'im mis'rable, she did, always a-bangin' me brothers and sisters about, makin' 'is 'ome a noisy racket. 'E no sooner walk through the door and she'd be a-yellin' at 'im, barkin' at 'im like a dog. Take me word for it, mate, and don't waste yer time on a wife 'n' kids. Do nothin' but take yer 'ard-earned money and keep you from drinkin' a beer when it suits you."

Nettle was stunned, bewildered. Such a wasted life! His mind raced for a response, for something worthwhile to say, and at last, he found it. "William," he said, "I want you to pray with me. Will you do that?"

"Pray?"

"Yes, William. There's a power in prayer that has sustained me through my hard times. I think it can do the same for you."

Barlow wrinkled his brow, then a huge smile crossed his face. "Let's pray for another beer, mate. You want me to pray? I'll pray for that."

But Barlow wasn't Nettle's only project. He was still expected to learn the ropes at the shelter, spending time in each of the numerous jobs that were necessary to keep the operation going on a day-to-day basis, and a few nights later he was back with Bill, the porter, passing out blankets in the sleeping quarters. The overnighters would come in, take a blanket from Nettle, and head to a long, narrow room with two large oaken beams traversing its length. Rough pieces of canvas were stretched between the beams, and the men slept on the canvas. When he first heard about the arrangement, and before he had seen it, Nettle thought of seamen in hammocks, rocking to sleep with the rhythms of the open sea, but the reality was nothing like that, and the actual arrangement lacked any of the adventurous dignity a landsman could envision for the life of a sailor at sea. The men were packed in shoulder to shoulder, and the room was dreadfully noisy with snores and coughs and breaking wind, and in the right light, the whole room shimmered with a living cloud of fleas.

He was watching this sad display with a heavy heart when Bill appeared at his shoulder.

"What are you about, sir, talkin' with Barlow the Butcher?"

"Excuse me?" he said, alarmed by the man's tone, even though he was a good six inches taller, and maybe forty pounds heavier.

"You become 'is reg'lar drinkin' mate's what I 'ear."

"I have not," Nettle protested. He stammered, trying to rise to his own defense, and finally managed to tell Bill his plan, how his goal was the man's salvation.

Bill just laughed.

"What's wrong with going after a lost sheep?" Nettle said.

"'E ain't no sheep," Bill said. "A devil, aye, but 'e ain't no sheep."

"What do you mean?"

"There's an em'ty warehouse down on the Brown Hay Road. D'you know it? A big, ugly brute of a buildin'?"

"I've seen it," Nettle said, cringing inwardly at the memory of the beggar and the hansom cab.

"Your mate used to be the union man there. 'Bout two years ago."

Nettle eyed him warily.

"Did 'e tell you 'bout the people 'e killed there?"

"Killed? What are you talking about?"

Bill sneered at Nettle. "Aye, I thought not."

"Tell me what you mean, sir. You cannot accuse a man of such a crime and not state your proof."

Bill only shook his head. "Nothin' was ever proved 'gainst 'im. Didn't 'ave no blood on 'is 'ands. None that the courts could see, anyway. But 'e killed 'em, all right. Just as pretty as you please."

Nettle searched the man's face for some indication that this was a joke. It had to be. He searched the creases in the old man's face, the cracked red map of lines that colored the whites of his eyes, but found nothing to indicate that this was a joke.

"When you say killed, do you mean . . . "

"I mean 'e murdered 'em. Sure as the Pope eats fish on Fridays. Murdered more'n an 'undred people. Men, wimmen, and children, just as pretty as you please."

Nettle felt his legs go to gelatin. He fell against the wall and said, "A hundred people?"

"Aye."

"But, how?"

"Why, 'e starved 'em. Locked 'em in that warehouse for full on twelve days. When they finally opened 'er up, every one of 'em, men, wimmen, and children, was dead as dead can be." Then he leaned close and said, "I 'eard tell some of them bodies was eaten on."

"That's impossible," Nettle countered. "How could he do such a thing?"

"I already tol' you, sir. 'E was the union man, and those people went on strike. The comp'ny tol' 'im to fix the problem, and 'e did."

"A man can't starve to death in twelve days," Nettle said.

"You've seen these men," Bill said. "Not a one's more than a week away from death's door."

"But somebody would have done something to stop him," Nettle said. "You can't just kill a hundred people and expect to get away with it. Somebody would have said something."

But Nettle didn't need to see the blank expression on Bill's face to know that wasn't true. Not here in the East End.

Feeling angry, and confused, and betrayed, Nettle ran from the peg house and set out for the coffee house where he and Barlow had been meeting in the afternoons. He knew no other place to look for the man, but as it turned out, it wasn't necessary to look anywhere else. He found Barlow in the back alley behind the shop, rifling through a paper bag of trash he'd found on the curb, pulling out little bits of orange peels and tearing what remained of the pulp from the pith with his blackened front teeth.

"Mr. Barlow," Nettle called out from across the street.

Barlow looked up and smiled. But then his smile fell. Perhaps he saw the savage expression in Nettle's eyes, or heard something sinister in his tone, but whatever it was, his expression instantly changed, and he took off running into the night.

Nettle didn't bother to chase him. It was enough, for the moment, to see him run. That was all the proof he needed that Mr. Barlow, also known as Barlow the Butcher, was a devil of the highest magnitude.

Some men snap by degrees. Like green wood, they bend a long ways before the tension takes its inevitable course. But other men break like porcelain. They cleave with sudden fury, shattering into thousands of irredeemable pieces, their edges left razor sharp.

Nettle was of the later sort, and when his mind snapped, it came with the illusion of sudden clarity. It seemed he was thinking clearly now for the first time and the path before him seemed clearer now than it had ever been before. He suddenly saw in Barlow, not an individual's face to put on all of humanity's troubles, but a cause of its misery, and there was only one thing to do with such causes. The fact that he had befriended such a beast, that he had bought such evil a drink, for God's sake, didn't terrify him so much as instill in him a sense of personal responsibility. His proximity had given him ownership over the ending to Barlow's sordid little history, and he set out to bring that history to a close.

He carried the banner that night, walking the streets of the East End without stopping for rest or sleep—indeed, without even feeling the need for rest or sleep—ferreting out the hiding places of the homeless, but with his mind on only one man.

He caught up with Barlow in a doorway, the man sitting on the top step, his knees bunched up to his chest and his head bent down between them, trying to sleep.

Nettle kicked his foot. "Wake up," he said. "I want a word with you."

Barlow thought him a policeman at first, and had already half pulled himself to his feet when the haze of sleep left him entirely, and he realized who was standing in front of him.

"You owe me an answer, Mr. Barlow."

But Barlow didn't stand still to give it. He turned and ran with all the energy a scared, weatherbeaten, and prematurely old man could muster.

Nettle followed him at a jog, yelling "I want an answer!" over and over again at Barlow's back, and as they slipped deeper and deeper into the warren of slimy streets that made up the bowels of the East End, a cold, light rain began to fall.

Nettle finally closed on him in a back alley off the Brown Hay Road, the streets deserted now and splashy beneath their feet. Barlow had curled up under a flight of stairs and was trying to hide his face with his arms.

"You have some explaining to do," Nettle said. The rain rolled off his face unnoticed.

Barlow stared up at him with abject fear.

"What did you do? Answer me!"

"For the love of all that's 'oly, sir, please don't yell. You'll—"

"I'll what? Wake the dead? Go on, you villain, say it! Say it! Are you afraid they'll hear us?"

Barlow looked seasick. His eyes pleaded for silence, but got none.

"Spill it!" Nettle roared. "Tell me what you did."

Nettle waited, and for a moment there was no sound but the pattering of a gentle rain on cobblestones, but then it came, as both Nettle and Barlow knew that it most assuredly would, the sound of slow, plodding feet dragging on the cobblestones behind them.

Nettle looked over his shoulder, and saw a small crowd of shamblers had appeared out of the mist. There were men, women, and even children in that crowd. Their faces were dark with disease and their cheeks empty from extreme hunger. Their eyes were carrion eyes, and a smell that could only be death's smell preceded them, filling the street with its sad, inexorable power.

A man in the front of the crowd raised his arms, and it looked like one of his hands had been partially eaten. He groaned, "Foooood," and Barlow jumped to his feet and tried to run.

"Where are you going?" Nettle yelled after him. "Don't you know you can't run from this?"

Barlow didn't make it very far, only to the middle of the Brown Hay Road. There, he stopped, wheeling around in a panic, surrounded by the dead on every side. They stepped out of every doorway, out of every alley, from behind every staircase, taking shape out of the shadows. He fell to his knees in front of Nettle and started to cry.

"Please," he begged.

"Tell what you've done," Nettle said.

Barlow looked at the groaning, starving dead, and he shook his head no. *No, no, no, no, no!*

"Say it," Nettle said. "While there's still time."

But there wasn't any more time. Barlow could no more belly up to the magnitude of what he'd done than he could force himself to stop breathing, and as the rotting dead shouldered their way past Nettle and closed on Barlow, all that he could do was close his eyes.

The dead tore at Barlow with their hands and their teeth, ripping his flesh like fabric. Nettle stumbled away, into the dark, and as he walked he heard Barlow's screams carry on and on and on. They seemed to go on far longer than it seemed possible for any one man to suffer, but go on they did, and they echoed in Nettle's mind even after the shrillness of them disappeared from his ears.

After that, Nettle wandered, his mind unhinged, until he began to see people. These he tried to tell what he had seen, but they flinched away from him, alarmed at the intensity in his eyes and the urgency in his voice and the complete lack of sense in his speech.

As day broke, a russet stain behind plum-colored smoke clouds, Nettle collapsed less than fifty feet from the doors of Stepney Green Hospital. He lay there, lips moving soundlessly, eyes still as glass beads, until an orderly from the hospital knelt beside him and said, "Hey, mate, are you hurt? What is it? Are you 'ungry?"

If the horror wasn't on Nettle's face, it was nonetheless there, in his mind. *Eat*, he thought, and sensed his body in complete revolt at the idea. *God no, I'll never eat again.*

# LONEGAN'S LUCK

## STEPHEN GRAHAM JONES

Like every month, the horse was new. A mare, pushing fifteen years old. Given his druthers, Lonegan would have picked a mule, of course, one that had had its balls cut late, so there was still some fight in it, but, when it came down to it, it had either been the mare or yoking himself up to the buckboard, leaning forward until his fingertips touched the ground.

Twenty years ago, he would have tried it, just to make a girl laugh.

Now, he took what was available, made do.

And anyway, from the way the mare kept trying to swing wide, head back into the shade of town, this wasn't going to be her first trip across the Arizona Territories. Maybe she'd even know where the water was, if it came down to that. Where the Apache weren't.

Lonegan brushed the traces across her flank and she pulled ahead, the wagon creaking, all his crates shifting around behind him, the jars and bottles inside touching shoulders. The straw they were packed in was going to be the mare's forage, if all the red baked earth ahead of them was as empty as it looked.

As they picked their way through it, Lonegan explained to the mare that he never meant for it to be this way. That this was the last time. But then he trailed off. Up ahead a black column was coming into view.

Buzzards.

Lonegan nodded, smiled.

What was dead there was pungent enough to be drawing them in for miles.

"What do you think, old girl?" he said to the mare. She didn't answer. Lonegan nodded to himself again, checked the scattergun under his seat, and pulled the mare's head towards the swirling buzzards. "Professional curiosity," he told her, then laughed because it was a joke.

The town he'd left that morning wasn't going on any map.

The one ahead of him, as far as he knew, probably wasn't on any map either. But it would be there. They always were.

When the mare tried shying away from the smell of death, Lonegan got down, talked into her ear, and tied his handkerchief across her eyes. The last little bit, he led her by the bridle, then hobbled her upwind.

The buzzards were a greasy black coat, moved like old men walking barefoot on the hot ground.

Instead of watching them, Lonegan traced the ridges of rock all around.

"Well," he finally said, and leaned into the washed-out little hollow.

The buzzards lifted their wings in something like menace, but Lonegan knew better. He slung rocks at the few that wouldn't take to the sky. They just backed off, their dirty mouths open in challenge.

Lonegan held his palm out to them, explained that this wasn't going to take long.

He was right: the dead guy was the one Lonegan had figured it would be. The thin deputy with the three-pocketed vest. He still had the vest on, had been able to crawl maybe twenty paces from where his horse had died. The horse was a gelding, a long-legged bay with a white diamond on its forehead, three white socks. Lonegan distinctly remembered having appreciated that horse. But now it had been run to death, had died with white foam on its flanks, blood blowing from its nostrils, eyes wheeling around, the deputy spurring him on, deeper into the heat, to warn the next town over. Lonegan looked from the horse to the deputy. The buzzards were going after the gelding, of course.

It made Lonegan sick.

He walked up to the deputy, face down in the dirt, already rotting, and rolled him over.

"Not quite as fast as you thought you were, eh deputy?" he said, then shot him in the mouth. Twice.

It was a courtesy.

Nine days later, all the straw in his crates hand fed to the mare, his jars and bottles tied to each other with twine to keep them from shattering, Lonegan looked into the distance and nodded: a town was rising up from the dirt. A perfect little town.

He snubbed the mare to a shuffling stop, turned his head to the side to make sure they weren't pulling any dust in. That would give them away.

Then he just stared at the town.

Finally the mare snorted a breath of hot air in, blew it back out.

"I know," Lonegan said. "I know."

According to the scrap of paper he'd been marking, it was only Friday.

"One more night," he told the mare, and angled her over to some scrub, a ring of blackened stones in the packed ground.

He had to get there on a Saturday.

It wasn't like one more night was going to kill him, anyway. Or the mare.

He parked the buckboard on the town side of the ring of stones, so they wouldn't see his light, find him before he was ready.

Before unhooking the mare, he hobbled her. Four nights ago, she wouldn't have tried running. But now there was the smell of other horses in the air. Hay, maybe. Water.

And then there was the missing slice of meat Lonegan had cut from her haunch three nights ago.

It had been shallow, and he'd packed it with a medley of poultices from his crates, folded the skin back over, but still, he was pretty sure she'd been more than slightly offended.

Lonegan smiled at her, shook his head no, that she didn't need to worry. He could wait one more day for solid food, for water that wasn't briny and didn't taste like rust.

Or—no: he was going to get a *cake*, this time. All for himself. A big white one, slathered in whatever kind of frosting they had.

And all the water he could drink.

Lonegan nodded to himself about this, leaned back into his bedroll, and watched the sparks from the fire swirl up past his battered coffee pot.

When it was hot enough, he offered a cup to the mare.

She flared her nostrils, stared at him.

Before turning in, Lonegan emptied the grains from his cup into her open wound and patted it down, told her it was an old medicine man trick. That he knew them all.

He fell asleep thinking of the cake.

The mare slept standing up.

By noon the next day, he was set up on the only street in town. Not in front of the saloon but the mercantile. Because the men bellied up to the bar would walk any distance for the show. The people just in town for flour or salt though, you had to step into their path some. Make them aware of you.

Lonegan had polished his boots, shaved his jaw, pulled the hair on his chin down into a waxy point.

He waited until twenty or so people had gathered before reaching up under the side of the buckboard, for the secret handle.

He pulled it, stepped away with a flourish, and the panel on the buckboard opened up like a staircase, all the bottles and jars and felt bags of medicine already tied into place.

One person in the crowd clapped twice.

Lonegan didn't look around, just started talking about how the blue oil in the clear jar—he'd pilfered it from a barber shop in Missouri—how, if rubbed into the scalp twice daily and let cook in the sun, it would make a head of hair grow back, if you happened to be missing one. Full, black, Indian hair. But you had to be careful not to use too much, especially in these parts.

Now somebody in the crowd laughed.

Inside, Lonegan smiled, then went on.

The other stuff, fox urine he called it, though assured them it wasn't, it was for the women specifically. He couldn't go into the particulars in mixed company though, of course. This was a Christian settlement, right?

He looked around when no one answered.

"Amen," a man near the front finally said.

Lonegan nodded.

"Thought so," he said. "Some towns I come across . . . well. Mining towns, y'know?"

Five, maybe six people nodded, kept their lips pursed.

The fox urine was going to be sold out by supper, Lonegan knew. Not to any of the women, either.

Facing the crowd now, the buckboard framed by the mercantile, like it was just an extension of the mercantile, Lonegan cycled through his other bottles, the rest of his jars, the creams and powders and rare leaves. Twice a man in the crowd raised his hand to stop the show, make a purchase, but Lonegan held his palm up. Not yet, not yet.

But then, towards mid-afternoon, the white-haired preacher finally showed up, the good book held in both hands before him like a shield.

Lonegan resisted acknowledging him. But just barely.

They were in the same profession, after all.

And the preacher was the key to all this, too.

So Lonegan went on hawking, selling, testifying, the sweat running down the back of his neck to wet his shirt. He took his hat off, wiped his forehead with the back of his sleeve, and eyed the crowd now, shrugged.

"If you'll excuse me a brief moment," he said, and stepped halfway behind the ass-end of the buckboard, swigged from a tall, clear bottle of nearly-amber liquid.

He swallowed, lifted the bottle again, and drew deep on it, nodded as he screwed the cap back on.

"What is that?" a woman asked.

Lonegan looked up as if caught, said, "Nothing, ma'am. Something of my own making."

"We—" another man started, stepping forward.

Lonegan shook his head no, cut him off: "It's not *that* kind of my own making, sir. Any man drinks whiskey in the heat like this is asking for trouble, am I right?"

The man stepped back without ever breaking eye contact.

"Then what is it?" a boy asked.

Lonegan looked down to him, smiled.

"Just something an old—a man from the Old Country taught this to me on his deathbed. It's kind of like . . . you know how a strip of dried meat, it's like the whole steak twisted into a couple of bites?"

The boy nodded.

Lonegan lifted the bottle up, let it catch the sunlight. Said, "This is like that. Except it's the good part of water. The cold part."

A man in the crowd muttered a curse. The dismissal cycled through, all around Lonegan. He waited for it to abate, then shrugged, tucked the bottle back into the buckboard. "It's not for sale anyway," he said, stepping back around to the bottles and jars.

"Why not?" a man in a thick leather vest asked.

By the man's bearing, Lonegan assumed he was law of some kind.

"Personal stock," Lonegan explained. "And—anyway. There's not enough. It takes about fourteen months to get even a few bottles distilled the right way."

"Then I take that to mean you'd be averse to sampling it out?" the man said.

Lonegan nodded, tried to look apologetic.

The man shook his head, scratched deep in his matted beard, and stepped forward, shouldered Lonegan out of the way.

A moment later, he'd grubbed the bottle up from the bedclothes Lonegan had stuffed it in.

With everybody watching, he unscrewed the cap, wiped his lips clean, and took a long pull off the bottle.

What it was was water with a green juniper leaf at the bottom. The inside of the bottle cap dabbed with honey. A couple drops of laudanum, for the soft head rush, and a peppermint candy ground up, to hide the laudanum.

The man lowered the bottle, swallowed what was left in his mouth, and smiled.

Grudgingly, Lonegan agreed to take two dollars for what was left in the bottle. And then everybody was calling for it.

"I don't—" he started, stepping up onto the hub of his wheel to try to reach everybody, "I don't have—" but they were surging forward.

"*Okay,*" he said, for the benefit of the people up front, and stepped down, hauled a half-case of the water up over the side of the buckboard.

Which was when the preacher spoke up.

The crowd fell silent like church.

"I can't let you do this to these good people," the preacher said.

"I think—" Lonegan said, his stutter a practiced thing, "I think you have me confused with the k-kind of gentlemen who—"

"I'm not confused at all, sir," the preacher said, both his hands still clasping the bible.

Lonegan stared at him, stared at him, then took a respectful step forward. "What could convince you then, Brother?" he said. "Take my mare there. See that wound on her haunch? Would you believe that four days ago that was done by an old blunderbuss, fired on accident?"

"By you?"

"I was cleaning it."

The preacher nodded, waiting.

Lonegan went on. "You could reach your hand into the hole, I'm saying."

"And your medicine fixed it?" the preacher anticipated, his voice rising.

Lonegan palmed a smoky jar from the shelves, said, "This poultice, yes sir. A man named Running Bear showed me how to take the caul around the heart of a dog and grind—"

The preacher blew air out his nose.

"He was Oglala Sioux," Lonegan added, and let that settle.

The preacher just stared.

Lonegan looked around at the faces in the crowd, starting to side with the preacher. More out of habit than argument. But still.

Lonegan nodded, backed off, hands raised. Was quiet long enough to let them know he was just thinking of this: "These—these snake oil men you've taken me for, Brother. People. A despicable breed. What would you say characterizes them?"

When the preacher didn't answer, a man in the crowd did: "They sell things."

"I sell things," Lonegan agreed.

"Medicine," a woman clarified.

"Remedies," Lonegan corrected, nodding to her to show he meant no insult.

She held his eyes.

"What else?" Lonegan said, to all.

It was the preacher who answered: "You'll be gone tomorrow."

"—before any of our hair can get grown in," an old man added, sweeping his hat off to show his bald head.

Lonegan smiled wide, nodded. Cupped a small bottle of the blue oil from its place on the panel, twirled it to the man.

He caught it, stared at Lonegan.

"I'm not leaving," Lonegan said.

"Yeah, well—" a man started.

"I'm *not,*" Lonegan said, some insult in his voice now. "And, you know what? To prove it, today and today only, I'll be accepting checks, or notes. Just write your name and how much you owe me on any scrap of paper—here, I've got paper myself, I'll even supply that. I won't come to collect until you're satisfied."

As one, a grin spread across the crowd's face.

"How long this take to work?" the bald man asked, holding his bottle of blue up.

"I've seen it take as long as six days, to be honest."

The old man raised his eyebrows. They were bushy, white.

People were already pushing forward again.

Lonegan stepped up onto his hub, waved his arms for them to slow down, slow down. That he wanted to make a gift first.

It was a tightly-woven cloth bag the size of a man's head.

He handed it to the preacher, said, "Brother."

The preacher took it, looked from Lonegan to the string tying the bag closed.

"Traveling like I do," Lonegan said, "I make my tithe where I can. With what I can."

The preacher opened it.

"The sacrament?" he said.

"Just wafers for now," Lonegan said. "You'll have to bless them, of course."

Slowly at first, then altogether, the crowd started clapping.

The preacher tied the bag shut, extended his hand to Lonegan.

By dinner, there wasn't a drop of fox urine in his possession.

When the two women came to collect him for church the next morning, Lonegan held his finger up, told them he'd be right there. He liked to say a few prayers beforehand.

The woman lowered their bonneted heads that they understood, then one of them added that his mare had run off in the night, it looked like.

"She does that," Lonegan said with a smile, and closed the door, held it there.

Just what he needed: a goddamn prophetic horse.

Instead of praying then, or going to the service, Lonegan packed his spare clothes tight in his bedroll, shoved it under the bed, then made the bed so nobody would have any call to look under it. Before he ever figured this whole thing out, he'd lost two good suits just because he'd failed to stretch a sheet across a mattress.

But now, now his bedroll was still going to be there Monday, or Tuesday, or whenever he came for it.

Next, he angled the one chair in the room over to the window, waited for the congregation to shuffle back out into the streets in their Sunday best.

Today, the congregation was going to be the whole town. Because they felt guilty about the money they'd spent yesterday, and because they knew this morning there was going to be a communion.

In a Baptist church, that happened little enough that it was an event.

With luck, nobody would even have noticed Lonegan's absence, come looking for him.

With luck, they'd all be guilty enough to palm an extra wafer, let it go soft against the roofs of their mouths.

After a lifetime of eating coarse hunks of bread, the wafer would be candy to them. So white it had to be pure.

Lonegan smiled, propped his boots up on the windowsill, and tipped back the bottle of rotgut until his eyes watered. If he'd been drinking just to feel good, it would have been sipping bourbon. For this, though, he needed to be drunk, and smell like it.

Scattered on the wood-plank floor all around him, fallen like leaves, were the promissory notes for yesterday's sales.

He wasn't going to need them to collect.

It was a funny thing.

Right about what he figured was the middle of lunch for most of the town—he didn't even know its name, he laughed to himself—he pulled the old Colt up from his lap, laid the bottom of the barrel across the back of his left wrist, and aimed in turn at each of the six panes in his window, blew them out into the street.

Ten minutes and two reloads later, he was fast in jail.

"Don't get too comfortable in there now," the bearded man Lonegan had made for the law said. He was wearing a stiff collar from church, a tin star on his chest.

Lonegan smiled, leaned back on his cot, and shook his head no, he wouldn't.

"When's dinner?" he slurred out, having to bite back a smile, the cake a definite thing in his mind again.

The Sheriff didn't respond, just walked out.

Behind him, Lonegan nodded.

Sewed into the lining of his right boot were all the tools he would need to pick the simple lock of the cell.

Sewed into his belt, as back-up, was a few thimblefuls of gunpowder wrapped in thin oilcloth, in case the lock was jammed. In Lonegan's teeth, a sulfur-head match that the burly man had never even questioned.

Lonegan balanced it in one of the cracks of the wall.

He was in the best room in town, now.

• • •

That afternoon he woke to a woman staring at him. She was sideways—*he* was sideways, on the cot.

He pushed the heel of his right hand into one eye then the other, sat up.

"Ma'am," he said, having to turn his head sideways to swallow.

She was slight but tall, her face lined by the weather it looked like. A hard woman to get a read on.

"I came to pay," she said.

Lonegan lowered his head to smile, had to grip the edge of his cot with both hands to keep from spilling down onto the floor.

"My father," the woman went on, finding her voice, "he—I don't know why. He's rubbing that blue stuff onto his head. He smells like a barbershop."

Lonegan looked up to this woman, wasn't sure if he should smile or not.

*She* was, anyway.

"You don't see its efficacy," he said, "you don't got to pay. Ma'am."

She stared at him about this, finally said, "Can you even spell that?"

"What?"

"Efficacy."

Now it was Logan's turn to just stare.

"Got a first name?" she said.

"Lonegan," Lonegan shrugged.

"The rest of it?"

"Just Lonegan."

"That's how it is then?"

"Alone, again . . . " he went on, breaking his name down into words for her.

"I get it," she told him.

"Regular-like, you mean?"

She caught his meaning about this as well, set her teeth, but then shook her head no, smiled instead.

"I don't know what kind of—what kind of affair you're trying to pull off here, Mister Alone Again."

"My horse ran off," Lonegan said, standing, pulling his face close to the bars now. "Think I'm apt to make a fast getaway in these?"

For illustration, he lifted his right boot. It was down at heel. Shiny on top, bare underneath.

"You meant to get thrown in here, I mean," she said. "Shooting up Molly's best room like that."

"Who are you, you don't mind my asking?"

"I'm the daughter of the man you swindled yesterday afternoon. I'm just here to complete the transaction."

"I told you—"

"And I'm telling you. I'm not going to be indebted to a man like you. Not again."

Lonegan cocked his head over to her, narrowed his eyes. "Again?" he said.

"How much it going to cost me?"

"Say my name."

"How much?"

Lonegan tongued his lower lip out, was falling in love just a little bit, he thought. Wishing he wasn't on this side of the bars, anyway.

"You like the service this morning?" he asked.

"I don't go to church with my father anymore," the woman said. "Who do you think swindled us the first time?"

Lonegan smiled, liked it.

"Anyway," the woman went on. "My father tends to bring enough church home with him each Sunday to last us the week through. And then some."

"What's your name?" Lonegan said, watching her.

"That supposed to give you some power over me, if you know?"

"So you think I'm real then?"

Lonegan shrugged, waiting for her to try to back out of the corner she'd wedged herself into.

"You can call me Mary," she said, lifting her chin at the end.

"I like Jezebel better," he said. "Girl who didn't go to church."

"Do you even know the Bible?" she asked.

"I know I'm glad you didn't go to church this morning."

"How much, Mister *Lonegan*?"

He nodded thanks, said, "For you, Jezebel. For you—"

"I don't want a deal."

"Two dollars."

"They sold for two bits, I heard."

"Special deal for a special lady."

She held his stare for a moment longer then slammed her coin purse down on the only desk in the room, started counting out coins.

Two dollars was a full week's work, Lonegan figured.

"What do you do?" he said, watching her.

"Give money to fools, it would seem," she muttered.

Lonegan hissed a laugh, was holding the bars on each side of his face, all his weight there.

She stood with the money in her hand.

"I *bake,*" she said—spit, really.

Lonegan felt everything calming inside him.

"Confectionary stuff?" he said.

"Why?" she said, stepping forward. "You come here for a matrimony?"

" . . . Mary Lonegan," Lonegan sung out, like trying it out some.

She held the money out, her palm down so she'd just have to open her fingers.

Lonegan worked it into a brush of skin anyway, said at the last moment, "Or you could just—you could stay and talk. In the next cell, maybe."

"It cost me two more dollars not to?" she said back, her hand to her coin purse again, then stared at Lonegan until he had to look away. To the heavy oak door that opened onto the street.

The Sheriff was stepping through, fumbling for the peg on the wall, to hang his holster on.

"Annie," he said to the woman.

Her top lip rose in what Lonegan took for anger, disgust. Not directed at the lawman, but at her own name spoken aloud.

"Annie," Lonegan repeated.

"You know this character?" the man said, cutting his eyes to Lonegan.

"We go back a long ways, Sheriff," Lonegan said.

Annie laughed through her nose, pushed past the lawman, stepped out into the sunlight.

Lonegan watched the door until it was closed all the way, then studied the floor.

Finally he nodded, slipped his belt off with one hand, ferreted the slender oilcloth of gunpowder out.

"For obvious reasons, she didn't bake it into a cake," he said, holding the oilcloth up for the lawman to see.

"Annie?" the lawman said, incredulous.

"If that's the name you know her by," Lonegan said, then dropped the oilcloth bag onto the stone floor.

The lawman approached, fingered the black powder up to his nose. Looked to the door as well.

By nightfall, Annie Jorgensson was in the cell next to Lonegan's.

"Was hoping you'd bring some of those pastries you've been making," he said to her, nodding down to the apron she was still wearing, the flour dusting her forearms.

"Was hoping you'd be dead by now, maybe," she said back, brushing her arms clean.

"You could have brought something, I mean."

"That why you lied about me?"

"What I said, I said to save your life. A little courtesy might be in order."

"You think talking to you's going to save me?" she said. "Rather be dead, thanks."

Lonegan leaned back on his cot, closed his eyes.

All dinner had been was some hardtack the Sheriff had had in his saddlebag for what tasted like weeks.

Lonegan had made himself eat all of it, though, every bite.

Not for strength, but out of spite. Because he knew what was coming.

"You're sure you didn't go to church this morning?" he said to Annie Jorgensson.

She didn't answer. It didn't matter much if she had though, he guessed, and was just lying to him about it, like she had with her name. Either way there was still a wall of bars between them. And he didn't know what he was going to do with her anyway, after. Lead her by the hand into the saloon, pour her a drink?

No, it was better if she was lying, really. If she was a closet Baptist.

It would keep him from having to hold her down with his knee, shoot her in the face.

Ten minutes after a light Lonegan couldn't see the source of was doused, the horses at the livery took to screaming.

Lonegan nodded, watched for Annie's reaction.

She just sat there.

"You alive?" he called over.

Her eyes flicked up to him, but that was all.

Yes.

Soon enough the horses kicked down a gate or a wall, started crashing through the town. One of them ran up onto the boardwalk it sounded like, then, afraid of the sound of its own hooves, shied away, into a window. After that, Lonegan couldn't tell. There was gunfire, for the horse maybe. Or not.

The whole time he watched Annie.

"Mary," he said to her once, in play.

"Jezebel to you," she hissed back.

He smiled.

"What's happening out there?" she asked, finally.

"I'm in here," Lonegan shrugged back to her. "You saying this doesn't happen every night?"

She stood, leaned against the bars at the front of her cell.

One time before, Lonegan had made it through with a cellmate. Or, in the next cell, like this.

He'd left that one there, though. Not turned, like the rest of the town, but starved inside of four days anyway. Five if he ate the stuffing from his mattress.

It had been interesting, though, the man's reactions—how his back stiffened with each scream. The line of saliva that descended from his lip to the ground.

"I've got to piss," Lonegan said.

Annie didn't turn around.

Lonegan aimed it at the trap under the window, was just shaking off when a face appeared, nearly level with his own.

It was one of the men from the crowd.

His eyes were wild, roving, his cheeks already shrunken, making his teeth look larger. Around his mouth, blood. He pulled at the bars of the window like the animal he was.

"You're already dead," Lonegan said to him, then raised his finger in the shape of a pistol, shot the man between the eyes.

The man grunted, shuffled off.

"That was Sid Masterson," Annie said from behind him. "If you're wondering, I mean."

"Think he was past the point where an introduction would have done any good," Lonegan said, turning to catch her eye.

"This is supposed to impress me?" Annie said, suddenly standing at the wall of bars between them.

"You're alive," Lonegan told her.

"What are they?" she said, lifting her chin to take in the whole town.

Lonegan shrugged, rubbed the side of his nose with the side of his finger.

"Some people just get caught up when they're dying, I guess," he said. "Takes them longer."

"How long?"

Lonegan smiled, said, "A day. They don't last so long in the sun. I don't know why."

"But you can't have got everybody."

"They'll get who I didn't."

"You've done this before."

"Once or twice, I suppose. My oxen gets in the ditch like everybody else's . . . "

For a long time, Annie just stared at him. Finally she said, "We would have given you whatever, y'know?"

"A good Christian town," Lonegan recited.

"You didn't have to do this, I mean."

"They were asking for it," Lonegan said, shrugging it true. "They paid me, even, if I recall correctly."

"It was that poppy water."

Lonegan raised his eyebrows to her.

"I know the taste," she said. "What was it masking?"

In reply, Lonegan pursed his lips, pointed with them out to the town: that.

"My father?" Annie said, then.

Lonegan kept looking at the front door.

Her father. That was definitely going to be a complication. There was a reason he usually passed the night alone, he told himself.

But she was a *baker*.

Back in her kitchen there was probably all manner of frosting and sugar.

Lonegan opened his mouth to ask her where she lived, but then thought better of it. He'd find her place anyway. After tonight, he'd have all week to scavenge through town. Every house, every building.

Towards the end of the week, even, the horses would come back, from downwind. They'd be skittish like the mare had been—skittish that he was dead like the others had been, just not lying down yet—but then he'd have oats in a sack, and, even if they had been smart enough to run away, they were still just horses.

Or, he hoped—this time—*a mule*.

Something with personality.

They usually tasted better anyway.

He came to again some time before dawn. He could tell by the quality of light sifting in through the bars of his window. There were no birds singing, though. And the smell. He was used to the smell by now.

Miles east of town, he knew, a tree was coated with buzzards.

Soon they would rise into an oily black mass, ride the heat into town, drift down onto the bodies that would be in the street by now.

Like with the deputy Lonegan had found, though, the buzzards would know better than to eat. Even to them, this kind of dead tasted wrong.

With luck, maybe one of the horses would have run its lungs bloody for them, collapsed in a heap of meat.

With luck, it'd be that ornery damn mare.

They'd start on her haunch, of course, finish what Lonegan had started.

He nodded, pulled a sharp hank of air up his nose, and realized what had woke him: the oak door. It was moving, creaking.

In the next cell, Annie was already at the bars of her cell, holding her breath.

"They can't get in," Lonegan told her.

She didn't look away from the door.

"What were you dreaming about there?" she said, her voice flat and low.

Lonegan narrowed his eyes at her.

*Dream?*

He looked at his hands as if they might have been involved, then touched his face.

It was wet.

He shook his head no, stood, and the oak door swung open.

Standing in the space it had been was the Sheriff.

He'd seen better days.

Annie fell back to her cot, pulled the green blanket up to her mouth.

Lonegan didn't move, just inspected. It wasn't often he got to see one of the shufflers when they were still shuffling. This one, he surmised, he'd fallen down in some open place. While he was turning, too, another had fed on him, it looked like. His face on the right side was down to the bone, one of his arms gone, just a ragged sleeve now.

Not that he was in a state to care about any of that.

This was probably the time he usually came into work on Monday.

It was all he knew anymore.

"Hey," Lonegan called out to it, to be sure.

The thing had to look around for the source of the sound.

When he found it, Lonegan nodded.

"No . . . " Annie was saying through her blanket.

"He can't get through," Lonegan said again. "They can't—keys, tools, guns."

For a long time, then—it could sense the sun coming, Lonegan thought—the thing just stood there, rasping air in and out.

Annie was hysterical in a quiet way, pushing on the floor with her feet over and over, like trying to back herself out of this.

Lonegan watched like she was a new thing to him.

Maybe if he was just seeing his first one too, though. But . . . no. Even then—it had been a goat—even then he'd known what was happening. It was the goat he'd been trying all his mixtures out on first, because it would eat anything. And because it couldn't aim a pistol.

When it had died, Lonegan had nodded, looked at the syrup in the wooden tube, already drying into a floury paste, and been about to sling it out into the creek with all the other bad mixes when the goat had kicked, its one good eye rolling in its skull, a sound clawing from its throat that had pushed Lonegan up onto his buckboard.

Finally, when the horse he'd had then wouldn't calm down, Lonegan had had to shoot the goat.

The goat had looked up to the barrel like a child, too.

It was the same look the thing in the doorway had now. Like it didn't understand just how it had got to be where it was.

The front of its pants were wet, from the first time it had relaxed into death.

Lonegan watched it.

In its other hand—and this he'd never seen—was one of the bottles of what Annie had called poppy water.

The thing was holding it by the neck like it knew what it was.

When it lifted it to its mouth, Annie forgot how to breathe a little.

Lonegan turned to her, then to the thing, and got it: she knew what that water tasted like, still thought it *was* the water, doing all this to her town.

He smiled to himself, came back to the thing, the shuffler.

It was making its way across the floor, one of its ankles at a bad angle.

Now Annie was screaming, stuffing the blanket into her mouth. The thing noticed, came to her cell.

"You don't want to—" Lonegan started, but it was too late.

*Make them take an interest in you,* he was going to say.

Like anything with an appetite, jerky motions drew its attention.

Annie was practically convulsing.

Lonegan came to the wall of bars between them, reached for her hand, just to let her know she was alive, but, at the touch she cringed away, her eyes wild, breath shallow.

"You should have gone to church," Lonegan said, out loud he guessed, because she looked over, a question on her face, but by then the thing was at the bars. It wasn't strong enough to come through them of course, but it didn't understand things the way a man would either.

Slowly, as if *trying* to, it wedged its head between two of the bars—leading with its mouth—and started to push and pull through.

The first thing to go was its one good eye. It ran down its cheek.

Next was its jaw, then its skull, and still it kept coming, got halfway through before it didn't have anything left.

Annie had never been in danger. Not from the thing, anyway.

She wasn't so much conscious anymore either, though.

For a long time, Lonegan sat on the edge of his cot, his head leaned down into his hands, the thing in the bars still breathing somehow, even when the sunlight spilled through, started turning its skin to leather.

It was time.

Lonegan worked his pants leg up, slid the two picks out, had the door to his cell open almost as fast as if he'd had the key.

The first thing he did was take the shotgun off the wall, hold the barrel to the base of the thing's skull. But then Annie started to stir. Lonegan focused in on her, nodded, and turned the gun around, slammed the butt into the thing until its head lolled forward, the skin at the back of the neck tearing into a mouth of sorts that smiled with a ripping sound.

When the thing fell, it gave Lonegan a clear line on Annie.

She was dotted with black blood now.

He might as well have just shot thing, he figured.

"Well," he said to her.

She was crying, hiding inside herself.

"You don't catch it from the blood," he told her, "don't worry," but she wasn't listening anymore.

Lonegan pulled the keys up from the thing's belt, and unlocked her cell, let the door swing wide.

"But—but—" she said.

Lonegan shrugged, disgusted with her.

"*What?*" he said, finally. "I saved your life, Mary, Jezebel. Annie Jorgensson."

She shook her head no, more of a jerk than a gesture.

Lonegan twirled the shotgun by the trigger guard, held it down along his leg.

The easy thing to do now would be to point it at her, get this over with.

Except she was the cake lady.

For the first time in years, he wasn't sure if he'd be able to stomach the cake, later, if he did this to her now.

"What's the name of this town?" he said to her.

She looked up, the muscles in her face dancing.

"Name?"

"This place."

For a long time she didn't understand the question, then she nodded, said it: "Gultree."

Lonegan nodded, said, "I don't think I'll be staying in Gultree much longer, Miss Jorgensson. Not to be rude."

She shook her head no, no, he wasn't being rude.

"I'm sorry about your father," he said then. It even surprised him.

Annie just stared at him, her mouth working around a word: " . . . why?"

"The world," he said to her, "it's a—it's a hard place. I didn't make it. It just is."

"Somebody told you that," she said weakly, shaking her head no. "You don't . . . you don't believe it."

"Would I do this if I didn't?"

She laughed, leaned back. "You're trying to convince yourself, Mister Alone Again," she told him.

And then she didn't stop laughing.

Lonegan stared hard at her, hated Gultree. Everything about it. He was glad he'd killed it, wiped it off the map.

"Goodbye then," he said to her, lifting the fingers of his free hand to the hat he'd left . . . where?

He looked around for it, finally just took a sweated-through brown one off the peg by the door.

It fit. Close enough, anyway.

For a moment longer than he meant to, he stood in the doorway, waiting for Annie to come up behind him, but she didn't. Even after the door of her cell made its rusty moan.

Lonegan had to look back.

Annie was on her knees behind the thing the Sheriff had become.

She'd worked his revolver up from his holster, was holding it backwards, the barrel in her mouth, so deep she was gagging.

Lonegan closed his eyes, heard her saying it again, from a few minutes ago: "But—but—"

But she'd drank the poppy water too. Thought she was already dead like the rest of them.

She only had to shoot herself once.

Lonegan narrowed his lips, made himself look at what was left of her, then turned, pulled the door shut.

Usually he took his time picking through town, filling saddlebags and feed sacks with jewelry and guns and whatever else would sell.

This time was different, though.

This time he just walked straight down main street to his buckboard, folded the side panel back into itself, and looked around for a horse.

When there wasn't one, he started walking the way he'd come in. Soon enough a horse whinnied.

Lonegan slowed, filled his stolen hat with pebbles and sand, started shaking it, shaking it.

Minutes later, the mare rose from the heat.

"Not you," he said.

She was briny with salt, from running. Had already been coming back to town for the water trough.

Lonegan narrowed his eyes at the distance behind her, for another horse. There was just her, though. He dumped the hat, turned back around.

Twenty minutes later, her nose to the ground like a dog, she trotted into town.

Lonegan slipped a rope over her head and she slumped into it, kept drinking.

All around them were the dead and the nearly dead, littering the streets, coming half out of windows.

Ahead of him, in the straight line from the last town to this one, there'd be another town, he knew. And another, and another. Right now, even, there was probably a runner out there from *this* town, trying to warn everybody of the snake oil man.

Lonegan would find him like he'd found the last, though. Because anybody good enough to leave his own family to ride all night, warn people twenty miles away, anybody from that stock would have been at the service Sunday morning too, done a little partaking.

Which meant he was dead in the saddle already, his tongue swelling in his mouth, a thirst rising from deeper than any thirst he'd ever had before.

Lonegan fixed the yoke on the mare, smeared more poultice into her wound.

If things got bad enough out there this time, he could do what he'd always thought would work: crush one of the wafers up, rub it into her nostrils, make her breathe it in.

She'd die, yeah, but she'd come back too. If she was already in the harness when she did, then he could get a few more miles out of her, he figured.

But it would spoil her meat.

Lonegan looked ahead, trying to figure how far it was going to be this time. How many days. Whether there was some mixture or compound or extract he hadn't found yet, one that could make him forget Gultree altogether. And Annie. Himself.

They'd been asking for it though, he told himself, again.

If it hadn't been him, it would have been somebody else, and that other person might not have known how to administer it, then it would have been one half of the town—the *live* half—against the other.

And that just plain took too long.

No, it was better this way.

Lonegan leaned over to spit, then climbed up onto the seat of the buckboard. The mare pulled ahead, picking around the bodies on her own. The one time one of them jerked, raising its arm to her, Lonegan put it down with the scattergun.

In the silence afterwards, there wasn't a sound in Gultree.

Lonegan shook his head, blew his disgust out his nose.

At the far edge of town was what he'd been counting on: a house with a word gold-lettered onto the back of one of the windows: *Wm. Jorgensson*. It was where Annie lived, where she cooked, where she'd *been* cooking, until the Sheriff came for her.

Lonegan tied the mare to a post, stepped into Annie's living room, found himself with his hat in his hands for some reason, the scattergun in the buckboard.

They were all dead, though.

"Cake," he said aloud, trying to make it real.

It worked.

In the kitchen, not even cut, was a white cake. It was smeared with lard, it looked like. Lard thick with sugar.

Lonegan ran his finger along the edge, tasted it, breathed out for what felt like the first time in days.

Yes.

He took the cake and the dish it was on too, stepped back into the living room.

The father was waiting for him, a felt bowler hat clamped down over his skull. He was dead, clutching a bible the same way the Sheriff had been carrying the bottle.

The old man was working his mouth and tongue like he was going to say something.

Lonegan waited, waited, had no idea what one of these could say if it took a mind to.

Finally he had to say it for the old man, though, answer the only question that mattered: Annie.

"I got her out before," he said. "You don't need to worry about her none, sir."

The old man just creaked, deep in his throat.

Walking across his left eyeball was a wasp.

Lonegan took a step back, angled his head for another door, then came back to the old man.

If—if the buzzards knew better than to eat these things, shouldn't a wasp too?

Lonegan narrowed his eyes at the old man, walked around to see him from the side.

He was dead, a shuffler, but—but not *as* dead.

It hadn't been a bad mixture, either. Lonegan had made it like every other time. No, it was something else, something . . .

Lonegan shook his head no, then did it anyway: tipped the old man's bowler hat off.

What spilled out was a new head of hair. It was white, silky, dripping blue.

The old man straightened his back, like trying to stand from the hair touching his neck now, for the first time ever.

"No," Lonegan whispered, still shaking his head, and then the old man held the bible out to him.

It pushed Lonegan backwards over a chair.

He caught himself on his hand, rolled into a standing position in the kitchen doorway. Never even spilled the cake.

"You've been using the oil," he said to the old man, touching his own hair to show.

The old man—William Jorgensson: a *he*, not an it—didn't understand, just kept leading with the bible.

Lonegan smiled, shook his head no. Thanks, but no.

The old man breathed in sharp then, all at once, then out again, blood misting out now. Meaning it was almost over now, barbershop oil or no.

Again, he started making the creaking sound with his throat. Like he was trying to talk.

When he couldn't get it out, and Lonegan wouldn't take the bible, the old man finally reached into his pocket, came out with a handful of broken wafers, stolen from the pan at church.

It was what Annie had said: her father bringing the church back to her, since she wouldn't go.

Lonegan held his hands away, his fingertips even, and stepped away again. Not that the wafers could get through boot leather. But still.

The bible slapped the wooden floor.

"You old thief," Lonegan said.

The old man just stood there.

"What else you got in there, now?" Lonegan asked.

The old man narrowed his half-dead eyes, focused on his hand in his pocket, and came up with the bottle Lonegan had given him for free. It was empty.

Lonegan nodded about that, got the old man nodding too.

"That I can do something about, now," he said, and stepped long and wide around the old man, out the front door.

The heat was stifling, wonderful.

Lonegan balanced the cake just above his shoulder, unhooked the panel on the side of the buckboard. It slapped down, the mare spooking ahead a step or two, until the traces stopped her.

Lonegan glared at her, looked back to the house, then did it anyway, what he knew he didn't have to: palmed up the last two bottles of barbershop oil. They were pale blue in the sunlight, like a cat's eyes.

He stepped back into the living room, slapped the wall to let the old man know he was back.

The old man turned around slow, the soles of his boots scraping the wood floor the whole way.

"Here," Lonegan said, setting the two bottles down on the table, holding up the cake to show what they were in trade for.

The old man just stared, wasn't going to make it. His index finger twitching by his thigh, the nail bed stained blue.

"I'm sorry," Lonegan said. "For whatever that's worth."

By the time he'd pulled away, the old man had shuffled to the door, was just standing there.

"Give it six days," Lonegan said, touching his own hair to show what he meant, then laughed a nervous laugh, slapped the leather down on the mare's tender haunch.

Fucking Gultree.

He pushed out into the heat, was able to make himself wait all the way until dark for the cake. Because it was a celebration, he even sedated the mare, cut another flank steak off, packed it with poultice.

He'd forgot to collect any water, but then he'd forgot to collect all the jewelry and guns too.

There'd be more, though.

In places without women like Annie Jorgensson.

Lonegan wiped the last of the mare's grease from his mouth, pulled his chin hair down into a point, and pulled the cake plate into his lap, started fingering it in until he realized that he was just eating the sweet off the top, like his aunt had always warned him against. It needed to be balanced with the dry cake inside.

He cut a wedge out with his knife, balanced it into his mouth, and did it again and again, until something popped under his blade, deep in the cake.

It was a half a wafer.

Lonegan stared at it, stared at it some more. Tried to control his breathing, couldn't seem to.

Was it—was it from *this* Sunday's service, or from last?

Was what was in the old man's pocket the whole take, or just part of it?

Lonegan's jaws slowed, then he gagged, threw up onto his chest, and looked all the way back to town, to the old man in the door, smiling now, lifting his bible to show that he knew, that he'd known, that he'd been going to get religion into his daughter's life whether she wanted it or not.

Lonegan shook his head no, no, told the old man that—that, if she'd just waited to pull the trigger, he would have *told* her that it wasn't the poppy water. But then too was dead certain he could feel the wafer inside him, burrowing like a worm for his heart, his life.

He threw up again, but it was thin now, weak.

" . . . no," he said, the wet strings hanging from his chin. It didn't—it couldn't . . . it didn't happen *this* fast. Did it? Had it ever?

His fingers thick now, he sifted through the cake for another wafer, to see if he could tell which Sunday it had been from, but all the shards were too small, too broken up.

Annie. Goddamn you. *Which Sunday?*

But—but . . .

The oil, the barbershop oil. Hell yes. It slowed the wafers.

Lonegan stumbled up through the fire, scattering sparks, the cake plate shattering on a rock, and started falling towards the mare. To ride fast back to Gultree, back to the old man, those two blue bottles.

But the mare saw him coming, jerked her head away from the wagon wheel she was tied to.

The reins held. The spoke didn't.

She skittered back, still sluggish from what he'd dosed her with, and Lonegan nodded, made himself slow down. Held his hat out like there was going to be something in it this time, really, come on, old gal.

The mare opened her nostrils to the night, tasting it for oats, then turned her head sideways to watch Lonegan with one eye, then shied back when he stepped forward, shaking her mane in warning, flicking her tail like she was younger than her years, and when he took another step closer, leading with the hat, she ducked him, and in this way they danced for the rest of the night, her reins always just within reach, if he could just time his steps right. Or what he thought was his reach.

# THE RICKSHAW PUSHER

## MERCURIO D. RIVERA

When I think upon the day that Father left us, I wonder whether the passage of time has distorted my memories or whether my perceptions were skewed from the onset by the type of overactive imagination that afflicts most ten-year-old boys. To this day, Mother insists that Father was a lover of wine and women so it should have come as no surprise to anyone that he would have run off to the West with Jiao, the village slut. Her discomfort with the subject is understandable, I suppose, but I've always sensed that she was holding something back about the real story of Father's abandonment of our family, about Liang, the rickshaw puller, and about that chilly night when the heavens wept fiery tears.

Liang began serving as Father's personal rickshaw puller in the summer of 1899, the year our rice fields were markedly bountiful. Father had made deals with British shippers for the export of our rice crop but it required him to travel quite often into Qufu for meetings with the Westerners. Liang, one of the young rice field workers, waited outside our house every morning at the first glimmer of dawn to transport Father in a rickshaw on his various errands.

I suppose I admired Liang the way any child admires an older boy, wanting to imitate him and get his attention. Father scolded me—and even swatted me across the side of the head on more than one occasion—for talking to Liang during our long trips to the city, which I considered great adventures. The youth, Father had explained, was below my station. Father and I would sit pressed together in the wooden rickshaw seat while Liang pulled us along narrow streets past the fish-market and colorful storefronts. Every time we visited the city, Father would make a regular stop on the way back, just outside our village, to visit Lady Jiao, a pretty young woman who lived alone in a wooden stilted house on the slope of a hill. Father made me wait outside in the rickshaw anywhere from half an hour to forty-five minutes. It was during these brief respites, which seemed to me to last for hours, that Liang and I would walk down to the creek together where he washed his face and practiced his exercises while chanting incantations to the great spirits.

"Where did you learn this?" I asked, wide-eyed, as he took deep breaths and struck curious poses, crouching and punching the air.

"My brothers in the Society of Righteous and Harmonious Fists," Liang said. "They come from honorable families like mine that have lost everything, all victims of Western imperialism."

I nodded though I had no idea what he meant by "imperialism." I was more interested in the stances he took, the exercises he performed.

"The Guizi have taken to calling us 'boxers,' though I don't know why."

"Don't you get tired?" I asked.

"Yes, but the great spirits enter my body and give me strength," he said. "And my job as rickshaw puller allows me to earn a steady income and to send money to my mother and grandmother in Yantai. Have you heard of our town?"

I shook my head.

"Once a fishing village in the Baihai Bay, now kept as a port for the British, the Germans and other Guizi."

Liang and I would always head back to the rickshaw after a few minutes so that we'd be waiting for Father when he emerged. I never told Father about my conversations with Liang. And Father, in turn, made me promise never to tell Mother about the stops at Lady Jiao's place. The business of men, he had explained, was inappropriate to discuss with women and the sooner I learned that truth the better. In hindsight, I suspect guilt drove Father to purchase expensive Indian silks at Qufu for Mother—which she loved—along with woven fabrics that she used to sew my clothes.

One night, as I stared out of my bedroom window, the heavens began to weep. Across the black sky dozens of stars fell, leaving behind tracks of fire.

"Father," I screamed.

Father charged across the hallway into my bedroom. "Wei, what are you doing up at this late hour? Will you never learn obedience?" he said, before slapping me across the side of my head.

I held back the tears for although the heavens might weep, a man never should. (Not even Mother cried whenever Father struck her and sent her flying into the wall or tumbling down the front steps of our house).

"Look, Father," I said, pointing out of my window. "Tears! Fiery tears!"

Father peeked out of the window and his mouth opened in surprise. One of the teardrops crashed into the rice fields with such thunderous force that our house shook.

After Father marched out of my room, I heard him shout at the servants to go inspect the fields. Because the moon was bright and full, I spied the two servants—Peng and Liang—from my bedroom window headed in the general direction where the blazing teardrop had fallen.

Although excited, I lay in bed and pretended to be asleep in case Father returned to my room. And in feigning sleep, the real sleep overtook me.

The next morning at breakfast I overheard Mother talking to the cook about Peng and Liang, how they'd been found dead next to a semi-buried boulder on the banks of the Yellow River.

"No! Not Liang," I said to her. "He can't be dead. The great spirit soldiers protect members of the Righteous Harmony Society like him."

"Oh, Wei." Mother hugged me but said nothing more.

When another servant who'd been sent to bury the bodies never returned, Father decided the spot was cursed and forbade anyone else from approaching it. He directed the remaining servants to erect a fence twenty feet around the area where the boulder lay half-buried in the soil. And no one said anything when the three corpses vanished, swept away by the rising river waters during a night of heavy rain.

Imagine my shock—and Father's—when we stepped out of the house the next morning and saw Liang standing in the courtyard, waiting for us as he had for many months. Only now he stood immobile and his skin had a sick, gray pallor. He did not utter a word or even nod at us.

Father ordered me to stay inside and, accompanied by six servants, went to confront the boy. There was a great commotion outside and while I never learned what happened, the next day when I joined Father for his regular errands to Qufu, the rickshaw had been redesigned. Liang no longer stood in front of us, facing forward, pulling the wheeled cart by twin wooden poles; now he was relegated to the rear, with wrists chained to the ends of the two poles.

"This rickshaw was imported from Japan," Father said, with a trace of contempt in his voice. "But I've adapted it to match the classic Chinese style for carts. Carts like these were used at one time to transport Confucius himself."

Liang now faced us while Father and I sat in the covered cart with our backs to him. I couldn't resist looking over my shoulder at Liang as he growled and slobbered and tried to move towards us. Because of the two five-foot wooden rods between us, he could never get close. Instead, he pushed us forward. Father would lean left or right and Liang would push the rickshaw in that direction. When we wanted him to stop, Father tossed a horse-feed sack over Liang's head, which prompted him to stop in his tracks. And so Liang became Father's loyal rickshaw *pusher*.

After the incident with the glowing boulder on the riverbanks, Liang never grew tired so Father used the boy's services days and nights for every conceivable errand. Every morning Mother and the servants stared from the windows, dread etched across their faces as we set out in the rickshaw. When we rode, Father advised curious onlookers to keep their distance from Liang, whom he said suffered from a form of pneumonic plague.

After several occasions when Liang ran us off the road in pursuit of passersby, Father had to put blinders on the boy's head so he could only stare straight ahead at us.

During one of our trips back from Qufu, I dared to ask Father, "What's happened to him? Why do pieces of Liang's skin dangle from his face and attract flies, which he never even bothers to swat?"

"Have you heard nothing of what I've said? He's suffering from a terrible malady," Father said. "You must stay away from him as you always have, only now more than ever. If you speak to him, if you even draw near him, I will beat you raw. Do you understand?"

"But if he's sick shouldn't we call the doctor?"

"Don't question me, boy!" Father scolded. "All that matters is that I no longer have to pay him for his services. This is a great boon to our family in these trying times. Now shut your mouth and stop being disrespectful."

I nodded and closed my eyes, bracing for Father's blow, but we had just pulled up to Lady Jiao's house so instead he smoothed his shirt and ran his fingers through his hair. It bothered me to think about Liang's mother and grandmother waiting for him to send them a portion of his salary, which they depended on to survive, a payment that would never come.

Before Father disappeared into Jiao's house, he chained Liang's leg to a tree while his wrists remained bound to the rickshaw's two wooden poles, which he could never set down. I thought Liang must be exhausted. And how hot he must have felt with that burlap sack covering his head. Worse, I had no doubt he had overheard Father say that he would no longer be paying Liang for his services.

I snatched the key from the rickshaw cart, where Father had left it, and unlocked the chain that bound Liang's wrists to the rickshaw poles. At last the poles fell to the ground and Liang could finally rest his weary arms. "Does that feel better? Are—are you worried about your mother and your grandmother, Liang?"

I pulled the sack off his head but instead of sitting and relaxing, Liang strained against the chain that bound his ankle to the tree and reached for me with his pale hands. I stood just out of his reach. And when I stared into his black, bottomless eyes a terrible fear overcame me, and I understood at last that the Liang I knew was gone, replaced with a snapping and violent creature that hurled itself at me repeatedly, only to come to a sudden halt as its ankle strained against the chain. Unsure of what to do, I decided to walk down to the creek to wash my face, as I normally did during these stops. I wondered how I would re-chain Liang's wrists to the poles, how I would get close enough to throw the sack over his head again so as to hide what I'd done from Father.

When I returned fifteen minutes later, Liang was missing. In all the years that have passed, whenever I wake up at night in a cold sweat, my heart galloping, wondering whether I'd imagined it all, it is this moment that haunts me. I found the chain still hooked around the tree trunk, but at the other end of it remained only Liang's foot, a splintered piece of bone jutting from its top. But no blood, not a trace. The front door to Lady Jiao's house gaped wide open so I assumed that Liang had gone to confront Father. At the time, I couldn't say I blamed him. Working full days and oftentimes at night, it didn't seem fair that Father had decided to no longer pay him.

My memory becomes hazier now as to whether I really crept up to the house and stared through a side window. Whether I really saw Father and Lady Jiao splattered in different shades of red, their eyes wide open, unblinking. Whether Liang really knelt at the side of the bed as if at a dinner table, pulling intestines from their stomachs and shoving them into his mouth like raw squid.

I ran home and arrived just as the sun was setting. When Mother questioned me, I confessed everything.

The next morning Mother went to Lady Jiao's house accompanied by the local authorities and when she returned later in the day, sat me down and told me that I had not seen what I thought I'd seen. That Father and Lady Jiao had, in fact, run off together. Although fear crept into her eyes on those rare occasions that she spoke about this matter, Mother explained that the Westerners had compromised Father's morals and that I should take it as a lesson.

As for Liang, it was rumored that the Westerners at the free port in Yantai had met with resistance from members of the Society of Harmonious Fists, including one who dragged his leg and proved invulnerable to bullets and other weapons. The two other missing servants presumed dead were also spotted late one night shuffling across a gangplank and onto an English ship that never arrived at its destination in London. The stories of these resistance fighters inspired others to believe that they too might gain the favor of the great spirits through a pure life of training and prayer, that they too might be able perform extraordinary feats of magic in defense of China.

These days I bear responsibility for harvesting my father's rice fields. With the Boxer Rebellion having been crushed long ago, I have no choice but to deal with the Guizi, though I make it a point to warn my own son about the dangers of Western influence. He's uninterested in the subject. How my ten-year-old reminds me of myself at that age: mischievous, disobedient, and so every month I fortify the fence that cordons off the land near the banks of the Yellow River. And, when exhausted or weak I cannot resist the temptation to peek over its top at the huge boulder from the sky, which to this day remains half-buried in the acrid-smelling soil surrounded by a gray and withering vegetation that never grows and never dies.

# THE REVENGE OF OSCAR WILDE

## SEAN EADS

"C'est lui! Dieu merci!"

*"Je vous remercie, Saints, pour la santé de Monsieur O.W.!"*

He bows to acknowledge the appreciation from eight pretty damsels in distress. Two divergent groups of shambling, decomposing Lazarus men have herded them into a terrible trap in the narrow street between the Panorama du Congo and the massive, barricading left wing of the Palais du Trocadero. An hour ago, they were modern, self-assured young ladies quite unwilling to let the men, their fathers and brothers and husbands, sequester them further. They were *armed*, after all, and no doubt confident in the sturdiness of their parasols. Now the skeletal remains of those umbrellas lecture them on their foolishness. Shreds of fine vibrant fabric flutter off the broken, twisted ribs, mimicking the crisp, massive flags high overhead on the Palais spires. But the women's gaze is not heavenward. If there is a god to them now, he walks this earth and his name is Oscar Wilde.

He has appeared seemingly out of nowhere and stands resplendent in an orange topcoat, a sunflower in the uppermost buttonhole and an elegant Webley Royal Irish 450 CF revolver in his right hand—the weapon a gift from his lover Bosie, the pretty poison he has picked and died from years ago. Wilde's head is bared to the breeze, his brown hair long and unkempt as in his younger days. Standing beside him, significantly shorter and appropriately serious and somehow vibrant in matching gray pants and shirt, is Albert Ayat—as of fifteen days ago the gold medalist in fencing at this, the 1900 Olympics here in Paris.

The sword Ayat lifts in salute to the ladies now is sturdier than a traditional foil but his accuracy and speed with it are unchallenged and deadlier for the heft. It cuts a nifty whistle in the air when his wrists flick it just so.

"I do not believe any of these Lazari include the one who bit poor Bosie, Ayat. Nevertheless the ladies require our attention—how dreadful."

"There are ten threatening from the left. I will take them," Ayat says. Wilde listens, slow on the translation. Ayat is difficult to understand when he's almost breathless. Wilde himself is nearly breathless just from looking at Ayat. But all that must wait. Ayat maneuvers toward the larger group of Lazarus men in that peculiar fencer's stance that seems both noble and ridiculous. Wilde turns, his sigh quickly changing to a gasp as he weaves away from one clumsy hand. Decaying fingernails rip the sunflower from his chest and crush the petals. Three lumbering creatures growl at him and close.

Wilde recomposes himself, brushes the flower's remains from the buttonhole and retreats several steps, coolly checking the Webley to find it loaded and in good working order. In the days before his downfall in England, when Bosie's father the Marquess of Queensberry threatened to assault him, Wilde threatened in turn to shoot him on sight. It had been a bluff—and Wilde was a very good bluffer. There was genuine fear in the little old bully's eyes when he thought the towering Irishman might kill him there and then. *I should have,* Wilde thinks. But in 1893 he was another man, civilized, Bosie's devoted fool. Wilde has been—and been with—many different men since then. Every dead incarnation of his being lives in whatever man he is now. But perhaps men always remain, inside, with the first person they ever loved, and remain the men they were at the time of that love's experiencing. Why else is he out here once more avenging Bosie's honor?

Bosie's father died many months ago. His passing did nothing to ease Wilde's troubles at the time. It did not elicit the strange recall to life he feels now. His greatest pleasure, before he shoots the nearest Lazarus man in the head, is imagining it is 1893 again and that Queensberry is charging toward him. A bullet would have undone much misery.

Wilde smiles and returns the first resurrected man to his rest. He dispatches the second and third attacker in short order, aiming at Queensberry's face each time. It will take more than Christ to bring these Lazari back now. But perhaps resurrection was always the devil's own work.

Behind him, Ayat has troubles. He is a genius with the blade and a fine physical specimen, though Wilde cares little for the curly moustaches that age the Frenchman's face past its twenty-four years, hanging off his lips like wilted petals on an otherwise vibrant flower. Careful and strategic in most circumstances, diagonal in his feints and parries—a chess-piece bishop with the sword of a chess-piece knight—Ayat has miscalculated. Wilde knows the root of his difficulties is the ladies and his eagerness to impress them. The young fencer leapt into the fray without realizing how the narrow confines and the Lazari's sheer numbers cheat his sword of its principal attribute—length. Now nearly encircled, he cannot swing or stab his way free. *A smitten fool,* Wilde thinks. But Ayat looks too wholesome and fresh to garner further opprobrium. The fencer's youth and vitality have made Wilde's heart his *Piste.*

He reaches into his left coat pocket for bullets to feed the Webley and then steps forward unflinching, gun outstretched. He sees Queensberry's right and left profile; he sees the back of Queensberry's head. Imagining well is the best revenge and the Lazari sate his imagination. Several minutes later, when the last resurrected man is returned to the dust, Wilde can only marvel at the Webley, saying, "The pen may be mightier than the sword, Ayat, but I believe I should like to compose only with this henceforth. There are several critics I have been meaning to send letters."

"Must you be so impossible, Oscar?"

"It is an impossible situation, Ayat."

The ladies rush toward them, their white gloved hands waving in welcome little surrenders to both men. The French women are very unlike the British, Wilde notes, especially in moments of excitement. Their initial hysterias are the same, but French ladies seem immune to fainting spells and are surprisingly adaptive to scenes of gore. Consider how they stand around these rotting corpses unfazed now that the danger has passed. Wilde accepts their praise, acknowledging his growing reputation as the knight-errant of this, the disturbed Exposition Universelle. It is as if no one remembers his dank, weary form haunting the city's cheapest cafés, a penniless, friendless alcoholic and shamed bugger, embracing a long and pathetic public suicide. Most likely some of these same women spat at him on the street only a month ago as their fine, intact parasols darkened him with shadow.

Their scorn was well deserved and earned, Wilde thinks, shuddering at an image he conjures of himself lying insensate in a gutter. It has been over three years since he completed the jail sentence that destroyed his soul. Disgraced, humiliated, divorced, he has lived these years in European exile, determined to conclude it here in Paris. There had been presumptive talk among his friends that he should write again—that his wit would be a magic balm to erase the past and soar him to even greater heights. None of them understood, not even his dear and loyal friend Robbie Ross, the impish boy who first seduced Wilde and unlocked the key of his being, stirring fresh life from an existence that was dead for reasons Wilde could not articulate to himself. He had a wife and darling children and yet he was not a living man until Robbie embraced him—Robbie who seemed to understand everything in the world in spite of his youth, or perhaps because of it. No, not even Robbie understood the prison experience, the years of hard labor, the hideous conditions that yet held sway over his mind. When Wilde dreams, he is there again, in the prison yard watching fair-haired youths bruised and worked until they shamble about so very much like the creatures he and Ayat just put down.

*Yet each man kills the thing he loves*
*By each let this be heard.*
*Some do it with a bitter look,*
*Some with a flattering word.*
*The coward does it with a kiss,*
*The brave man with a sword!*

Wilde shudders again and the women mistake it for something else and offer their comfort. A glance at Ayat's dripping blade makes him remember the conclusion of his poem, his only attempt at writing since his release. "The Ballad of Reading Gaol" had been an anonymous hit with the public and it had pleased him, the master of paradoxes, that everyone had missed the poem's ultimate paradox. Even Robbie and Bosie had missed the intent of that line—*For each man kills the thing he loves.* Had Wilde not also said, "To love oneself is the start of a lifelong romance?" The poem was a statement of intention, a suicide note that announced he planned to kill himself by living.

He had embarked on this plan by drinking and whoring as much as he could, each day a meaningless and wincing preamble to a long and stuporous night. He wanted only to rot where he stood and decay as he walked, until nothing remained. Yes, it was a prolonged suicide, and a successful one until the phenomenon of the Lazarus men. Wilde may have seen the very first of their kind, three weeks ago. He had fallen into a gutter across from a man who seemed quite dead, no doubt a murdered tourist. Wilde had even slurred a question to him about what it was like. Then the dead man rose and stumbled into the crowded night. A hallucination or mere mistake, Wilde thought at the time, though now he is certain it was a Lazarus man and he wonders if his drunken impotence then bears some responsibility for the present chaos. *And for poor Bosie's condition.*

"These ladies are lovely, are they not, Oscar?"

Ayat gallantly swipes the sword's blood across his right pants leg and then kisses the hand of the girl he has decided, Wilde assumes, is the loveliest. The ladies are quiet and indeed all of Paris seems so. How many of its citizens have been killed—and killed again? He thinks of Bosie, stripped half-naked and sweating in his sheets at the hotel, his throat bandaged from the bite that happened three days ago. He hears the young aristocrat calling out, fading away. The auditory vividness of it startles Wilde. *What am I doing out here, attempting to avenge a death that has not even happened—and* won't *happen!* He wonders if this self-assurance is a bluff or a mad reliance on a technicality. There is one point of universal agreement in these days of penumbral confusion: a Lazarus man's bite is fatally transformative. Bosie will die and yet he will *not* die.

Wilde considers how best to excuse himself. Ayat will want to accompany him. Even the allure of beautiful, willing women is not enough to sever the sudden warrior bond between them. They have now fought four battles together, Ayat having sought Wilde out for his renewed fame. Wilde was, of course, quite drunk when the first incidents occurred and multiplied. The attack at the Velodrome de Vincennes supposedly killed over three hundred people, though it had not proven easy to distinguish victims from attackers in many instances. Wilde realizes, from what little he can remember, that nothing short of divine providence acquitted his escape at the simultaneous attack on the Champ de Mars. For he had defended a child using the heavy cane of someone already felled. Wilde was a very large man, not athletic but powerful all the same. Fueled by alcohol and rage, a powerful anti-societal vengeance suddenly electric in his spine, Wilde bashed heads with such furor that no less than ten skulls were certified split open from his blows. Reflecting on it in later sobriety as he wittily held court before admiring Frenchmen and the child's injured mother (bitten, poor creature, but at the time this was no cause for alarm), he realized he had no idea if the people he had struck—men only, there was at least that balm—were innocent people or their resurrected assailants.

He has not touched a drop of alcohol since.

"See the ladies to safety, Ayat. I have urgent business elsewhere."

The Olympic fencer protests but there is nothing he can do. Wilde holds up an imposing, callused hand. "We will find each other later, dear boy. You may rest assured."

"Yes, Oscar."

Ayat is breathless now in a different way as he turns back to the women. Wilde smiles, wondering if the ladies are in even more danger now. But the Frenchman is young and no doubt lacks expertise. A pity, he thinks, checking the Webley again before starting off. Youth is wasted on the inexperienced.

He could expect a tedious walk to the Hôtel d'Alsace under normal circumstances, Paris' population having swelled by many thousands on account of the Exposition and the Olympics. Now the streets are shockingly deserted and the Eiffel Tower, which Wilde considers an appropriate idol to worship if these are indeed the Last Days, stands a lonely sentinel's watch from across the way. He walks faster than he has in years and his heart feels it. He thinks of what he will say when he re-enters their room. He knows he must sound self-assured and fluid. Somehow he believes only a display of great confidence will keep Bosie alive. *Bosie, you must not die and you will not die as long as you have my love. Therefore, Bosie, I can assure you of a splendid immortality.*

Truth be told, while he has always been known as an amazing speaker, with wit at will, his speech is seldom as extemporaneous as it sounds. He has held imaginary conversations with himself since he was a boy, working on lines and rehearsing clever dialogue and bons mots to summon only slightly altered according to need. His employment and delivery is so quick and seamless that it truly feels spontaneous. But true ease in talking comes from art, not chance, to paraphrase Pope, and he believes Pope is always better paraphrased than taken directly. When faced with subjects he cannot even conceive of, much less practice for, Wilde knows he sounds like a stuttering fool, even a simpleton. Bosie's charming torment is his ability to create hour after unbroken hour of such instances, and Wilde humiliates himself in base incoherencies for the sake of love.

The entrance to the d'Alsace is like that of other hotels since the crisis, barricaded and patrolled by three armed and watchful men. Their guns train on Wilde before he is ever properly in shooting distance. Wilde stops and adjusts his posture and bearing to make sure neither in any way resembles the stumbling shuffle of the Lazari. He calls loudly to them in his Irish brogue and their fingers relax off the triggers. "Monsieur Wilde," one says, nods politely and clears a path for him.

"If only decent theatres could afford armed gunmen to keep out the public, plays might finally be performed in their perfection before absolutely no one. I've always said the unfortunate fact of drama is that it must be witnessed."

"*Oui, Monsieur,*" another guard says, and gives Wilde a glare that reminds him not everyone has buried his past with the risen dead.

He hurries up to their room—Bosie's room, really, since he pays for it with money inherited from his father's estate. In bed, Bosie's head thrashes right and left, dank blond tresses sweated heavily to his forehead. Death's skeletal hand has gift-wrapped his throat in thick white gauze over a necrotizing bite wound. The rest of his body does not move and this horrifies Wilde. It is as if the Death has asserted dominion everywhere else and what life there remains has gathered in Bosie's head for a doomed last stand.

Shots fire from outside the window. Wilde looks in that direction, sweating.

"So cold," Bosie says.

Wilde whips off his topcoat and presses it like a blanket of fire across the slight body.

"Dear boy," Wilde says. "Have you been unattended all this time? I left specific instructions—"

"Don't leave me again," Bosie whispers.

Wilde swallows. How those four words recall memories both tender and hard! Bosie once had the flu and Wilde nursed him devotedly, never leaving his side as he suffered. Then suddenly Bosie recovered and Oscar was stricken by the same malady. From the open window of his sickroom in their rented lakefront house, he endured the sound of his restored lover frolicking jubilantly with several local youths, Bosie having left him to sweat out his own illness in parched solitude.

Wilde forces his hands to open. He has clenched more fists in the last two weeks than he ever did during his three trials or even in prison itself, when the indignities and outrages he'd experienced built into a bitter torrent he directed entirely at Bosie—through a letter. The prison guards had finally allowed him to write something, and the resulting unsent letter presented an accusation, an entire trial and a sentencing of Bosie for his crimes. He had fallen so far, and for what? Bright blue eyes, a pretty face that launched and sank exactly one ship—Wilde's own? Writing the letter released a rage he would not know again until his moment on the Champ de Mars. *A love letter to my messiah,* Wilde thinks to himself in derision. It was longer than any letter composed by the Apostles. Here in bed before him is his love's Laodicean church.

"I can't breathe," Bosie says. His chest heaves in short demonstrative bursts.

Wilde touches the handsome youth's forehead. "Bosie, as long as you have my love, you will not die. I promise you immortality. Splendid immortality, Bosie."

"Oh, Oscar," Bosie says, coughs once, and dies.

Fifteen minutes later, men carry the body outside, Wilde protesting. There is fierce debate about what comes next. A German doctor staying at the d'Alsace wants the corpse left inside for observation. Wilde too wants Bosie left in bed. In truth, he is anxious to return the body upstairs because he intends to disrobe and sleep with it, holding Bosie until he feels the life return again. He has seen this happen with his own eyes. The resurrection starts with a tremendous shiver and shake, like the uncoiling of some terrific spring inside the body cavity. The arms shoot up and the knees bend as an extension of that energy. Meanwhile a hissing noise comes from the mouth as dry, inflexible and now unnecessary lungs try to fill. From Bosie's lips the hiss will sound soft as poetry.

*One can survive everything, nowadays, except death.* Wilde cannot remember when he said or wrote that. It does not matter—the Lazari have rendered it false.

*Hurry back to me, Bosie.*

"Le corps doit être brûlé."

Wilde stirs from his grief and hope, rethinks what he has just heard and translates. His hands move forward, shaking. "My Bosie is to be burned? I'll not allow that!"

"It is the government's orders. All dead must be cremated."

*When I am dead cremate me.*

Wilde rubs his temples, fighting unwanted memories of Bosie's father. Around him an argument ensues between the hotel's manager and the armed guards. The rapidity of the exchange and Wilde's inner distractions trouble his ability to understand. The gist is who shall take Bosie's corpse to the designated place of disposal. The crematorium is apparently not close and transportation has become exceedingly difficult and confused. The government has commandeered all the motor vehicles and there are things happening in the streets that have startled the horses. All serviceable horses are also government requisitioned, and the Lazari are known to prey on them when human meat does not present itself. A coach now out of the question, the one choice seems to be carrying Bosie across the city on a stretcher.

"I will not allow my staff to be exposed to such risks. I hired you specifically—"

"You hired us to guard the door. Well, we're guarding it."

"How much more do you want?"

"Couldn't pay us enough. Defending a fixed position is easy. Being out in the open, a moving target? Find yourself a few Americans. They seem foolish enough."

"Brave enough," Wilde says, bringing all attention where it properly belongs, on him. "I have been to that exotic land, gentlemen, and dwelt among their roughnecks. I have met recently a young man from a place called Arkansas—how I should love to flee there one day. Americans themselves do not flee. They are a people blessed by the music of Apollo and the ingenuity of Hephaestus. They—"

One of the gunmen strikes a match and holds it over Bosie's body. "No need to risk the crematorium. Get kerosene. We'll burn the body right here."

"In front of the Alsace? My god, the stench! No, my patrons cannot be exposed to such—"

The gunmen's leader just smiles. "To such what? Barbarism? Indelicacy? Inhumanity? It will be much worse when they see this thing rise to drink our blood."

"I believe you are confusing this hideous condition with vampirism. If you read the celebrated novel by my friend and countryman Stoker, you will realize they are not the same," Wilde says.

"He's an English aristocrat, isn't he? He was a vampire in life. What he returns as won't be so different. Get the kerosene."

Wilde's gaze shifts to the manager's reaction. The little Frenchman's forehead blisters with beads of sweat, telling Wilde that he has already decided to acquiesce. Before the manager can take a step, Wilde produces the Webley. The unexpected quickness of his hands combined with his great height and bulk stupefy them all. No guard even attempts to raise a weapon as Wilde's aim alternates fast before each face.

"If Lord Douglas must go, then so shall I."

"You'd carry him alone through these streets?"

"They seem quite deserted now."

The manager attempts to plead with him, though Wilde knows this is only for the sake of politeness. Removing the body is his chief concern and Wilde was a considerable headache to him before the crisis. In his view, if Wilde leaves with the body, so much the better.

Wilde holds the Webley out a moment longer and then pockets it. He stoops, gathers Bosie into his arms, and like some self-saddling mule Wilde slings him over his right shoulder. The weight stoops him and antagonizes his back, but Bosie feels most familiar to him as a burden to bear. Wilde realizes he did harder labor in prison and ponders that God laid him low in order to toughen him for the present nightmare. It is a perfectly Protestant fantasy, but Wilde is determined to die a Catholic. He takes one step and then another. It will be a slow journey but the weight is not unmanageable. Nothing truly is except for checking accounts.

"I shall entertain you, my dear resting Bosie," Wilde says some ten minutes into the journey. His pace is slowed even more because he stops constantly to turn and check his blind spots. The streets remain empty but the Lazari have a way of suddenly swarming in spaces that were clear only moments ago. They move with no grace at all, but so slow and inexorable that their footfalls are soundless. Those wearing shoes make a telltale scraping noise, but most come barefooted. The long dead come only on bone. *They lumber,* Wilde thinks. It is an odd word to describe a walking style and he wonders at its etymology. He assumes it means wooden and stiff, without joints, as how a tree might stalk its prey. But that association is too obvious, especially for English diction. Probably the meaning evolved from a root word long dead and resurrected in fifty other disparate expressions having little to do with one another. The paradox of dead meanings existing parasitical and hidden in living words pleases him.

Wilde smiles, remembering his promise to entertain Bosie. He begins to gallop a bit, as if he bore one of his own small children on his back (but no, he shall not think of them now, their mother is dead and it is too horrifying to imagine them alone in another country and surrounded by Lazari). His voice booms out, turning the street into a stage—

*"Alas, poor Yorick! I knew him, Horatio: a fellow of infinite jest, of most excellent fancy: he hath borne me on his back a thousand times; and now, how abhorred in my imagination it is! my gorge rims at it."*

Wilde stops, winded, and kneels to gentle Bosie's body to the ground. He pants for air as he strokes the angelic face and adjusts the white gauze that has slipped to reveal the wound. Looking at the purple and red gouge, Wilde only now realizes own lips were not the last to feel the heat and pulse of Bosie's throat before he died.

"Alas, poor Yorick," he whispers to himself. A famous speech from a play with many famous speeches—but why did his mind select *that* one? He is a living Yorick looking at his dead Hamlet. Suddenly he is certain the world has gone terribly wrong, that Bosie should live many decades more and that, by standing here breathing, Wilde is a resurrected man as unnatural as the Lazari. *I was dying and every part of me deserved the death.* He feels, even in the face of Bosie's end, the complete bloom of health and vitality. This flower he'll keep in his buttonhole at all costs. He looks down at his lover and repeats Hamlet's speech up to the point he set Bosie down. As Wilde's fingertips stray into Bosie's sweat-stiffened hair, he finishes: "Here hung those lips that I have kissed I know not how oft."

He bends to kiss them now and forces himself not to recoil at their cold, rubbery texture. Bosie's mouth does not open and Wilde's tongue encounters a barricade of teeth as perfect as prison bars.

"Come back to me, Bosie. *Wake.*"

How long will it take? Hours? *Days?* He pushes back from the body and ponders. Vaguely he hears the wounded gait of four, perhaps five, of the resurrected approaching from the east. Blinking away a few tears, Wilde straightens his back and turns to look over his right shoulder. Nine, he counts in astonishment. Six appear quite fresh—they wear fashionable clothes and are obviously recent victims of the very Lazari they have now become. The other three have spent at least ten decades in the ground, garbed as they are in shreds of Jacobin simplicity that doubtlessly resembled rags even a hundred years ago. Complete decomposition of the genitals at least manages to keep them from being altogether indecent.

As he stands, the Webley trembles in his grip. He has already imagined the prospect of reloading. His fingers rub against each other in the left coat pocket—the pocket is empty. He does not have enough bullets for the situation. *How could I have made such an oversight?* So many things never occur to him until it is too late; sometimes his life seems nothing more than a string of neglected chances at foresight and planning. He thinks of Ayat, leaping into action without thinking. *Who in Hades am I to criticize his judgment?*

Wilde closes one eye, raises the gun and prepares to duel. The pistol's strong recoil sends a bolt of pain through his broad wrist as the closest attacker drops, a third eye newly minted in its forehead. Wilde retreats three steps and then automatically circles closer, like an indecisively suicidal man. The brave imperative to assert himself between the Lazari and Bosie waxes and wanes against his terror.

His second shot isn't good enough—the shoulder. The impact flings the Lazarus woman onto her back and the entire right arm disconnects and shatters into splinters. Maybe it will be enough. But no—the remaining body rises a moment later, oblivious to its loss. The left arm juts out, fingers opening and closing, a hideous mimic of the creature's lipless mouth.

"You're nearly as stubborn as Sarah Bernhardt," Wilde says, firing his third shot into her head.

He shoots again and again, more careful with his aim. The bullets find and fell their targets. But five more Lazari approach.

And one bullet remains.

For myself, Wilde thinks, and even turns the gun around to stare down the barrel. A head shot will assure he stays down. But does he want that? The question surprises him so much he spares a second to consider it. In that space, he imagines himself rising, finding Bosie waiting on him. Is there love among the Lazari? There is clearly greed and gluttony and endless hunger. Is love so different than these things? Is love, as he's known it, any less base?

Sweat breaks across his face and pools on cheeks that have become sallow and pitted with age. So hideous, he thinks, staring at the monsters as he backpedals. The notion that he could become one of them willfully, that he would be mindless in his carnal pursuits . . . *my God,* he realizes: he already mirrors them. He has lived their existence even before his reputation and his fortune fractured. He had only better skin on a better public face.

The gun goes to his temple, his eyes wincing shut against the planned violence. Then he hears a familiar whistle and looks to see the head of the Lazari farthest from him go flying across the street. The decapitated body drops, revealing Ayat in all his glory, holding a sword so ostentatious that Wilde can only marvel. He brings the sword back to him and leaps into a pose—*a la coquille.* Wilde cries out, drops the Webley, falls to the ground and kicks away from a lunging Lazarus man. The remaining four step over Bosie and swipe down at Wilde's clothes.

"Now it is my turn to save you, dear Oscar," Ayat shouts as he thrusts the blade through the next man's neck. An elegant twist turns the blade flat and with the slightest flick the steel sweeps away bone and flesh. The head lolls backward and tumbles atop the body that collapses underneath it.

"Oscar, what are you doing? Move!"

Wilde has scrambled back as far as he can go. The Lazari have forgotten him, pivoting to indulge Ayat's fervor. *Move,* he thinks. He looks for the Webley. It is there—out of immediate reach. His gaze trains on Bosie.

The great coil has sprung inside him. The body twitches with new energy, a scene such as only Mary Shelley could imagine. For the second time in half an hour, Wilde thinks of a scene out of literature and inverts his role inside it. Aesthete, poet, playwright, doomed martyr—all the identities he has created for himself—and in reality he is Bosie's construction entirely. He is the Creature watching his Creator come to life.

He bares his neck for Bosie's teeth.

"Oscar!"

Somehow Ayat has lost his sword. It rattles across the ground with a sound that makes Wilde wince. It is a sound like a perfect gem being dropped on the floor and stepped upon until it powders.

Bosie hisses and sits up.

"Dammit, Wilde, your gun! Shoot something!"

Ayat is breathless again. His French is so hard to understand. Wilde takes a deep inhale, wondering if he'll miss it—breathing. Not here, perhaps. The air is wonderfully poisonous in Paris. He much prefers England where they show their toxins with more discretion, in the heart.

Bosie's eyes are pale blue cataracts that fix on Wilde's slumped body. He crawls, still hissing, his body so lithe and exotic and *seductive* that Wilde's erection actually hurts in his pants. *Take me, consume me,* he thinks. There seems so little remaining to him that Bosie has not already devoured, why shouldn't the flesh yield too? Wilde begins to undo his shirt.

Ayat meanwhile dodges one clumsy blow and throws himself along the ground, rolling to escape being surrounded. He rolls all the way to his fallen sword and takes it up. Wilde's attention flickers a moment at him. Beautiful, daring Ayat—so much more worthy than Bosie in nearly everything, a man of hard effort and harder employment, not the bratty, untalented poet son of a crazed aristocrat, himself possessed of terrible poetic pretensions and sensibilities. *When I am dead cremate me.*

He looks at Ayat and then back at Bosie and wipes away a tear with the back of his hand. Poor boy, raised by such a tyrant and likely touched by inherited madness. It excuses everything. It *must.*

Ayat beheads the remaining Lazari. The last one he toys with, dancing just out of reach as leisured swipes sever the right hand and then the left, followed by both arms at their shoulders by making an exaggerated, cleaving swing. He whittles away the Lazarus man, clipping extremities as a tailor might break off an excess of buttons. It is an unexpectedly cruel performance only Bosie could appreciate.

"Do you know what sword this is, Oscar? It is the Austerlitz Blade—the personal sword of Emperor Napoleon, forged by the great Biennais! How I longed to hold it as a boy every time I saw it at the Army Museum. I am a God with this weapon. I am—who is it to you British?"

"I am not British, dear boy."

"I remember now—yes, I am St. George!"

He delivers the decisive blow and then waxes on, addressing his enthusiasms to the blade at such lengths that it takes a minute to realize Wilde's silence. He turns—and shouts something Wilde cannot understand. Gibberish is gibberish in any language, though he wonders how it must look, with Bosie nearly on top of him and Wilde shirtless, waiting for the dry teeth, imagining how his own blood will warm his lover's cold mouth.

"Oscar!"

Ayat rushes toward them. Wilde realizes his intent and something in Bosie realizes it too. His muscles still have strength and quickness to them. He turns in to Ayat's charge, dodges at the last moment and bites into the Frenchman's leg. The Austerlitz Blade strikes the building a mere inch from Wilde left ear and again falls abandoned. "No, Bosie," Wilde cries. His lover smothers over the shrieking fencer, whose arms flail in impotence without a weapon.

"No!"

Wilde staggers up, a walrus in his movements. He seizes Bosie by the waist and literally throws him to the side. He finds Ayat on the ground, coughing up blood. Bosie had started to bite his throat open.

"Not like this," Ayat manages. "Kill me, Oscar. I don't want to . . . come back."

*All men kill the thing they love.*

Bosie rolls over. The cataract gaze locks onto them as he hisses.

"I—I can't, Ayat."

"If you love me," Ayat says.

*The brave man with a sword.*

"But I am not brave, Ayat," Wilde says, his melodious voice cracking. "I'm not like you, I cannot use the sword." The fencer has no idea what he's talking about. "I cannot even give you a kiss. But here," he says, forcing the Webley into the Frenchman's hand as Bosie manages to stand and shuffle toward them.

"Oscar."

"We'll do it together. I shall help you, if you lend me your strength. Oh, I am a fool. What strength have you left to lend? I am a pitiless borrower, Ayat. Here, both our fingers on the trigger—"

Ayat's face shatters with the blast.

Wilde does kill Bosie afterwards, but not straight away. He takes up Ayat's stolen blade and breaks into the nearest building and climbs the stairs. From the second floor window, he watches Bosie walk about in what appears to be stunned circles for twenty minutes before he suddenly decides on a direction. From his vantage point, Wilde detects the reason for this sea change—a child, lost and terrified, is standing in the middle of the road a block over. Bosie has caught the scent. Wilde's breath hitches and he knows what must come next. He cannot permit such an outrage.

The memory of the deed lingers and refuses to stale. What's so horrifying is the freedom each sunrise brings since Bosie's beheading. He is at first philosophical about it, telling himself that he now realizes death is merely the state in which the striving mind finally perceives the Nothingness it has always suspected was there. He is a delight among the refugees fleeing across France to the Channel, an absurd entertainer, a legend, a perfect Christ. "The best way to conquer death is by not dying," he says, and somehow to the people who have lost their friends and families, their very future, to the Lazarus plague, this statement proves the very essence of cheer.

There are rumors everywhere. The horrors that infected France have moved across Europe and there are reported outbreaks in England itself. This news makes the Channel crossing very tense, as someone announces the British military will either sink the vessel before it docks or else execute them all as soon as they got off. This image is so vivid to mad minds that several men and women jump overboard at the halfway point and are soon out of sight, swimming, swimming.

Wilde however hopes the outbreak *has* happened in England. He counts on it, for Bosie's death troubles him with freedom. He senses his past life with Bosie no longer counts and that he can now live unfettered—almost. One chain remains about his neck, and perhaps around Bosie's too, if his spirit lingers. But Wilde knows how to break it, and so he crosses back to the country that persecuted him.

All of Western Europe seems to be accompanying him, and nothing stanches the invasion. Wilde encounters no Customs clerk to whom he can declare his genius or Ayat's sword or the more precious thing he carries in a black satchel. Wilde steps onto English soil three years after vowing to never return. In a way, he has not broken his pledge. The Wilde who made it no longer exists.

*When I am dead cremate me.*

Months ago Wilde heard—and delighted in—a rumor that Bosie's father, despite the wishes stated in his absurd poem, was not cremated but instead buried vertically with his head pointing down, his gaze directed at more eternal fires. If true, his plan may work. Queensberry's body is still far away, on the estates of Kinmount House in Scotland. It will be an arduous affair getting there, especially if every city in England and its countryside teem with Lazari. He already knows this must be the case. The wind is tainted with a familiar chill and scent, even this close to the sea. Survivors call it the Lazari's Breath and it is a combination of mass, mobile decomposition, and a sweating terror.

Wilde watches the refugees flock west—thousands of them with thousands more on the way. They are heading for larger ports with ships they will storm, if necessary, to seek shelter in America. Wilde remembers his own trip there decades ago as he stalks northward, stopping just once to set the satchel down so he can grasp Ayat's sword with both hands. It did belong to Napoleon, after all—who is Wilde to deny anyone a thwarted dream? *(And perhaps the Emperor too has risen and even now stumbles and slouches through the Arc de Triomphe in an abandoned Paris, his hand still famously tucked into his shirt, disconnected from any arm.)* With a cry, he takes the sword and plunges it into the ground, releasing it to quiver like a living thing reveling in territorial conquest and triumph. Wilde admires the weapon's grace and beauty, forged from steel and silver, shining with gold gilt but bronzed with dried blood.

Taking up the sword again as he retrieves the satchel, he says, "Bosie, we are on our way."

The journey takes weeks. The sword conquers armies of Lazari. Wilde lacks Ayat's skill but his stamina and ruthlessness, powered by a monomaniacal fixation, keep him moving. It is more exciting, more electrifying, to dispatch British Lazari. He no longer even sees the business as gruesome—each is a small revenge and freedom leading to the greater one ahead.

If doubts possess him, he need only sleep to have all confidence restored. Each night his dream is exactly the same. He stands in Reading prison watching a young man's execution. He cannot remember the man's name, only that Wilde has sworn eternal love to him. The youth is hanged until death and then his body is lowered to the ground. Almost at once the body resurrects and becomes vibrant. Shocked, the prison officials hang him again. The body thrashes on its rope endlessly and the warden and all the guards flee in terror. The gates are left open and everyone escapes except Wilde, who stands pressing his forehead against the man's bound legs and weeping.

"We are here, Bosie."

The grave of Bosie's father, John Sholto Douglas, Marquess of Queensberry. *When I am dead cremate me.* Perhaps the monster's wishes were carried out after all—perhaps digging will reveal a vessel of ashes where the body should be. Wilde strikes his spade into the earth, snarling at the labor of it, willing the dirt to yield.

A half hour later he finds signs of—O wonderful paradox!—*life.*

The rumors are true. Bosie's father has been buried vertically upside down. There is no coffin at all, just a body jammed into the earth. Wilde's spade finds the feet and the feet are—*moving.* A thin layer of dirt pulses like a beating heart and Wilde clears it to reveal two worn and filthy soles. He gasps, falls back and hastens to the satchel.

He pulls Bosie's head from within and sets it atop the tombstone. "Now at last I understand Salome," Wilde says, considering the head. The desiccated blue cataracts leer straight ahead at Wilde as he resumes digging. Queensberry's legs kick in greater strides as Wilde disencumbers them. It takes almost three hours before he can drag the body out of its hole.

The Marquess is clearly ravenous and Wilde recognizes a hunger that is unchanged by death. Had he been buried like a normal person, he would have clawed his way to the surface weeks ago. Wilde swallows, angered by his fear of the familiar, rotting face. He did not come all this way to indulge fear. Queensberry suddenly lunges stiffly at him and Wilde shrieks and bashes his head with a powerful backhand. The fear goes, replaced with a long nourished rage that seizes all of his being. He will use the sword.

*There is no God,* Wilde thinks. And if there is a God, what he does next is perhaps not technically a sacrilege, an immorality so vile that even the most decadent of men would turn from the very idea in horror. It is not necrophilia if the body is resurrected, after all, and he pins Queensberry into the dirt before the grave and shames the father in front of the son.

When it is finished, he takes Ayat's sword and beheads the Marquess and puts it on the tombstone next to Bosie's. The air around Kinmount House fills with laughter and the echo of heavy footfalls. It is Wilde, his long arms swaying in the air as his body writhes, a man veiled with life, and he is dancing, dancing, dancing.

# EARLY 20$^{TH}$ CENTURY

# THE GRINGO

## SILVIA MORENO-GARCIA

"I know him. That gringo was a famous writer."

Light trailed through the leaves, tracing funny shadow patterns on the ground. The resurrected man dangled from a thick rope, twitching every few minutes and moaning.

The resurrected were sturdy and the soldiers who'd hanged this one had done a poor job, merely hoisting him from the branches like a broken piñata. When you're going to have a hanging, you'd better have it right but Catalina had seen many idiots tie a rope and get it all wrong. Even with regular prisoners, never mind the resurrected, they'd muddle it. There was nothing worse than watching a poor sod slowly suffocate because someone had not figured how to break his neck properly.

Catalina smirked, taking a puff on the cigarette and handing it to her fellow soldadera. Catalina smoked a cigarette each afternoon and another one at night. *Religiously,* Lola said, possibly because everything had to do with religion for Lola.

*Small things. It's the small things that count,* Catalina's dad used to say, and she found herself in agreement more and more these days.

"You read any of his stuff?" Catalina asked.

Before the Revolution Lola had been studying at an exclusive girl's school in Cuernavaca. She spoke French and English, and knew how to dance the waltz. Not that it mattered now. What mattered was carrying weapons and cleaning them, shooting the Federales with a steady hand, and Catalina could do that even if she couldn't read none too well.

"He had a story about a hanged man who thinks he's not really dead," Lola said.

"It sounds like he saw it coming."

Lola handed Catalina the cigarette back. Catalina crossed her arms and stared at the twitching gringo. An old guy, gray-haired. What did he think he'd be doing down in Mexico, following the troops at his age? And then a Cemetery Man had the gall to bring him back, to have his withered hands drag supplies across the arid fields.

Catalina understood the logic of the Federales: they needed cannon fodder. Hell, everyone needed cannon fodder. It didn't matter if you were fighting for Zapata or Villa, everyone wanted more soldiers. Kids of twelve or thirteen were being "recruited" at gunpoint. Before the Revolution, the henequen fields were harvested by groups of resurrected. Now the Federales had the dead fighting for 'em.

"What do you want to do about him?" Lola asked. "Are we cutting him down?"

"Cutting him down," Catalina said, chuckling. "He'd kill us."

The man moaned. A low, guttural sound. The resurrected were pretty stupid but also pretty strong. Without a Cemetery Man to control him, he'd be extra stupid and violent. Catalina didn't want to take any chances.

"It doesn't seem right to let him stay like this. The crows are going to peck him."

"The crows are going to peck all of us."

Catalina looked at the man and wondered if it had been villagers who'd hanged him or Revolutionaries like her. She wondered if they'd done it for sport, 'cause the more she looked at the rope, the more it looked like they'd just left him there for fun.

She thought about six months back, when they'd passed through a scorched village reeking of death. The streets were littered with corpses. The Federales had taken everything. The horses, the cows, the chickens. But they'd somehow left behind the pigs. Big, fat pigs which were happily munching on the corpses.

When her company had gone through, a few soldiers, for kicks, decided to tie a couple of pigs up and burn them. They weren't hungry. They wanted to hear them squeal.

Pigs eating men and then the men eating the pigs. And a guy hanging from a tree, probably because it was a merry sight. Just like the pigs squealing had been funny.

She grabbed the Mauser and aimed, slowly squeezing the trigger. The shot sent the birds in the tree flying; created echoes which splashed across the fields.

The man who had been a famous writer twitched one last time and his moaning ceased.

"We should say a prayer," Lola said.

"Next you'll want to bury him. You'd have made a good nun."

Lola did not reply. She knelt, closed her eyes and pressed her hands together, head politely bowed.

"Our Lord in Heaven, we ask that you receive the spirit of our brother Ambrose. Amen."

"Amen," Catalina repeated.

Lola rose, wiping the dirt from her skirts. She glanced at Catalina.

"If I die, will you make sure I have a cross with my name on it?"

"Like a cross with your name is gonna do you any good."

"Just promise."

"Don't think about that," Catalina said.

Lola stared at her. Catalina smoked her cigarette, finally shaking her head.

"Well, that's enough scouting for a day. I say we head back and meet with them others," Catalina muttered.

They turned around, back towards Rio Frio. Catalina gave the dead gringo one last look. At least he'd be eaten by the birds. That was better than being pig food. That was better than being resurrected. Small things. It's the small things that count.

She flicked her cigarette away.

# THE END OF THE CARROLL A. DEERING

## BOB HOLE

"Oh, I saws them, I did." Jacobson muttered. Once he demanded men at the tap call him Captain, but lately even he had forgotten the title except on the rainiest, the bleakest of nights. "I saw them poor blighters up on that ship."

The fellow seated beside him snorted at the edge of his stein.

"Crew all was stumblin' 'round the foredeck. They was groanin' and callin', I tells ya." Jacobson had not been near the water in years. His skin no longer a tan from sun and salt but the pasty gleam of too much time indoors. "It *was* the *Deering*, comin' back from Rio. Last stop was Barbados they said. No mistakin' the five masts of that schooner. Maine wastes trees."

"True enough, but many a man has been known to mistake things at sea." His listener sipped his beer. "At night." He was amused and baited the old seaman. He had traveled all the way from New York because Jacobson's tale deserved to be preserved in the ragged, untrimmed edges of the pulps.

"Not as close as I got! Them things weren't human . . . least not anymore." Jacobson finished his mug, then clanked it on the wooden table with a sharp thunk. Perhaps a sign to both visitor and pub that he wanted his third of the evening. "They'd stopped in Barbados."

Putting his own mug down in front of him, his companion said, "What of it? What were they hollering, then?"

"So much wind. First I swore I heard them callin' out 'sleet.' A hard-bitten January, cold in '21 as to set all the grinders in Diamond Shoals chatterin' in men's mouths.

"Then they came closer. Then I knew what they was callin'. Didn't think I could feel the chill more that night. But near as soiled myself. Can tell you that. Tell you that now." Jacobson stared out the grungy window of the pub. The shoreline was miles away but not to his eyes. "Barbados." He repeated the word as if some catechism. "Just like the others."

"What others?"

The captain turned back to his visitor. "*Cyclops*. She left Barbados just like the Deering, but in '18, three years ago. Three hundred eight souls 'board. All lost. There were stories then."

The man from New York was losing patience. "Out with it."

"Cursed waters, ships abandoned. Lost if lucky. Crews gone missin' 'twixt here and Bermuda."

"But the *Deering* wasn't lost. She came aground at Hatteras."

"An' her crew all gone." The captain turned back to the window and chewed a bit more at the lower lip hidden beneath his beard. "Taken by the sea, I hope . . . Salt water heals all things, I hear . . . " His voice trailed off.

The visitor groaned and paid the tab. He rose and shook out what water remained on his overcoat. "Tell me at least what you heard them hollering?"

The captain, his eyes locked somewhere past the window, shuddered. "Meat, Mr. Munsey. They was callin' fer meat."

# PROMISED LAND (WINEVILLE, 1928)

## RICHARD E. GROPP

*Promised land. Promised land. Promised. Land.* The fever burned through his flesh—words without thought, echoing through the empty cavern of his skull.

*Promised land.*

West by night. The mid-day sun was too scalding now, doing awful things to his skin. And he remembered, at times, where he was going—but never where he was. Or exactly who he was.

*California.* He was going to California. The beach. The stars. Home to all of those magical picture shows, flickering black and white across his barely-remembered hometown screen—so alien to his family, a source of ridicule, scorn, and Father's angry fists whenever he showed up too late to work the fields. Too busy daydreaming. Too busy imagining himself up there on the screen, in tux and tails and rakish grin.

And the daylight didn't just hurt his skin now. His eyes, too—the sun burning bright in one, the other turned blind, then gone. Plucked out. Soft and wet on his tongue. He'd dug into the eye cavity for more, but there was nothing there, just crumbling flesh sloughing off against bone. And his flesh, too, was bad: tasted tough and bitter, when he wanted warm and sweet and alive.

It had started with a single bite. He had stowed away on the back of a farmer's truck, heading to California (*the promised land, the promised land, the promised land!*) only to find that he wasn't alone. A shadow in the corner, a salivating beast in overalls, waiting for a fresh hot meal. He'd managed to tumble out of the back of the truck before that *thing* could rip more than a single bite from his forearm.

And then the fever had struck, and he lost days and days and days. And his skin . . .

So he hid during the day and moved at night, following the setting sun. His feet didn't hurt, despite all the walking, but his joints made horrible sounds, popping and crackling under his disintegrating flesh. *Must be in California by now.* He'd started out in Arizona, surrounded by dead crops and crumbling farmhouses. And he wished he could see his father now. That old man, beaten down and angry at the world, angry at his family, angry at his dying fields.

The thought of Father's fleshy, callused right fist made his stomach scream with hunger.

## PROMISED LAND (WINEVILLE, 1928)

He caught a cat in the dark, in the woods. Domestic. It must have been domestic; it didn't even run. And then he saw farmhouse lights beyond a wall of trees. And heard the screams of disturbed birds. A chicken ranch.

There were people in the yard, and as soon as he saw them, his arid mouth filled with saliva, and he bit off a chunk of his own tongue—dead, pale imitation of human flesh.

"I said, do it!" A yelling voice, a looming Father-shadow next to the nearest chicken coop. "Or you're next, you little whoreson. A shallow grave and quicklime . . . to make sure we never get caught. And that's more than these Satan-lure catamites deserve!" Then he stalked off, and the front door slammed shut, leaving one quaking shadow to drag a child-size lump across the field, to a spot near his hiding place.

The urge was great—and growing greater—to hunt and eat, to bite down on something that breathed and bled. Something human. But he couldn't do it. He remembered Hollywood. He remembered glamour on a screen, elegance and beauty, and he couldn't kill. That wasn't him. That wasn't his destiny.

So, despite his hunger, despite his overwhelming desire for the flesh of this trembling teenager, he stood in the trees and watched. He watched as a scared boy dug a little hole for a little body. And when the teenager was finally done, and disappeared back into that run-down shack, he darted out and dug up the freshly turned earth.

The dead-boy flesh wasn't particularly good—not warm, not filled with beating blood. But it *was* flesh, and it sated some of his hunger. Not as much as the shaking teenager would have done, or the horrible Father-man—or any of the others he could smell cowering inside that horrible, horrible shack.

But he wasn't a monster. That wasn't a role he wanted to play.

There were multiple graves in the Father-man's field, out behind the chicken coops. All children. A terrible crop planted over days, or weeks, that would never grow. And when he was done, when the graves were empty and his stomach full, he closed his eyes and tried to feel the pull of the promised land in the distance. It wasn't far now. He could sense it.

And, once again, he started shambling west, toward Hollywood.

He was going to be a star.

# TELL ME LIKE YOU DONE BEFORE

## SCOTT EDELMAN

As the star-speckled black of the sky gave way to an unbroken dark blue canvas that promised a dawn, a thin man, his shoulders slumped as if he had been carrying the world upon them, rose from where he had been hiding amidst the brush.

He slapped at the dry earth which clung to the folds of his well-worn clothing. The grim expression on his sharp features softened slightly as he was swallowed by the resulting cloud of dust.

He stared down into the valley to where he knew a ranch was nestled several miles away, miles he'd had no remaining juice to cover the night before. Even though a new day was on the verge of being born, he still could make it out by but a few pinpoints of campfire.

He smiled then, a change in expression so slight that it would have been perceptible only to someone who had known him for many years.

But there was only one friend like that who still walked God's green Earth. And he was many miles away, the miles growing greater each day. Or so this weary man hoped.

Besides, that friend was supposed to be dead.

The man had made it to the start of another day, something which he'd been wise enough not to count on. He wished he could have made it to the ranch the night before, where surrounded by others he might have been lulled into a false sense of security which would have let him get some rest, instead of a broken sleep which left him as exhausted now as before he lay down, but fatigue had overtaken him there among the sycamores, and that was that.

He heard a scraping at his feet, and looked down to see a small rabbit, its bones bent, its eyes glowing, dragging itself toward him through the brown grass. Before he could react, it leapt at him, though because its frame was crippled, it could only propel itself to the top of his left boot, and no further. The wretched thing drove its incisors into the thick leather at the man's calf.

He shrieked, and struggled to kick at it with the heel of his other boot, but his angle was all wrong, and so he struck it with only glancing blows. He fell, even as he was doing so telling himself how stupid he'd been to let his throat get within the creature's reach. The rabbit dropped its jaws, a noxious liquid spilling forth, and as it readied itself for another leap, one which would end this terrifying dance, the man's scrabbling fingers chanced on a medium-sized rock. He scooped it up and slammed it hard against the thing's skull.

The coney dropped to the man's side, still wriggling, preparing for another attack, and so he quickly rolled to his knees, bashing at it again with the rock. But it kept coming, not giving up until he caught its skull directly. He brought the rock down once, twice, again, so many times he lost count.

Only then did it lie still.

The man fell back, gasping for breath, shuddering not only from the close call, but also from the memories which had haunted him ever since the night he'd pulled the trigger, embers which the violent encounter had stirred into a raging fire. He'd been haunted even before that dreadful dusk, but he'd thought that with his ultimate action, once the bullet flew, it would surely be over.

Turned out all he'd done was trade one kind of haunting for another.

He lay on his back until the sky had turned a bright cloudless blue, a color that told him he was free of any further such encounters, at least until night began to fall once more. He stood then, looked down at the ranch the morning had revealed. He'd hoped that might be the place to rest for a spell, but he now saw that he still needed to put a few more miles on his boots.

He sighed. That had been much too close. He couldn't afford to linger.

There would be other ranches.

There would have to be.

He listened for a moment to the rumble in his belly, and then moved on.

During the day, as he picked his way through the willows that lined the banks of the Salinas, hoping that it would cover his tracks and knowing at the same time that hope was pointless, he hunted for food. During the days, he could. That was when the things, and most importantly, the thing (though it hurt to call him that) which hunted him could not.

He was hungry, but even so, he hesitated when he saw his first rabbit that morning. Daylight or no, the flood of the reanimated had taught him to be wary. And there'd been so many of them killed over the years. His friend had been clumsy that way. Who knew how long they would keep coming, the parade of the damned? So his first live one of the day got away. But then, spurred on by the increasing volume of the rumbling in his gut, he shook off his close call at dawn and was able to bring himself to bring one down.

And he needed to. He had to keep up his strength, and the cans of beans he'd borrowed—he preferred to call it that rather than use the word "stolen"—had only lasted so far. He'd thought events had taken a bad turn in Weed, but on the night when he'd had to make that horrible choice, to do that terrible thing to the friend who'd trusted him more than anybody else in the world, they'd gotten worse. As worse as he thought it was possible for a life to get.

He'd been wrong. He'd been wrong about a lot.

He worried that, warm meat settling in his belly or no, he could only go on so far.

But he would have to try.

He reached the next ranch in the late afternoon, when almost all of the men were still out in the fields. He'd done that sort of thing before, shown up too late for work and gotten a meal without having to toil for it, but in the old days, that action had been a choice, and he hadn't been alone.

Of course, however it seemed, he really wasn't alone now. That's why he had to keep moving. But he'd grown wearier than usual these past few days, and had to take the risk. At least briefly.

He entered the bunkhouse and found one lone ranch hand begrudgingly sweeping the stained floor. The hand paused, leaning against his broom, and eyed the intruder warily.

"Well, aren't you the special cuss," he said. "Waltzing in here like this with the day's work just about done."

"No, I ain't nobody special. Name's George. George Milton."

George held out a hand, but the man refused to take it, keeping his fingers wrapped around the broom handle.

"Sorry," he continued. "Hitched a ride, and meant to be here early, but I got dropped off one ranch over. Had to hoof it from there. Mighty impressive spreads in these parts. Took a mess of hiking to get me here."

"You're damned lucky we're down a few hands, otherwise the boss would send you on your way like *that*." He snapped his fingers, and that action somehow broke his resolve. His grimace blossomed into a smile, and he held out a hand. "Name's Willie."

"Pleased to meet ya, Willie," said George, as the two men shook.

"So how come you're short?" asked George, after the pleasantries were done. "Times like these, no one just walks away from a job without a good reason."

"You'd think so," said Willie, his brow wrinkling. "Only, that's what done happened. Three guys just took off in the middle of the night during the last week alone, one at a time, without even the decency to say why or goodbye. Lucky for you, they didn't take any of their stuff, so since it don't look like you're carrying much in the way of supplies, you're welcome to their leftovers."

Normally, George would be grateful for that spot of good luck. There was only so much he could carry, so he'd had to leave a lot behind. But he didn't like the sound of this. Turning your back on three squares and a cot was crazy, with what the you ess of ay was going through in the '30s, with both food and work so scarce. Just wasn't done. Not by anyone. And certainly not by three from the same ranch, so close together.

But he didn't have time to think much further on the puzzle, because that's when the men returned from their long day in the fields.

They were glad to see him, or made a show of being so anyway, because being down a few men, their routine had become even more brutal than usual. And he was glad to see them, too, because in those few minutes of exchanging names and slapping backs, in the midst of a dozen or so men laughing, cursing, spitting, he felt almost normal. By the time the introductions were over, he had trouble remembering most of the names, but it didn't matter that he couldn't keep them straight, because he knew their types well.

Maybe they'd been bucking barley. Maybe they were just back from haying. It didn't really matter. Guys like that were the same all over.

Here was the joe who blamed the world for all of his problems, there the silent one who might be stupid or might not, but since he rarely opened his mouth, few could tell for sure (George quickly moved on from that one for fear of remembering too fully once more), here the one with the tripwire temper who was quick to anger, there the lazy bastard who hoped no one would notice but knew everyone did . . .

There the calm and steady one, the one George could tell people listened to. That last one's name he'd make sure to remember. Jackson. He was the rarest type of all, the peacemaker, a sort not always found in the muddle of men on ranches and farms. And he might come in handy.

Then the dinner bell rang and George met the boss around a long table as plates of tough meat and tougher rolls were passed around, and the men gobbled them down like candy. The meat tasted like horse—it was a sign of the times that he could identify the flavor, for once he'd never have been able to do that—but he was glad of any meal he didn't have to kill for himself.

The boss, a barrel-shaped man named Dix, didn't question him much, so George didn't have to explain what had happened in Weed, or what happened not so very much later a few miles south of Soledad. George wasn't a very good liar, so he wasn't sure how well he would have been able to hide the truth, but the boss seemed too needy to go hunting after possible distressing facts anyway.

After the meal, the guys pitched a few horseshoes, and smoked a few cigarettes, but they were all too worn out for much more fun than that, the men from their work, George from his long hike and close escape. Only after he'd crawled into bed did he remember that he'd intended to ask about the men who'd vanished, find out what kind of people they were, if there was a simple reason why so many workers would have gotten skittish enough to bolt so close together.

But then sleep overcame him, and he was off in dream, telling the same old story again, the story his friend had always treated as new, the one about a little house on a couple of acres, and a vegetable garden, and the rabbits.

Always the rabbits.

George jerked awake at dawn, when the sun's first rays crept into the room. He had learned what that first light meant. He'd survived another night, and nothing could get at him until another one fell. The work to come that he would normally have cursed as backbreaking would instead be a relief, because it would tell him that he was alive. Even a poorly cooked breakfast, with bits of shell mixed into the scrambled eggs, didn't dampen his mood, and when he leapt with the other men into the wagon and headed out for the barley, he was filled with as much happiness as his present life could muster.

As he worked that day, watching the sun track across the sky, he found himself wishing it would move more slowly. Ever since he'd done what he'd done, there was no end of things out there looking for him.

The big lummox had snuffed out so many of them. Only they hadn't stayed snuffed out. He couldn't even get that right.

But George must have made a mess of it big time as well. He'd shot Lenny, seen him fall. He'd shot him in the sweet spot, right where he was supposed to, supposed to so that his friend's long troubled journey would all be over.

Only it wasn't.

When he got back to the bunk house at the end of the day, he discovered that a rope had been stretched between two trees out front, a sheet tossed over it to hang limply.

"What do you suppose that's about?" asked George.

"I don't rightly know," said Jackson. George had attached himself to the man, hoping to borrow some of his calm. "Been here a piece but never seen it done before."

They shrugged and passed the setup by, heading in for another overcooked meal. When they pushed back from their plates, Dix stood up, and leaned forward with his palms flat on the table.

"I have a treat for you fellers tonight," he said. "As soon as it's fully dark, we're going to have ourselves a picture show."

The men chattered excitedly as they rushed outside.

"What do you think it's gonna be?" said one.

"I hope it's a dancing picture," said the quiet one, who surprised them by speaking up at such length. "I like them dancing pictures."

"Don't matter to me much," said George. "As long as it takes me away from here."

"Oh, it ain't so bad here," said Jackson. "We got food, a place to lay our heads. And sure, Dix can be tough at times, but believe me, I've seen worse. Who could want anything more than that?"

George could, and he wasn't the only one. He could think of a few others who would want more as well, and he knew exactly what it was they'd want. How he was the one who'd made them want it. And how he had gone ahead and ruined it for them all.

You couldn't blame the big lummox. He didn't know what he was doing. But George . . . he was supposed to know better. All that came after. That was his own damn fault.

Dix directed the men to set up rows of crates in the wide space between the bunkhouse and the stables, and then they sat there, working at their toothpicks, spitting in the dust, waiting for the purple sky to turn black. George didn't like being exposed out in the open like that, but he couldn't figure any way around it. He pressed himself into the center of the men. The boss carried out a projector and fussed with it, not letting any of the others help him with the delicate machine. That didn't stop him from cursing at Willie as the hand played out a length of cable that ran from the small generator which usually kept the boss' house lit.

"Settle down, men," shouted Dix. "I don't exactly know what we got ourselves here, but from what they tell me, it's supposed to be a doozy."

George shifted uncomfortably on his crate, and was relieved when the utter darkness was broken by a beam of light. One of the guys nearest the screen laughed and jumped up, throwing his silhouette on the sheet, but a shout from Dix returned him to his crate. Soon the night was pierced by a beating of drums, and the words *WHITE ZOMBIE* stretched before them.

"Hey, look," someone shouted, as Bela Lugosi's name appeared, "it's got that vampire guy in it."

George didn't know what the hell he was talking about. He wasn't much for picture shows, at least not lately, not when he'd had more important plans for his money. But not just with *his* money . . .

Best not to think of it. Best not to think of any of it, the missed picture shows, the skipped visits to fine parlors, all sacrificed in pursuit of—

Forget it. Forget it all.

Maybe this movie, whatever it was, would take his mind elsewhere. But based on how it began, it served only to refocus him more fully on his problem. Off in a country not really so distant and yet as far away to him as the moon, dead men walked, dead men who were at the same time somehow undead.

"Haiti is full of nonsense and superstition," said one character to another, but to be either of those, a thing had to be untrue, didn't it? George understood all too well the truth of his situation, that there could be life after death, though not much of one, and as the movie went on, his skin prickled with recognition. And when, about fifteen minutes in, the camera closed in tight on a huge bull of a man, his eyes wide, his soul gone, looking as if he could crush you with one hand, it all became too much. He leapt up from the center of the men, almost knocking a few of them over, ignoring the boss when he shouted at him to stay.

He fled, circling to the opposite side of the bunkhouse, cursing. He crouched down there, leaned his back against the wall, and with shaking hands rolled himself a cigarette. He could barely steady his hands to bring match to tip, and it wasn't until he'd smoked it halfway down that his trembling stopped.

Jackson was suddenly there with him.

"Mind if I join you?" he asked.

George shook his head, and waved with his free hand at the patch of ground beside him.

They sat there quietly for a while. George wanted to say something, anything, to cover the sound of the movie which whispered at them around the corners of the bunkhouse, but he couldn't think of a damn thing.

"So what was that all about?" Jackson finally asked.

George had half a mind to tell him everything. He remembered another man like him, one who took George under his wing after the deed was done. He got George stinking drunk, and made him think that life could go on after what he'd had to do.

Life went on all right, but not the way either of them had thought. Now Slim was dead, George was on the run, and there was something after him, which though no longer capable of running, seemed pretty much unstoppable. But how to begin to tell something like that?

Before George could speak, a shuffling sound came from out of the desert, one which could barely be heard over the movie's buzz on the other side of the bunkhouse. George noticed it first, his senses having been made more alert to such things due to his recent situation.

Jackson noticed him squinting, and followed his gaze.

"What are you looking at?" he asked. "I don't see anythi—why, would you look at that!"

A small dog crawled toward them in the darkness, one of its front legs broken. Even so, it managed to close the gap between them quickly. George pressed his back more forcefully against the wall of the bunkhouse, unable to move any further, even as Jackson stood up and took a step toward it.

"Jackson, no!" George shouted.

But before Jackson could heed George's warning, he was on his knees beside the thing, reaching out to stroke it. It responded by biting hard into the meaty part of the man's thumb. Jackson yanked back his hand, but the animal wouldn't let go, and so was pulled into the air as he jumped up. He leapt around in pain, flinging his hand about, snapping the animal this way and that to no avail. It clung to him with the hunger of another world.

Jackson's yelps finally propelled George to action. He slid his work gloves from where they were tucked into his belt, and grabbed the thing by its hind legs, angry memories flooding back. He knew who had broken that one leg. He knew who had killed it. And yet not even those injuries, sudden, foolish, and fatal, had been enough to stop its vicious hunt. It had still kept coming, tracking him, sensing him out, and if George didn't act quickly, it would turn the man who'd come between them into another victim of his unwise choices.

He pinched at the hinge of its jaw, forcing it to release its grip, and hurled it to the ground. He brought down his heel, catching it in the midsection as it made to escape, flattening it as surely as if it had been run over by a wagon wheel, but though it burst, intestines spilling out, that wasn't enough to stop it. It still struggled for them. He slammed down his heel again and caught it near one ear, while Jackson continued to yowl in pain, cradling his arm, unable to help. George could hear a crunch of bone, but because of his angle he didn't think that had been enough to take care of it.

Though its lower jaw now hung at an ugly angle, he could see that he hadn't yet finished it. It moved away from the two men, more quickly than George thought would have been possible, and he had a choice. He'd always had choices. Wasn't that what had brought him here? Too many had died because of him, and so he knelt beside Jackson, held him as the creature vanished into the night.

"What the Hell was that thing?" said Jackson, puking. He slumped against George. "Oh, I don't feel so good."

George helped Jackson to his feet, and saw that they were still alone. Good. The fact that they were still by themselves meant that thanks to the sounds from the movie and the whoops of the men, no one had heard anything. There was still time, time to save Jackson and time to keep his secret.

But not much. Jackson's eyes were dilated. His tongue lolled in his mouth.

"Do you want to live?" asked George. Jackson jerked his head, but George couldn't tell whether the man was nodding or shaking it. "Jackson, listen to me. You want to live, don't you?"

Jackson was beyond answering, so George answered for him. He dragged him into the bunkhouse through the back door, and laid him down on his cot. He got a knife, a candle, and a bottle of whiskey, and then took a brief furtive look out the front door.

The men were still mesmerized, not giving a damn that two of their comrades were gone. George pulled back from the door, avoiding even the slightest glance at the screen. That would be too much, even now. *White Zombie* be damned.

George lit the candle, and held the blade of the knife over the flame. He poured the whiskey, first on the heated knife, then down Jackson's throat. The man hardly had the power to swallow, and barely even had the power to choke. George crushed one corner of the bed sheet and jammed it in Jackson's mouth.

George held the knife against the base of Jackson's thumb, which by then was almost black, and oozing a foul pus. He held the knife an inch below the bite marks, pressed it against the part of flesh where the skin was already turning from pink to gray.

"There's no other way," said George. "I wish there was, but there ain't."

He took a deep breath and sliced as cleanly as he knew how, while Jackson howled through the cloth, which thankfully dampened the sound of it, and then fainted. George poured another slug of whiskey onto the wound, then wrapped the hand tightly with scraps from a shirt that had been abandoned by one of the men who had vanished.

Having just encountered the undead cur, he now was pretty certain where they had gone.

He'd answer Jackson's question when he woke, tell him *exactly* what that was all about. He swore he would. Because though he may have decided he'd just have to get used to being one of the loneliest guys in the world, something which he never thought he'd have to be, there was no way out of this life alone.

Tonight proved that.

The men never saw how the movie played out, whether or not the fancy-pants hero managed to save the day against "that vampire guy." George ended it all when he came running out of the bunkhouse, screaming, his eyes wild. He sprinted up to the boss, shouting hysterically, grabbing his collar, calling out Jackson's name. They all followed him back inside and found Jackson stretched out there, his hand a ball of bloody cloth.

George tried to explain what had happened, what he wanted them to think had happened, but couldn't be heard over the chaotic questions from the men. Dix had to fire a shot into the ceiling to shut them up. With the room silent, George was barely coherent, or at least tried his best to be, and Willie insisted he down some whiskey, which helped in his pretense, especially considering he'd already taken a few shots on his own before sprinting outside.

He explained how a coyote had attacked them as they'd been talking there quietly in the dark, and how they'd fought it off, but not before Jackson had lost a thumb. One of the men, who'd almost finished high school, and had done some book reading, peeled back the sodden makeshift bandages. George could see that the blood ran red, thank god, and so what he'd done had been worth the funny look the man then gave him. George looked away as the man did his best to sew up Jackson's hand, though he heard him explain that he wouldn't be able to return to work for at least weeks. George then saw the guy whispering to Dix, who walked over to him angrily.

"Are you sure you're telling us what really happened?" he barked.

George protested that he had, and Dix seemed to take his word for it. At least at first, for he did glare back at him suspiciously after he returned to stand over Jackson.

George hoped that once he woke, the man would be able to keep his story straight. George's life, George's plan, depended on it.

George's life? Hah!

One way or another, it would have to end.

George spent the next day toiling in the field while wondering how Jackson was doing, what he was saying, and how everything could have gone so wrong. Nobody was in the mood to talk much, and the men kept their distance from him, so he had plenty of time in which to wonder.

He'd sworn, though his intentions then were not what they were now, that his aim had been true. He'd pressed the barrel of that gun right where the spine and the skull joined, but he must have closed his eyes, or looked away at the last moment, or done something to stop the shot from firing straight. How else to explain it? It was love that had caused him to do what had to be done, but he guessed that it was also love which had left space for the mistake which had allowed his friend to come back.

The day passed quickly, because even though he pressed himself to work like a dog, harder than he ever had before, in an attempt to forget, he wasn't really there, since that attempt was a failure. He was instead off in that clearing in the brush where it had all gone down—Had it truly been only a few weeks before? That seemed impossible—but also lost in the night before, when in the instant Jackson was attacked he had made a decision. So he was in those two places, not out under the hot sun. He had no way to undo either of those events, but he could damn well make sure that there would be no other such events in the future. If only Jackson could remember what George had whispered to him through his delirium.

By the look Dix gave him when the crew returned at the end of the day, it seemed as if he had. George nodded at his boss, and the man nodded back without judgment. As the rest of the men ran to the dining table, George slipped away to sit himself down next to Jackson's cot. Jackson, propped up by a pile of sweat-soaked pillows, was clear-eyed, and appeared fully himself again.

"I'm sorry," said George, his voice cracking.

Jackson studied George, taking his measure of him, and then nodded.

Then George told him everything.

He told him all about Lenny, big as an ox and just as dumb, and how Aunt Clara had asked him to watch out for the poor bastard, and all the promises he had made, and livin' off the fat of the land, and what happened to drive him and Lenny out of Weed, and about Curley, and Curley's wife, and it all tumbled out breathlessly, right up until that horrible night in the clearing near the brush by the river.

And through it all, Jackson kept nodding, his expression revealing nothing. So the tale he never thought he'd tell anyone kept pouring out of him, those impossible things that came after, how Lenny, and the things he had killed, had started to come back. Back for *him*.

Finally, there was nothing more left to tell. Nothing. Except—

"I need your help," said George.

Jackson held up his crippled hand.

"Help?" he said, snorting. "What can I do? What good would I be?"

"More good than what all of the others could possibly be put together," said George. "After what you seen, you'll believe."

Then George told him of his plan.

"Will you do it?" said George. "As far as I can figure, that's the only way to make it stop."

Jackson whistled.

"You're a crazy bastard, you know that?" he said. "Crazy as a wedge."

"Maybe. But that don't mean it won't work. Will you help me?"

This time, Jackson didn't hesitate.

"From the sound of it, you saved my life," he said. "Wouldn't seem right not to."

George reached out to shake Jackson's hand, then frowned, letting his own undamaged hand fall back into his lap.

By the time George finished laying out what the two of them would do next and got to the dinner table, most all of the food was gone, but it didn't really bother him. His hunger had been dampened by his plans. He mopped up some gravy with a heel of bread and mulled them over. That would have to be enough for now.

Once the meal was done, and the men poured outside to unwind with jawing and horseshoes, with one an excuse for the other, and it was never clear which the excuse and which the thing that had brought them there, he snuck back in and made his way to the deserted kitchen. He packed a bindle with half a loaf of bread, a rind of cheese, and a couple of cans of beans. Such a theft had become far too familiar to him, and he hated that, but depending on how things went, one way or another, this would be the last time he did this.

He returned to his bunk, hid the supplies under his covers, and pretended to sleep. When the snores of the other hands began to echo through the room, he slipped to his feet, tucked his boots under one arm, and made his way over to Jackson. He nudged the man, who snapped awake.

"It's time," he whispered.

George grabbed Jackson's things so that he wouldn't have to use his bum hand to fumble with them, and led him out the door, feeling crazy for doing so as the darkness swallowed them.

They hadn't been on the road for more than a couple of hours before they came upon Curley's wife shambling toward them in the moonlight.

Seeing her make her way unerringly in his direction through the bramble, each step clumsy yet determined, George realized that if they hadn't left when they did, this encounter might have occurred at the ranch, and then he would have been responsible for even more wreckage than he'd spread so far. Three men whom he did not know were already dead. He wouldn't have been able to bear the burden of more.

Her right leg was twisted in a way a leg shouldn't be able to go and still function, while her left shoulder seemed dislocated, the arm that hung straight down from it dangling limply.

"Damn you," screamed George. "You done this! If not for you, we still coulda been back there, still hoping, still dreaming, still pulling together our stake. But you had to go and mess things up, didn't you, you had to—"

Jackson dropped his good hand on George's shoulder.

"She can't hear you, George," he said. "There ain't nothing left inside of her to hear."

"Maybe you're right," said George. "Considering what we gotta do to that woman, I sure hope so."

George pulled out the pistol he had taken, a theft for which he hoped Dix would forgive him, but Jackson tapped his wrist with cold metal of his own and shook his head. George could see that he was grasping his baling hook.

"Save your bullets," said Jackson. "From what you been telling me, we're going to need them."

The two men separated, moving in wide circles to take up positions on opposite sides of the woman, their hands filled with curved steel. That she moved toward George without hesitation, whether from conscious thought or just some primal animal instinct that remained, ignoring Jackson as if he was nothing more than part of the landscape, told him, as if he needed any more convincing, that all his running had been pointless. He could never run far enough that she, or something like her, would not have been able to follow him.

As George looked at her then, her once shining sausage curls now dull as they hung from a grizzled flap of scalp, the splotch of red smeared across her mouth no longer lipstick but rather fresh blood, the hatred he'd been carrying around for her suddenly vanished. Whether that was going to make what was about to occur easier or more difficult he could not reckon.

He didn't have much time to figure that out, either, because he could see Jackson coming up behind her, beginning to make his move, and so he dashed in and dropped to his knees, swinging wildly to slash at the tendons in her calves. Unable to die or not, that would at least slow her down. As she bent toward him, he rolled to one side, and as he hacked at her again, Jackson joining him, she toppled like a downed oak.

With her face in the earth, Jackson leapt upon her, pressing both knees into the small of her back. He plunged his hook into the base of her neck, tearing through the gray flesh. George was right there with him, alternating his blows so that they only slashed her, and not each other, their hooks occasionally getting stuck in her skull and needing to be pulled free. The ichor flew like ribbons in the wind each time they raised their fists to the sky, and they did not halt their attack until what had once been Curley's wife stopped wriggling beneath them on the ground. Then they fell back, gasping for breath, dropping their weapons into the dry earth.

George poked at her with the toe of his boot. He felt the bile rise in his throat, felt as if he was about to retch, but he somehow managed to hold himself back.

He'd only known the woman for a little while, and still it had been difficult. But Lenny . . . Lenny was like a brother. He couldn't imagine how much more painful that would be.

He looked across her broken body at Jackson.

"The next one won't be so easy," said George.

Jackson looked at the blood seeping through his bandages, and nodded. He glanced down at Curley's wife, and suddenly grew solemn.

"She deserves a decent burial after all she's been through, don't you think," he said.

"She's already had one," said George. "And one is more than most of us ever get. Besides, we just don't have the time."

So they piled stones on her until she could no longer be seen, though George doubted that any animal would be drawn in by what was left of her and be tempted to feast. He said a short prayer to keep Jackson happy, even though he believed in God less now than ever.

They stood silently for a moment, until George could bear no more, and then they continued on.

As George led Jackson back, back to where this final chapter had begun, the journey made him feel as if they were traveling not just in space but in time. If only that were possible, if only he could have undone it all with different choices, instead of what was coming. But that was wishful thinking, and he had no more wishes left.

He did not follow a path which would lead them there directly, because he did not want them to meet head on the one who followed, but rather force this to be ended where it seemed right that it should be ended. So they circled back around the far side of the valley, made their way as far up the foothills of the Gabilan mountains as they had the energy to spare.

George wanted no possibility they would meet at some random midpoint. Rather, he wanted to draw his friend back, back to that place in the brush by the sandy banks of the Salinas River.

Lenny would remember that place, even with all that had occurred, even with what he had become. George had made sure to drum that hiding place into his feeble brain until it stuck like tar. If all else was burned away, that would remain. George was sure of that.

It took them several days to reach the spot, and several further encounters with pets which Lenny, when living, had not been able to help but kill, and by the time they arrived, night had already fallen. George could barely see the outlines of the place, but in his bones, he knew. This was where his friend had been reborn.

"What do we do now?" asked Jackson.

"We wait," said George. "It shouldn't be long now until he returns, until it's over."

He knelt, ran his fingers through the soil on the patch of ground where his friend had fallen.

"I don't know that I'll be able to sleep," he continued. "But I have to at least try. Why don't you take the first watch?"

George threw himself down under a sycamore tree, and closed his eyes, but even though he was exhausted, his eyelids atwitch with fatigue, sleep would not come. Somehow beyond conscious thought he must have sensed that he should be aware of that stretch of final moments before he did what he had to do, and not pass through them unconscious. He looked at the branches above him, and then closed his eyes to think about his next step, and when he opened them, he found that he must have fallen asleep anyway, for Lenny was there, crouched beside him.

George quickly glanced over to where Jackson was supposed to be keeping watch. The fool was slumped over, having fallen asleep, instead of preparing to do to Lenny what they had done to Curley's wife. He cursed, not at Jackson, but at himself. It was too much to have asked of him, after he'd already undergone so much.

George looked back at Lenny, who sat there as if frozen. He could have been a statue in the moonlight, rather than a man, a dead man, but still a man. George could make out a wound at the base of his throat, the bullet hole not where he would have imagined it to be. He hadn't been able to look before, but now he knew for certain he must have pointed the gun down at the last instant, missing the brain completely. It had been enough to kill him. It just wasn't enough to keep him killed.

They sat there, unmoving, and in George's mind it was almost like the old days, a night like any other in a long string of nights, and he was being asked to tell him like he done before, asked this time not with words, but with silence. And he knew that he would answer that request, as he always had.

"Guys like us are the loneliest guys in the world," said George in a whisper, not because that's what he intended, but because that's all that would come out at first. "They got no family, nothing to look ahead to. But not us. No, not us. Because I got you to look after me, and you got me to look after you!"

George looked over at Jackson, his sleep unbroken by the bizarre conversation occurring so close beside him. George raised his voice, hoping to rouse the man.

"We're gonna get the jack together and get a little place," he continued. "We're gonna live off the fat of the land."

That's when Lenny would normally have punctuated the speech by clapping his hands together. George hesitated, leaving a space for the old familiar answer. He waited, looked for any movement, however imperceptible, from his old friend, but none came.

"We'll have chickens, and a vegetable patch—and rabbits. Rabbits, Lenny. *Rabbits!*"

George was shouting now, but no matter how loud the words came, Jackson would not move. He could see then in the moonlight that the man wasn't sleeping after all.

Arrayed around him were dozens of undead mice in various stages of decomposition, and all the other animals Lenny had in his clumsiness put down. Every watchful eye was aglow. The puppy they'd encountered earlier sat curled in Jackson's lap, its intestines draped over the man's legs like ribbons.

His neck was bent and broken, and what George had earlier taken to be a shadow from the brim of the hat pulled low over his eyes had actually once been a waterfall of blood, a waterfall now stilled. George looked back at Lenny to see a matching patch of color smeared across his face.

George stood slowly.

"I guess I'm not going to get to tell you about the rabbits no more, am I?" he said.

Lenny answered by also getting to his feet, and once he started rising, he kept on rising. George tilted his head back to look him in the face, the way he'd had to for years. He was surprised that even though it hadn't been that long, he'd already forgotten how amazingly tall Lenny had been. His friend stepped closer, but George did not retreat. There would have been no point.

And besides, all was as it should be.

He'd made a promise to Lenny's Aunt Clara, a promise to watch over him, to make sure no harm came to her addled nephew.

He'd failed. Failed them all.

Failed Lenny, and Clara, and Candy, and Crooks. And now Jackson.

And himself. Most of all, himself.

He'd made endless promises, and he failed to deliver on any of them, and whatever happened next in the remaining moments of his short, hardscrabble life, he deserved it.

Everybody in the whole damn world was scared of each other.

But George wasn't scared no more.

Not even when Lenny's teeth ripped through his stomach to what lay beneath.

George had always told Lenny that someday his friend would be living off the fat of the land.

As his life seeped from him, as he began to lose consciousness, he managed in his last moments to be strangely comforted by the sudden awareness that even though the alfalfa and chickens and rabbits would now be forever out of reach, even though he had fulfilled no other promise on this Earth, he had at least fulfilled that one.

# THE FATED SKY

## AIMEE PAYNE

Amelia Earhart never meant for any of it to happen. The newspapers, the endorsements, that Lady Lindy nonsense, she could have done without it. All she ever wanted to do was fly. It was the only thing that mattered to her.

She scanned the eternity of water in front of her. It looked different than it had from the air. Up there, she still felt like she could get beyond it. From the ground, it was impassable. If she got out of this—and she fully expected to—that's exactly what she'd tell the press.

She rested her hand on the Lockheed Electra's bright aluminum skin. Setting down on the reef had ripped the right landing gear free so the plane canted to that side. It hurt her to see that damage done to the most beautiful plane she'd ever owned, but she hadn't dumped it in the drink. And as long as it sat on the left gear, she could run that engine. And if she could run that engine, she could work the radio. And if she could work the radio . . .

A groan sounded from inside the plane. Amelia's train of thought chugged to a halt. She never should have hired Fred Noonan. She knew better. Best navigator in the world or not, the man was a drunk.

She shielded her eyes and turned toward the island. More like a tiny ring of coral around a shallow lagoon. The noise of the bickering frigate birds grated on her already raw nerves. From above, the island had looked like a scythe blade. Not the best of omens.

She pushed the thought away. "Not time for that, yet." But they were words and the wind took them to a place with only water and storms to hear.

From the back of the plane, Noonan called out for his mother, his wife, and finally Amelia. Amelia cursed as she climbed onto the wing. Stupid man. His wife wasn't so important when the British girl with skin so white she looked grey had been nuzzling his neck in that bar in Lae.

The smell inside the Electra knocked her back onto the wing. Noonan lay draped over the extra fuel tanks. They were bone dry, as he should have been more than a day after his bender.

"For heaven's sake, Fred. How much did you drink?"

He lifted his head. Amelia took a step back. The whites of his eyes were red. Not bloodshot but bloody. "Not drunk. Sick." His voice could have rubbed rust off the plane.

"And how." She climbed through the cockpit and into the cargo area. Hot air stung her face. Sitting in the sun, the Electra hoarded heat like an oven. "We have to get you out of here. Or you'll broil."

He shifted onto his side. Amelia covered her mouth with her hand. She knew she wasn't the sweetest smelling flower in the bunch, but good lord, the man smelled rotten.

He sat up. Amelia squelched the urge to gag. She would have to touch him, put her arm around him, let him lean against her. She squared her shoulders. Her father hadn't raised to her be a jittery Jane.

Maybe the ocean would rinse some of the stench off him.

Noonan allowed her to pull him to his feet. Good lord, the smell, she thought as she led him to the plane's side hatch. But she didn't vomit.

She shouldered the hatch open. The saltwater breeze cleared some of Noonan's miasma. Amelia hopped out first, then helped him down onto the reef. They faced the island. The shore seemed farther than it had been before.

*I'm going to die here,* she thought.

This time she didn't push it away. Know your opponent, her husband always said. On a deserted atoll in the Pacific Ocean, she could take her pick: the ocean, the weather, the island . . . the whole world. But she was no shrinking violet. And she wasn't alone.

"Let's go, Fred."

He groaned an answer. The shore wasn't far, maybe a hundred yards or so, but Noonan's weight made every step a hard landing. By the time they'd covered half that, Amelia's legs shook and sweat streamed down her back.

Noonan muttered the whole way. Most of the time it was gibberish too mushy to understand. But every so often, he'd speak clearly—strange words that didn't mean anything together. They were almost to the beach, when he finally made sense.

"Bit me," he said.

Amelia's feet shuffled from the clean coral shelf onto beach sand. Her balance threatened to desert her. She gritted her teeth and steadied her screaming muscles.

"What's that?"

"That dame," he said, his voice clearer. "She bit me." He pulled Amelia to a stop. "The crazy twist bit me."

"We have to get further up, under the trees." Amelia braced herself against him and stepped forward. Noonan didn't budge.

"What the Sam hell are you playing at, Fred Noonan?" She slipped out from under his arm, fully expecting him to topple into the surf. He stood steady as granite.

"You ain't listening, Mary Bea. That girl bit me." He threw out his arm. Right above his wrist, far enough under his cuff she would never have seen it if he hadn't showed her, was a red and purple bite. There was a good chunk taken out of the flesh, too.

But what truly worried Amelia was the fact that he'd just called her Mary Bea. Mary Bea was his wife, number two from what Amelia heard. And if he couldn't tell the difference between them, his condition was very bad indeed.

"Are you trying to tell me you haven't been hitting the sauce?" She goaded him, hoping he'd follow her into the shade of the jungle.

He stared at her. After a few seconds, his eyes cleared. "Amelia?"

"That's right, Fred."

"I didn't have a drop."

"We were in a bar."

"Not a drop since Delhi. Even then it was just a sip with dinner."

When she thought back to it, she didn't remember him drinking anything. She remembered the girl, though.

"Why did she bite you, Fred?"

He shook his head. "Don't know. One minute we were talking about my ma's people in London, the next her teeth are buried gum deep in my arm." He held it up again. It looked even worse than it had the first time, with a greenish pus clinging to perfect little tooth marks. Good lord, could it really have gotten that much worse that quickly?

*Infection,* she thought. *And us hundreds of miles from the nearest doctor.* For the third time since landing the plane safe and sound on the reef, she thought of Death.

Noonan stared down at the bite. "I'm going to die here."

"You see that?" She pointed down the reef to the hulk of an old steam freighter run aground. "That means the island isn't uncharted. Someone will think to look sooner or later. All we have to do hang in there and keep sending out distress signals. They'll find us."

He stared at the wreck. "That's the *Norwich City.* Ran aground on Gardner back in '29."

"Gardner. That puts us in the Phoenix Islands." She smiled with as much cheer as she could muster. "Phoenix is a good sign, right?"

The corners of Noonan's lips stretched the tiniest bit. Close enough. Amelia gestured toward the edge of the jungle. "You think you can make it to the trees on your own?"

He stared up the beach like a man at the end of a long journey. "I think I can. Where you going?"

"Back out to the plane." She gestured over her shoulder. "We'll need supplies."

They both knew the "supplies" on the Electra didn't amount to much. They were never in flight long enough to need much more than a sandwich or two and water. But there was a first aid kit, and a few things they could use to build a makeshift shelter.

Noonan nodded. Amelia left him to make his own way up the beach. She waded out to the plane. Before she crawled inside, she scanned the water. Tides were probably low this time of day. The water would get deeper. Whether it was deep enough to lift the plane and wash it out to sea, she could only wait and see.

She crawled inside and scavenged anything that would be useful and stowed it in a pack, including a pocketknife, hammer, and long screwdriver. Water was the main thing. They didn't have much, but until they could find fresh water they'd need every drop. That meant two half-empty canteens. A little bag from New Guinea contained some bread, cheese, and meat. Under it sat a rather large bottle of Kentucky bourbon. She took that, too. As she climbed out, she grabbed the first aid kit mounted near Fred's navigation station.

When she got back to the beach, Noonan lay face down in the sand not twenty feet from where she had left him.

"Noonan!" She dropped their provisions. Kneeling next to him, she rested her hand on his side, her breath backing up in her chest. He couldn't be dead. What would she say to his wife? And the newspapers . . . Amelia could see the headline now: *Lady Lindy Loses Luck, Costs Navigator's Life.*

Noonan's ribcage expanded almost too slowly to feel, then gradually deflated. She fell back onto the sand, her relief whooshing out of her with her held breath. Still alive. How much longer, though?

She walked back down the beach and retrieved the things she'd gathered from the plane. She got the provisions back to shore. She thought Noonan was sleeping when she got back, but his eyes opened when she drank from the canteen.

"Water?"

She trickled some into his open mouth, careful not to let the canteen touch his lip. She offered him a piece of the bread, but he shook his head.

She washed Noonan's bite wound with seawater, then smeared it with the analgesic balm from the first aid kit. She would have bandaged it, but the only spare fabric was their grubby clothes. Besides, she thought, the air might do it some good.

Through the rest of the day, she offered Noonan bits of bread but he always shook his head. He accepted water—as much as she would give him—but it made little difference. By the time the tide went out again, he refused a drop.

Sometime in the late afternoon, Amelia drifted off. She dreamt about the little house in California. When she woke, only the top rim of the sun still shone over the horizon. The constant squawking of the birds had lulled to an occasional brief squabble.

Sweat ran off her in streams. Her throat felt like she'd swallowed half the beach. She swished water from the canteen around her mouth. "Sorry I conked out, Fred. I bet you're thirsty."

She cupped her hand around his chin to steady him. In spite of the heat, his skin felt clammy and loose. She recoiled. Not good, she thought. Not good at all.

She snapped her fingers in front of his face. "Fred!"

He didn't move.

She took notice of the dried blood and pus that caked the shirt cuff over Noonan's wound. Amelia fetched seawater with the tin first aid kit container. She poured water over the cuff to loosen the crust then pulled it back.

She gasped, and reared back. The flesh around the bite had turned grey. Black lines radiated up to his elbow and down to his palm. It smelled even worse than before, like a dinner plate left in the sink to rot. Her gorge rose.

*No. You will not disgrace yourself.* She'd heard the little voice before. It was the one that kept her in the air when everyone told her the sky was a man's domain. It was the voice that never let her quit. For the first time, she noticed how much it sounded like her mother.

Noonan smacked his cracked lips. Relief washed through her. She drizzled water from the lighter of the two canteens into his mouth. She'd done the same for her father when she was a girl. He might have drunk too much, but Edwin Earhart was a good man. He loved his family and did the best he could under the circumstances. He was the one who took her to the airfield for her first flight. Noonan got her lost out here, but he found this island. Somewhere in the Phoenix Group, he said. She owed him.

When Amelia had gotten all the water she could into him, she chewed on bread crust and watched the waves hit the reef's edge, then slide over its flat top and back again. The plane wasn't far from that edge. At high tide, a wave with a strong enough backwash would pull the Electra right over. Only God knew how deep the Pacific was out here. If she couldn't hail someone, they'd never find her.

Noonan moaned, so she gave him more water. When he settled again, she lay back on the sand and stared up at the sky. She knew she should start searching for a source of fresh water, but her body refused to cooperate. Even with the nap, it wasn't enough. Before landing on this deserted rock, she'd spent twenty hours in the air. Dragging Noonan's sorry ass onto shore had sapped the last of her strength.

She closed her eyes. The island was the altar of a vast, empty cathedral, abandoned by its congregation and god. Amelia wasn't sure she believed in God anymore, not after nursing the boys sent home from the war. Or maybe there was a god, and he'd gotten tired of all her silly exploits. Her persistent bending of his rules about which creatures ruled the sky angered him. He laughed and plunked her down on this little speck of nothing to die, her feet firmly planted on the ground.

After a while the roaring lullaby of wind and sea soothed her mind into sleep. She dreamed of the world consumed by storms of fire and water and air. She stood on a flat rock the size of a tabletop with no way to fight.

A sudden stillness woke her sometime in the fuzzy hours between midnight and morning. She sat up, not sure where she was or how she got to be there. Her hand knocked against Noonan's canteen, the one with only a drop or two left inside. She remembered. *Yes, I am stranded.*

She scooted across the sand. Her hand reached for Noonan's chin to steady him while she trickled water onto his lips. His flesh was cold and oddly rigid, like a thing instead of a man.

"Fred?"

She patted his cheek. He didn't respond. She laid her head against his chest. Nothing. She jerked up, grabbed him by the shoulders and shook. "Fred!"

He didn't move.

When Amelia realized that he was no longer with her, she dropped him and shoved backward like a crab until her legs gave out. "You're not dead, Fred Noonan. Not from a ridiculous bite. They're coming for us any minute now."

She repeated, "They're coming," until her throat hurt. Even after she couldn't say it anymore, it bounced around the inside of her skull.

She didn't know how long this went on, but by the time she came out of it the moon had dove from its perch high in the heavens to skim along the black horizon. The ghost of the plane rested out on the reef. Further? She couldn't tell.

*You need to pick yourself up by the bootstraps, Meeley.*

"Yes, Mama."

It wasn't really her mother. She wasn't that far gone, yet. The part of her that would not—could not—wallow in self-pity needed a voice. Amy Otis Earhart's was a good one, no nonsense and impossible to ignore.

Amelia needed to get back to the plane.

The water was higher now. First it wet her to the knee, then the thigh, and finally the waist. She'd left the side hatch open when she pulled Noonan out, and water had filled the half with the broken landing gear.

She climbed up through the cabin to the cockpit, then crawled out onto the wing. She was afraid to look at the propeller. If even the tip dipped into the water, it wouldn't turn. No turn, no power for the radio.

The prop cleared the water by inches, but clear was clear. Before Amelia settled into the cockpit, she traced out the edge of the reef. It was closer than she remembered. She rocked back and forth. Beneath her the Electra shifted.

*Dear God.*

She didn't have the energy to deal with that now. Losing the plane would break her heart, but she could get another. Lockheed wasn't going anywhere, and damn it, neither was she.

She climbed into the pilot's seat and started up the engine. For the next four hours, she broadcast her name, rough coordinates, call letters . . . anything that might tell the *Itasca* where she was. The outgoing tide pulled her closer to the reef's edge.

No one answered.

When she started fumbling the numbers, she turned off the plane's engine. "I can sleep, then start again later," she told herself. She settled into the seat. Her mind drifted back to the house in California. G.P.'s house. Her husband. Even after six years, the word still seemed strange to her . . . hollow. She drifted off to sleep thinking of the little carob tree in the back yard.

This time when Amelia dreamed, the world was a wasteland. Flat grey earth stretched in every direction with nothing green or alive to break the desolation. Noonan stood next to her, staring out at the waste. "I burned her," he said.

Amelia's feet rooted to the ground. Then, instead of barren land, a black ocean surrounded the little plot of earth where they stood. Noonan grabbed her wrist. His skin felt cold and loose. He lifted her hand to his mouth, like he was going to kiss it. She tried to pull away, but it was too late. His teeth sank into her wrist.

She woke screaming, but the pain didn't go away. She glanced down at her wrist and screamed again. A brownish-red pincer clamped down on her wrist. She jerked sideways, pulling the monster half into the cockpit.

That's when she saw it was a crab. One of the biggest goddamned crabs she'd ever seen, but a crab just the same.

She pried the pincer open. Not an easy task considering the creature was the size of a terrier and pretty intent on carrying her away.

As soon as she was free, she squirmed out through the hatch onto the wing. The sun-scorched aluminum warmed the soles of her shoes as the climbed back into the water. In the shade of the wing, she caught her breath . . . let her heart settle back into its normal rhythm.

"Jesus," she said, her voice shaking. First that dream, then the crab: she was lucky she hadn't had a coronary right then and there.

*Still alive, Meeley.*

"Yes, Mama," she mumbled, breathing deep.

*Can't leave that animal in the plane. It might chew through the wires. And then where would you be?*

It sounded like something her mother would say, but that last bit about the wires told her she wasn't crazy. Not yet, at least. The voice was still just another part of Amelia. The part that kept her awake in the dark hours of the night when someone had to fly the plane. The part that kept her alive.

She felt steadier. The little flutter in her gut had dwindled to a slight hiccough. Might as well handle the crab now, she thought. Besides, she wasn't ready to deal with what was waiting for her on the beach. Not just yet.

She sloshed through the water to the plane's open side hatch. That was the whole problem right there. The crab never would have gotten inside if she had secured her plane. It was her own damned fault.

Considering how scared she'd been only a few moments ago, removing the crab was easy. She came up through the cabin and grabbed one of its back legs. It was so heavy, she worried that instead of getting the thing out of her plane, she'd just end up pulling the leg off.

She didn't. The crab writhed and bucked. She let go of it twice, but managed to get it out in the end. Once it skittered away across the reef, she closed the plane's side hatch.

She faced the island. She couldn't stay out here forever. Fred Noonan required burial. She needed to find water. She could always eat crab if today's little adventure indicated how easy they were to catch.

She walked back to shore. She could be alone. There was a picture of her in her high school yearbook with the caption "the girl in brown who walks alone." She knew how to do it. Preferred it, really, even though she had married Putnam. But being alone with people around was a very different proposition than being alone with the sand and the sky.

An odd, scraping sound vibrated up through her feet. Birds erupted from the coconut trees. Amelia whirled around just in time to see the Electra tip sideways over the edge of the reef.

"No." Her voice, so weak, couldn't rise over the chatter of birds. She fell to her knees. Not the plane. Not after everything else.

The wing swung up, throwing a glittering trail of water through the air. She reached out, as if she could catch it, pluck it from the sea and set it back on its gears. But even if she were large enough, strong enough, it was too late.

The plane slipped under the waves. The engine wouldn't turn now. The radio was dead.

She slammed her fist down, shredding the skin over her knuckles. This wasn't how it was supposed to end. Not like this. It would have been better if she'd crashed the damned plane on landing. At least she would have been closer to the air.

She sat there for a long time, watching the empty space where the plane used to be. Her brain tried to sketch out the lines of the wings. Maybe if she stared long enough she would wake up and find out this was a nightmare.

*Still alive, Meeley.*

"Shut up, Mother."

*You still have chores.*

"I'm on an island. There are no chores."

The voice that wasn't her mother didn't answer. And she did have chores. She had to find water, fresh water. And food. But first she had to bury her navigator.

She stumbled through the sand to where she left the pack, the first aid kit, and canteens. Fred Noonan's body was gone.

Amelia searched the island. She walked the outer ring of beach, then made her way into the lagoon and circled it, too. She trekked through the coconut grove, searching for fresh water. The jungle was denser than it looked from the beach or the air. Scrub and tall, unfamiliar trees with huge trunks that grew so close together she could barely squeeze between them in places seemed to fight her every step. She suspected she circled the same stand of trees two or three times before she moved on. The damned island wasn't even that large.

She pushed, sweating and hungry, through the brush. Her pack with the last crust of bread and nearly empty canteen caught on a branch. She jerked it free.

Maybe he wasn't dead, she told herself. She had been exhausted and dizzy from thirst. She could have made a mistake. What if he woke? He could have been hallucinating and wandered into this damned mess. He'd called her Mary Bea.

She pushed another branch out of the way. It whipped back, laying a sharp track of fire down her cheek. "God damn it!"

The ever-present bird chatter wound up. Amelia cursed again. The damned birds got even louder. If she couldn't get some peace and quiet, she thought she might go mad.

"Shut up!"

They didn't. She heard them in the trees, their huge black wings rustling against the leaves. Scavengers, most likely, waiting for her to die.

They came closer. Amelia slumped again the trunk of one of the big trees, defeated. Let them take her. At least she'd be out of this God-forsaken jungle.

She sank to the ground. She rested her head against the trunk and closed her eyes. The rustling grew closer. The birds chattered. Then, under the birds, something groaned.

Amelia's breath caught. She scanned the jungle. "Fred?"

She waited. The birds' calls sounded like laughter now. *Stupid woman. Stupid for getting lost. Stupid for losing your navigator. Stupid. Woman.*

She buried her face in her hands. It was over. All of it. She'd never get out of this. Never.

Then she heard it again. Under the sound of the retreating birds, came a groan.

"Fred!" He wasn't dead. Not yet, anyway. There was still hope. She leapt to her feet and plunged headlong into the jungle. "Noonan! Wait!"

She yelled his name until her voice turned rough, but he'd disappeared again. She continued searching, though. It gave her purpose. Reminded her she wasn't dead.

For three days, she searched. When the water ran out, she drank the juice inside coconuts, drilling into them with the sharp end of the screwdriver. What if what she heard had been some animal? Or worse, her imagination? What if she wandered around this island, wearing herself out for nothing?

She didn't let herself think about Noonan's body, lying unguarded on the beach while she slept in the plane. She tried not to imagine giant crabs crawling out of the surf for him. What if she did find him and there were only bones to bury?

She was up in a coconut tree, knocking coconuts onto the sand below when she heard the plane. At first, the engine's buzz sank into the sounds of the ocean, the wind, the birds. But then she saw it.

"Hey!" She almost fell waving her arms. "I'm here!"

But they couldn't see her. They were too high, looking for the plane. That's when she saw the man stumbling between the trees. Relief so strong it loosened her grip on the tree washed through her. Her body shifted sideways over the drop.

"Fred!"

His head tipped up, as if he was sniffing the wind.

Amelia half-slid, half-climbed down the tree. She jumped the last ten feet. She hit the sand hard. Her ankle rolled and something crunched. Pain spiked up through her leg to her knee.

"Damn it!"

The plane circled over the far end of the island. She couldn't make it in time, not on that ankle. But all Fred had to do was walk out onto the beach.

"Fred!" She pointed at the sky. He sniffed their air again. "Get the lead out of your ass!"

This time, he didn't sniff the air. His head turned toward her on a slow pivot. His mouth hung open. Green and purple tinted the hollows of his cheeks. Mucus—dried, dark, and bloody—crusted his nose. He shuffled toward her.

"Fred, go to the beach!" He acted like he hadn't heard her, but he must have. She limped forward, her ankle screaming with every step. Overhead, the plane's engines buzzed louder as they came back around the island. "Turn the hell around!"

He did not turn around. He walked, shuffled really, right for Amelia.

The smell reached her first. Rot. She scanned the ground for the screwdriver she used to break into the coconuts. There, near the base of the tree with her supply pack. Noonan was getting closer. She hopped on one leg back to the tree. She slung the pack over one shoulder and scooped up the screwdriver.

Fred moved slowly, but he didn't stop. Amelia braced her back against the tree trunk and held the screwdriver in front of her. "Go to the beach, Fred, or we'll both die."

He didn't answer, just kept pushing forward. That's when Amelia noticed his eyes. She forgot the plane. She didn't remember what color Noonan's eyes were when they landed on the island, but it sure as hell wasn't milk white.

She pointed the screwdriver at him, the tip shaking with the trembling of her hand. "Don't come any closer, Fred."

Every step he took toward her, away from rescue, drove a shaft of icy fear further into her heart. The sound of the plane grew fainter. They were lost, alone, abandoned. Noonan was past caring. Amelia was trapped here, like a mouse under the great bowl of the sky.

Noonan's hands curled into grasping claws as he came near. Strands of saliva hung from his lips. The sickness couldn't be airborne or she'd already be ill. That meant whatever virus infected him had come from the bite.

He stumbled closer. G.P. used to tell Amelia, "You are the thing with feathers." But the real line was: "Hope is the thing with feathers." From Emily Dickinson.

*Hope. I am hope. And Fred is the last man I'll ever see.*

He was only about six feet away now. Amelia's fist tightened around the screwdriver's handle. "Fred, you're very ill, but you need to stay back."

He lurched forward, his hands scrabbling at her arms. Amelia felt the screwdriver hit flesh and sink in. She staggered back, the screwdriver still clutched in her hand.

At first, she couldn't tell where she'd stabbed him. Then she saw it: a hole in his neck just above his collarbone on the right hand side. He hadn't even flinched.

Her fingers opened. The screwdriver fell and stuck tip down in the sand. Though it was against every fiber in her body, she wheeled around and stumbled into the jungle.

Amelia set up camp at the western end of the island near the lagoon. She drank coconut milk and rainwater. She ate crabs, and once a turtle. Every night she lay under the open sky, hoping for her mother's voice or another dream to tell her what to do. Never had her life been so purposeless.

She sat in the water at the edge of the lagoon soaking her sore ankle. Only a sprain.

When she was ten, maybe eleven, she had found a rat in the yard near the street. She wanted to bury it. Her mother wouldn't let her. "They carry disease," she'd said.

So Amelia did what she did back in those days. She went to the library. She learned one very important fact about rats. They spread the bubonic plague.

She had wanted to protect her family, so she went into the house and got her father's .22 rifle. She spent the rest of the day wandering around Atchinson, searching for rats. That's what her father had been talking about in her dream.

More than once during her short treks into the brush to gather firewood, she'd heard Fred and his avian companions rustling through the jungle. She could ignore her fear and revulsion, but the guilt drove her back to the little camp near the lagoon.

So far, she'd managed to avoid him. It couldn't last forever, though. She wasn't ill. He was deathly ill, and seriously wounded. All she had to do was wait him out. If she couldn't, and he came for her again, she might have to do something drastic. She wasn't ready for that.

She stood and made her way back up to the campfire. Thank God for the stupid jar of freckle cream. Amelia had always hated the freckles sprinkled across her nose. They made people treat her like a child. But that jar had a base shaped like a lens. Once it was rinsed out, all she had to do was use it to direct the sun into a little pile of tinder . . . and wait.

Noonan's words from the dream echoed through her head. She said them out loud. "I burned her."

The screwdriver hadn't worked. If Fred came for her, she'd have to burn him. She wasn't sure how, though.

She gathered more wood from the scrub forest and built up the fire. She didn't want to kill Noonan. She hadn't known him long. He wasn't even the first man she'd hired to navigate. All those hours in the plane hadn't drawn them closer. Loud engines meant they couldn't talk. Only pass notes. Still, she didn't dislike him.

She took a coconut from the pile near the campfire. She wasn't sure how much longer she could last on coconut water. Breaking through each husk and shell weakened her more now than it had a week ago. And she needed at least three to slake her thirst.

She reached into the pack for the screwdriver. She'd gone back for it, a feat that took every ounce of courage she could muster. Then she'd boiled it in salt water for what seemed like hours to make sure it didn't carry any of Noonan's infection.

As she pulled it out, her knuckles grazed Fred's bourbon. She dug it out, too. The first swallow burned all the way down her throat and slugged a fiery fist into her gut. Fire. She took another mouthful and spat it onto the fire. The flames roared up, making her lie all the way back.

Amelia sat back up and looked at the bottle. A tiny, feathered thing fluttered in her chest.

Splash Noonan with that, and he'd go up like a torch.

She took another drink. She didn't care anymore. Not one little bit. The world could be what it was going to be. Dead men could dance the Lindy Hop for all she cared. All her life, she had tried her damnedest to be the best she could be. Even the setbacks couldn't keep her down. Crash the plane in Hawaii? Fix it and start over going the other direction. Never give up. Never, never, never.

But all that determination meant nothing. She felt tears squeeze out the outer corners of her eyes and roll toward her ears. She'd been holding onto them since she realized she'd missed Howland with its landing strip and the Coast Guard standing by. It didn't matter if she cried. There wasn't anyone here to see. No one would ever see her again. No matter what she did, she would die here. Alone.

Amelia slept hard that night, clutching the half-empty bottle tight to her chest. When she woke, her head and mouth felt as though they'd been packed with moldy cotton. She couldn't stand, so she crawled to the lagoon.

She vomited twice on the way.

When she finally reached the water, she splashed handfuls over her face then rolled back onto the sand. Her throat ached for water. Fresh, cold, clear water from the well outside her grandparents' house in Kansas.

She lifted her hand to shade her eyes and realized she'd dragged the bottle down to the water with her. She knew it wouldn't do her any good, not in the long run. But for now, at least her throat wouldn't be so damned dry.

She heard her mother's voice for the first time in days. *Meeley, don't.*

"You can't stop me." Amelia sat up and lifted the bottle to her lips, anticipating the burn.

The burn. She lowered the bottle so fast it slipped from her fingers and landed on the beach on its side. Golden brown liquid glugged out.

"Damn it!" She snatched the bottle upright. One of the few things she had from home, and she was pouring it all over the ground. She'd gone mad. That was the only explanation for wasting her one best weapon against Fred Noonan.

Birdcalls stabbed at her aching head. She didn't know if the world was gone or not. She didn't know how long Fred could last in his state. She didn't think anyone would come for them, but what if they did? What if some well-meaning captain brought Fred aboard before she could warn him?

Amelia's mother was out there, house sitting in California. Her *mother*. If it came down to keeping her mother from whatever plague Noonan carried, she had to try.

As if on cue, the late Fred Noonan dragged his reeking self out of the trees. Once she saw him, Amelia couldn't believe she'd missed his smell, like sour eggs. Of course, she still had the stink of slightly used coconut bourbon crab clinging to her nose and throat. And the damned birds. She should have known.

He didn't notice her at first. She patted her hand across the ground, never lowering her eyes. She'd dropped the screwdriver near the campfire after prying open last night's coconuts.

Fred shuffled forward. Amelia abandoned her search for the screwdriver. The damned thing hadn't done her any good last time. She reached for one of the twisted branches from the fire, and held it out in front of her.

She held the bottle in her other hand. Simple plan. Splash Fred with the bourbon then light him with the burning branch.

Noonan didn't cooperate. Instead of coming for her he scuffed along the edge of the trees.

"Oh, for Pete's sake," Amelia muttered.

Noonan's head swiveled in her direction. She'd assumed he hunted by smell. As bad as he stank, she couldn't smell much better at this point. Now he relied on his ears.

"Hey, Fred."

He turned his body. The birds quieted. Amelia felt thousands of bright, black eyes trained on her. Whatever happened next, the birds stood as mute observers, distant and unmoved.

"Are you even Fred anymore?" Amelia asked. "Or did you stop being Fred on the beach?"

The questions were meant to keep him coming, but once she said the words she realized she wanted answers.

Of course, he didn't answer, just stumbled his weary way forward. She could outrun him even on her sore ankle, but that hadn't done her any good the last time. Here Fred was again. Her father was right. Never run.

The real question was: would Amelia deserve to die if she burned a sick man to death? She didn't know the answer.

Amelia let him come closer. Closer. Closer. Finally, she gave the bottle one good shake. Clear brown bourbon arced through the air and splashed down across his shoulder. The second stream hit him in the face. One last drink, Amelia thought, with something like affection.

He reached out for her. Amelia jabbed forward with the burning branch. Fire raced across his chest and over his shoulder, but he kept coming.

Damn it.

She swung the bottle. It smashed across his temple. The flames on his shoulders flared. Amelia's feet tangled under her. She fell back. As she hit the sand, a sharp pain stabbed into her back just under her shoulder blade.

She gasped, and the pain exploded through her chest. The damned screwdriver. She tried to breathe but couldn't get more than a sip of air. She tasted blood. *I'm drowning,* she thought. *I was supposed to drown when the plane came down, and now it's caught up to me.*

She stared up at the sky. It pressed down on her like the ocean. The last days were all a dream, she thought. I'm dead.

Off to her left, Noonan wandered through her campsite. Goddamned tears ran down her face and into her ears for the second time in as many days. Damn it. Failed.

*Not yet, Meeley. Look.*

Her mother's voice. And for once, Amelia obeyed. Even though her head felt light, a circus balloon pulling at its string, it took most of her strength to turn it toward Noonan.

He faced her from the far side of the roaring campfire, cheery flames flick-ering on his chest and shoulders. Damn it, she thought. What are you waiting for?

Then it came to her. She hadn't made a sound since she fell. He couldn't find her.

"Fred," she said, but it was barely more than a whisper. She tried to force more air into her lungs, but it hurt too much. She tried to move her cold, numb arms. They didn't respond. Already dead.

Damn it. Damn it. Damn it.

She closed her eyes. That was it. She could only hope Noonan rotted away before anyone came to this god-forsaken rock.

Hope.

She thought of G.P. "You are the thing with feathers." She used to think he'd been calling her a bird.

She gritted her teeth and breathed in. With every ounce of strength left to her she reared up, then dropped back down, driving the screwdriver deeper into her back.

A ragged, groaning, scream hurtled at the sky. Noonan jerked toward her. His feet stumbled over the burning logs of the fire. He fell to his knees. The fire hit his bourbon-soaked clothes. He didn't scream. He didn't thrash. But he burned.

Amelia hiccuped. Blood ran from the corner of her mouth. Her pain faded. It was done.

Birds flew over, their silent vigil over. When the search plane didn't see her, she'd compared the sky to a giant bowl trapping her here. But now she saw it wasn't a bowl. It was endless. And she was ready.

# THE CROCODILES

## STEVEN POPKES

I could not make a silk purse from a sow's ear. But I went over the data again to see if I could find a tiny tatter of bright thread in the otherwise disappointing results. There had to be a better use of a well-educated chemical engineer than cannon fodder. Willem, my wife's uncle, called me.

"Max," he said, a happy disembodied voice over the phone. "Very sorry about your work and all that. How was it going?"

It didn't surprise me he already knew. "We didn't get the results we'd hoped for," I said. "But there are other areas in the war effort where fuel filtration research would be entirely applicable. Aircraft engines, for instance—"

"No doubt," he said, chuckling. "However, by an astonishing coincidence I was planning to call you anyway. I have a good use for your skills."

"Oh, really?" I said with a sinking feeling. I had no desire to work for the Gestapo. Uncomfortable work at the very least.

"Yes. There's a Doctor Otto Weber doing some very interesting biological work in Buchenwald. He can use your help."

"What sort of work?"

"I'm sure I'd be the wrong person to discuss it with you, not being a scientist or an engineer. I'll work out the details of the transfer and send round the papers and tickets."

"I really ought to find out how I can be of service—"

"There's always the regular army. I'm sure a man of your caliber—"

"I'll be looking for your messenger."

"Fine. Oh, and Max?"

"Yes?"

"Weekly reports. On everything and everybody. All right?"

"Of course," I said.

You don't argue with the Gestapo. Even my Elsa's uncle.

Otto Weber was a thin, elderly gentleman. Once he had been quite tall. He was now stooped with age. His eyes were washed out and watery, like blue glass underwater. But his hands were steady as he first lit my cigarette, then his own.

Weber called them tote Männer. Once he showed me their decomposing condition and single-minded hunger, I thought the term apt.

Weber was brought the first host in 1938 and had to keep the disease alive with new hosts from the Gestapo—which they were always willing to supply, though in small lots so he never had more than a few laboratory subjects at a time. He was never told where that first host came from but he surmised South America. Later, in 1940 when the laboratory was at Buchenwald, the Gestapo supplied him with a slow but steady trickle of Gypsies.

What he had discovered when I joined the project in 1941 was that infection was only successful by fluid transport from the infected host, infection was in two phases, and there were at least two components to the disease.

In one experiment, Weber took fluid from a toter Männ and filtered three samples, one through a 100 micron filter, one through a 50 micron filter, and one through a Chamberland filter. The 100 micron wash caused full infection. The 50 micron also caused a partial infection involving quick and sudden pain, followed by an inevitably fatal stroke. He called this partial infection type I-A. The Chamberland wash caused a particularly quick and virulent form of rabies—Weber referred to that as type I-B. Hence, Weber's hypothesis of two components for a full infection, one large and the other the rabies virus. He had isolated a worm as the possible large component in that, when collected and washed of any contaminants, it seemed to cause an I-A infection similar to the infection caused by the 50 micron wash. When the Chamberland wash was recombined with the worm, full infection ensued.

Weber had even characterized the partial infections and the stages of the full infection. I found it interesting that the partial infections were both dismal, painful affairs, while the full infection showed up first as euphoria, followed by sleepiness and coma. The subject awoke in a few days as a toter Männ.

Even so, I was surprised that there hadn't been more discovered in four years. After all, Weber had the tote Männer themselves and their inherent ability to infect others. The Gestapo was willing to provide a constant, if limited, supply of hosts. But Weber's horror of contagion was so strong that every step had to be examined minutely until he had determined to his satisfaction that he could properly protect himself and his staff. Dissection was a long and tedious process; vivisection was almost impossible. I suppose I could not blame him. Even a partial infection would be fatal and full infection always resulted in another toter Männ. No one wanted to risk that.

Thus, my first task was the design and construction of a dissection and histology laboratory where Weber could disassemble the subjects in safety. It was not a difficult task. I came to Buchenwald in July. By the end of the month I had the design and began construction. Weber dissected his first wriggling subject by the first of September.

My fuel work had been much more interesting. It was exacting, exciting work with great applications. Here, I was barely more than a foreman. The war in Russia seemed to be going well and I wondered if I should have protested more to Willem.

But Elsa and our son Helmut loved Weimar. The city was pretty in a storybook way. It didn't hurt that the bombers left Weimar largely undisturbed, instead striking in Germany proper. It lent the city a relative calm. Several young couples had taken over the empty housing. This was early in the war and food and petrol, though rationed, were still plentiful.

I didn't work weekends and the three of us spent many summer days in the Park on the Ilm. It occurred to me, during those pleasant hours watching Helmut playing in front of Goethe's House, that this was, perhaps, a better use of my time than the factory or the lab.

Within a week of opening the new facilities, Weber made some astonishing discoveries. Histological examination of the brain tissue of the tote Männer showed how the worms nested deep in the higher functioning brain—clearly explaining why there were only tote Männer and not tote rats and tote cats. He speculated that there could be tote gorillas and tote chimpanzees and went so far as to request animals from the Berlin Zoo. The Zoo was not cooperative. Weber reconsidered his New World origin of the disease and attributed it to Africa or Indonesia where the great apes lived. It stood to reason that a complex disease found suddenly in humans would require a similar host in which to evolve prior to human infection.

However, the worms were only one half of the disease. The virus followed the nervous system through the body, enabling worm entry into the brain but also enabling the growth of strong cords throughout the body. This was further proof of the two-component infection model Weber had developed. In the case of partial infections of the worm or the virus, the process only went so far. Forced by the absence of the virus to remain within the body's major cavities, the worm caused fevers and paralysis, blocking blood vessels mechanically, causing a heart attack or stroke. The virus enabled the worm to penetrate directly into the brain, leaving the heart and circulatory system intact—at least for a while. Without the worm, the virus merely crippled the nervous system, causing fevers, seizures, and great pain. The cords only appeared when both were present. Weber was convinced by the pathology of the disease that the tote Männer virus was a variant of rabies, but the biological history of the virus, the worm, and the virus-worm combination was mysteriously speculative.

I dutifully reported this to Willem, along with descriptions of Weber, his assistant, Brung, and his mistress, Josephine, whom we had met at dinner in Weimar earlier in the summer. Unsure whether Willem's desire for detail extended to the subjects, I included the names of the last couple of Gypsy hosts left from the Buchenwald experiments and the newer Jews we had appropriated from the main population of the camp. Weber was curiously reluctant to use the handicapped and mentally deficient and he hated using Poles. Perhaps this stemmed from some event in his past of which I was unaware.

Willem paid his niece a Christmas visit, visiting our laboratory only coincidentally. He was impressed with our progress. "With the tote Männer we will crush Russia," he said over drinks that evening.

Weber paled. "There will be problems using the tote Männer in winter," he said obliquely.

"Eh?" Willem looked at me. "Speak plainly."

"The tote Männer cannot thermoregulate. This doesn't show up in laboratory conditions but below ten degrees Celsius the worms do not function properly. By freezing they die and the host dies with them."

Willem considered that. "We can clothe them."

Weber grew excited. "They do not generate enough heat. Humans maintain temperature. Cats maintain temperature. Crocodiles do not. They do not eat—the hunger for brains is no more than the desire of the disease to perpetuate the infection—the way horsehair worms cause crickets to drown themselves. They do not consume what they put in their mouths. Metabolism keeps the body temperature above ambient somewhat like large lizards. Clothing lizards would have no more effect than clothing tote Männer."

"I see," Willem said. He patted down his vest until he located his cigarettes and lighter. "I'm going out on the porch for a smoke. Max, will you join me?"

Weber looked as if he'd swallowed a lemon. He rose as if to join us but Willem waved him back. "Don't bother. This gives Max and me a chance to exchange a little gossip."

Outside, we lit our cigarettes and watched the snow fall.

"It's true what Weber said? We can't use them as soldiers?"

I thought for a moment before answering. "Comparing them to crocodiles is apt. You can't make a soldier out of an animal. And it's too cold for them in the east."

"Then what good are they? Is this all for nothing?"

"I did not say they could not be a weapon."

"Tell me."

"The crocodile simile is better than you know. They are very fast and very strong. There is so little to their metabolism that they are hard to kill. And they are terrifying—you've seen them. You know. We must be able to make some use of them." I shook my head. "I don't know enough yet. I need to perform some experiments. Weber has discovered the basic science. Now it is time to apply some German engineering."

Willem nodded. "I'll do what I can." He grimaced. "Two weeks ago the Japanese attacked the Americans. The Americans declared war on Japan. We declared war on each other. They allied themselves with the British, which brings them into the war in Europe."

"The Americans are too far away. They don't have the strength of mind to make much difference."

"So we thought in the last war. The point is I may not have much time to give."

The goal was to deploy tote Männer to a suitable front and have them wreak havoc on the enemy while leaving our own troops alone. The tote Männer would terrify and demoralize the enemy. Our troops would march in behind them, clearing the area of enemy soldiers and tote Männer alike. Simple.

Only, we did not have a means by which we could create a large number of tote Männer simultaneously or a means by which we could be sure they would discriminate between our soldiers and the enemy.

Weber attacked the discrimination problem while I considered issues of scale.

Buchenwald was too small and low volume to be useful to us. Auschwitz was more appropriate to our needs. However, Auschwitz was already overwhelmed with the volume of its operation.

In October, the Birkenau expansion of Auschwitz had begun. It was scheduled to be complete in the spring. Willem had shown me copies of the plans. It was clear that only minor modifications to the Birkenau plans would accommodate our needs much more easily than building an addition to Buchenwald or moving to Auschwitz proper.

In January of 1942 I kissed Elsa and Helmut good-bye and boarded the train to Krakow. From there, I took a car west. It was beautiful country, full of gently rising mountains over flat valleys. Curiously unspoiled either by industry or by the war.

Auschwitz was a complex, not a single camp like Buchenwald. There were several smaller camps near the headquarters. Birkenau was farther west. Here, construction was going on apace in spite of the winter weather.

The foundations for gas chambers and crematoria had already been laid. But that didn't matter as far as I was concerned. The addition of some larger chambers and holding areas was an insignificant change to a well-managed engineering project. I went over the modifications in detail with the chief engineer, a man named Tilly.

Willem had sent me with a certificate of authority. That gave me the full support of Tilly and the chief of the camps, Rudolf Hoess, even though they did not know the reason for the modifications. I finished working out the details in two weeks.

I spent a few days in Krakow. I planned to move Elsa and Helmut into an apartment in Krakow and then travel to work by automobile. It was not far and the roads were good. If that proved impractical in a hard winter—something difficult for me to predict as the weather was now mild—I could just stay in the camp for a few days or come home on weekends.

When I returned, I found I had been gone just long enough for both Elsa and Helmut to miss me terribly. It made for a sweet homecoming.

Weber was reluctant to plan the move but saw my logic. He was preoccupied with the discrimination problem. Since the tote Männer were attracted to normal humans as hosts, he had reasoned that it was easier to *attract* them to a particular prey rather than *repel* them from a particular prey. He had performed several experiments with different hosts to see if there was any preference for differing types, such as racial subtype, diet, or other variables he could control.

I looked over the data and noticed that there was a marked difference in attack percentages not according to his typing but to the time the subjects arrived at the camp. Those subjects that were at the camp the longest were the most attractive to the tote Männer. I showed my figures to Weber. He instantly grasped the significance in ways I could not. The older inmates at Buchenwald were considerably thinner than the newer inmates since the rations were short. Fat utilization caused excretory products to be exuded by the skin and from the lungs. Weber reasoned these were what attracted the tote Männer.

Immediately, he called Willem for a mass spectrometer and a technician to run it.

We were all very tired but elated at this new direction. We decided to take a few days off. Elsa, Helmut, and I went for a trip into the mountains.

Birkenau opened in March of 1942. Weber and I stopped work on the subjects, except to keep an incubating strain alive, and took the month to pack up the laboratory for the move. In May, we moved the equipment, materials, and tote Männer to Birkenau. Once the planning for the move was complete, Weber supervised the staff and aides Willem had supplied. Elsa and Helmut traveled down to Krakow by train and took up residence in the apartment I had leased for them. As for myself, I left Buchenwald and returned to Berlin for meetings with representatives of Daimler-Benz and I. G. Farben. The delivery mechanism for the tote Männer still had to be devised.

The mood in Berlin that spring was jubilant. The army was driving toward Rostov and trying for Stalingrad. Sevastopol was about to fall to Germany. The use of the tote Männer could only be necessary as a last resort. A doomsday scenario. The Reich would never need it.

Personally, I felt the same. Still, I had no wish to help in canceling the project unless I could find better work. So I met with the Daimler-Benz mechanical engineers and utilized the I. G. Farben labs. I had brought with me a pair of tote Männer for testing purposes.

Not being a mechanical engineer, the problem of deployment was more difficult than I had initially imagined. Tote Männer were a curious mixture of toughness and fragility. You could shoot a toter Mann until he was merely chopped meat and he might continue to advance. Blowing apart his brain would kill the worms and stop him. But the tote Männer were so resilient and resistant to anoxia that they could still advance with their hearts shattered and their sluggish black blood pooled beneath their feet.

However, their flesh was soft enough and loosely enough attached to their bones that heavy acceleration, such as dropping them with parachutes, would cause them to come apart. Clearly, they had to be preserved long enough to reach their target.

The Daimler-Benz engineers were the best. On a chalk board, they drew up several ways of conveying them to enemy lines. The simplest idea was a cushioned cage dropped with a parachute. An impact charge would blow the doors off the cage and the tote Männer would be free. The engineers didn't like the idea. They said it lacked elegance and style.

I pointed out the tote Männer could tolerate significant time without ambient oxygen, operating as they did largely on a lactic acid metabolism. They tossed the cage idea with abandon and attacked the problem again, coming up with a sphere containing carefully restrained tote Männer. A compressed-air charge would open the doors and break loose the restraints. This had the advantage of being quiet.

I only donated a little knowledge here and there as needed, letting their minds fly unfettered. It is a grand thing to watch engineers create works of imagination with only the germ of a requirement, a bit of chalk, and some board to write on. When they found I had brought a couple of tote Männer for experiments, they were overjoyed. I tried to explain the danger but they did not listen until one of their own number, Hans Braun, was bitten. He and his friends laughed but stilled when I came over. Wearing surgical gloves and a mask I carefully examined the wound but I already knew what I would find.

"You are an idiot," I said as I sat back.

"It is a small bite—"

"It is a fatal wound." I gave him a pack of cigarettes. "You have been killed by that thing out there."

"But—"

"Shut up." I couldn't look at him: tall, healthy, brown hair and a face in the habit of smiling. "You have been infected. By tomorrow, you will feel wonderful. You will want to kiss and fondle your friends out of love for them. Then, after a few days, you will—still enormously happy—feel an overpowering urge to sleep. Sleep will turn to coma. Then, after three days, you will be one of those things out there."

His hands trembled. "I didn't realize—"

"No."

Hans steadied himself. "There is no hope?"

"None."

He nodded and for a moment he stood straighter. Stronger. I was proud of him.

"Do you have a gun?"

"I do. Is there a furnace where we can dispose of the body?"

He nodded, shakily. "Will you accompany me?"

"I would be honored." And I was.

After the funeral, realizing the power and speed of the tote Männer and the infection they harbored, the Daimler-Benz engineers were more careful.

In a couple of weeks, my part was done and I took the train to Krakow to have a long weekend reunion with my Elsa and Helmut. The following Monday, I drove to Birkenau to address the problem of tote Männer production.

Elsa had mixed feelings about the rental. While she liked the apartment itself and the proximity of Park Jordana, she found the leftover debris and detritus disturbing. These were obviously Jewish artifacts and Elsa's excitement might have come from a mixture of womanly wariness of another female's territory combined with an aversion to having anything Jewish in the house. I assured her that the original owners would not be returning and she relaxed somewhat.

Helmut had no reservations about his new environment. Finding small objects of indeterminate origin covered with unfamiliar characters fastened in unexpected places gave mystery to the place. No doubt he observed I was more inclined to answer questions about this or that artifact than I was about the American bombers or air raid drills or what Father did at work. I protected my family as best I could from such things.

For the next several months we were collecting the breath and sweat of subjects into vials, injecting the vial contents into the mass spectrometer, and determining what was there. Then we concentrated the effluvia and tried it on the tote Männer themselves. Immediately, we found that the tote Männer were not attracted to merely any object smeared with the test substances, only when those attractants were applied to a possible host. Weber thought this quite exciting. It suggested that the tote Männer had a means of detecting a host other than smell.

In October of 1942, we hit on a combination of aldehydes and ketones the tote Männer found especially attractive. I synthesized it in the growing chemistry laboratory we had been using and applied it to a collection of test subjects. Control subjects who had no application of the test attractant were also present in the experiment and were ignored until the test subjects had been thoroughly mauled. At that point, the controls were attacked. We made careful note of this as it would strongly influence how troops would recover an infected area after the enemy succumbed.

We had proved our attractant in place by the end of October of 1942. But the war appeared to us to be going so well, our little military experiment would never be needed. We would win the Battle of Stalingrad in a month and concentrate on the western front.

That changed in November.

The Battle of Stalingrad evolved into what I had feared: a siege over a Russian winter. The Red Army began their counteroffensive along with the winter. Like Napoleon, the German army was stuck.

The Germans lost ground in other places. Willem suggested if I could hurry up the program, I should.

We were in part saved by problems encountered by the Daimler-Benz engineering team. Developing a deployment methodology had been proved harder than the engineers had foreseen. They had broken the problem into three parts. The first, and most easily solved, was how to restrain and cushion the tote Männer until they could be released. The remaining two issues revolved around deploying on an advance and deploying on a retreat. In both cases, they resolved into two kinds of scenarios: how to deploy the *first* time and how to deploy *after* the first time. If secrecy was kept (and Willem assured us the enemy did not know what we were working on), then the first deployment would be relatively easy. Deploying on a retreat could be as simple as leaving sealed containers transported by trucks to the target zone to be opened pyrotechnically by remote control. Similar containers, with additional cushioning, could be released by parachute.

But once the secret was out and the Allies were looking for tote Männer delivery devices, we would need a means to overcome their resistance. This had stalled the Daimler-Benz engineers. I saw presentations of stealth night drops, blitzkrieg raids with tanks carrying large transport carts—one enterprising young man demonstrated a quarter-scale model trebuchet that could catapult a scale model container holding six tote Männer as much as three kilometers behind enemy lines. Not to be outdone, his work partner showed how bracing a toter Mann could enable it to be fired from cannon like a circus performer.

These issues so dwarfed our own minor problems that we were given, for the moment, no close scrutiny and I had the opportunity to address shortcomings in our own production.

In February 1943, Russia won the Battle of Stalingrad. Willem warned us that we would have to expect to send tote Männer against Russian troops before long. I argued against it. It would be foolish to waste surprise in an attack that could not work. At least, it would not work until summer.

I went home and spent a week with Elsa and Helmut. Each morning I sat down and drew up production schedules, scrapped them, smoked cigarettes, and tried again. In the afternoon, I played with my son. It was cold in Krakow and with the war not going very well, heating fuel was hard to come by. I was able to requisition what we needed due to my position but even I couldn't get coal for the theater or the restaurants. Often, we spent intimate evenings together with just ourselves for company. I didn't mind. Elsa and Helmut were company enough.

All that spring Willem told us of defeat after defeat—I don't think we were supposed to know what he told us. I think we served as people in whom he could confide as his world crumbled. Germany retreated in Africa. The Warsaw uprising. The Russian advance.

I buried myself in my work. I resolved that if there were to be a failure in the program, it would not be where I had control. Production was, in my opinion, our weak point. Weber's approach to creating tote Männer was haphazard and labor intensive. I wanted something more robust and reliable. Something more *industrial*.

I came to the conclusion that our production schedule had to revolve around the progression of the disease. For three days there was a strong euphoria. Often, the new hosts tried to kiss anyone who came near them, presaging the biting activity of the fully infected toter Mann. Sometime on the third day, the host fell into a sleep that progressed rapidly into coma. Breathing decreased to almost nothing. The heartbeat reduced to a slow fraction of the uninfected. Body temperature dropped to nearly ambient though the infected were able to keep some warmth above room temperature.

The coma period lasted as long as five days, though we saw it end as soon as three. Arousal was sudden, so often precipitated by a nearby possible victim that I came to the conclusion that after three days, the toter Mann was ready to strike and merely waiting for the opportunity.

After that, a toter Mann was mobile for as much as ten weeks, though during the last weeks of infection the toter Mann showed significant deterioration.

Therefore, we required an incubation period of six days, minimum. Effectiveness could not be counted upon after eight weeks. This gave us a target window. If we wanted, for example, to deploy on June first we had to have infected our tote Männer no later than May twenty-fifth. This was the time domain of our military supply chain.

The first order of business was to synchronize the incubation period. I performed a series of experiments that showed that, as I suspected, once the coma period had been entered the toter Mann was ready to be used. However, there was unacceptable variation in the time between exposure and coma. We couldn't reliably produce tote Männer in six days.

The new Chief Medical Officer, Mengele, delivered the necessary insight. Zyklon B was the answer. Though the standard Zyklon B dose would kill the subject quickly, a reduced dose weakened the subject sufficiently to allow infection almost instantly. Commander Hoess was able to supply me with enough experimental data that I could proceed with my own tests. We introduced the gas, waited for ten minutes, then sprayed the subjects with an infecting agent. The remaining three days were sufficient for subjects to recover from the gas just in time to provide healthy hosts for the organisms. This method had the added bonus that the same production chambers could serve two purposes.

By November, when the march up Italy by the Allies had begun and Germany seemed to be losing on all fronts, we could incubate as many as a thousand at a time, six days after exposure. The trains supplying the rest of the camp came in full and left empty so by using the empty trains for transport, we could send tote Männer anywhere in Germany or Poland. Delivery to the deployment launch point would have to be by truck. We were ready. Now, it was up to the Daimler-Benz engineers to deliver our tote Männer the last kilometer to the enemy.

Christmas 1943 was uneventful. Weber and I worked on various refinements to an already prepared system without damaging it too badly. My teachers back in Berlin had taught me the idea of Schlimbesserung: an improvement that makes things worse. At that point, the natural tendency of idle minds and hands to improve a working system into uselessness was our only real enemy.

Given that, we resolutely turned our attention away from the weapons system we had devised to a different problem we had discussed a year before: why deliver tote

Männer at all? The worm and virus were perfectly able to create tote Männer for us. Why did we have to supply the raw material?

Delivering a disease substance was perilously close to delivering a poison gas—something forbidden us from the previous war. However, we had already made some excursions into the territory with the production and delivery of tote Männer attractant—a colloid I had developed that would evaporate into the proper aldehyde and ketone mix the tote Männer found so irresistible. We had also attempted to deliver an infecting gas along with the Zyklon B but the attempt had failed. The worm succumbed to the Zyklon B before the subjects.

Creating an inhalant that carried both the worm and virus proved to be an interesting problem. The virus was stable when dry and the worm could be induced to encyst itself. However, it took time for the worm to decyst and by the time it did, the subject was fully infected with an undirected virus. Rabid humans made a poor host.

We went back to the colloid I devised for the attractant. Colloids are neither liquid nor solid but partake of the traits of both. Gelatin is a colloid. By adding nutrients to the colloid so that the worm could stay alive and not encyst, the virus could be delivered along with the worm when both were at their most infective stage. It was interesting work for a couple of months. Weber was quite elated with it. He called it the Todesluft.

In May of 1944, Willem paid us another visit. This time, he took both Weber and myself aside and spoke to us privately.

"It is clear the Allies are preparing a counterinvasion. The likely location is somewhere across from England on the coast of France." He held the cigarette to his lips thoughtfully.

"We're ready," I said boldly. "We've been ready for months. What do the Daimler-Benz engineers say?"

Willem breathed out smoke. "They have made several methods available to us. Since this is to be the first deployment, we have chosen the retreat scenario. We will place the tote Männer in a bunker in the path of the Allies and detonate it when they come."

"Are we expecting to be overrun?"

Willem shook his head. "Of course not. The tote Männer are a backup plan only. We will deploy them behind our own lines and only release them if we are forced past them. If the front line holds, we will not release them at all."

I nodded. "How many?"

"We estimate six thousand."

I thought quickly. "It takes six days for each group. Six thousand will take us thirty-six days."

Willem smiled at me. "Did you know of the expansions of Birkenau commissioned early last year?"

"Of course," said Weber. "They were a dreadful nuisance."

"They are about to pay for themselves," retorted Willem. "I developed Max's original plans for Birkenau beyond his conception. The new facilities can serve as incubator."

"How many?"

"At least forty thousand at once. Six thousand should not be a problem." He pulled from his briefcase a set of plans.

I looked them over. I was impressed with the innovations I saw. "This is better than I had hoped."

"I'm glad you are pleased. When can the first squad be ready?"

I looked over the plans again and did some figuring on a piece of paper. "May 12, if Daimler-Benz can provide the bunkers and the transportation."

"I've been assured this will not be a problem."

"Then we will be ready to deploy."

Willem pulled a map from his briefcase. "Our sources say we will be struck here." He pointed to the map. "Pas de Calais. That is where our defenses are located and just three kilometers behind them, our tote Männer. The Allies will not know what hit them."

This was by far the largest group of tote Männer we had ever attempted to create. Weber took a fatherly approach to them. When the hosts entered the euphoric stage and called to him with affection, he responded, calling them his "children" and other endearments. I found this unnerving. When the tote Männer were finally ready and installed into their transportation containers I was glad to see them go. Weber watched them leave with a tear in his eye. I went home to my wife and son.

But, of course, the Allies did not strike at Pas de Calais but at Normandy, over three hundred kilometers to the southwest. The tote Männer were in their bunkers. The Daimler-Benz engineers had packed them like munitions. There was no way to extract them without releasing them.

It was terrible timing. All of the available tote Männer were in Calais and the next squad would not be ready for deployment until June 9: three days!

Willem conferred with his staff and said that if we could drop enough bunkers in the Cerisy Forest and fill them with tote Männer, we would let the Allies overrun the forest and open the bunkers.

At this point the new squad was just entering the coma stage. We'd found the tote Männer were vulnerable to jostling during this period and had always transported them toward the end of the coma. But desperate times require desperate measures. Willem and I led the crew that took the newly comatose tote Männer, eight thousand strong, and trucked them to the forest. Meanwhile, three large prefabricated bunkers were erected on the sites. I barely had time to phone Elsa to say I would not be home that night. Weber, affectionate to the tote Männer as before, elected to stay and incubate the next squad. I was just as glad not to have him along.

The bunkers were not particularly explosive proof but would stop bullets. They looked more like officers' quarters than anything else. We locked them and moved away to nearby Trévières. This was June 8th. By the afternoon of June 9th, the tote Männer would be alert. When fired, the bunker would first explode a smoke bomb containing the colloid and attractant we had devised to mask the area. A few minutes later, small explosives would release the tote Männer and break the outside walls. The tote Männer would have to do the rest. We hoped the smell of nearby prey would waken them to fury as we had observed in the lab.

The time passed slowly, punctuated with small arms fire and a few large weapons. The wind moved back and forth, sometimes bringing us the firecracker smell of the battlefield and then replacing it with the pine smell of the forests.

The afternoon came. An odd aircraft I'd never seen before, called a *Storch*, was made available to us. The pilot, Willem, and I boarded the airplane along with the radio equipment. The heavily laden craft took off in an impressively short distance and in a few moments we were high enough to see the bunkers and, worse, the advancing Allies. Willem pressed the button.

Smoke poured out of the three buildings. I could not hear the reports as the internal explosives ignited but there was motion—furious motion—through the smoke. Seconds later the advancing Allies were running down the hill away from the smoke. Directly behind them were the tote Männer.

The tote Männer were much faster than the humans they pursued and more clever than ever I would have guessed. One toter Mann leapt from human to human, biting and clawing, not even pausing to enjoy the "meal." Eight thousand tote Männer poured over the Allies. Guns didn't stop them. They were in and among the soldiers so quickly none of the supporting artillery or machine guns could fire. The smoke switched over them and we could no longer observe.

"Fly over them," Willem ordered, "So we can look down."

"Sir, we will be shot."

"Fly over them, I say," Willem shouted and brought out his pistol. "Or I will shoot you myself."

We flew over the churning mass of tote Männer and humans. They took no notice of us. All of their attention was focused on the horrifying apparitions among them.

"Good," said Willem grimly. "Return."

It was a safe bet that each of the tote Männer had likely managed to bite at least three soldiers. Assuming an overlap of twenty percent, that meant better than thirteen thousand Allied tote Männer would be awakening in a week. This was a conservative estimate, assuming the infected soldiers would not infect others during the euphoric period.

We landed and General Marcks himself joined us. Willem told him of the adventure and the anti-tote Männer equipment—mostly flame throwers and protective jackets—waiting in trucks not ten kilometers distant. The Allied invasion would not succeed.

And it did not.

The Allies, so demoralized by the Reich's new weapon, were unable to advance. German bombers were able to sink support craft in the channel. The war stalled in western France all that summer.

When I returned to Krakow in July to see my wife I still smelled of burning diesel and gunpowder. She made me bathe before I could kiss her.

The Daimler-Benz flying barges were deployed. These, I had not known about. They were gliders filled with forty or fifty tote Männer, towed overnight by bombers and released near the front to land where they would. The crashes released most of the tote Männer but mechanical relays released the remainder. Willem informed us that there were now highly localized tote Männer infections in Britain, where wounded men had been returned before they had turned completely and before the Allies had realized what they were dealing with.

But the Russians continued to advance. They were no less ruthless than the tote Männer and had devised a simple but effective defense. Any group of tote Männer they found they slaughtered without regard to coincident casualties. We estimated they were killing as much as ten percent of their own men with this technique. But it was effective. It was only a matter of time before they reached Germany.

The Allied advance had not been routed as we'd hoped but only stalled as they tried to cope with their own problems. Had Germany remained the fighting force it had been at the beginning of the war, this would have been enough. However, now the Allies had a foothold in France and would not give it up. Anti-aircraft batteries were brought over the channel and the bombers could no longer eliminate the shipping. Soon, the Allies would figure out a method of containing the infection just as the Russians had done. A stalemate in this war would inevitably lead to an Allied victory.

Willem created the Todeskommandos. These were the last paratroopers still left in the Luftwaffe. They were infected without their knowing and dropped far behind enemy lines. Their mission was to spy on the enemy and return in two weeks' time. Of course, they transformed in less than half that time and infected the Russians.

I refused to participate in this activity. I would not be a party to infecting unwitting German soldiers. Willem did not press me at that point though I knew a day of reckoning was coming. Knowing this, I persuaded Willem to loan me one of the Daimler-Benz engineers—preferably Joseph Bremer, a friend of Hans Braun and the engineer who had later proposed the trebuchet. I liked the way his mind worked. Willem sent him to me with the warning that something needed to be done about the Russians.

Bremer, being a mechanical rather than a chemical engineer, immediately saw solutions to the issues we had not solved. We had to maintain the environment of the worm and virus for the duration of delivery and then spray it out into the surrounding area without shredding either. Weber and I had already determined that *inhaling* the inoculum would not infect the host unless some portion was swallowed. The worm needed to actually enter the digestive tract to enter the blood stream. The only result from a purely pulmonary inoculation would be a sterile partial infection.

It was Bremer who devised an irritant to be added to the mixture. The irritant would not be poisonous in any way but would cause a mucous flow from the nose. The subjects would be forced to swallow. It worked in Birkenau experiments with great success.

By this time, Hitler had been sending V1's against Britain for a few weeks. My purpose was to be able to replace the explosive in the V1 with a Todesluft canister and infect the Allies in their home territories.

Once we had the Todesluft device perfected, we approached Willem with it. Willem at once saw the possibilities but denied us the chance to try it out in a V1. Instead, he told us of a new rocket, vastly more powerful and accurate. It was to be called the V2.

The bombers over Berlin never stopped during that summer. Up until we released the tote Männer, Auschwitz, Buchenwald, and the other camps had been spared for some reason. By July, we had a version of the Todesluft device ready for the V2 and after the first few reached their targets, the Allies, realizing where our production facilities must be located, started bombing the camps. I had to drag Weber from our burning laboratories. He wanted to save his "children." I triggered the containment-failure devices and incinerated the last remaining tote Männer squads but saved inoculum samples and the Todesluft devices to operate elsewhere. It was curious: the incubation pens and the holding areas were completely destroyed but the gas chambers survived the bombing.

I had thought to travel immediately to Krakow to be with Elsa. But before I could, Elsa showed up at the camp. Weber, Elsa, Helmut, and I were able to find safety in the basement of the headquarters building. I managed to locate an intact phone and called Willem to tell him where we were.

The bombing ceased in a day or so. The inmates were taken care of and we had food and water. Power was restored the following day.

Weber liked to be near us. Something profound had come undone in him. He mourned the death of his squad over and over. On the third day he accosted me out in the street as I cleaned up the front of the building.

"Could it have been the Jews?"

"What are you talking about?"

"The failure of our tote Männer."

I sighed. "The tote Männer did not fail."

"How can you say that? Germany is *still* losing the war!"

I considered responding to this. How could any single weapon ever win a war on its own? It was *our* failure, not any failure of the tote Männer. But that would only have encouraged him. "We haven't lost yet."

He ignored that. "We made tote Männer out of the Jews. Perhaps there was a Judengeist that impaired them."

"What would you have done instead? Made them out of Germans as Willem did?"

"I should not have been so reluctant to use Poles," Weber said and sat on the bench, sunk in apathy.

I continued shoveling broken concrete and shards of wood out of the street.

Willem showed up that night. He was half-drunk and I was surprised he'd managed to drive all the way from Berlin. Morose and untalkative, he refused to speak until after dinner when Elsa had taken Helmut and herself to bed.

"The Americans are smarter than we are."

"Beg pardon?" I said, ready to defend German intelligence.

"It had to be the Americans. The British would not have considered it."

"Considered *what*?"

Willem stared at me. "Of course. How could you know? They have been raining tote Männer on Berlin. All over Germany."

"That's impossible. Did they drop them out of the bombers? Did they think we would be intimidated by smashed body parts?"

Willem shook his head. "Nothing so complex. All they did was harness them to a big parachute and then tie them together with a bow knot so they would not escape during transport. Then they shoved them out the back of a bomber on a strip line. It undid the bow knot and released the parachute. Some of them were killed, of course. But so what? Between ours and the ones generated from their own ranks, they have enough."

"How were they released from the parachutes?"

"We found a wind-up spring clip. When the spring wound down, the clip opened and they were released. Diabolical simplicity."

I drank some wine. "There are tote Männer in Berlin." I tried to frame it as a logical proposition. I could imagine them lurching through the city.

"There are tote Männer all over Germany. There are tote Männer in London from the V2 Todesluft attack. Von Braun even managed to extend the range of the V2 with a V1 attachment. There are tote Männer in Moscow. Tell me, Weber. How many tote Männer must there be to become self-sustaining?"

Weber peered at him owlishly. "They cannot be self-sustaining. Eventually all of the raw material would be used up."

"You are so comforting," Willem said dryly.

I stared at the wine bottle. "When will they reach here?"

"They were behind me when I crossed the border. One day? Two days? They move slowly but steadily and they will be brought here by our scent."

We had all underestimated them. They were in the camp by morning.

They had broken through the barbed wire holding the inmates easily. The inmates were bit and mauled by the hundreds. The guards died when they insisted on firing on the tote Männer and the tote Männer, of course, did not fall.

The scent of the inmates was so strong that it overpowered our own smells. The tote Männer did not know we were there. We took care to remain hidden in the headquarters building. With so many possible hosts around, the tote Männer ignored the buildings. Each time a few seemed to take interest, there was another inmate to attack.

Elsa refused to let Helmut near the windows. During a lull in the fighting she sat next to me as I watched through the window.

"What are those things?" Elsa said quietly. Her face was milk white but her voice was calm. "Max? Uncle? What are those things?"

"We call them tote Männer," I said.

"Is that what you were building in the camps? Is that your weapon?"

"Yes."

She shook her head. "Did they escape from another camp?"

"No." Willem laughed dryly. "The Allies were kind enough to return these to us."

"Helmut must not see them."

"Yes," I said. "More importantly, they must not see us."

She nodded.

Eventually, the inmates were all infected. We had discovered in experiments that infected hosts were ignored by tote Männer. But there were still so many of them our own scent remained undiscovered. The tote Männer wandered off in small groups, heading east toward Krakow.

The remaining freed inmates, now euphorically infected hosts, were not so ignorant as the tote Männer. They tried to enter the headquarters building. Willem and I defended the place as best we could. Hoess and Mengele tried to gain entrance by sweet reasonableness and grumbled when we shot at them. They wandered off arm in arm.

By the end of the third day after the attack, we saw hosts finding small places to sleep. That evening the camp was entirely still.

"We have to leave," Willem insisted. This was Monday morning. By Wednesday night we would be fighting for our lives.

"I'm ready," Elsa said. "Those *things* will not hurt Helmut. I will kill him first."

I nodded. It pleased me that Elsa understood the situation. "Where shall we go? *Our* tote Männer are to the west and south. *Their* tote Männer are to the north and east. We have no petrol—the depot was blown up in the bombing."

"What shall we do, then?" demanded Willem.

"They are not very intelligent—as I said a long time ago, think of them as crocodiles. They can use their eyes but largely they depend upon scent. Therefore, we can block ourselves up in one of the gas chambers. They are air tight."

"We will smother," said Elsa.

"No." I shook my head. "We have three days. I can devise air circulation. It will be slow and diffuse up through the chimneys. But I do not think it will be sufficient to cause the tote Männer to attack the chamber. We can hold out for help."

It took most of those three days to set ourselves up. We had to change the locks on the doors so we could get ourselves out and convert the exhaust fans to give us a little air. We stockpiled as much food and water as we could carry. I even built a periscope through which I could observe the courtyard in front of the chamber and the areas around.

We were carrying one of the last loads into the chamber when a toter Mann leapt on Willem from the roof. Willem grabbed his pistol as he hurled the toter Mann to one side. Weber cried out and wrestled with Willem. The toter Mann attacked both of them. Finally, Willem threw down Weber and emptied the clip of his pistol into the toter Mann's head. He turned to club Weber but Weber climbed the wall and was gone. Willem turned his attention back to the toter Mann, which had ceased moving as its head had ceased to have any shape. The worms wriggled out like thin spaghetti.

Willem looked at me and held up his arm. His fingers and wrist were bitten. "Do I have any chance at all?"

I shook my head.

"Well, then." He replaced the clip in the pistol. "Perhaps I have time enough to kill Weber for this."

"Don't wait too long," I advised. "Once you start to feel the euphoria you won't want to kill him at all."

"I won't."

He nodded at me and I saluted him. Then I went inside the chamber and sealed the door.

Which brings me to the present.

It has been ten weeks since we sealed the door of the chamber. No one has come to help us. Sure enough, the tote Männer have not detected us though they often walk around the building sensing something. Our scent is diffuse enough not to trigger an attack.

But they do not wander off as the previous tote Männer did. They have remained. Worse, instead of degrading in ten weeks as our experiments suggested, they remain whole. I am now forced to admit that the deterioration we observed in our experiments was more likely the result of captivity than any natural process.

I watch them. Sometimes a group of them will disappear into the surrounding forest and then return with a deer or the corpse of a man or child. Then they eat. We never took an opportunity to observe their life cycle. It seems that once the initial infection period is over, they can, after their own fashion, hunt and eat.

We ran out of water two days ago. We ran out of food nearly a week before that. Helmut cries continuously. The sounds do not appear to penetrate the walls of the chamber—at least, the tote Männer do not respond.

I had planned to hold out longer—perhaps attempting an escape or braving the tote Männer to try to bring back supplies. It is now September. Surely, the impending winter would stop them. Then, when they were dormant, we could leave. But in these last days I have witnessed disturbing changes in their behavior. I saw one toter Mann walking around the camp wrapped in a rug found in one of the camp buildings. A small group of five or six gathered around a trash barrel in which smoldered a low fire. At first, I thought the disease might have managed to retrieve the host memories or that the hosts were recovering—both indicated disaster for us. We would be discovered.

But this is different. The tote Männer stand near the fires until they smolder and only then move away. They drape blankets and clothes completely over their heads but leave their feet unshod. Whatever is motivating them, it is not some surfacing human being but the dark wisdom of the disease itself.

They are still tote Männer and will infect us if they can. There is no hope of escape or holding out.

Always the engineer, I prepared for this. I kept back a bottle of water. In it, I dissolved some Demerol powder. Elsa and Helmut were so thirsty they did not notice the odd taste. They fell asleep in minutes.

I am a coward in some ways. The idea of me, my wife and my child living on only as a host for worms and microbes horrifies me. Death is preferable. Nor do I trust drugs. The faint possibility they might come upon us in our sleep fills me with dread. I have my pistol and enough bullets for Elsa and Helmut and myself. If they find us we will be of no use to them.

I believe that you, Germany, will triumph over these creatures, though that victory will no doubt be a hard one. The Third Reich will not live forever as we had hoped but will, no doubt, fall to the tote Männer. But good German strength must eventually prevail.

For my own part, I regret my inability to foresee my own inadequacies and I regret that I must die here, without being able to help. I regret that Elsa and Helmut will never again see the sun and that they will die by my hand.

But you, who read this, take heart. We did not yield. We did not surrender here but only died when there was no other way to deny ourselves to the enemy. You will defeat and destroy them and raise your hand over a grateful Earth.

It is there waiting for you.

# GEDENKSCHRIFT AUTHORS

**Paul M. Berger** has sold stories in such magazines and anthologies as *Strange Horizons, Interzone, Polyphony 6, Twenty Epics, All-Star Zeppelin Adventure Stories*, and *Ideomancer*. The story of his battle against giant Japanese spiders was the first true-life memoir published in *Weird Tales*. Berger has been a Japanese bureaucrat, a Harvard graduate student, an M.I.T. program administrator, an Internet entrepreneur, a butterfly wrangler, and a Wall Street recruiter, which, in the aggregate, may have prepared him for nothing except the creation of speculative fiction. He is a founding member of the well-regarded and increasingly impressive writing group Altered Fluid. Paul lives in New York City.

**Christopher M. Cevasco**'s short fiction has appeared in *Black Static, The Leading Edge*, and *A Field Guide to Surreal Botany*, among many other magazines and anthologies. He was also the editor/publisher of the award-winning *Paradox: The Magazine of Historical and Speculative Fiction* from 2003 through 2009. Chris writes in Myrtle Beach, South Carolina, where he lives with his wife and their two young children. Visit him at: christophermcevasco.com.

**S. J. Chambers** is the co-author of *The Steampunk Bible*, and has had fiction published in *New Myths, Mungbeing, Yankee Pot Roast, Thackery T. Lambshead's Cabinet of Curiosities*, and in the forthcoming *Starry Wisdom Library*.

**Sean Eads** is a writer and librarian living in Denver. His short fiction has appeared in the *Journal of Popular Culture,* the *Oregon Literary Review,* and *Shock Totem*, among others. He has two novels out, the thriller *Trigger Point* and the darkly humorous *The Survivors*.

**Scott Edelman** has published more than seventy-five short stories in magazines such as *Postscripts, Rod Serling's The Twilight Zone, Absolute Magnitude*, and *Science Fiction Review*; as well as the anthologies *The Solaris Book of New Science Fiction, Crossroads, MetaHorror, Once Upon a Galaxy, Moon Shots, Mars Probes*, and *Forbidden Planets*. A collection of his zombie fiction, *What Will Come After*, is available. He has been a Bram Stoker Award finalist five times.

**Richard E. Gropp** lives on a mountain outside of Seattle with his partner of fifteen years. It is a small mountain. He studied literature and psychology at the University of California, Santa Cruz, and has worked as a bookstore clerk, a forklift driver, and an accountant. His debut novel *Bad Glass*, made *Library Journal*'s year-end list of Best Books 2012 in Science Fiction/Fantasy.

**Samantha Henderson** is writer and poet whose work has appeared in *Strange Horizons, Realms of Fantasy, Weird Tales*, and many other publications both in print and online. She resides in Covina, California by way of England, Johannesburg, Illinois, and Oregon.

**Bob Hole** is a science educator in Northern California. He has been fantasizing about being a writer all his life. This is his first sale.

**Dayna Ingram** writes things for you to read. Not a lot of things, but she's still young. Check out thedingram.com for more info about her other zombie-centric thing, *Eat Your Heart Out*.

**Victoria Janssen** writes both fiction and nonfiction. Her fiction includes numerous erotic short stories and three erotic novels. She is a voracious reader, especially of fantasy, mystery, young adult speculative fiction, and historical romance.

**Alex Jeffers** has published six books in several genres, most recently the collection *You Will Meet a Stranger Far from Home* and novel *Deprivation; or, Benedetto furioso: an oneiromancy*. His short fiction has appeared sporadically since 1975 in spec-fic anthologies and magazines, lit-fic journals and anthologies, and on line. He reveals no secrets at sentenceandparagraph.com.

**Stephen Graham Jones** has eleven novels and three collections on the shelf. He's been a Stoker Award finalist, a Shirley Jackson Award finalist, and has been an NEA Fellow. He has some hundred and fifty stories published. He teaches in the MFA programs at CU Boulder and UCR-Palm Desert.

**E. L. Kemper** lives in Victoria, British Columbia, Canada. Between cloudbursts Erinn and her partner walk the dog from coffee shop to coffee shop until it gets too bleak out, then she packs the dog in a bag and joins the birds heading south (or declares it "happy hour" when travel funds are tight). The rest of the time she renovates and writes horror stories that unsettle, provoke, and resonate. She is a member of the Horror Writer's Association and has a column in their monthly newsletter. "The Cost of Moving the Dead" is her first story to see print. For more about Erinn visit her blog at erinnkemper.com.

**Rajan Khanna**, writer, musician, and sometime bon vivant, is a member of the New York-based writing group, Altered Fluid. His fiction has appeared or is forthcoming in *Shimmer Magazine* and *Beneath Ceaseless Skies* (among others) and has received Honorable Mention in the Year's Best Fantasy & Horror and the Year's Best Science Fiction. He sometimes writes articles for Tor.com and occasionally narrates podcasts for sites like *Podcastle*, *Lightspeed*, and *Pseudopod*. Khanna also writes about wine, beer, and spirits at FermentedAdventures.com. He currently resides in New York.

**Ed Kurtz** is an author, exploitation cinema buff and tarantula wrangler. He lives in Texas. His short fiction has appeared in *Needle: A Magazine of Noir* and *Psychos: Serial Killers, Depraved Madmen, and the Criminally Insane.*

**Carrie Laben** was asked to write this story because the editor knew she has a deep fondness for birds. Laben lives in Brooklyn, where she writes software user manuals and other still more dire things for a living, but this is a big improvement over milking cows and selling used books to agitated mental patients. Her fiction has been published in *Apex Online* and *Clarkesworld* as well as the anthologies *Phantom* and *Haunted Legends.*

**L Lark**'s speculative fiction and poetry have appeared in various literary magazines, including *P'an Ku* and *Coastlines*, as well as in the anthologies *Lycogeny* and *Boys of Summer*. She was the winner of the 2007 Broward College Creative Writing Award, as well as the 2010 Aisling Award for Fiction, given by Florida Atlantic University. Her flash fiction piece "Five Houses on the Shore" was recently published in issue nine of *Innsmouth Magazine.*

**Richard Larson** was born and raised in St. Louis. His stories have appeared in venues such as *Strange Horizons*, *Subterranean*, and *ChiZine*, as well as the anthologies *Beyond Binary* and *Wilde Stories 2011.* He also writes criticism for *Slant Magazine* and *Strange Horizons*, and he's currently pursuing an MFA at New York University. He lives in Brooklyn.

**Livia Llewellyn** is a writer of horror, dark fantasy, and erotica. A graduate of Clarion 2006, her fiction has appeared in *ChiZine*, *Subterranean*, *Sybil's Garage*, *PseudoPod*,

*Apex Magazine*, *Postscripts*, *Nightmare Magazine*, and numerous anthologies. Her first collection of short fiction—*Engines of Desire: Tales of Love & Other Horrors*—was published in 2011 by Lethe Press, and nominated for the Shirley Jackson Award for Best Collection. You can find her online at http://liviallewellyn.com/.

**Jonathan Maberry** is a *New York Times* bestselling author, multiple Bram Stoker Award winner, and freelancer for Marvel Comics. His novels include *Assassin's Code*, *Flesh & Bone*, *Ghost Road Blues*, *Dust & Decay*, *Patient Zero*, and many others. Nonfiction books include *Ultimate Jujutsu*, *The Cryptopedia*, *Zombie CSU*, and others. Jonathan's award-winning teen novel, *Rot & Ruin*, is now in development for film. He was a featured expert on the History Channel special *Zombies: A Living History*. Since 1978 he's sold more than 1200 magazine feature articles, 3000 columns, two plays, greeting cards, song lyrics, and poetry. He teaches the Experimental Writing for Teens class, is the founder of the Writers Coffeehouse, and co-founder of The Liars Club. Jonathan lives in Bucks County, Pennsylvania, with his wife, Sara, and their dog, Rosie. Jonathanmaberry.com.

**Alex Dally MacFarlane** lives in London, where she is pursuing an academic life. When not researching, she writes stories, found in *Clarkesworld Magazine*, *Strange Horizons*, *Beneath Ceaseless Skies*, *The Mammoth Book of Steampunk*, and *The Other Half of the Sky*. She is the editor of *Aliens: Recent Encounters* (Prime Books). Visit her online at alexdallymacfarlane.com.

**Joe McKinney** is the author of several horror, crime, and science fiction novels, including the four part *Dead World* series; the science fiction disaster tale *Quarantined*; and the crime novel *Dodging Bullets*. McKinney has also worked as an editor, along with Michelle McCrary, on the zombie-themed anthology *Dead Set*, and with Mark Onspaugh on the abandoned building-themed anthology *The Forsaken*. His short stories and novellas have been published in more than thirty publications and anthologies. In his day job, McKinney is a sergeant with the San Antonio Police Department. Before promotion to sergeant, Joe worked as a homicide detective and as a disaster-mitigation specialist.

Mexican by birth, Canadian by inclination, **Silvia Moreno-Garcia** lives in beautiful British Columbia with her family and two cats. She writes speculative fiction (from magic realism to horror). Her short stories have appeared in places such as *Fantasy Magazine*, *The Book of Cthulhu*, *Imaginarium 2012: The Best Canadian Speculative Writing*, and *Shine: An Anthology of Optimistic Science Fiction*. Her first collection, *Shedding Her Own Skin*, is out in 2013. Moreno-Garcia is the publisher of Innsmouth Free Press, a Canadian micro-publishing venture specializing in horror and dark speculative fiction.

**Adam Morrow** is an expat of Boston, living with his husband in Andalucía. He is an enthusiast of Near Eastern studies. "The Wedding of Osiris" is his first publication.

**Rita Oakes** writes horror, dark fantasy, and historical fiction. A graduate of the Odyssey Writing Workshop, she enjoys history, travel, and Belgian beer—sometimes at the same time. Her work has appeared in *Paradox*, *Aeon Speculative Fiction*, and *Beneath Ceaseless Skies*, as well as in the anthologies *The Many Faces of Van Helsing* and *Time Well Bent*. She currently lives in New Jersey. Visit her website at ritaoakes.com.

**Elaine Pascale** has been writing for most of her life. She took a break from fiction in order to give birth to two children and a doctoral dissertation. She lives on Cape Cod, MA, with her husband, son, and daughter. She teaches at a private Boston university. Her writing has been published in several magazines and anthologies. She is the author of *If Nothing Else, Eve, We've Enjoyed the Fruit*. She enjoys a robust full moon, chocolate, and collecting cats.

**Aimee Payne** first became obsessed with Amelia Earhart after watching an episode of the '70s television show *In Search Of*. . . with her father. She lives in Jacksonville, Florida, with fellow writer Will Ludwigsen and an assortment of cats and dogs. All are trained to recognize the undead.

**Steven Popkes** is a sort of Science Fiction Writer/Software Engineer. Born in Southern California and, nearly being a native Angeleno, he spent most of his life moving. California to Alabama to Seattle to Missouri. He has an M.S. in Neurophysiology, which explains some of the wonderful scientific details in "The Crocodiles." Recent short story sales include to *Asimov's Science Fiction*, *The Magazine of Fantasy and Science Fiction*, *Daily Science Fiction*, and Gardner Dozois's *The Year's Best Science Fiction*.

**Mercurio D. Rivera** (mercuriorivera.com) was nominated for the 2011 World Fantasy Award for his short fiction and his stories have appeared in markets such as *Black Static*, *Interzone*, *Asimov's*, *Nature*, *Year's Best SF 17*, edited by Hartwell & Cramer (HarperCollins 2012), and *Solaris Rising 2*, edited by Ian Whates (forthcoming). His works have been translated and published in China, Poland,

and the Czech Republic. His collection *Across the Event Horizon* is being published in 2013 by NewCon Press.

**Nate Southard**'s books include *Scavengers, This Little Light of Mine, Red Sky, Just Like Hell, Broken Skin*, and *He Stepped Through*. His short fiction has appeared in such venues as *Cemetery Dance, Black Static, Thuglit*, and the anthology *Supernatural Noir*. A graduate of The University of Texas with a degree in Radio, Television, and Film, Nate lives in Austin, Texas with his cat. You can learn more at natesouthard.com.

**Molly Tanzer** lives in Boulder, Colorado along the front range of the Mountains of Madness, or maybe just the Flatirons. She is a professional writer and editor, among other things. Her debut, *A Pretty Mouth*, was published by Lazy Fascist Press in September 2012, and her short fiction has appeared in *The Book of Cthulhu* (Vols. I and II), *Fungi*, and the forthcoming *Geek Love: An Anthology of Full Frontal Nerdery*. She blogs—infrequently—about writing, hiking, cocktail mixing, vegan cooking, movies, and other stuff at mollytanzer.com, and tweets as @molly_the_tanz.

**Lee Thomas** is the Lambda Literary Award and Bram Stoker Award-winning author of *The Dust of Wonderland, In the Closet, Under the Bed, The German, Torn, Ash Street,* and the newly released *Like Light for Flies*. Lee lives in Austin, Texas, where he is working on a new book. You can find him online at leethomasauthor.com.

**Raoul Wainscoting** is an occasional writer of speculative fiction and full-time nerd. In addition to the story reprinted in this anthology he has a story in Graveside Tales' *The Beast Within* werewolf-themed anthology.

# PUBLICATION HISTORY

"Good Deaths" copyright © 2013 by Paul M. Berger. Original to this volume.

"A Frenzy of Ravens" copyright © 2013 by Christopher M. Cevasco. Original to this volume.

"The Good Shepherdess" copyright © 2011 by S. J. Chambers. First published on the author's blog. Reprinted with permission of the author.

"The Revenge of Oscar Wilde" copyright © 2013 by Sean Eads. Originally appeared in *Stupefying Stories*. Reprinted with permission of the author.

"Tell Me Like You Done Before" copyright © 2009 by Scott Edelman. Originally appeared in *The Dead That Walk: Flesh-Eating Stories*. Reprinted with permission of the author.

"Promised Land (Wineville, 1928)" copyright © 2013 by Richard E. Gropp. Original to this volume.

"Hung from a Hairy Tree" copyright © 2013 by Samantha Henderson. Original to this volume.

"The End of the Carroll A. Deering" copyright © 2013 by Bob Hole. Original to this volume.

"Seneca Falls: First Recorded Outbreak of Strain Z" copyright © 2013 by Dayna Ingram. Original to this volume.

"Blood Marker" copyright © 2013 by Victoria Janssen. Original to this volume.

"The Hyena's Blessing" Copyright © 2013 by Alex Jeffers. Original to this volume.

# THE EDITOR

**Steve Berman**'s curriculum vitae includes editing over a dozen anthologies (including *Bad Seeds: Evil Progeny* for Prime Books), nearly one hundred articles, essays, and short stories sold, and a young adult novel, *Vintage: A Ghost Story*, a finalist for the Andre Norton Award for Young Adult Science Fiction and Fantasy. He does have a voodoo doll collection. He resides in New Jersey, the only state in the Union with an official devil.

# ALSO FROM PRIME BOOKS

**Trade Paperback | 360 pages | 978-1-60701-403-4 | $15.95**

In *Shades of Blue and Gray*, editor Steve Berman offers readers tales of the supernatural — ghost stories that range from the haunts of the battlefield to revenants on the long march home . . .